Praise for *The Me I Used to Be*

"Jennifer Ryan takes family drama to a new level in this tangled emotional web of a novel. Secrets come to light, love is rekindled, and redemption is found—all in the glorious golden sunshine of the Napa Valley. I loved it!"

—Susan Wiggs, *New York Times* bestselling author

"*The Me I Used to Be* is Jennifer Ryan at the height of her story-telling best. Page-turning, powerful, with high-stakes drama and unforgettable romance. I couldn't put it down!"

—Jill Shalvis, *New York Times* bestselling author

"Gripping and emotionally compelling, *The Me I Used to Be* is a beautiful story of losing yourself, starting over against all odds, and coming out triumphant. I was hooked from page one!"

—Lori Foster, *New York Times* bestselling author

"Ryan (*Dirty Little Secret*) delivers an intoxicating blend of hair-raising suspense, betrayal, and true love with this gripping contemporary set in the rich vineyards of Napa Valley. . . . Ryan's fans will devour this outstanding tale, as will the many new readers she's bound to win."

—*Publishers Weekly* (starred review)

Summer's Gift

By Jennifer Ryan

STAND-ALONE NOVELS
Summer's Gift
The One You Want
Lost and Found Family
Sisters and Secrets
The Me I Used to Be

THE WYOMING WILDE SERIES
Max Wilde's Cowboy Heart
Surrendering to Hunt
Chase Wilde Comes Home

THE MCGRATH SERIES
True Love Cowboy
Love of a Cowboy
Waiting on a Cowboy

WILD ROSE RANCH SERIES
Tough Talking Cowboy
Restless Rancher
Dirty Little Secret

MONTANA HEAT SERIES
Tempted by Love
True to You
Escape to You
Protected by Love

Summer's Gift

a novel

JENNIFER RYAN

AVON

An Imprint of HarperCollinsPublishers

SUMMER'S GIFT. Copyright © 2023 by Jennifer Ryan. All rights reserved. Printed in the United States of America. No part of this book may be used or reproduced in any manner whatsoever without written permission except in the case of brief quotations embodied in critical articles and reviews. For information, address HarperCollins Publishers, 195 Broadway, New York, NY 10007.

HarperCollins books may be purchased for educational, business, or sales promotional use. For information, please email the Special Markets Department at SPsales@harpercollins.com.

FIRST EDITION

Designed by Joy O'Meara

Title page and chapter opener photograph © Aleksandr Ozerov/Shutterstock

Library of Congress Cataloging-in-Publication Data has been applied for.

ISBN 978-0-06-309415-4

23 24 25 26 27 LBC 5 4 3 2 1

For you, the reader.

As Summer would say, "I wish you good times, good wine, and good love in your life."

Charles Sutherland had money, power, and the most precious gift of all: his granddaughter, Summer Sutherland Weston. And he'd lied to her, her entire life.

He couldn't take the guilt and shame of his behavior anymore. His sweet girl deserved the truth.

So he was going to fix this situation, because his Ladybug deserved the world. Most of all, she deserved to be loved.

In business, he could solve anything one way or another. But he didn't know how to fix his Ladybug's feeling that her mother never loved her.

Would Summer forgive him for what he'd done at his daughter Jessica's behest?

He'd spoiled Jessica to compensate for his long work hours and leaving her alone all the time after her mother died. He knew it was wrong, and he did it anyway, making her believe that anything she wanted would be handed to her on a silver platter.

He'd done better by his granddaughter, raising Summer to work hard and take the reins of Sutherland Industries one day. And that day was coming sooner rather than later.

He stood in his office doorway and watched Summer and the first step of his plan play out.

"You won the monthly office raffle!" Kennedy, one of the executive assistants, informed his granddaughter.

Summer stared at the gift bag on her desk. "But that's not fair. I'm a Sutherland. This should go to someone else." Summer didn't want any special treatment and tried to hand the package back.

Kennedy held her hand up to stop her. "It's okay. This month, your grandfather put five gifts in the raffle. They came from the company Sutherland Industries just acquired. You're not taking the only one given out. It's fine. Besides, every employee is eligible to win."

Summer opened the package and held up the box inside. "I have to say I was intrigued by these when we did the research on the company."

Kennedy did exactly what he knew she'd do and pushed Summer to open the DNA test kit. "Don't you want to know if you have a long-lost relative, or if you're descended from royalty?" Kennedy's excitement ignited his granddaughter's.

Summer laughed that off, but Charles saw a spark of an idea light her eyes. "I've often wished that my uncle had a secret love child out there somewhere."

Charles frowned. He'd expected Summer to wonder about her father, not his brother, who'd passed away three years ago, leaving Summer his estate. He'd had no other immediate family besides Charles to inherit.

Charles and Jessica had done too good a job of lying to Summer about her father. Now she didn't even think about the man she never knew.

Kennedy pushed again and pointed to the boxes on her desk. "The others have already done their tests. I'm going to mail them back right now. Do yours and I'll send it, too."

Summer shrugged. "Why not?" She opened the kit, and Kennedy spelled out the instructions and even helped Summer set up the online account and register her kit.

Summer spit into the tube, then Kennedy affixed the barcode sticker on it, packaged it back up to ship, and beamed a smile at Summer. "In three to four weeks, you'll know everything."

Charles hoped so.

Though he didn't want her to know he'd set this all up.

His granddaughter picked up a call.

Kennedy met him by his office door. "This is such a wonderful idea, trying out the company's product this way." Kennedy had no idea why he'd really done it.

"I hope the kids enjoy them."

Kennedy's eyes brightened with excitement. "I confirmed with the biology teacher at the school this morning. They received the kits, and the kids are doing them today, too. What a fun science experiment. Nothing like this existed when I went to school."

Everything was going according to plan.

Now all he had to do was wait for the results to come out and the dots to be connected.

Summer would finally get what she'd always wanted but had given up on.

Maybe this would make her happy, even if it made her angry with him.

Chapter One

Four weeks later . . .

$\mathcal{H}$aley Weston rushed into the kitchen with her laptop open and held it up to her parents. "It's here! It's finally here!"

Her mom stirred something in a pot at the stove.

Her dad pulled plates out of the cupboard to set the dinner table.

Cody sat at the breakfast bar reading some report. He worked with Haley's dad at the company they owned together, but he was close enough to all of them to be family. "What's here?"

Her sister Natalie walked in and sat next to Cody. "What is it now?"

Haley ignored Natalie's exasperation and turned the laptop to Cody, who always encouraged her in everything. "The DNA test I took in biology class. I got the results."

"You did what?" her dad asked.

Her mom turned the stove off and faced them. "I signed the permission slip. The kids took one of those DNA tests to find out their ancestry and traits. It sounded educational and fun."

"The results show where my DNA comes from across the globe. That was kind of boring, because we mostly know where we come from." She bounced on her toes, her excitement building again. "But there's something even better."

"What?" her dad asked, moving closer to look at the report.

She pointed to the mind-blowing revelation in black and white on the screen. "I have a sister."

"Duh." Natalie rolled her eyes.

Haley sneered at her older sister. "*Another* sister."

"What?" Her mom sounded confused. "Nate?"

Her dad took the laptop, held it closer, and stared at it. "This can't be right. No way."

"It is," Haley assured him. "DNA doesn't lie, Dad. Someone named Summer Sutherland Weston is my half sister." Then it hit her: in all her excitement, she hadn't thought it through. "Wait. That means—"

"Your father has another child he didn't tell me about," her mom accused, looking both hurt and angry.

"Because I didn't know." Her dad's face paled.

Cody winced and tried to look like he wasn't witnessing all this.

Haley's stomach tightened. Maybe she shouldn't have blurted it out that way.

Her dad looked stunned and shook his head. "This can't be right. Why wouldn't she tell me? Why didn't Summer come looking for me? She has my name," he said, his voice filled with wonder and a question all at the same time.

Mom planted her hands on the counter, leaned in, and stared hard at Dad. "I take it you know her mother."

"Sutherland. Jessica Sutherland. We were together one summer."

Haley grinned. "That's why she's named Summer." She loved how it fit together. Her dad, some girl he fell for, a summer of fun and love. She caught herself in another daydream. Her mom often told her to not get so excited and spin such wild stories in her head—and out loud.

Her mom did not look happy about any of this. Haley should have thought of that and done this privately with them.

Too late.

She hoped her mom understood she hadn't meant to spring this on her like this.

Everyone always said Haley was too young to understand such relationships, but she thought it kind of cool and normal to be young and fall in love—again and again. Until you find the one.

Dad found Mom. They fell in love, married, had a family. The usual.

Mom probably had other boyfriends before Dad. Of course, she didn't have a child he didn't know about. But Dad didn't know about Summer, either, so this would probably all work out.

She hoped.

Her dad sighed, like what happened in the past didn't matter. "I was twenty. She was eighteen."

"So this is true." Natalie's eyes narrowed. "You have another daughter."

Dad looked across the breakfast bar at Mom. "I have another daughter."

"What are you going to do about it now that you know?" Mom asked.

Haley wondered that, too. She really, really wanted to meet her sister.

Dad didn't hesitate. "I'm going to find her."

Haley cheered on the inside, because everyone still seemed concerned about something that felt really great to her. Summer was family.

Mom turned away from Dad and left the kitchen. Dad put the laptop on the counter and went after her.

Uh-oh.

Haley hoped they didn't fight. They rarely disagreed about anything. But this was definitely something.

Natalie glared at her. "Nice job."

Haley looked at Cody, hoping for support. "I got excited. I didn't think about what it really meant. I thought I'd find out we're related to a serial killer and help capture him, like on all those cool podcasts. I never expected another sister."

Cody tried to hide a grin. "Putting away a serial killer would have been really cool." Cody turned serious. "It's a surprise to everyone. Once the shock wears off and your mom and dad talk about it, everything will be fine. Obviously, this happened before they met. He wasn't hiding it from her."

Haley frowned. "Why doesn't he know about her?"

"Who cares?" Natalie interjected. "I say leave it alone. She obviously wants nothing to do with him or us, or she'd have found him by now. I mean, she has his last name, so she knows who he is."

Cody's eyes narrowed with concern. He grabbed the laptop and typed something in, his eyes filling with surprise, and something she didn't understand. "Here she is." Cody turned the computer toward them.

Haley's smile made her cheeks hurt. "She's beautiful. Look at her. She kind of looks like Dad, a little. Maybe even a little like me."

Natalie stared at the picture. "Looks like a spoiled rich girl to me. Look at what it says about her. Heir to the Sutherland Industries fortune, inherited her great-uncle's real estate holdings, one of Texas's elite." Natalie rolled her eyes. "I bet her conceitedness is as big as Texas, too."

Look who was talking. Natalie loved being the oldest, the most spoiled. She had to have everything her way. She loved to be the center of attention.

Natalie hadn't met Summer yet, but she was already jealous.

"That dress is killer." Haley wished she looked like her big sis.

"Probably costs more than she gave at the fund-raiser she attended." Natalie pretended not to be interested in Summer at all. But, come on, Summer was pretty and sophisticated and rich.

Cody couldn't seem to take his eyes off the screen.

Haley bumped her shoulder to his. "What do you think? Do you think we'll get to meet her?"

Cody met her gaze. "I'm not sure. But I know your dad is going to want to track her down and get some answers."

Chapter Two

Nate followed his wife into their bedroom, closed the door, went to her, and took her by the shoulders. "I swear to you, Miranda, I didn't know anything about Summer." Anger shot through him again like a lightning bolt. He released Miranda and paced their room. "I can't believe Jessica kept this from me." They hadn't parted on good terms. She'd packed up and left while he was at work. But things hadn't been so bad that he wouldn't have supported her and their daughter—if only she'd let him know.

Miranda pulled him out of his thoughts. "Would you have stayed with her if she told you about the baby?"

"We were so young. Jessica . . . she was rich and spoiled, looking for a good time and a chance to be whoever she wanted to be away from her stern father. She thought being with me, someone so different from the country club, prep school boys she'd known, was fun. Until reality set in that I couldn't give her the life she'd run away from to have a fling with me."

"Did you love her?"

It was so easy to fall back into the memories of that summer twenty-five years ago. "In the moment, when it was new and exciting and everything was wild . . . yeah. I loved being with Jessica. But after a while, it became clear that I wasn't enough for her. I barely had a dime to my name. I had an idea and a plan. She wanted to use her daddy's money to pay for all of it. I wanted to make it on my own, not be handed something her father would probably claim as his own because he paid for it. I wanted to show her that I could build something from the ground up."

Pride shone in Miranda's eyes. "And you did."

"After she and I parted ways, yes."

Miranda eyed him. "Was it amicable?"

Nate shrugged. "She was disappointed I didn't want to do things the easy way, because for her, everything was easy with Daddy's money. I was frustrated she didn't understand I wanted to earn it. It got to the point I felt like she didn't believe in me. She thought I wasn't good enough." Nate raked his fingers through his hair. "Apparently so much so that she didn't think I'd be a good father to our daughter."

Miranda frowned and shook her head. "You're a wonderful father."

He held his arms out wide, then let them drop. "Why did Jessica give her my name but not let me see her?"

Miranda's lips pressed tight. "I don't know her, or why she'd do this, so I can't say. But I find it odd that your daughter obviously knows your name and never came looking for you for answers."

"Well, I'm damn well going to find out why. Jessica can't keep hiding her from me forever. Not anymore." He took two steps toward their bedroom door and stopped short.

Miranda blocked his path. "Hold on a minute."

He tried to relax and be patient.

"I know this is a shock and a surprise." Miranda's measured tone kept him on alert.

"For both of us." He wanted her to understand he hadn't expected this at all, and he understood this would change things in the family.

Miranda nodded. "So maybe you should proceed with caution."
He went still. "What do you mean?"

"If Summer knows who you are but has never come to see you, maybe it's because she doesn't want you in her life." Miranda put her hand on his chest. Her eyes filled with sympathy. "I'm sorry if that hurts your feelings, but it could be true. For whatever reason."

His mind reeled with all the possibilities of how and why it had happened like this. "And what if that's not the case?"

"Then maybe finding out what the real reason is first, before you rush into her life unannounced, would be a better way to handle things. It would give you both a chance to come together when it's right for both of you."

He implored her with a look. "She's my daughter. I don't know anything about her. I missed everything in her life. What if, whatever the reason is for that, she hates me for not being there? What if she thinks I abandoned her? I can't live with that."

"You don't know that's the case. We don't know anything right now, except her name."

"So what are you suggesting? That I send her an email? Call her? How do I go about approaching her that doesn't seem like I'm inserting myself into her life if she doesn't want me in it?"

"Send Cody. He can be the buffer and find out why Jessica didn't tell you and why Summer never came looking for you. Summer is an adult now, right? She wouldn't need permission if it's what she wanted to do."

Nate sighed, his heart sinking. "Because she doesn't want to know me."

Miranda wrapped her arms around him. "I'm sorry. I didn't mean it like that. I just meant, there must be a reason. Maybe once you know it, you'll know how to go about introducing yourself to her."

Nate thought of something. "If she took the DNA test thing, too . . . I mean she had to have taken it to be in the system and to be matched with Haley . . . So maybe she's looking for family. Maybe she's looking for me."

Miranda nodded. "Maybe so. But I still think sending Cody is the best course of action to ease into this."

Nate deflated as the urge to go see her immediately waned and caution took hold. "I just want to meet her."

Miranda put her hand on his cheek. "I don't want you to get hurt, if she doesn't want to see you."

He appreciated that Miranda wanted to protect his heart.

Nate capitulated, because it would be a huge blow to have his own daughter turn her back on him to his face. "Fine. Maybe you're right. Only I don't know that I'll be able to let it go if she declines and sends Cody back here with bad news."

"One step at a time. You know who she is. Hopefully soon you'll know what really happened and why you were denied your daughter."

He was relieved to see that Miranda's initial hurt and anger had faded, and now she was perturbed that he'd been left in the dark about having a child. "I'll go speak to Cody and have him on the next plane to Texas."

"How do you know that's where she is?"

"That's where Jessica and her father lived. He owns and runs Sutherland Industries. I'm sure Cody can do some Internet digging and get more information on her before he leaves."

"He's probably already gotten started." Miranda left the bedroom ahead of him.

Nate let out a relieved breath that they'd gotten through the initial shock. He bet Natalie and Haley had a lot of questions for him. He had a lot himself and no real answers to give his girls.

And he hoped he could answer any questions Summer had, and they could forge a relationship. He'd missed twenty-five years of her life. He didn't want to miss a single second more.

$\mathcal{C}$ody arrived at the Sutherland offices in Dallas two days after the Weston family received the news about Summer. He wasn't surprised by Nate's request that he make the initial contact with Summer. Nate's emotions were all over the place. Most of the time, he was happy and excited, albeit with a healthy dose of wariness. Other times, his anger spilled over as he blamed Jessica Sutherland for keeping his daughter away from him.

Cody heard an earful about the spoiled rich girl who ran away from home one summer looking for a chance to stretch her wings and rebel a little. She'd made it all the way from Texas to the California coast and Carmel, where she met Nate on the beach. She had a romantic notion about living near the ocean—surfing, bonfires, fun in the sun with new friends. But it soon became clear Nate's going-nowhere job that paid shit, his tiny apartment, and his mounting school debt didn't offer the country club benefits she grew up with. Before long Jessica was looking for ways to convince Nate to let her use her family money to upgrade them to the lifestyle she enjoyed and missed.

Nate wasn't the kind of guy to take a handout. Cody thought a woman would appreciate that trait in a guy who wanted to provide for himself and her. Instead, Jessica went back to the life she loved more than the boy she spent the summer with and never contacted again.

Cody was all for finding Summer and getting some answers, but he'd had to fight Nate to wait a couple days so they could get some basic background on the woman. He didn't want to go in blind.

Nate was a wealthy man now. Cody didn't want anyone, not even Nate's daughter or her selfish mother, coming after him for money, not after he'd been denied his daughter all this time.

As a lawyer, Cody knew the value of doing his due diligence. So he hired a local Texas private investigator to do a background check and gather information on Summer Sutherland Weston, the woman who never really smiled.

He thought again of all the pictures the private investigator had taken over the last two days. There were pictures of her at the local coffee shop ordering her morning high-octane fuel: a double espresso. There were photos of her eating lunch alone, sitting on a bench under a shady tree. Of the fifty or so photographs, the only photo he'd seen where she actually looked happy showed her crouched down petting an oversized puppy as a man and young girl stood beside her. That frozen moment had disturbed him the most.

On one count, he'd been struck by her smile and how it changed her face completely. She was beautiful without the smile, but with it she was a punch in the gut—stunning.

And then he'd looked at the man looking down at her with an appreciative grin on his face and lust in his eyes, and Cody got hit by a wave of unfamiliar jealousy.

He'd been surprised both by his reaction and by the fact that it had hit him so hard and swift from only looking at a photograph.

He didn't even know her, and yet . . .

He was a man who trusted his gut instincts, because they usually proved to be right. They'd saved him in his personal life when the woman he'd thought he loved turned out to be a cheater with the acting skills of an Oscar winner. He'd fallen hard for her sinful body and her deceptive smile until his gut had told him to surprise her at her place instead of meeting her at her favorite restaurant. Something told him she was holding something back.

Turned out, she was hiding a boyfriend. Cody had caught her just outside her apartment, saying good-bye with her tongue down his throat and his hand on her ass. She was even wearing the stunning diamond necklace he'd given her just two days before.

He'd been played for a fool. That had been a first for him. It was the only time he'd given his heart to a woman and opened himself up to be hurt. He'd learned his lesson and kept his heart on lockdown from that moment on, except when it came to family.

He still dated. With caution. And a mutual understanding to keep things fun and casual.

Cody stepped off the elevator into the executive offices on the twenty-second floor of the Sutherland Industries building and stopped short, struck by the beauty across the office. Summer Weston stunned in photos. In person, she could bring a man to his knees.

Even him, he reluctantly admitted to himself, because he couldn't deny the intense attraction he had to her.

Those gorgeous blue eyes, the color of a bright summer sky, were offset by her dark brown hair. Too bad there was no joy or laughter in those eyes. He wondered what in her life had made her so reserved and sad. And then his damn gut clenched when she traced a finger over her cheek and tucked a strand of rich brown hair behind her ear before answering the phone with an efficient greeting. He wanted to follow the curve of her cheek with his tongue and lips as he buried his fingers in the mass of mahogany silk.

He shifted his weight and just watched her.

So far, she hadn't really noticed him. He was just another client dressed in a business suit waiting his turn for a meeting with one of the executives. She was one of six executive assistants manning desks outside the executive offices, like sentries guarding the doors of the castle. Only she guarded the door to the CEO, her grandfather.

The PI had supplied some decent intel.

Summer ran things for her grandfather—going over proposals, discussing business with the people who came to meet with her grandfather, and summing up the situation, letting visitors know whether they had a chance in hell of getting the CEO's approval.

Cody had heard that old saying that behind every great man was a woman helping him to succeed. Charles Sutherland had Summer Weston standing in front of him making sure things were done right.

The detective hadn't come up with anything really personal on her. He'd said she was a hard worker, efficient and competent. She had a bachelor's degree in business management. Cody thought that was a concession to pressures from her grandfather, whose expectations were high, his standards even higher. He was considered a ruthless businessman, though he had a real sense of fair play.

His daughter, Summer's mother, Jessica, was considered a temptress. She'd seduced, married, and divorced four wealthy men. That didn't include the numerous lovers she'd taken over the last twenty-plus years.

She'd taken every one of her ex-husbands for as much as she could get. So why hadn't she demanded her due from Nate?

Time to get some answers.

Cody approached Summer's desk, ready for those gorgeous blue eyes to lock on him and the electric attraction running through him to sizzle even as he fought it.

"Can I help you?" Her voice was like a gentle rain, soft and soothing.

For a second, he didn't know what to say.

She tilted her head and studied him. "I don't have anything on the schedule for another twenty-seven minutes." She eyed him. "Did my mother send you?"

"You could say that," he said vaguely.

•   •   •

Summer liked the smooth, deep, slow rumble of his voice. It perked up her nerve endings and drew her complete attention. It was the kind of voice a woman would never tire of hearing.

She looked at him from the top of his golden head to the tips of his expensive polished shoes. His dark blue suit was perfectly tailored to fit his broad shoulders and lean waist. She had to admit, this time her mother had tried to set her up with a very good-looking man.

Most of the time, the men she sent after Summer were businessman-soft with a wealth of entitlement issues that matched their hefty bank accounts.

There was nothing soft about this man, from the strong set of his jaw to his long, elegant fingers that could curl into sledgehammer-sized fists and crush anything he slammed them into, namely a table when he objected to his opponents' arguments.

"Lawyer, right?" When his eyes narrowed, she knew she'd hit the mark. "Lawyers love to answer a question without actually answering it. So, what is it this time? My mother knows your mother, they had lunch, hatched a plan to get the two of us together and meld family names and bank accounts, and produce beautiful heirs?"

One eyebrow quirked. "This has happened before?"

She shrugged with indifference. This scene had played out countless times, though she had to admit never at her office. Usually the men approached her at whatever social event her mother guilted her into attending. It had gotten to the point that she suspected any man who asked her out as a setup. So she simply turned them down without ever considering one of them could be the man of her dreams. Any man her mother wanted for her couldn't be trusted.

She'd learned that the hard way.

She wasn't about to make the same mistake twice.

"Too many times to count," she answered him. "You probably come from a wealthy family, born and bred with the best of everything, attended the best schools, graduated summa cum laude from college and law school, became a partner in your family's lucrative practice, and now your parents can't wait to see you happily settled with a wife from an equally acceptable family, and then you'll have two kids."

She saw the cool look in his eyes, the way he seemed to flex and tense, and the set of his mouth thinned like the thought of those wealthy, entitled boys was beneath him.

She changed her mind about the handsome stranger. It wasn't often she second-guessed her initial impression of someone. Most of the time, she was dead-on. This man was worth a second look. That he intrigued her and set off a little flutter in her belly interested her even more. "On second thought, you're different from the others. I'll give you that. You actually worked your way through school with determination and grit to become the successful man you present today."

The intensity in him eased. "What made you change your mind?"

"The look in your eyes. You look like a man who doesn't take anything for granted."

"I try not to."

She believed him and relaxed. He definitely was not one of the snotty brats her mother usually sent after her.

"Please accept my apology." She tried to play it cool, even though she was anything but, with her nerves going haywire on the inside.

"I appreciate the fact that you came here to please my mother and indulge her delusions. If you'll excuse me, I have work to do. I'm sure you're a busy man yourself. I won't waste any more of your time. Tell my mother we had a lovely time, but you find me boring and unappealing."

"She'd believe that?" His eyes filled with shock and disbelief. "Would anyone ever actually say that about you?"

She remained resigned and irritated that her mother kept doing this to her. "She'd believe that and more. And yes, it's been said. More than once." And it still stung.

"If that's true, or you simply believe that it is, I'm sorry. Maybe you just need to look in a mirror and see what I see."

Though the compliment set off those butterflies again and she felt herself blush, she waved it away.

He studied her even harder. "Listen, while your mother is part of the reason I'm here, she didn't send me."

Embarrassed, her cheeks flushed even hotter. "Oh, god. I'm sorry. I've read the situation wrong." This was not her day. Not with him, anyway. "I hope I haven't ruined some business deal for the company."

"Not at all. This has nothing to do with business," he assured her, leaving her even more confused.

"She really didn't send you?" she asked, genuinely puzzled.

"No. Your father did."

The blood drained out of her face. Every thought in her head evaporated. Her whole body, including her heart, went numb.

She didn't know what to say and just stared at the stranger, dumbstruck.

"Miss Weston." The man planted his hands on her desk and leaned in close. "I'm Cody Larkin. In addition to being your father's lawyer, I'm also his business partner and friend. He sent me here to talk to you."

When she didn't respond, he tried to get her attention again. "Miss Weston."

After all this time, he'd sent his lawyer. He hadn't come himself.

The crushing disappointment wasn't new, but it hurt even more that he'd made contact through an intermediary so he wouldn't have to speak to her himself.

"What's his name?"

Cody stood to his full height again, stunned disbelief in his eyes. "Nathan Weston. Everyone calls him Nate."

At least her mother hadn't lied about his name. "Why now?"

Cody paused, his concerned and wary eyes locked on hers. "He just found out about you two days ago. His daughter received the results of a DNA test she did in biology class. It revealed that you'd taken the same one . . . and you were matched as half siblings."

Summer's heart clenched with the shock.

Her father didn't know about her! She had a sister!

She didn't want to believe it.

He didn't know? *How could he not know?*

"Didn't you get your results from the test you took?"

"I . . . I've been so busy with work and an issue at one of my properties . . . I hardly ever check my personal email. My work one . . . It just never stops."

"Why did you take it?"

"I won it in the office raffle. I thought maybe my great-uncle had a love child out there somewhere, or something."

That eyebrow went up again. "It never occurred to you that you'd find your father's family?"

"I didn't know he had one. I don't know anything about him."

"How is that possible? You know his name. You could have found him easily."

Simple. She'd stopped wanting anything from the man who didn't want her.

At least, that's what she'd been told. Over and over and over again.

She thought she'd lived her life in a blissful state of numbness for many years because of her mother's idea of rearing a child while bouncing her around from home to home, school to school, and stepfather to stepfather. Summer had been wrong. She hadn't been numb. She'd simply ignored everything around her.

This was numb.

Unable to feel anything, she was surprised she could still take in a breath and her heart still beat. She knew once the numbness wore off, the pain would come, and it would cut deeper than anything her mother had ever done to her.

She wondered if there were any pieces of her heart left that her mother hadn't torn to shreds over the years.

Her mother had lied. Over and over and over again.

How could she lie about something so important?

How could she tell her daughter her father didn't want her?

Summer took that in and let it fill her mind along with all her other dark thoughts.

All these years, Nate didn't even know he had a child who desperately wanted her father.

An all-too-familiar laugh brought her out of her thoughts.

Her elegant, beautiful mother walked off the elevator in a flowing floral dress, her gaze directed at the man walking beside her. He was her sole focus. He was the most important thing in Jessica's world.

Right now, anyway.

Because Jessica loved everything new, especially love.

But when it got old . . .

Jessica Sutherland liked to keep things fresh and exciting. She lived for the thrill.

Summer managed to stand, amazed her unsteady legs held her

up at all. She wanted to run, because facing this meant facing a lifetime of lies.

She wanted to grab her mother's perfect hair and shake her until her bones rattled. Perhaps then some kind of understanding would rise up to replace her mother's selfish nature.

All were futile thoughts. Her mother didn't have an unselfish bone in her body.

"Summer, darling, I was just coming to see you."

Summer managed to recover her voice and maintain her cool disposition in front of everyone in the offices. "Mom, what have you done?" It wasn't what she wanted to say, but it would have to do. Causing a scene outside the executive offices would set off her grandfather's temper.

"Darling, really, you knew Roger and I were flying off for a long weekend away. Since we were in Vegas enjoying the nightlife, we decided to bite the bullet. We got married!" Her mother beamed, the flush of romance and new love making her euphoric.

Summer saw the stunning diamond solitaire sparkling on her mother's left hand, taking up the entire space between knuckles as she held her hand pressed to Roger's lapel, showing off the brilliant rock to its full advantage.

She wasn't surprised by her mother's sudden marriage. That was Jessica.

"You should have seen it, darling. Roger set up this little impromptu wedding service in the hotel's garden by this gorgeous koi pond with candles floating on the water and exotic flowers scenting the air. It was over-the-top glorious."

Just the way Jessica liked everything.

"Anything for you, my love." Roger smiled adoringly at his new bride.

Jessica frowned at her, that familiar look of disappointment coming over her because Summer didn't gush over her mother's announcement. "Please don't start one of your lectures." Waving her hand to dismiss anything Summer might say, Jessica went on, completely oblivious to Summer's distress. "Wait until you see the pictures." When that didn't get the response Jessica wanted, she resorted to that disappointed look again. "Darling, you look pale. Obviously, you're working too hard. And I've told you a hundred times dark colors don't suit you. They wash you out. You should wear something soft and pretty. It would bring out the color in your cheeks. A little lipstick wouldn't hurt, darling."

She caught a glimpse of Cody's shocked disbelief that her mother would say something like that in front of others.

It didn't surprise Summer at all.

"Mom!" Summer tried to restrain the urge to smooth her hand over her charcoal sheath dress or fuss with her hair. Her mother always seemed to find something to criticize. Summer ignored it, like all the other times, and tried to focus on the bizarre situation she found herself in. "Does Grandfather know?"

"Of course, darling. Your grandfather was the one to put Roger and me together."

Roger held tight to Jessica's waist, watching Summer with his usual patience and indulgence. "Summer, you know how much I love your mother. If I'd known how upset you'd be by our getting married without you, I would have flown you to Vegas to join us."

Summer had to actually shake her head to clear it.

Did they really believe she cared about them getting married?

She liked Roger. She'd liked most of the men in her mother's life. A long time ago, she'd resigned herself to the fact that they held her mother's attention above Summer—until they didn't anymore.

"Roger, this has nothing to do with you marrying my mother." She looked directly into Jessica's merry eyes. "This is about my father."

Jessica rolled her eyes. "Darling." She placed a perfectly manicured hand on Summer's arm. "You know how much I loved your father. He didn't want us, darling. I've spent my life searching for the kind of love I found with him. I have it now with Roger."

For now, Summer wanted to say, because she knew it wouldn't last. Love came easy to Jessica Sutherland Peters Burke Elliot Marlow, now Scott.

Had she missed one?

No. That was all of them. At least, the ones Jessica had married.

"You said he didn't want *me*. How many times did I ask about him? How many times did you tell me he didn't want *me*?"

The pain was swift and sharp. All these years, she'd felt like she wasn't good enough, something about her was lacking because her own father didn't want her.

Lies. More of Jessica's carefully constructed fabrications. And she wanted to know why.

Cody swore under his breath.

Jessica tried to placate her. "Darling, I thought you were long past this. Perhaps you need a vacation. A day at the spa and the salon will do wonders for you. We'll go tomorrow. Roger won't mind our having a girls' day out, will you, darling?"

"Of course not. I hate to share you, but Summer is your daughter and she deserves to spend time with you. Besides, Charles and I have a lot of business to discuss now that you're my wife."

Summer knew just what that meant. Another marriage set up and executed for profit. Oh, her mother was undoubtedly in love with Roger. She was always in love with the man she was with, but the side benefits of pleasing her father and ensuring some huge business deal were a bonus. And the men of course saw the advantage in marrying Charles Sutherland's daughter.

Cody took a step closer to Summer and dropped his voice low, though they didn't have privacy with her mother and brand-new stepfather just a few feet away. "Miss Weston, maybe it's best we discuss this privately. You and I can go somewhere and talk and we can figure this out."

"Who are you, handsome?" Jessica looked Cody up and down, sizing him up and obviously liking everything she saw. "You look exactly like what my stubborn daughter needs. That sexy drawl might even melt Summer's cool composure." Jessica looked at Cody as though he'd be a definite possibility for her next lover if she hadn't just gotten married.

Summer let her hostility fly. "Where are my manners? Mom, I forgot to introduce you to Cody Larkin. He's a lawyer." She waited for her mother's favorable reaction to Cody having a lucrative job. "He's here on behalf of his friend and client." She paused for dramatic effect, then dropped the bomb. "Nate Weston."

Her mother's face paled.

"Who apparently just found out *two days ago* that he has a grown daughter!" Summer hadn't meant to shout the last part of that, but her anger got the better of her.

If she hadn't been waiting for it, she wouldn't have seen the slight squint of her mother's left eye telling her that her mother had indeed lied and was worried about being caught.

She took a menacing step toward her mother and stood within a breath of her. Her mother's exotic perfume scented the air between them. She was an inch taller than her mother and looked into Jessica's brown eyes directly. "How could you? I've forgiven you more times than I can count for the terrible things you've done. There were many times I thought what you'd done was as close to unforgivable as you'd ever get. I was wrong. I will never forgive you for this. Ever."

Panic filled Jessica's eyes. "You belong to me, darling. You and me . . . we're all we need."

What her mother meant was that Summer was the one person she counted on to be there no matter what. She needed Summer's love. She trusted Summer when all the others let her down. Summer was the only person Jessica believed would never leave her.

Maybe that came from losing her own mother so young.

It didn't excuse Jessica's behavior.

"I won't let Nate take my little girl away from me. It won't happen. I won't allow it. He will not come between us. Darling," her mother implored, "whatever this man told you is a lie."

Summer felt more than saw Cody take a step to move around her and confront her mother.

Summer sidestepped and cut him off. "You're lying. You've been lying to me my whole life."

"You're going to take *his* word for it?" The cracks were showing in her mother's carefully erected facade.

"Yes. Because he has integrity. He wouldn't lie. Not about this." She knew it to her soul, Cody Larkin had a stake in coming here on her father's behalf.

Cody leaned in. "Miss Weston, let's go have a cup of coffee and discuss your father's request."

"There's nothing to discuss, Mr. Larkin," her mother snapped. "You tell Nate she isn't interested in anything he has to say. It's too late for him to come after her now. I raised her. She's *my* daughter! He's got two of his own."

"Mom! That's enough." It hit Summer hard that her mother knew her father had a family. Which meant she'd known the whole time how to get in touch with him and hadn't.

Cody didn't back down. "Mr. Weston has every right to contact his daughter and request a meeting with her, if for no other reason than to tell her himself that he had no idea she existed. You took away his parental rights. While there's nothing I can do about that now, I will fulfill my client's wishes and speak with Miss Weston on his behalf."

Summer pressed two fingers to the bridge of her nose and hoped the ache behind her right eye didn't bloom into a full-fledged migraine before this awful day was over.

"Really, darling, this isn't the time or place to discuss this ridiculous matter."

Ridiculous matter? Well, that said everything, didn't it? They were only talking about her life.

Roger took Jessica by the shoulders. "Darling, you've kept something extremely important from her. Don't you think you owe her a proper explanation?"

Jessica gave Roger her famous pout.

Summer turned her back on her mother, who just didn't get it, and went to the one person who would understand—and had some explaining to do.

"Where are you going?" her mother called, the panic in her voice warranted. No doubt she recognized Summer's intentions. Jessica wanted to keep her father out of it.

While her grandfather drilled into Summer the value of education and a work ethic built on achieving success by working hard and earning what you achieved, he'd spoiled and indulged his only child. Worse, in adulthood, he gave Jessica the freedom to do as she pleased. Consequences were never foremost on Jessica's mind and easily dealt with when you had Charles Sutherland there to clean up the mess left in your wake.

Not this time. Her mother was going to answer for this.

Summer wasn't about to let her grandfather off the hook, either. He would account for his part in breaking her heart.

So she barged right into his office spoiling for a reckoning.

Chapter Four

The door to Charles Sutherland's office flew open and his grand-daughter marched in with fury and fire in her eyes. "Grandfather, I need to speak with you privately. *Now*."

Charles took note of his granddaughter's squared shoulders and the stubborn tilt of her chin. This was a side of her he didn't often see. Sometimes, he wished to see it more. "Summer, whatever has you riled will have to wait. I'm in a meeting."

Summer barely spared a glance for the two men seated in front of him. "I'm your granddaughter and I want to talk to you. *Right now*," she snapped. She hardly ever used the fact that she was his grand-daughter to get her anything. It was a source of pride for her to earn her own way and do things for herself. This time, she wanted to be heard, and she wasn't going to be put off for business or anything else.

Charles leaned back in his chair and looked over Summer's shoul-der. His daughter, Jessica, looked a little frazzled as she stood beside the man he'd handpicked to be his newest son-in-law. After all these years, he hoped Roger would be the one man who could rein in her penchant for always having someone or something new in her life.

He sensed a family squabble brewing, most likely stirred up by something Jessica had done.

Still, it wasn't like Summer to come to him spoiling for a fight. Certainly not in the middle of the day, in his office, while he discussed business with employees.

And when it came to situations involving her mother, she usually came to him privately with a sense of calm resignation.

This was different. And once he recognized the man who came in behind Summer, he had a feeling he knew why. He caught himself before he smiled. His plan had finally worked, though he couldn't let on that he was behind it.

Cody Larkin certainly looked like he had something on his mind, and he wasn't leaving until he got what he wanted. Charles recognized that kind of quiet determination and respected it.

He looked at the two men sitting in front of his desk. "Gentlemen, if you'll excuse me. We'll resume this tomorrow morning." Charles waited for the men to gather their papers and walk out of his office.

Jessica was smart enough to close the office door before he began the conversation.

Summer knew him well enough to give him a chance to temper his anger and begin in his own time.

"Now, *Granddaughter*, why don't you tell me what's all hellfire important that you came into my office, unannounced, to break up a very important meeting?" He punctuated the statement by slamming his fist down on his desk. Not surprisingly, his ire didn't even make Summer flinch.

She stalked closer to his desk, planted her hands on top of it, leaned over, and spoke directly at him. "You have always told me the unvarnished truth. You'd better do it now."

Yep, he liked seeing Summer in command. He'd chosen his successor well.

"Did you know Mom kept my existence a secret from my father?"

Charles didn't have to answer; she knew the truth already, because he knew everything about Jessica and how she lived her life. One mistake and disaster after another. He'd created the spoiled, entitled woman, so he cleaned up after the mess.

Summer's eyes filled with disappointment, and it killed him. "How could you do this to me? All these years I thought he didn't want me. *You* let me think he didn't want me." Shattering hurt filled her eyes.

Sometimes, a man had to take a blow. This was one of the very few times he was going to take one to the heart without fighting back. He was a hard man, knew that unequivocally about himself. But she'd been something special in his life. With her, he'd been able to let down his guard as much as he was able.

"I'm not a man who apologizes often. You, better than anyone, know that." He released a deep sigh and continued to look her directly in the eye because she deserved that respect. "I'm sorry, Ladybug. I never wanted to hurt you."

"Don't! Don't use that name with me when you know I'm angry and hurt."

Resigned to the fact that there was no way out of this discussion, he tried to set things straight. "All right, Summer. At the time, your mother was reckless and impulsive."

"Nothing has changed." Summer had stopped being quiet, or even polite, when it came to her mother's bad behavior years ago.

Jessica let out an indignant huff.

Charles ignored them both and continued. "You know the basic story. She refused to go to college, opting to take off on her own to see the world. She got as far as Carmel, California, where she met your father. They had a brief affair."

Summer pressed her lips tight. "Three months. One season. She named me Summer because she said that time was *so special*." The thick sarcasm didn't escape him. "More than likely, it was a reminder that summer affairs have consequences."

Jessica once again huffed out her indignation, but she still didn't say anything. She'd spun a tale for Summer about being madly in love with her father.

Charles understood Summer's ire, because Jessica was always madly in love. It never lasted. It never meant more to her than the next guy she fell for deeply, madly—fleetingly.

"Your mother came home at the end of the summer and announced she wanted to go to college after all. Things with your father hadn't turned out the way she hoped. Within weeks, she knew she was pregnant. She wanted to keep you but not marry him. I could have gone after him, but he didn't have the means to support you, and quite honestly, he had plans for his future, plans that would have fallen apart if he'd had to use what little he had to support a child."

Summer steamed. "She didn't need his money. Not when she had you."

"You're right. But your mother made it clear that if Nate knew about you, he'd want to pay his fair share. It was a hard decision, but I thought, at the time, giving him a chance at his dream made the most sense, since Jessica and I could give you everything you need."

"Everything but my father. And how did that turn out for me when she got tired of taking care of a baby, a toddler, the child she wanted to keep all to herself but not actually raise?"

He didn't know what to say. "I supported her decision to keep you. I went along when she refused to tell your father about you. I never said I liked it." In fact, he hated it. "I couldn't believe she told you he didn't want you. In fact, I confronted her about it several times when you were a little girl. You were just so persistent in asking questions that she felt she had to give you an answer, any answer."

"I wanted my father. Was that so hard to understand?" Misery filled her soft voice.

"No, Ladybug. You had every right. Your mother made a mistake. And so did I." He saw the look in Summer's eyes and knew she understood all too well the kinds of errors Jessica had made over the years. All of them had been hurtful in some way to Summer.

"Let's just get the whole truth out, Grandfather." The look in her eyes didn't bode well for him. "Nate didn't come from a wealthy family. He couldn't spoil her the way she'd become accustomed to."

"Summer, darling, that's not fair."

Summer turned to her mother abruptly. "Do you really want to talk about fair?" She folded her fingers around the malachite paperweight on his desk.

In rare instances of pure rage as a child because of something her mother had done, Summer had thrown things and liked to see them smash to pieces. He'd often thought it represented her heart shattering in her chest, the shards ripping her soul to pieces.

Jessica didn't see the damage she inflicted. Charles saw it all too clearly in his granddaughter's eyes.

He knew it was his fault.

Cody slowly reached out and put his hand over Summer's. Instantly, she calmed and leaned into him. He leaned into her. It lasted a brief second, just enough time for Charles to see something spark between them before they caught themselves and separated, Summer leaving the paperweight on his desk. Cody took a few steps back and tore his gaze from Summer.

Interesting.

"Summer, give your mother a chance to explain." Roger held Jessica's hand and guided her to the sofa. He held her close as tears welled in Jessica's eyes.

Summer wasn't swayed by the tears. They came too easily for Jessica.

Charles ignored them as well.

"There's nothing left to say. She lied. Grandfather lied. My mother forgot Nate the moment she came home and found someone new to shower her with attention." Summer glared at Jessica. "I can only imagine what you told Thomas. That my father abandoned you, I suppose, would garner you the most sympathy. He played your hero and married you two months after having me, if I remember correctly."

"It wasn't like that." Jessica brushed a tear from her cheek.

"It was exactly like that," Summer snapped. "At least, you didn't compound the lie by making me believe he was my father." Something made her eyes go wide. "Why did you give me his name? You could have kept his identity a secret by naming me Sutherland."

"I wouldn't let her." Charles showed a rare sign of weariness by running his hand across the side of his head through his more gray than brown hair. "I hoped that once you were born, she'd do the right thing and contact your father to let him know he had a daughter. She didn't. She wouldn't."

"No. Of course not." Summer shook her head. "She had a new love in her life and was wrapped up in wedded bliss, newlywed joy, and all the other lovely new things she likes so much. Until it fades," she added scathingly.

Jessica fumed. "Summer, I won't tolerate you speaking to me like this."

"I don't care, Mom."

"He wouldn't have been able to provide for you," Jessica tried to defend herself even though it was next to useless. Summer was formidable when she was mad and hurt. "I did the best I could and raised you the way you deserved to be raised . . . with wealth and privilege."

Summer rolled her eyes and balled her hands into fists at her sides. "You abandoned me to nannies. I spent more time with them and Grandfather than I did with you."

"That's not true." Jessica pouted.

Charles hated to admit Summer was right.

"When will you learn happiness doesn't come from money and things?" Summer said.

"He didn't want you!" Jessica believed her own lies.

"He didn't even know about me!" Summer turned to Cody. "Do you have any idea what it's like to be told over and over again that your own father doesn't want you?"

Charles felt every ounce of Summer's pain in his own heart.

"I begged, over and over again, for them to just let me see him once. To let me speak to him. If he saw me . . . If I told him what a good girl I'd been, maybe then he'd change his mind. But the answer was always the same. He didn't want to see me. He didn't want to know me. So I begged the man in the moon, I wished on every star, I swore I didn't need money from the tooth fairy or a present from Santa. All I wanted was one moment with him." Tears slipped unchecked down her cheeks. "I searched everywhere for a four-leaf clover to bring luck, only to be told by the gardener that there weren't any weeds on the grounds. I cried to Grandfather and he had a whole field planted for me. But no matter how many I found, all I had was bad luck. He never came for me."

She stared at Cody, who looked back at her with compassion and sorrow. "I tried to be the best at everything. If I was a good girl, surely he'd want me. I got the best grades. I made the best science projects. No matter what it was, I tried the hardest and did my best. And then one day I wondered, how would he know if I was the best student in my class, or the best at kickball, or made the biggest and best papier-mâché volcano?" She hung her head. "He wouldn't." She looked at Cody again. "Because he didn't want me. He didn't care. He wasn't going to show up for the school play or a soccer game. Only one person never missed anything." She turned to Charles. "You were pushy and demanding, but always on my side and at everything I did even when Mom was off with whoever she loved more in the moment."

Her mom gasped. "That's not fair. I always loved you best."

"No, it wasn't fair." She met Charles's gaze again. "And neither was you being my everything and lying to my face every time I begged you to find him and make him want me. It wasn't fair that you kept me from him."

"No, it wasn't, Ladybug. I wanted to give you everything, but I didn't give you that, and I'm sorry for it. I could make excuses, I always do when it comes to your mother, but there isn't one for what I did. Just know I, too, gave into my selfishness, because I wanted to keep you all to myself, too. I saw in you everything I'd done wrong with your mother and everything I could do right by you. Everything I have will be yours. Everything I've become over the last twenty-five years is because you made me a better man."

Summer's tears fell in earnest. "All you had to do was tell me the truth."

"I wanted to so many times. And then you stopped asking and I thought it for the best because your father had moved on and had children of his own."

"I am *his* child, too! He'll never forgive me for not looking for him."

"There's nothing for him to forgive, Summer," Cody assured her. "I'll tell him everything I learned here. He'll understand it wasn't your fault."

Summer suddenly went still and a look of dawning understanding came into her eyes.

Charles's gut fluttered with nerves.

"I only found out the truth because of the DNA test. And my father found out because his daughter took one, too." She leveled her glare on him. "You put the DNA test in the raffle. You made sure I got one."

Charles had hoped his plan wouldn't seem so obvious.

Cody caught on, too. "Haley said the test kits were donated to her school."

"From the very company Sutherland Industries now owns, no doubt." She raised a brow at Charles. "All you had to do was tell me. It's been twenty-five years. Why now? Why this way?"

"You think it's easy to look you in the eye and tell you I lied to you about this and break your heart?" It cut him deep, and he deserved it. "I need to know that when I'm gone, you have someone else who loves you more than anything, the way I do."

"He doesn't even know me."

"He wants to," Cody assured her. "He wasn't sure why you never reached out to him, so he sent me, hoping you'd agree to meet him." Cody took a step closer to Charles's granddaughter. "He sent me to bring you home."

"Where is he?"

"Still in Carmel. I may not be the man in the moon, but I can make your wish come true. I have a plane waiting to take me home. Come with me. You can see him today."

Summer's eyes went wide. "Do you really think he wants me to come to California?"

Charles hated that Summer questioned whether Nate wanted anything to do with her.

Cody reassured her. "I know that's exactly what he wants. I mean, he'd come to you for sure, but it might be best for you to come back with me. Give you and Nate some space away from here to connect."

Summer raised a brow. "You mean away from my mother."

Cody nodded. "Nate's going to need some time to cool off before that reunion."

"Summer isn't going anywhere," Jessica shouted. "She has a job and a life here."

"The job, yes. The life—" Charles shrugged. "That's debatable. Which is why I did this. Summer believed her father didn't want her, so why would any other man?"

"I don't think that," Summer defended herself.

"Really?" Charles asked. "If you're not here, you spend all your time alone in your condo."

"Because all I do is work for you, I have no time for anything else. Even my friends tease that you keep me chained to my desk."

Charles knew he needed to back off at work. She knew her job. She could run this company without him now. She deserved the personal life he'd always put on the back burner for himself and regretted. He wanted more for her. He knew Summer wanted more for herself, too, but was afraid of putting herself out there and getting rejected.

"You brush off every man who even looks at you like he wants a date. The ones who ask, you dispatch without even taking the time to get to know them."

"That has nothing to do with my father and everything to do with *her*." Summer pointed the finger at Jessica.

"I only ever wanted your happiness," Jessica interjected.

"By pushing me to get married to one eligible bachelor after another."

"I wanted you to find love and ensure a solid future for you."

"You manipulated me. You went behind my back and set me up with a man you knew had a very specific agenda, and you didn't care that he was using me. You never gave any thought to my feelings." That experience had soured Summer on relationships.

Charles didn't miss the anger in Cody's eyes.

He needed to stop this before Summer dove deeper into Jessica's misdeeds and faults. "That's water under the bridge." Charles hated that Jessica had interfered in Summer's private life. The young man had wanted a leg up in the company and had used his granddaughter as a means to get it. He'd been smooth, doing and saying all the right things. Summer fell hard for him, but ultimately saw the ruse when it became clear he hadn't felt for her what she felt for him. He'd been cruel in the end, telling her the position at the company appealed to him more than she did anyway.

It still made Charles seethe. His granddaughter certainly deserved better. But it seemed the people closest to her always hurt her. Himself included.

He wanted to change that, which was why he'd done this.

He hoped the short-term strife would lead to them all being closer without this secret between them.

He hoped Summer and her father forged a bond that made Summer happy and gave her someone else she could count on. Because Charles wasn't going to be around forever. And the thought of leaving her just with her mother . . . Well, Summer needed someone who put her first and thought about her feelings and wanted her happiness.

Summer turned to Jessica. "You and I will settle up when I get back."

Jessica leaned forward. "No matter my many mistakes, I always loved you."

Summer took a step toward her mother. "You loved me with lies. You loved me by making me think my own father didn't want me. You loved me with criticism and the pressure to love you no matter how many times you put me last or neglected to think of me first."

Cody took her hand. "I've known Nate a long time. He took me in when I didn't have anyone. He's a good man. Kind, caring. That's why I can tell you, more than anything, you matter to him." Cody met Charles's gaze, then looked at Summer again. "Since you've been kept completely in the dark about Nate, I'll fill you in about him, his family, and the business he built from the ground up."

"Without my family's money, you mean."

Cody nodded, seemed to realize he was still holding Summer's hand, and released it.

Summer clasped her hands together in front of her, like she didn't know what to do with them anymore.

Charles hid a grin and wondered if what was simmering between them would turn into something good in Summer's life.

But Charles let that go and spoke to Summer about her father and the amazing success he'd had over the years. "What your mother never knew about Nate was that he's brilliant. When she met him at twenty, Nate had already finished his bachelor's degree in mechanical engineering. He had an idea but not the money to build it. I made sure he met someone who knew business and finance."

Cody gasped at his intervention. "You set him up with my dad?"

Charles nodded. "I didn't know him well personally, but I knew he was damn good at his job. And I admired Nate for his ingenuity and entrepreneurial spirit. Nate built a prototype while your dad found them investors. Together, they built W. L. Robotics."

Summer glanced at Cody. "Weston and Larkin?"

Cody nodded. "My father ran the business side of things until he passed away and left his share to me and my sister."

Sympathy filled Summer's eyes. "I'm so sorry for your loss."

Cody accepted the condolences with a nod.

Summer pinned Charles in her gaze. "And let me guess, you secretly invested."

Charles wanted to play it off but couldn't lie to her again. "Yes. You can thank your father for your trust fund. All the money in it came from him."

Cody swore under his breath. "You sneaky . . ."

Charles grinned. "Tell Nate he provided very well for her."

Jessica huffed. "Why didn't you tell me any of this?"

"You wanted Summer all to yourself and left Nate in the past,"

Charles snapped. "It's not an excuse for what I did, Summer, but I thought about telling Nate about you all the time. But then what would happen? You'd go visit him. You'd want to stay, because he was a good family man, a hands-on father to his other two girls. Your mother would have been jealous and demanded you come back. She'd have played an ugly game of tug-of-war with you caught in the middle."

"It wouldn't have been like that." Jessica pouted.

He looked at Summer.

She gave him a nod that she understood all too well he was right.

She looked at Cody again. "Nate proved her wrong."

Cody grinned. "Yes. He did. In a very big way."

"Good for him." She looked so proud of her dad. Then her eyes turned stormy again when she looked at Charles. "You and I are going to have a long talk about this, Pappy."

Cody caught himself before he laughed at the nickname Summer used only in private.

The look Charles shot him told him to keep his damn mouth shut. "I look forward to it, Ladybug. Chocolate cake, liquor-laced hot chocolate, and a heated discussion. My favorite kind of evening."

"Over a game of chess," she added, and gave him a cocky grin.

He rolled his eyes. "I should have never taught you how to play."

"I wouldn't want your over-inflated ego to go unchecked."

"Huh," he huffed out, and sat back deeply in his chair, content that the two of them would be fine in the end. Oh, she'd have her say, put him in his place, and whip him at chess, but she'd already decided to forgive him. She was still his little girl.

Summer sighed before turning back to Cody. "When do you want to leave?"

Cody stuffed his hands in his pockets. "As soon as you're packed.

There's plenty of room for you at the house. Stay as long as you like."

"You can't be serious about leaving with this man!" Jessica protested. "You don't even know him."

"I'm going. There's nothing you can say to stop me."

"But I just got back. Roger and I want to celebrate our marriage. I thought we'd throw a huge party at the house. You have to be there."

"I'll be at the next one," Summer said in all seriousness.

This time Charles had to catch himself before he laughed.

"No offense, Roger." Summer truly didn't mean it as a joke or a jab. It was just reality when it came to Jessica. "Enjoy being a newlywed, Mother. After all, this is your favorite part."

Jessica turned to Charles. "Dad, you can't just let her leave. She has responsibilities to you and this company. She can't just leave!" Jessica leaned into Roger for support. "You can't do this. You can't pick Nate over me. Daddy, stop her!"

"She's a grown woman. She knows her own mind." Charles had expected Summer to want to meet her family once she found out about them. He'd hoped she'd make the discovery without him getting caught meddling, but everything was in the open now.

As much as he wanted to hold on tight to Summer, he needed to let her go and do this on her own. He'd steered her into working for him, knowing full well one day the company would be hers. But he wanted her to want it. And lately, he'd seen how she went through the motions with efficiency and an expertise she'd gained being by his side all these years. But she wasn't happy.

And he wanted her to be.

Personally, and professionally.

Summer proved him right by laying out her next steps. "Amanda and Leslie will cover for me and hire temps to see to their other duties," Summer said emphatically.

"It takes two people to cover for you?" Cody asked.

Summer gave Cody an appraising look. "Yes. It does."

Charles's chest puffed out with pride. "And those two won't be half as good as you."

Her eyes went wide with surprise at his rare praise. She deserved it. "Of course, you'll be able to reach me on my cell for anything *important*."

"When do you think you'll be back?" he asked, because although he'd never admit it, the office wouldn't run smoothly without her here. And he'd miss her.

"I have thirty-two days of vacation time saved up. Maybe that's enough time to make up for the twenty-five years I missed with my father. Maybe it's not. We'll see."

Jessica stood. "You can't possibly think to spend . . . what? Like six weeks with your father. Summer, please. We need to talk about this. Give me a chance to explain," Jessica pleaded.

"I don't want to hear any more lies or excuses for the inexcusable. I just want to meet my dad, get to know my sisters, and be a part of a family who doesn't expect me to be anything but me. For once, I'm going to do what I want to do." Summer eyed her mom. "I think it's time I took a page from your book and left all my responsibilities behind for an adventure of my own."

Summer walked to the door Cody held open for her without looking back, making Charles so damn proud that she'd taken the reins of her life.

Chapter Five

Summer heard her mother's outburst through the thick door at her back and didn't even consider stepping back into that mess. She stopped at her desk and stared at all the work there. A whirlwind of emotions swamped her.

"You can't just walk out of here, can you?" Cody took a seat in front of her desk. "Go on. Take some time to do what you have to do to leave without feeling like you're putting your grandfather in a bind. Even if he deserves it." Anger filled Cody's blue eyes.

"I'm sorry."

He shrugged. "Don't apologize. I get it. I was in the middle of a contract negotiation when Nate sent me here. I had to hand it off, and all I can think about is whether my replacement will get the concessions we want." He pulled out his phone, probably desperate for information from his office.

"I'm sorry you had to come here and miss it."

"I'm not," he assured her. "Nate protected and looked out for me, nearly my whole life. When he asks, whatever he asks, I'm there for him, the way he's always been there for me."

A burst of jealousy joined all the other emotions swirling inside her. "It must be nice to have someone in your life like that."

Cody frowned. "Based on what I witnessed today, no one truly has your back."

She shrugged. "My grandfather has always been there for me. But he's . . . complicated. He treats my mother one way, me another."

"And it makes you angry that he expects your best and cleans up when your mom is her worst."

"That's just it, he can't make right what my mother has done to me. But he was a better version of himself for me than he was for her. I saw that growing up. I see it now."

"Why go through all this trouble to get you and your dad together and not just simply tell you where he was and that he didn't know about you?"

Her mother's voice grew even louder.

Cody shook his head. "Right. To avoid that scene."

"He has another meeting in thirteen minutes. I need to hurry and get out of here before he kicks her out of there."

"Don't worry about me. I've got two hundred and nine new emails to read."

She checked her inbox. "Is that all? I've got three hundred and thirty-six, just from the time we met."

He shrugged one shoulder. "The demands of the job."

She liked that he understood her position here and that she was more than just an assistant. Still, she offered what she'd offer anyone visiting the office. "Can I get you a cup of coffee or something?"

"No, thank you. I'd like to get out of here as much as you do and as quickly as possible before your mother tries to tell you again why you shouldn't leave with me."

"Don't take it personally. She's just afraid I'll like my father more than I like her."

"Do you like her at all?" The question seemed genuine and not meant to hurt her feelings or disparage her mother.

"She's my mom. She has her moments. It's in-between those moments that make it hard to like her sometimes. I have to remind myself that she doesn't mean to hurt me. What she does isn't done out of malice, but unconscious selfishness. What she wants to do, she does without thought to consequences, because everything, in her mind, can be fixed."

"You can't fix a broken heart. You can't fix missing twenty-five years with your father."

"No, you can't. But I can choose to stay angry and tarnish this chance I have to get to know him with it, or I can let it go and meet my father with an open heart and mind and see where that takes us."

"I'll give your mother credit for one thing. She gave you a lot of practice at forgiveness."

Summer laughed under her breath. "I guess she did."

"You're down to ten minutes," Cody reminded her.

Summer wrapped things up the best she could before she and Cody stepped onto the elevator. As the doors closed, her grand-father's office door opened. Her mom walked out, eyes bloodshot and puffy, her mouth set in a pout. Roger had his arm around her and whispered in her ear, probably trying to cheer her up.

Her grandfather spotted Summer and gave her a sad smile and a wave good-bye.

She returned the smile just before the doors closed.

"It's going to be all right. You'll love Carmel." Cody held the door for her to step out into the lobby. "I Ubered here from the airport. Should I get us a car?"

"Mine is in the lot." She led the way out of the building to her car. While she drove home, Cody took a business call. She didn't pay attention to anything he said and got lost in her own thoughts. Before she knew it, they were sitting outside her condo.

Large windows dominated the three-story structure. Luxury living. Sutherland Terrace boasted more high-powered executives, doctors, lawyers, and high-tech engineers than first-time home-buyers looking to build some equity to take them to the suburbs and white picket fences. It had all the amenities money could buy. A pool, spa, workout facility, conference/banquet facilities, and the finest security money could buy.

Her place was the largest on the property, a corner unit with a spectacular view from the third-floor rooftop terrace.

"Is this one of the properties you inherited from your uncle?"

"Yes." Along with a few others and several homes around the world. All of which she rarely used.

And she should, because what good was having all the properties if she never used them?

She glanced at Cody's expectant gaze. "Lucy, one of my past stepsisters, who became my best friend, is also my business manager. She oversees all of the properties."

Cody sat back and relaxed. "You're more interested in Sutherland Industries than the real estate?"

"I don't know. I never really thought about it. I've always worked for my grandfather. I can remember coloring at my grandfather's desk when I was little. He'd hold meetings. I'd listen. Even when I was little, he'd ask my opinion about whatever they were talking about. People thought it was cute."

"But your grandfather was teaching you the business even back then."

"Always. He made me feel important, like my opinion mattered."

"I bet that made you feel good when your mom did as she pleased and didn't ask you whether it was okay with you."

She didn't answer. She didn't have to. Cody knew the score on that one.

"I grew up with wealth and privilege," she said plainly. "Everything was the best money could buy. When I decided to move out of my grandfather's mansion, I moved into my very own complex because my grandfather said I needed someplace safe and befitting the manner in which I should be living. It's expensive to live here, but it's not very . . . homey."

She looked up the hard angles and deep gray color of the building and wanted to shudder. There was nothing warm and inviting about this place. It didn't say welcome home to her. She'd made the inside home, but she always felt a little twinge of something when she drove up and realized she owned this place, and she didn't even like it.

"It certainly does have a certain fortress quality about it," he admitted.

The landscaping in front of the property was bright and cheerful and welcomed you to come inside—if you could get past the gates. But here, it was more understated and sterile.

"You should have the landscapers add some more flowers, or something," he suggested.

She frowned. That would help. So would a new paint color. She should take care of it. If she felt this way, she could only imagine how her tenants felt. She should contact Lucy and order the changes.

"My life was handed to me on a platinum platter with twenty-four-karat gold engraving. My mother wants to see me married to a suitable man. My grandfather wants me to take over Sutherland Industries sometime in the next ten years. My uncle left me his real estate holdings."

She sighed. "The things I want are so intangible that the harder I try to grasp them, the easier it is for them to slip through my fingers like smoke."

"Perhaps you need to find something solid to hold on to for a change."

She looked into his compassionate eyes. "I know you're doing this for my father, but thank you for listening and putting up with me and my family drama."

She opened her door, but didn't exit when Cody put his hand on her shoulder, sending a blast of warmth through her system.

"Summer, I get that this isn't easy for you. You can lean on me. And I hope you do, because I'd like to get to know you better."

"I suppose we'll see each other a lot, since you're so close to my dad."

Cody nodded. "Yeah. We're practically inseparable."

She sensed something more to that comment but didn't ask. "I better get packed."

Cody met her at the front of the car. They walked into her place together. She watched him look around her place and liked that he seemed to find it surprising.

The outside was a modern structure, but in here was the feel of a cottage. Rich caramel-colored floors dominated the space. The first floor boasted a wall of windows that overlooked a private patio. Dozens of houseplants complemented the flourishing courtyard garden. The outside space was small, but she'd packed in the flowers and greenery. There was a single lounge chair with a small table on the slate patio.

She loved to sit out there soaking up the sun and reading a book. Alone.

The kitchen, dining area, and living room were all just one large open space. Huge photographs of single trees and forests surrounded the room. The sofas were warm brown leather and looked well used. A vibrant blue blanket lay rumpled at one end where she liked to watch TV or stare into the fire.

A thick, chunky wood table dominated the dining room, with a bench seat on one side and suede-covered chairs on the other. The kitchen had all the modern conveniences done in stainless steel, surrounded by simple white Shaker cabinets.

"This place is not what I expected. It's so . . . warm and inviting."

"Make yourself at home. I'll be upstairs packing. Can I get you something from the kitchen?"

"I'm fine. I'm just going to make another call."

She assumed he was calling her father with an update and to set up their first meeting. A riot of nerves trembled her system. "I'll be upstairs if you need anything. It shouldn't take me long."

"Summer, I know you're a little numb right now. Things will be okay. You'll see. Nate is looking forward to meeting you." Maybe if he told her enough times, she'd believe it.

She slipped away, silently taking the stairs up to the third floor. Her rooms took up the entire space. She had a large sitting area near the bank of windows. It gave way to her huge bed and led to her bathroom and walk-in closet. She normally walked into the space with a feeling of being surrounded by the things she loved. Today, the space felt as vast and empty as her heart. She didn't take any joy in seeing her mementos around the room. Her bed didn't look inviting. It looked empty and too big for one.

It had never bothered her before. But then, there hadn't been a man in her home, a man she couldn't look at without feeling something vibrate and wave through her system like a stone being dropped into a still pond. Those ripples went out and alerted her whole body that something—no, someone—had invaded her system, and he wouldn't be cast out easily.

No, Cody Larkin was a stone, solid as granite. If she grabbed on to him, he wouldn't slip through her fingers. He'd be a firm handhold on this cliff she found herself clinging to, hoping the fall wouldn't be too bad if she was let down one more time.

And that was exactly what she feared the most. If her father turned out to be anything like her mother, disappointing her at every turn, she wouldn't survive.

Walking through her room, she headed straight into her closet.

Pulling out her suitcase, she lifted it on top of the counter in the center of the room and threw open the lid. She stood there looking at all her clothes, shoes, and bags.

She froze, unsure what to take or leave.

Cody stood in the doorway. She felt him, more than saw him.

"I spoke to your dad. He can't wait to see you. Miranda, Nate's wife, is cooking up a big family dinner." He entered the room, closing the distance between them. "Summer, you need to pack, so we can go."

Standing there with him so close, she soaked up the comfort his mere presence offered. "What does one wear to meet their father for the first time, I wonder."

"Your birthday suit," he said, making her laugh. "It's what I was wearing when I met my dad."

She shook her head. She wanted to make a good impression. She desperately wanted him to like her.

"Light colors and lipstick, according to your mother." He sounded upset on her behalf. "Personally, I think you look great in that dress. You'd be beautiful in anything."

She turned and caught the earnest look in his eyes, right before his lids dropped and the hooded sultry look he gave her sent the butterflies in her belly fluttering.

She was being absurd. Her father wouldn't care what she was wearing.

Cody's gaze turned inquisitive. "Is your mom always like that?"

"Always." Summer rolled her eyes. "If I was wearing pink today, she'd have told me that shade didn't suit me. Then she'd remind me how she only wants the best for me and go on to tell me exactly what that is."

"Seems to me, you know what's best for you. You graduated with honors, have a good job. You've got a great place, even if the outside is too modern for your taste. You care for what's yours. You surround yourself with things that mean something to you, or have sentimental value."

"How do you know all that?"

"We hired a detective to give us the basics on your schooling and background, but your place says a lot about you."

"You hired someone to spy on me?"

Cody raised a brow at her incredulous and shocked tone. "I didn't want Nate to walk into the situation blind. We had a ton of questions and no answers for why Jessica would hide his child from him. We wanted some basic information. Nate was desperate to know anything and everything about you. What was in the file is nothing compared to what I've already learned from simply meeting you and seeing your place. The garden is well tended and thriving because you put a lot of hard work and heart into it. The pictures of you and your friends all show you smiling and happy. You don't care so much about their family background and bank account balance, like your mother, but that they're good people."

She appreciated that he saw more than the surface, but . . . "How can you tell that from a picture?"

He went back into her room and brought the picture that was on a table near the windows. He set the picture on the counter beside her suitcase and stood very close to her, like he liked her right beside him. For a second, she thought he sniffed her, but dismissed it.

He smelled fantastic. Something light, like lime, sunshine, and rain.

"Look at the picture."

She'd rather look at him.

"What do you see?"

"Me and four of my closest friends on graduation day. We'd just gotten our diplomas." She looked at all of them wearing their caps and gowns, arms around each other's shoulders with their diplomas grasped tightly in their hands. The culmination of four very hard years of study.

She really needed to stop working so much and spend more time with them.

"But, if you look closer, you're the only one wearing dime-sized diamond earrings and five-hundred-dollar shoes. The others have nice, but inexpensive jewelry. Their shoes and clothes don't come from a high-end boutique."

She raised a brow. "How do you know that?"

"I have an ex who liked expensive things." He didn't look happy about her, or like he wanted to talk about it, so she left it alone.

"So what if they didn't come from wealthy families like mine?"

"Exactly." Since she wasn't packing, he started for her, pulling down several pairs of slacks from the rod, taking them off the hangers, and placing them in the suitcase. "Your mother has spent her life looking down on others because of what they don't have. It's one of the reasons she left your father. You aren't like that at all."

"One of the reasons?" She definitely wanted to know what other reasons he knew about.

"We both know your mother wouldn't have stayed with your father, even if he had been suitably rich. She'd have found another reason to end the relationship. She always does. Her four marriages prove that."

"Five, now."

He nodded. "I stand corrected."

"I don't like being reduced to just another file on your desk." She watched him toss three pairs of jeans on top of the four lightweight sweaters he'd added to the suitcase.

Cody held her gaze. "You're a hell of a lot more than a few facts in a file."

They stared at each other across the counter with her suitcase between them for a long moment. She wanted to think the looks he'd been giving her meant something, but ultimately concluded that his relationship to her father meant he had a vested interest in making sure she wasn't out to hurt Nate. "Tell me about your relationship with my father."

"I've known Nate since I was six. I owe him more than I can ever repay. My loyalty to him made me come here with the intention of making sure you weren't like your mother."

"Spoiled. Selfish. Greedy."

"Exactly. But now that I've met you, it's going to be my pleasure to take you to see him. You are going to make him so happy."

"How can you be so sure?"

"Because you're a woman worth knowing. Because you have everything, but what you value can't be bought. You live a charmed life, yet you know what it feels like to be abandoned, lied to, and hurt down to your core."

"You don't even know me."

"I know enough. I want to know more." His gaze was intense.

"You don't look very happy about that."

"Yeah, well, that's about my past, not you." He turned back to her clothes and pulled down several blouses and started folding them and putting them into her suitcase. "You like to keep people at arm's length."

She agreed. "I have a bad habit of expecting the worst from people."

"I can understand why." He took a step closer. "But you're warming up to me."

"You think so," she teased, wondering how this had suddenly turned even more personal.

He nodded. "It's not so easy to dismiss someone who's genuinely interested in you, is it?"

He towered over her at six-two. His shoulders were wide, his hands big. Everything about him was strong and firm, even the set of his jaw. But it was that damn cocky smile he gave her that made her want to smile back at him. The man knew he was something to look at and had the intellect and personality to match it, and he enjoyed the attention. "I can honestly say you're not a man anyone could easily dismiss."

A teasing light came into his eyes. "And yet you tried."

"Only because I thought my mother sent you. I'll remind you, I apologized for my initial reaction."

"I'll take the compliment. I have a feeling that's as close as you'll come to giving one." He held her gaze for a few seconds, that sexy grin on his handsome face, then turned and plucked her favorite sky blue cardigan from a shelf and put it in the suitcase.

She'd spent a lot of years pushing men away.

Just as she had that thought, Cody settled his hand over hers on the tabletop. "The sooner you realize I'm not like the men your mother's been pushing on you, the sooner you and I can move on to getting to know each other."

"I want to get to know my father," she hedged, though he had her full attention and that of every nerve ending in her body with that simple touch.

"You will. If you'll just uproot those pretty feet of yours and finish packing. That is, unless you want me pawing through your underwear."

She blushed from her collarbones to her cheeks.

"God, you're beautiful." Surprise lit his eyes and shone on his face that he'd blurted that out. He turned back to her clothes and selected a few everyday dresses.

"Stay out of my panties." A split second later, she heard her own words ring in her ears. The blush moved into the lobster realm as she felt the heat in her cheeks intensify.

Cody looked over his shoulder and raised an eyebrow as one side of his mouth crept up.

The laugh bubbled up from her belly and burst out her mouth. She pointed a finger at him. "Don't say a word!"

He held up both hands and laughed himself. "You should do that more often."

"What?" She tried to catch her breath.

"Smile. Laugh. It looks so good on you. And you don't do it often enough."

She found her composure. "How would you know?"

"Because in the dozens of pictures the private investigator took of you, there was only one photo of you smiling." He saw her think about it. "Your dad thinks you're unhappy. I know you are."

She didn't know what to say.

Was she unhappy? Maybe she was just bored with her life. She wasn't sure. If someone asked her if she was happy, she'd probably say yes without thinking twice about it.

There certainly hadn't been much to smile about lately. She'd watched her mother and Roger grow close over the last few months. Her mother's happiness always seemed to make Summer sad. Probably because she knew her mother's bliss meant Summer would be ignored until things hit a rough patch and declined from there, and Summer was meant to pick up the pieces and make her mother happy again.

Was that why she shied away from relationships? Was she too afraid to even try because she assumed they would end in disappointment? She had good reason to think that after her last disastrous relationship. But not all men were like the power-hungry men her mother pushed on her.

Cody wasn't like them. He didn't want to use her as an advantage, or a means to get to her grandfather.

At least, he didn't seem that way.

While turning down the men her mother set up for her had been prudent and protection against being used, she'd dismissed other men's advances for no good reason.

"Summer."

She loved the way he said her name and the rich sound of his voice. "Yeah."

"We need to go."

She redirected her thoughts to the task at hand and pulled out undergarments and socks appropriate for what he was packing. She had to admit, he'd picked most of her favorites. She watched him carefully slide several of her dresses into her garment bag. He had an efficient way about him. She watched him scan her evening gowns and select one after careful consideration. It was a gorgeous gown, burgundy with a beaded bodice and straps that crisscrossed in the back. It draped from under her breasts to just below her knees. When she walked or moved, the dress looked like it floated as it clung to every curve of her body. It was her favorite gown and fit her to perfection.

Even her mother couldn't find fault with her in that dress.

"Why do I need a dress like that?"

"Your father and I have a benefit to attend a week from Friday. You'll be my date."

"You're very sure of yourself." She took the gown from him and held it against her chest, like a barrier between him and her heart.

He reached out and gently cupped her forearm in his warm hand. When their eyes met, he lightly brushed his fingers against her too-sensitive skin. "Will you go to the benefit with me? Please." When she hesitated, he added, "Your father will be there with us, if it helps."

"Why are we packing all of this?" She took a step away and pressed her fingers to her temples with the gown draped over her elbow.

He took the gown and hung it in the garment bag with the other dresses. "You told your family you'd stay with your dad for six weeks." He looked so hopeful she meant it.

"That was just to rile my grandfather. His office will be a disaster inside of two days. He and everyone else will be reminded that I'm more than just the granddaughter of the CEO."

"It never hurts to let them know how valuable you are to them," he confirmed. "Still, don't you want to take the time to really get to know your dad, your sisters, maybe even yourself a little better? I'm sure it feels overwhelming to have a whole other family waiting to meet you. But I'll be there with you."

That actually made her feel better for absolutely no reason that made any sense.

Somehow, in such a short time, and without any real reason to back it up, she trusted him.

Mind made up, she tossed shoes and other clothes into a second suitcase. "I just want things to be different."

Cody caught her by the arm. "Nate is nothing like your mom and grandfather. He's a great dad to his girls, to me and my sister. You'll see. He doesn't want to turn you into something he wants you to be. Maybe some time with him will show you, you don't have to live your life like you don't have choices. You do."

A tear slipped down her cheek. "How do you, a stranger, know me better than my own mother?"

He cupped her face and brushed his thumb across her cheek, wiping away her tears. "We have a few things in common. Your mother is nothing compared to mine."

"What did your mother do, set you up with a woman who only wanted your money and name? Mine's tried to do that a hundred times."

"No, I managed that all on my own," he said bitterly. "We have that in common, too. As for my mom, she walked out the door when I was five and my sister was three and she never looked back. She left by choice because she didn't want to be a wife and mother. Your mother might have lied about your father, but she loves you in her own way. She wanted to keep you all to herself. Selfish, but kind of sweet in its own way. Now that your father knows about you, he wants you, too. My mother didn't want us. That's a knife that cuts deep and makes you bleed. It never scars over and it never heals. Ask my sister."

She didn't have to because she'd spent her life thinking Nate didn't want her.

They stood so close together, their bodies seeking comfort where their hearts seemed hesitant to go. His hand was still on her face. "I don't need to ask your sister. I can see it in your eyes." She knew that kind of hurt.

"If your father had known about you, he'd have wanted you. He wants you now. He loves you already."

"I'm sorry that bitch you were with used you and your mother left you," she whispered, their gazes locked, breaths and heartbeats somehow in sync.

"It's crazy, but somehow hearing you say it makes it feel a little better when nothing else ever has." His mouth hovered over hers, his breath washed over her skin, warm and sweet.

Mesmerized by everything about him and the way he made her feel, she jumped when the doorbell rang. The noise vibrated through the room and broke the intimate spell.

It took him a second to let her go. Regret and need warred in his eyes. "Sorry."

Her heart sank the minute he said that.

"I should have held off ordering a ride to the airport until after we were done packing."

Her heart beat a little faster, knowing he didn't regret their . . . whatever was happening between them.

"Finish packing while I go down and tell them we'll be ready in a minute." His hand brushed hers as he passed and left the room.

The ache of unfulfilled desire swept through her and made her smile. She was beginning to see why her mother liked the opening act to all her relationships. It was exciting experiencing all the firsts with someone you found attractive and intriguing. She found it wonderfully scary, feeling drawn to someone so forcefully that it was like there was some magic energy pulling them together.

She pressed her fingertips to her lips and wished he'd kissed her.

Then she realized she was doing what her mother always did, thinking of the immediate gratification of being with a man and not thinking about the future and the consequences of jumping into a relationship with someone she barely knew.

Focus on your father, Summer. Not the hot guy in your house, touching you gently with those big hands. Don't screw this up. Stop it. Stop it. Stop it.

She shut out her thoughts, slipped out of her dress, and changed into a comfortable pair of slacks. She went to the shelves to grab a sweater, but spun around when she heard something behind her.

Cody stood there, staring at her in bare feet, slacks, and her black lace bra, his gaze hungry and locked on her.

She snagged a sweater and held it against her chest.

Cody seemed to shake himself out of his trance. Swallowing hard, he said under his breath, "Damn."

She tried not to grin and failed.

Cody stumbled over his next words. "Yeah. Sorry. Not really. The car . . . yeah . . . it's here. We should . . . go." He stuffed his hands in his pockets. "Ready?"

For him. "No." But he meant to leave. And she wasn't ready for that, either.

He slowly turned and walked back into her bedroom, giving a fleeting glance at the white iron bed before he disappeared again.

She easily pictured them in it. His tanned skin against the white sheets. His hands moving over her. Their mouths and bodies locked together.

She needed to focus on getting out of here and seeing her father.

It only took her a few more minutes to finish dressing for the plane ride. She gathered her toiletries from the bathroom, made sure she had everything she thought she'd need for an extended stay with her dad, then closed up the two suitcases and zipped up the garment bag, and headed downstairs with what she could carry herself.

Cody waited on the second-floor landing, hands planted firmly on the railing as he leaned against it and looked out the bank of windows toward the city landscape. He looked intense, like he was doing some serious thinking of his own.

"All set?" He turned and finally looked at her. His gaze swept over her dark hair, down the bright raspberry-colored sweater, her black slacks, and stopped at her pink-tipped toes poking out of the strappy heels she'd chosen. They were more comfortable than they looked.

"Do I look okay?"

Cody laughed under his breath. "Gorgeous is more like it."

She didn't know what to say. "Thank you." It didn't seem enough for the way he looked at her.

"Did it ever occur to you that your mom is jealous of the way you look so effortlessly?"

"No."

He shook his head.

"You've seen her. She's beautiful. Men trip over themselves when they see her."

"She has nothing on you. Your beauty isn't just skin deep. It comes from within, too." Cody seemed to catch himself. "Yeah. We need to go. You should get a coat. It's cold in the morning and evening in Carmel this time of year, with all the fog."

"Um, okay, I'll be right back." She draped the garment bag over the suitcase and headed back upstairs for her coat and the second suitcase.

Hormones. They were making her crazy. The headache building behind her eye didn't help her think straight, either. She needed to stop ruminating on the gorgeous man, who saw too much, knew her too well, and made her think and wish for things she didn't think she'd ever have in her life, before he stole her abused heart.

She hoped her brain would start firing on all cylinders sometime before she reached California and her father's home. There, she could focus on family and not the unexpected draw of the man who'd somehow shown her in just a short time that he actually saw her.

She didn't exactly know what to do with him, but she liked having him around.

Maybe too much.

Because he was dangerous to her poor heart. Even though she knew it, she didn't think she could resist him.

$\mathscr{B}$etween boarding the plane and landing, Cody knew a couple of new things about Summer: She'd been on private planes before, but didn't take it for granted. She was polite, never snooty. She didn't expect others to do things for her. And she had a massive headache and never complained about it.

He slipped into his car beside her outside the hangar where the plane now sat parked. "Are you okay?"

She gave him one of those smiles she didn't really mean. "I'm fine. Just a headache." She clasped her hands in her lap.

"You're nervous." It didn't take a genius to figure that out.

"How long until we get there?"

"Depending on traffic, maybe half an hour at the most. I texted Nate to let him know we're on our way. He can't wait."

"I can't believe this is happening." She'd been quiet for most of the flight, though he did give her a quick overview of the family. The rest of the time, he'd given her the time and space she needed to settle into this new reality. He'd mostly worked, answering emails on his phone. "Just take it one step at a time, one day at a time. If you get overwhelmed, we'll go out and do something, just the two of us."

"How do you think my dad will feel about that?"

"I'm more interested in knowing how *you* feel about it."

"Nervous," she admitted.

"At least you're honest." He started the car. "I am, too. Nervous, that is." He caught the soft blush on her cheeks and barely there grin and knew she was feeling something happening between them just like he did. He drove away from the hangar and onto the main road.

"Nice car." Amusement rang in her voice. She checked out the sleek dashboard and chrome controls.

"I knew you'd like it the second I got into yours." He grinned at her.

"Why didn't you tell me you had the same exact Porsche as me?"

"I wanted to see the look on your face when you saw my car." He glanced over at her. "The smile on your face was worth waiting for." He reluctantly turned back to the road.

"Can I ask you something?"

"Anything," he encouraged her, meaning it.

"You're a successful lawyer, business owner, you're rich, handsome—"

"Starting a file on me?" he teased.

"No."

"That's a list," he pointed out. "What's the question?"

"Women, and not just the ones who want something, find you immensely appealing."

"Immensely?" He couldn't help but grin at her again. "Still not a question."

"Why haven't you tried again with someone? There must have been dozens of nice women you've dated."

He heard what she didn't say. "You're safe with me, Summer. I don't want anything from you, except your company, friendship, and trust. Maybe those things turn into something more. But to answer your question, I got burned by someone I thought I could trust. Someone I thought cared about me the way I cared about her. I didn't see the end coming until it was too late and the damage had been done. We have that in common." He turned onto the highway and headed down the coast. "I know you've been hurt in the past. I would never do that to you, because I know how it feels to give everything to a relationship and find out the other person is betraying you. Or in your case, using you."

She turned to him. "Let's not be those assholes."

"Deal. And to add to my answer, yes, there have been other nice women in my life. But I'm not dating anyone right now. You have definitely captured my attention."

Another of those barely there grins tilted her lips.

He really couldn't deny the attraction between them. It felt like a hell of a lot more than chemistry. He truly wanted to know everything about her.

He worried about what Nate would think, but it didn't diminish the desire to be with her at all.

They shared a comfortable silence as he drove and she stared out the window. As the minutes passed, he felt the tension in her grow. "What's wrong?"

"It seems the closer we get, the more nervous I am. I have no idea what to say to him. I don't know anything about him. This is all happening so fast. I have a thousand questions circling my mind. There are so many things I want to know, so many things I want to ask him."

"We're only a few minutes away."

"It's so odd to be this old and to have never heard his voice or seen his face. You have no idea how strange it is to miss something you've never had."

"I have some idea." Despite his mother abandoning him, he missed her. He'd lost his father when he was fifteen and missed him more each day.

She gave him a sympathetic frown. "I can't imagine what it was like for you to lose both your parents so young."

"I had my sister. We had Nate and Miranda and the girls. We're all family now. Sometimes when I feel like I'm alone, I remind myself that I have all of them. And now you do, too. You have me." It made him nervous to put himself out there like this.

She settled beside him, the tension in her easing. "Was he angry that my mom didn't tell him about me?"

"Understatement of the century. But he knows there's nothing he can do about it now. He knows that you wanted to see him. That makes him very happy. Don't be surprised if he begs you to stay."

Cody took the turnoff and slowed on the long driveway. "We're here." The huge house came into view.

The land was beautiful. Tall, old trees lined the wide driveway. Flowers bloomed in front of the house. And the house . . . It was magnificent. Shaped like a wide U with the entrance in the center of the eight-thousand-square-foot space.

Nate and his family lived on the left side. Cody and his sister, Brooke, lived on the right.

Both sides had basically the same setup. Living spaces on the first floor, bedrooms upstairs. Eight bedrooms, eight full baths, two half baths. In the open part of the U off the back of the house was a pool, spa, and garden area. Farther back on the property, the ocean pounded the cliffs.

He loved it here.

He wanted Summer to love it, too.

Cody drove around the circular drive and parked in front.

Summer placed her hand over her stomach. "I feel like I'm going to be sick."

"Take a breath. You're fine. It's all going to be okay."

The front door opened and Alex ran out, yelling behind him, "Papa, they're here!"

"Oh, my god, he has a grandchild."

"That's my nephew, Alex. Your dad is the only grandpa he has on our side of the family."

She paled. "Are we related?"

"Hell, no!" He ran a hand over his face. This had been one of the longest days of his life. While he'd filled her in some about Nate, Miranda, and her sisters, he'd not talked about his family. "Alex is my sister's son. He's five. When we were teenagers, our father died suddenly of a heart attack, and Nate became our guardian. He's watched out for us all our lives."

Understanding dawned in her eyes. "You live here with him?"

"Yeah," he said, and smiled. "Why? You thought you were going to get rid of me?"

"You don't seem to be inclined to be gotten rid of." She grinned, but it didn't quite make it to her eyes because everyone, including Nate, walked out of the front door to greet her.

"You're catching on. Now let's go; they can't wait to meet you."

Chapter Seven

Summer stared out at all the people, her family, waiting to greet her. Butterflies swarmed her belly. Her heartbeat seemed off kilter. Her mind swirled with questions and possibilities and a little fear that this was a mistake and would only bring more disappointment in her life.

But then her father smiled at her. He looked so happy. Tall, with dark brown hair like hers—though his was threaded with silver at his temples even though he was only forty-six—he had the same light blue eyes that she saw in her mirror every morning.

She came from him. He wanted her in his life.

She sighed. The tightness in her chest eased.

She didn't know him yet, but something inside her recognized him.

She exited the car, not surprised that Cody came around the front to take a spot by her side. The little boy was the first to run over and he excitedly asked, "Will you be my aunt?"

Stunned by the request, she didn't know what to say.

Cody put his hand on his nephew's head. "She's not your aunt, buddy."

Alex frowned. "But Papa is my papa, even though he's not. Meme is Meme. Natalie and Haley are my aunts. So she's the aunt, too."

"Who can argue with that kind of logic," Cody said with genuine affection for the little boy. Cody raised a brow at her.

In for a penny . . . She squatted and held out her hand. "Hello, Alex. It's very nice to meet you. I'm your aunt, Summer."

Cody brushed his hand over her shoulder.

Alex grinned so big his cheeks puffed out, then he threw his arms around her neck and hugged her tight.

She hugged him right back and felt something in her heart shift.

She'd been an only, lonely child growing up. She'd wished for a sister or brother, but always took the wish back, because she wouldn't wish her mother on a sibling even to have company in her misery. But here she was, sister to two young women, and an aunt to one sweet little boy.

Maybe he wasn't blood, but he was hers now.

Just like how she felt about Lucy.

Summer picked up Alex as she stood. "I think I'm going to keep you."

Alex giggled and grinned at his uncle. "I like her."

"I like her, too," Cody admitted. He put his hand to her back. "Come on, Aunt Summer. Papa's waiting."

They walked up the wide stone path toward the porch together. Everyone watched their approach and started moving closer to meet them partway.

Cody kept things light. "Have you been a good boy for your mama while I was gone?"

"Yep. We went down to the beach and collected shells. Can I show Aunt Summer?"

"Later. Papa wants to see her and spend some time with her."

Summer couldn't take her eyes off her father. He stared right back at her. In his eyes, she saw regret, but also pride, and a whole lot of anticipation and joy.

But it was the youngest girl, her fourteen-year-old sister, who rushed forward next and wrapped her and Alex in a hug. "I knew you'd come. I'm Haley. I'm the one who took the test and matched with you. How come you didn't come see us when you got the results?"

Taken aback, Summer wasn't quite sure how to answer, except to tell the truth. "Work kind of consumes my life. I can barely keep up with those emails, let alone find the time to check my personal ones. I hadn't seen the results yet when Cody showed up at my office." Summer shrugged and glanced at her dad. "I thought maybe I'd discover I had a cousin, or something."

"I thought I'd find a serial killer in the family," Haley blurted out.

The shock must have shown on Summer's face.

Haley quickly added, "A sister is better."

Summer smiled. "You only got one new one, I got two." She looked to the other girl, who'd moved closer to Cody. "It's so nice to meet you, Natalie. Cody told me you recently turned eighteen and are about to graduate high school in a couple of weeks."

"Dad's buying me a new car for graduation," she boasted.

"Summer drives the same exact car I do," Cody chimed in.

Natalie frowned.

Summer changed the subject and addressed her father's wife. "You must be Miranda. Thank you for inviting me to your beautiful home."

"We're happy to have you." Her smile dimmed with hesitation. "Surprised, but happy," she assured Summer. "There's a room ready for you. While you're here, we want you to feel like this is home." The sentiment sounded genuine, but Summer suspected Miranda had concerns about her coming into the seemingly close family.

Summer tried to reassure her with a polite smile. "Thank you. That means a lot."

The other woman standing next to Nate came forward with her

hands out to Alex. He went right into her arms. "You, my big man, are too heavy to be carried around all the time."

Cody made the introduction. "Summer, this is my sister, Brooke. Brooke, Summer."

"Welcome," Brooke said. "I look forward to getting to know you."

"And I, you."

Brooke was obviously close to her brother, judging by the knowing smile on her face as she looked from him back to Summer. They looked a lot alike, same golden blond hair, same nose, same blue-gray eyes. Brooke was about her height, not Cody's six-two. She was as pretty as he was handsome. Alex took after her, too.

With her hands empty, Summer didn't know what to do with them and clasped them in front of her.

Cody took a step closer, but addressed her father, who seemed as stunned as she was to be standing here together. "I like her, Nate. I think we should keep her."

Somehow, greeting everyone else seemed easy. But with her father, all she could get out was a quiet hello.

"The pictures don't do you justice. God, you're beautiful."

"Thank you." She couldn't help the small smile. Even though they didn't have a history, his opinion mattered to her. More than she realized. "I've never even seen a photo of you. I have to say, it's strange to look at a face so close to my own." She glanced at her sisters. "So many faces that resemble mine."

"The second I knew about you, I wanted to see you. I was overjoyed to find out I had another daughter. I prayed you'd agree to see me."

"I'm sorry about . . . well, a lot of things."

"Nothing for you to be sorry about. Your mother made you believe I didn't want you. Nothing could be further from the truth. I hope to prove that to you."

"I'm just happy we have this opportunity to get to know each other now."

"Me too." Her dad's shoulders relaxed. "Did your mother tell you anything about me?"

"She did. In her way."

Her dad seemed to understand. "She hasn't changed."

"Not in all the time I've known her," Summer confirmed. He was just an arm's length away. She could reach out and touch him if she wanted. She just stood there.

Nate opened his mouth, then shut it, obviously thinking better of whatever he wanted to say about her mom. "Cody and I spoke briefly earlier. I hear Jessica got married."

"You can say it. Again."

"How many does that make?"

"Five."

Nate frowned. "You must have felt very much like a bystander watching the parade of men coming and going in Jessica's life. While she'd love the spectacle and excitement of it, I imagine as her child you'd feel very left out."

"I got used to it." She appreciated that in some small way he understood that her life hadn't been easy.

Cody shifted his weight. "Her mother wanted her to stay to attend some wedding celebration. Summer told her that she'd be at the next one. Funniest thing I've ever heard."

"It's funny because it's true," Summer said, and for the first time turned from her father to look at Cody. He smiled at her, and it went a long way to easing the tension inside her.

Nate addressed the elephant in the yard. "It's strange to have a daughter I don't even know."

She nodded her agreement. "I've always been Jessica Sutherland's daughter or Charles Sutherland's granddaughter."

"Were you close with any of your stepfathers?"

She shook her head. "I was not on the agenda for them. They had other priorities."

"I see."

The sadness in his eyes said he understood all too well that Jessica hadn't married to find a suitable father for Summer. She'd married for whatever advantage it gave her or the man she adored, until she didn't.

"Grandfather was the constant in my life. He's always been very good to me. The stable, loving one in my life. She's . . ."

"Jessica," he finished for her. "She's still a spoiled rich girl who thinks of nothing and no one but herself." His anger was swift and deep.

She understood it all too well. But what could she say? Her mother was exactly like that much of the time. Her mom had her moments, but they were few and far between, and often came when she needed to make amends for something she'd done to upset Summer.

"Let's go inside?" Miranda waved her hand toward the front door. "Nate, you can show Summer to her room. I'm sure she'd like a chance to freshen up before dinner. We'll eat when you're ready." Miranda gave her a soft smile.

Cody turned to Natalie and Haley. "Help me with your sister's bags." Cody waited a second longer to make sure she went in with her dad.

Summer heard Natalie behind them. "How long is she staying?"

"Six weeks. Maybe longer." Cody's voice held a note of hope that eased Summer. He wanted her here.

"That long?" Natalie asked, exasperated. Her newfound sister wasn't on Team Summer.

"I hope she moves in for good." Haley's excited voice rang out just before Summer walked through the front door.

She and Haley were going to get along just fine.

$\mathcal{S}$ummer followed Nate into the glass-enclosed foyer and to the right.

"I hope you don't mind being on Cody and Brooke's side of the house. Though we have a guest room on our side, we thought you'd be more comfortable in this room." Nate opened the door.

Summer stepped into a lovely room, dismissing the furnishing for the spectacular view. The private courtyard had a small pond with a waterfall that trickled down rocky steps and a lounge chair surrounded by flowering bushes and deep green ferns.

"Oh, my god, it's beautiful."

"Cody said you'd like it. He said your place is filled with plants. I hope they'll be okay while you're here."

"There's a concierge service in the building to take care of everyone's homes when they're away."

"Fancy." Her dad grinned. "You own the place, so I'm guessing you implemented that service."

A blush heated her cheeks. "A lot of people in the building travel extensively. It made sense."

"You're a smart businesswoman."

The praise meant a lot coming from her father. "I try to be. But I also have a good management company."

Nate nodded. "Because you're busy working with your grandfather."

She appreciated that he said "with" not "for." "Sutherland Industries will be mine one day."

He held her gaze. "Is that what you want?"

She shrugged a shoulder. "It will be mine whether I want it or not, so it's best to know how to run it for when that time comes."

"You could simply hire someone to run it for you."

"I could. But how will I know if they're doing a good job, or keeping to the company's values if I don't understand it? Real estate is easier to oversee from afar than a company with employees and customers. Dealing with a problem usually means hiring a plumber or contractor. But in business, if you don't understand how all the departments work together and how things are supposed to be done, it's easy to make a mistake that could cost the company a lot of money. And employees their jobs."

Nate's eyes filled with admiration. "Your grandfather taught you well. It's not all about making money."

"People matter," she agreed. "I'd love to know more about what you do, how you built the company, what you're working on now."

Nate grinned. "We have a lot to talk about and learn about each other. Right now, I just want to take it in that you're here. You're my daughter."

"And you're my dad." She tilted her head and stared at him. "I've never said that to anyone."

"I'm sorry. And also, I'm not. But I'm also sad because when I think about how different your life would have been if I'd been in it . . . it makes me angry. But I want you to know, none of that anger is directed at you."

"I haven't even begun to let myself think about and feel the impact of what my mother has done." Tears filled her eyes.

Her dad didn't hesitate. He hooked his arm around her shoulders and pulled her right into his chest. She wrapped her arms around his back and inhaled his scent, feeling for the first time the love of a parent like she'd never felt it before.

"It's okay, sweetheart. We'll get through this. Everything is going to be fine." He kissed the side of her head.

She hugged him tighter.

Cody and her sisters found them just like that. Cody draped her garment bag over the bed. "Everything okay?"

She stepped back, wiping tears from her eyes.

Her father did the same.

It touched her so deeply that he felt as keenly as she did about this moment. "Dad and I were just . . . commiserating with each other about the impact my mother's poor decisions have had on my life and his." She didn't bring up her grandfather's part in all this.

"Are you always this diplomatic?" her dad asked. "Because I don't think I can be that neutral when it comes to what Jessica did to us."

"It's a habit," she confirmed, because being angry when her mother wasn't contrite was just wasted time and effort.

"Your phone's ringing," Natalie pointed out.

Summer dismissed it. "I should probably shut it off for a while. She'll wear out the battery."

"It's your mom?" Haley asked.

"Probably. That or Sutherland Industries has fallen and my grandfather is begging me to come back and put everything to rights again. Either way, I'm not answering right now." She pressed her thumb to the ache pounding behind her eye.

Cody moved closer. "That headache still hasn't gone away."

"I'm fine. It's just been a hell of a day."

Her dad touched her arm, the caress soft and soothing. "We'll let you settle in and have a few minutes of quiet. Meet us in the dining room on the other side of the house when you're ready."

"I'll be there soon."

Her dad and the girls left her room.

Cody hung back. "Do you like the room?"

"It's perfect."

The cocky grin came back. "I knew you'd like it. You'll probably spend a lot of time on the other side of the house, but Brooke and I are happy to share our space with you. Our bedrooms are upstairs. Mine's the last door down the hallway. I got the ocean view." He looked proud of that. "Down the hall from here, you'll find my office next door, then the kitchen and living space at the back. Feel free to raid the fridge and pantry. On either side of the house," he added. "I'll give you the full tour later."

"Thank you."

He stuffed his hands in his pockets. "Do you want help unpacking?"

"No. I'll do it. It will give me a chance to take a breath and settle into this reality. I mean, this is real, right?"

He took her hand and a buzz of heat shot through her. "Real enough?"

"Yes."

"I'll leave you to it, then. Take something for that headache." He squeezed her hand, stared at her for a moment longer, then left her room.

She stood looking at the trickling water outside and sighed with the first moment of contentment she'd felt since she discovered the truth.

She didn't want to keep her family waiting for dinner, so she hurried to unpack her suitcases.

Maybe if she settled in, she'd feel like she belonged.

So she put away her clothes in the huge dark wood dresser with the deep drawers that looked amazing in front of the palest of blue walls. She hung her dresses, blouses, and slacks in the walk-in closet and put away her toiletries in the bathroom vanity drawers. The huge marble shower called her name. The hot water on her tense shoulders would be amazing. Later.

She left her purse on the bedside table, but took her phone with her.

Why? Guilt.

She wouldn't pick up for her mother. But if her grandfather called to check on her, she'd let him know she was okay.

She mustered her courage and finally left her room, though it had been only about fifteen minutes. She felt strange walking across the huge glassed-in foyer and into the other side of the gorgeous house that felt like a home, with all the personal photos, toys on the floor in the living room, someone's homework open on the coffee table, and the smell of dinner in the air.

This was nothing like the home she grew up in, or any of the places she'd visited, being dragged behind her mother.

The only place she'd ever felt this was in her grandfather's home office. There, he had pictures of her growing up through the years. She'd done her homework at his big desk while he worked. They played chess in that room. They talked in that room.

She'd always felt safe and wanted in that room. She hoped to find that feeling here, too.

Voices carried from the dining area, where everyone sat at the long wood table in black leather chairs.

"Does she have other brothers and sisters?" Haley asked Cody.

Summer answered for him. "I've had twelve stepsiblings throughout the years. I'm only close to one of them."

"Lucy," Cody added, letting her know he'd been listening.

"Yes. She is like a sister. She manages my real estate. The other steps mostly lived with their mothers and only visited their fathers on weekends and holidays. It was like having strangers in the house. Kind of like I imagine it feels for all of you having me here."

"It won't always," her dad assured her. "Come and sit."

She passed Natalie, then Cody, and found her spot between him and her father. Miranda sat across from Nate. Haley sat across from Summer. And Brooke and Alex sat across from Cody and Natalie.

Cody stood and held out her chair.

Her dad watched with a slight frown on his face.

Cody's sister, Brooke, smiled hugely at her brother and covered a laugh with a small cough. Apparently, everyone knew Cody was interested in her. Not that it was difficult to see. Neither of them could hide the sizzling attraction.

"So, do you have a boyfriend or husband?" Natalie asked.

Cody took his seat between them. "No. But not for lack of her mom trying to set her up."

"What?" her dad asked, and passed her a platter of pork chops.

She put one on her plate and handed the rest to Cody, then explained her mom's unhelpful matchmaking and how she had mistaken Cody for yet another setup.

Natalie frowned. "Like Cody needs help finding a date."

Summer bumped her shoulder to his. "I'm sure he doesn't."

"I have one with you next Friday."

"You're taking her to the benefit?" Natalie asked, perturbed though she tried to hide it.

"Yes," Cody said, making his intentions perfectly clear. "I thought your dad would like to have her there to spend the evening with us."

"Then she can go with him."

"Natalie," Miranda scolded. "That's enough."

"What? All of a sudden she's part of . . . everything." Natalie folded her arms over her chest and sank into her seat.

Summer knew coming into the family wouldn't be easy, but she didn't expect one of her sisters to be outright upset about it. "I don't have to go if—"

"You're going," Cody and her dad said at the same time.

Her dad touched her arm. "I'd really like you to come. We go as a family every year."

Cody scooped a pile of rice pilaf onto her plate. "Besides, you can't let me go alone."

Brooke grinned at her brother. "If you do, he'll be swarmed by women who will drape themselves all over him. He'll have such a miserable night," she teased.

"Please save me from all that," he mock-begged Summer.

She laughed. "And take you away from all your adoring fans?" She liked getting in on razzing Cody. It made her feel a part of things.

"You and my sister are going to get along great," he grumbled, and filled her salad bowl before passing the serving bowl behind her to her dad.

She bumped his shoulder again. "I'm not backing out if you want me to go."

Cody grinned and nodded, then filled her glass with white wine.

She looked to her father to be sure he wanted her to go.

"It'll be the perfect evening to have all my beautiful girls with me."

She thought it sweet that he looked across the table at Miranda to include her, too. They obviously had a close relationship that had sustained them for about twenty years.

She wanted to get to know her stepmother and asked, "How did you two meet?"

Miranda smiled at Nate. "I work at a real estate office in town. Your father came in looking for some commercial space to lease. We spent a lot of time together looking at one building after the next." She eyed Nate. "After all that, he ended up leasing the very first space I showed him and asked me out to dinner."

Summer turned to her dad and caught the utter look of love in his eyes.

"I didn't need to see the other ten properties. I just wanted to spend more time with her."

Summer sighed. "That's really sweet. And you've been together ever since."

"Twenty-two years together," Miranda confirmed. "We celebrated our twentieth wedding anniversary in April."

Summer had never seen her mother look at a man the way Miranda gazed at her father, her eyes filled with love and adoration. "How did you celebrate such a momentous occasion?"

Miranda gave Summer's dad another knowing smile. "We went to Belize and stayed in this private villa right on the ocean."

"I love Belize. I have a house there." Summer noted that everyone stared at her.

"You do?" her father asked.

"My great-uncle left it to me, along with seven other homes around the world. Wherever he went that felt right, he bought a place so he could go there whenever he wanted."

"Do you travel a lot?" Haley asked.

"When I was young, I'd spend school breaks with my uncle somewhere in the world, when I wasn't with my grandfather."

"Where was your mom?" Haley asked.

"Somewhere else. With someone else." It had been a long time since acknowledging a truth like that broke through the numbness of it all and made her sad.

"She did that a lot, I guess." Her father fumed beside her.

She shrugged. "It's hard to complain when I'd visited twelve countries by the time I was eighteen. The things I saw, the adventures I had. My uncle and grandfather did their best when she wasn't around. And school kept me busy most of the time."

Her dad turned to her. "I would have liked to see your amazing volcano."

She giggled.

Apparently Cody hadn't left out any details about what they talked about earlier.

"You'd have liked it. I used a robotics kit that had these hydraulic-like arms. I made the volcano in five pieces, each attached to an arm. I programmed them to move so it looked like the mountain quaked before it erupted. The boys were so jealous that I got better distance with my lava explosion than they did. It made a huge mess, but I won first prize."

Miranda's eyes filled with delight. "You take after your dad."

"I've always liked to tinker with things. Grandfather never got upset when I took things apart, except the one time I took apart a sixteenth-century clock made out of gold parts."

"Was he mad you couldn't put it back together?"

"No. I put it back together, it just took me a few tries to get it right. He just wanted me to stick to modern things, like the toaster oven, that could be replaced. While I liked taking things apart, putting them back together often got pushed aside because of homework and stuff."

Haley leaned in. "But how are you at freshman algebra?"

She leaned in toward Haley with a big smile. "I rule at algebra. Math has always been my thing. It helps a lot in business."

"You definitely take after him, then," Natalie grumbled.

Haley looked superior. "Natalie sucks at math. I'm really good at it. Like you."

"Everyone is good at something. You just have to find what that something is," Summer encouraged Natalie, hoping to score some points, or at least cool some of Natalie's hostility.

Natalie ignored her.

Cody tapped his elbow to Summer's. "You've barely touched your dinner."

She dug into the rice pilaf.

"Cake," Alex shouted from across the table.

"Soon," Brooke told him. "But you have to finish everything on your plate."

"What kind of cake do you like?" Summer asked the little boy.

"Chocolate." He gave her a very serious face, like that was the only acceptable choice.

"A man after my own heart. Chocolate is definitely the best."

"Uncle hides chocolates in my room for me to find."

Brooke glared at Cody. "I told you to stop doing that."

Cody didn't look contrite in the least. "I know. I ignored you. It's guy stuff, right, buddy?"

Alex gave another serious look and nod, totally with his uncle on that one.

Natalie dropped her fork on her plate, then looked at Summer across Cody. "If your mom is so awful, why didn't you look for Dad? Why not demand he take you, instead of her? Are you just like her and you don't care about him at all? Because he thought you didn't want anything to do with him. He thought contacting you would open up a can of worms and you'd make him pay up."

Summer's heart sank and tears threatened, but she held them back.

Nate leaned forward and addressed his daughter across Summer. "Natalie, you are way out of line. Apologize, then go to your room."

"I'm eighteen, Dad. You can't send me to my room."

"You live under my roof. You follow my rules."

Summer pushed her chair back from the table.

Cody reached for her. So did her father.

She held up her hands to ward them off. "I think I need some air."

"It's too cold to go outside," Cody warned.

She didn't care.

She didn't want to be responsible for ruining what had started out to be a comfortable family dinner.

She didn't want Natalie to feel hurt or threatened by her presence.

And it hurt to think the younger woman thought Summer was anything like her own mother.

She fled, leaving through the first door she could find, only to discover she'd ended up in the backyard by the pool.

Chapter Nine

*N*ate pushed his chair back to go after his daughter and apologize.

Cody put his hand on Nate's arm. "Give her a few minutes to collect herself. She's not going anywhere. She's overwhelmed and not feeling very welcome at the moment." Cody turned his hard gaze on Natalie.

"What?" Natalie looked unaffected. "Everything I said was true. You two are fawning all over her without asking what she really wants from us."

Nate raked his hand over his head. "All you had to do was be polite. Or quiet."

Natalie folded her arms over her chest and refused to look at him.

Cody's obvious attraction to Summer may have made Nate's young daughter even more upset because she worshipped Cody. They were good friends, almost like brother and sister. And Natalie tended to be territorial around Cody because he'd been hurt in the past.

Miranda spoke to Natalie. "Your outburst was hurtful. Not just to Summer, but to your father. He doesn't think Summer wants anything but a relationship with him. You made it sound like she came here with an agenda and we were all waiting for her to play it out."

Natalie glared at her mother. "You can't seriously tell me that you're fine with some other woman's kid coming to live with us."

Miranda sighed. "She is your father's daughter and she is welcome here. It's not her fault she was born, or that her mother kept her from your dad."

Nate appreciated Miranda's support, though he knew deep down she was still processing this stunning surprise like the rest of them. "We've barely scratched the surface in getting to know Summer, and her getting to know us. You had no basis to accuse her of something like that."

He gave Natalie something to think about. "You and Summer have some things in common. You've both led a charmed life. She's inherited a great deal of wealth. I provide you with just about everything your heart desires. You've attended the best schools, you've gone on lavish vacations, you live in this beautiful home by the sea. But you have something she's never had. A mother and father who love you unconditionally. You have our unyielding support. The safety of knowing you are wanted and loved and there is a place for you with us always."

Natalie's lips pressed tight. "She had her uncle and grandfather for that."

Cody huffed out a frustrated breath. "She had nannies and tutors who looked after her while her grandfather was running a multibillion-dollar conglomerate and her uncle was traveling the world. You of all people should know family is more important than money." Cody turned toward Natalie and looked her in the eye. "She has all the *things* that can be bought. Do you think she's ever been loved the way this family loves you?" Cody shook his head. "What does she want? Maybe just for one person to see her for who she is and to love her like no one ever has. But you know what probably seems even more impossible? A family who wants and accepts her and won't abandon her."

Natalie sat up. "*We* didn't abandon her."

"No. You pushed her right out the door." Cody sat back in his chair and stared across at Brooke, who shared a meaningful look with him, because they knew what it was to be left by their mother. And to lose the one person who loved them best, their dad.

"I'm sorry," she said to Cody.

He didn't even look at her. "I'm not the one who's owed an apology."

Natalie sighed, then looked at Nate. "Sorry, Dad."

Cody rolled his eyes. "Summer is owed the apology."

Nate tossed his napkin on the table. "All I wanted was to show Summer that she belongs here with us. I get that it's strange to have her here. We all need time to get used to it and to get to know her. But, Natalie, you need to accept that she is my daughter and your sister, and she has a place here just like you do."

Natalie didn't say anything. She stood, gathered as many dishes as she could carry because it was her night to do the dishes, and walked out.

Miranda sighed. "I'll speak to her. She's just upset that all the attention is on Summer."

"As it should be." Cody didn't usually chime in when Nate and Miranda were talking about the girls.

Nate let it go.

Miranda eyed Cody, then went to the kitchen.

Brooke stood and helped Alex out of his chair. "We'll go have cake in the kitchen before I take him for his bath and stories."

Haley followed Brooke with her empty plate.

Nate and Cody sat in silence for a few minutes.

"I'm sorry, Nate. I couldn't let it go. Not when it comes to Summer. What her mother did to her . . . I only know a little bit and it's enough to make me want to rage at her."

"How do you think I feel knowing that if I'd even once

considered that Jessica could have been pregnant . . . Everything could have been so different for Summer. I missed everything." He slammed his fist down on the table, making his dinner plate and silverware shake and clatter.

"Tell Summer you're angry you weren't there. Make her believe you will be there for her always now. And never forget Jessica told her over and over again that her own father didn't want her."

Nate smacked his fist on the table again. "Damn her."

"Straight to hell," Cody agreed. "Go out there and talk to Summer. Say all the things out loud she wishes one of her parents would say to her."

"I wish I had the words to erase all the bad in her past."

"If only. And a piece of advice . . ."

"What?"

"You don't need to tell her how rotten her mother is. She already knows, and it breaks her heart."

Nate knew Cody was right. He didn't want to put Summer in the middle of his and Jessica's fight. He wanted Summer to be happy.

"Are you interested in my daughter?" Nate blurted out the question because he'd never seen Cody like this. Cody had certainly never spoken to Natalie the way he did tonight, defending Summer.

"I'd like to evade the question, because I don't want there to be any kind of strain between us. But I've never lied to you. And I won't start now, or give you some vague answer." Cody turned and looked at him. "She's different, Nate. There's something inside me that is drawn to her. Every time I look at her, I want to make her happy."

Nate thought about Cody dating his daughter. He guessed if he was going to choose a man for her, he couldn't do much better than Cody.

Of course, Summer could make up her own mind, but he felt better knowing that Cody wouldn't hurt her if he could help it. Cody might have spent the last several years casually dating women, but he was never hurtful.

Nate would watch and wait to see if something actually developed between the two of them.

"I'm going to make it clear to Summer that this is her home. She has a place here now and every day in the future. No matter what happens in her life."

Cody nodded and met Nate's gaze again. "I understand what's at stake." Possibly Cody's place here if things turned sour between him and Summer. "I know what I want and what this could be for us. I didn't expect this, but I'm ready for it." Cody had finally found someone worth letting go of his past and trying to build a future with.

Shock came first. Then Nate thought about how often he'd wanted Cody to find a partner like Nate had in Miranda. Though Cody had dated often, he never seemed to connect with any of the women. Not in a way that didn't leave him free to walk away without a second thought.

Summer clearly had his full attention and devotion, if the way he'd put Natalie in her place said anything.

This could be a really good thing for the both of them.

Or turn into a disaster that left them both broken.

Nate had always been a glass–half-full kind of man, and he'd give them both his support and encouragement, because finding someone who looked at you the way he'd seen them look at each other was rare. And he didn't know two people who deserved it more.

"Just promise me one thing." Nate held Cody's earnest gaze. "If you don't feel for her, what she deserves someone to feel for her in a relationship, you'll let her down easy."

Cody nodded. "I know she'll do the same for me. But I'm hoping we'll have a hell of a lot more of the good stuff than the bad, and that will turn into something worth holding on to."

Nate stood and slapped his hand down on Cody's shoulder. "Then I'll keep my nose out of it and go make it clear to Summer that, unlike her mother, who breaks every pretty promise she makes, I'm a man of my word. I love her, and she can stay here as long as she wants, and this is and will always be her home."

Chapter Ten

Summer stood in front of the beautiful pool. The sprawling patio and lawn were just behind her, the stars were sparkling overhead, and the ocean waves crashed in the distance out beyond the darkest part of the yard. The beat of the waves echoed in her aching chest.

She wrapped her arms around her and tried to stay warm as the swift breeze blew in from the sea, giving a cold bite and salty smell and taste to the air.

She should have gone to her room, but she'd always preferred wide open spaces to think. In retrospect, she should have taken a little time before she came barging in here.

Of course her father had questions about her wants and expectations. Anyone would. Especially if they personally knew her mother.

She just never expected her father to think she wanted anything from him but a chance to get to know him. Her stepmother probably wasn't excited about a surprise stepdaughter upsetting her kid.

Summer thought having two new sisters would make them instant best friends, but she should have known better. Look at how many husbands her mother had—men with their own kids. They'd all come and gone from her life. And while they were in it, there had always been some tension and jealousy.

Why would this time be any different?

She'd taken her father's attention away from Natalie and Haley. While Haley seemed open to being friends, Natalie remained cautious and questioning, wary of the stranger in her house. Summer wondered if Natalie wanted to protect her dad and family, or if her obvious feelings for Cody made her act out that way.

Either way, it didn't matter. Right now, Summer's future with her father seemed tenuous at best.

What was she thinking, leaving her home and job and jumping on a plane with no plan? How were they going to overcome twenty-five years of separation?

Her eyes glazed over and she swallowed hard. She didn't want to cry. It wouldn't help. It never had.

She pressed the heel of her hand to her head over her eye and massaged the building headache, knowing if she wasn't careful, she'd have a full-blown cluster migraine. That was the last thing she needed.

"Summer, are you all right?"

The concern in her father's voice, the pain in her head, and the ache in her heart sent tears falling down her cheeks. When she turned to him, she saw the concern in his eyes as he came to her and stopped short in front of her.

"Please don't cry, honey. Natalie is . . . Natalie. She's never easy about anything. It takes her time to come to terms with new things that disrupt her world. You should have seen her when we brought Haley home from the hospital. She wanted to know when we were taking her back."

Summer grinned. "It's clear she's wondering the same about me."

"She's wrong about you, too. I know you don't want anything from me. You deserve a hell of a lot, but I know you're not here to ask for it."

"I have everything I need, except the one thing I've always wanted."

"Me?" Her dad looked pleased, but also unsure that's what she meant.

"Yes. I wish I could explain what it's like to know your father doesn't want you. I spent my whole life thinking I wasn't good enough for you to stay."

Immense pain filled his eyes, along with a healthy dose of bitterness. "I didn't do that to you, Summer."

"She did. And even though I know her reason why, and I know it's not true, it's really hard to change how I feel inside. I know it will come, but right now, hearing how Natalie feels about me being here, the tension I sense in you because you're angry with my mother . . . It's a lot to process."

She took a shuddering breath and said the one thing her heart wanted him to know. "I've missed you every day of my life."

He closed the distance and wrapped her in his arms. "Aw, honey, if I'd known about you, I'd have been in your life every day. I'd have been the father you needed and wanted. You have to believe me. I am so proud you're my daughter." He hugged her close, but leaned back and looked into her eyes. "Nothing and no one is going to keep me from you ever again. I love you, Summer."

Hearing the words undid her. "I love you, too."

"Every time I look at you, I feel like I need to do a double take."

"It's the eyes." She met his. "It's strange to see my eyes on someone else. Growing up, I always thought I looked like you. I mean, I had to because I don't really look like Mom."

"Your face is definitely an improved version of mine, but if memory serves, she was just about your height and build."

Summer grinned. "That build is what draws men to her."

Her father's cheeks pinked. "I'll admit, she caught my eye."

Summer smirked. "I'll bet."

"But I remember other things about Jessica. The way she walked with confidence. The way her head tilted when she laughed. The way her shoulders elegantly shrugged off whatever didn't suit her."

"She has that down to perfection."

"You take things to heart. You worry about others, your mother the most. You worry about what others think and how they feel around you. I saw it at dinner. You wanted to reassure Natalie."

Summer walked to the edge of the pool and stared down at the clear water. "I don't blame Natalie for her suspicions."

"I wish Jessica had been a better mother to you."

Summer shrugged. "I think she wanted a best girlfriend more than she wanted a child. She can actually be good at the friend part sometimes. The mother thing . . . not so much."

"She and I will settle up one day. But that isn't for you to worry about. I just want you to be happy here with me for as long as I can get you to stay."

She had to admit, now that she had him in her life, going back to Texas seemed sad and lonely and more of the same life she had been existing in rather than really living.

Maybe it was time to take a good, hard look at her life and decide what worked and what didn't for her now. The one thing she knew for sure, she wasn't ready to leave.

It finally felt like that missing piece inside her had clicked into place. She knew who she came from now. Maybe that would help her better understand who she was and who she wanted to be.

What did this new future look like?

Over her father's shoulder, she spotted Cody watching them from the living room window. Their gazes connected and he just stared at her.

Strange. She didn't know how to describe the feelings he brought out in her, because she'd never felt anything like them.

She met her father's earnest gaze. "I'd like to stay awhile. Long enough that I feel like we really know each other." She loved that he nodded his agreement right away. "A little distance between me and my mother right now is probably best. And though she's worried about me and what I'll do next, she's got a brand-new husband to distract her." As if her mother knew she was talking about her, Summer's cell phone vibrated in her pocket. She pulled it out and confirmed that with caller ID.

Her dad's eyes narrowed. "Jessica again, I take it."

"She's called every half hour since I left. I can only imagine how insane she's making Roger right now with all her *Poor me* and *Do you see what I have to put up with*," she said in a dramatic tone, then continued, "*How could she do this, just up and leave and not let me explain. Why can't she see I did all of this for her?*" She held her father's gaze. "It's always the same. I'm her daughter, therefore I have to forgive her and love her like no one else does."

Her dad stuffed his hands in his pockets, as chilled as she was standing out here in the wind and cold. "I see."

"No. You don't. I do it all the time. Eventually, no matter what she's done, I forgive her. Because someday—sooner than I'd like to think about—I won't have Grandfather, and she's all I'll have left. But that was before, and this is now. And I have you."

"Yes, Summer, you do. And your sisters and Miranda. Maybe it doesn't feel like we're all family yet, but in time, I know it will."

"Which is why I can't do it this time. I can't just let this go like I did all the times before. Do you have any idea what it's like to be the levelheaded one all the time? To be the one person she turns to time and again to cry on my shoulder, only to turn her back on me to go out looking for the next Mr. Right? I have never felt like I mattered. Nothing I do is ever enough. And still, I keep trying. Why?"

Her dad shook his head, his gaze filled with remorse and anger. "I'm sorry. That isn't the kind of life I want for you."

She huffed out a frustrated breath and closed her eyes for a second to help ease the tension aching across her brow. She looked at her father. "We're doing it again. I'm sorry. You're sorry. She'll say she's sorry. What good is that when we're stuck in this situation because of her selfishness?"

"How about you and I set that aside and just get to know each other better. We'll leave Jessica for another time."

"Sounds good to me." She pressed her fingers to her temple.

"That headache is getting worse."

"It's fine. Some sleep and I'll be good as new."

Her dad put his hand on her shoulder. "For what it's worth, I think you're perfect."

A surprised smile bloomed on her lips. "Thank you. But you're my dad. You might be biased."

"I'll always tell you the truth. But if you don't believe me, Cody certainly thinks you're special." He stepped beside her and looked at her as she looked sideways at him.

"He's not like all the men my mother tried to set me up with, or anyone I ever dated. He's . . . different," she said evasively.

"That's exactly what he said about you." Her dad grinned.

"I'm afraid I didn't make the best first impression. I had no idea he was there on your behalf."

"I think you made quite an impression on him." He turned to face her. "I can't remember ever seeing him unable to take his eyes off a woman. If you think I'm mad at Jessica for what she's done, he's right there with me."

"He told me his mother left them when he was just five. That must have been really hard on him and Brooke."

"Probably a lot like how you felt thinking I didn't want you."

"Similar, but he remembers having her in his life and rejecting him. I can't imagine your mom is there one day and gone the next because she decided to just up and leave. I never had you in my life. I didn't have to watch you walk out on me."

"No. I never would have done that to you. Even if Jessica and I didn't stay together, I still would have been in your life."

"I know that now."

"I hope you do, Summer. And I know it's not my place to tell you who you should or shouldn't have in your life . . . I just wanted to say that Cody is a guy worth taking a chance on. I can tell you from experience, he's a great friend. I trust him with business. I trust him with my family and my life. I trusted him to bring you home."

She nodded, appreciating the fatherly advice and how he was endorsing Cody without pushing her to or away from him, but leaving it up to her to decide.

"I'd just like to see you happy. I hate to think that Jessica's life has made you so closed off that you'll end up alone."

"You mean like I already am?" The sad, disturbing thought had occurred to her many times. It left her scared that time was getting away from her and she didn't have anyone with whom to share her life and make memories. "Thank you for looking out for me."

"Cody's like a son to me." He paused, then gave her a cocky half smile. "But that doesn't mean I won't kick his ass if he breaks your heart."

She laughed. She couldn't help herself. He looked downright pleased about the possibility of protecting her. "Let's hope it doesn't come to that. Besides, I just met Cody. I barely know the man."

"As long as you're here, sweetheart, you're living with him. That kind of closeness lends itself to getting to know somebody very well."

She looked back at the house and saw Cody in the living room talking to his sister. "Cody and Brooke are lucky to have you. It couldn't have been easy for you to become their guardian when you had two daughters to raise, too."

"They needed me. Without their father, I wouldn't have been able to start the business and build it into what it is now. We worked our asses off to do it. I only wish he'd lived long enough to see how successful it's become."

She liked him like this. He was easy to talk to and he thought like she did. "Cody and Brooke must miss him a lot."

"They were very close with their dad after their mother left them. Brooke lost her husband last year. He died serving overseas. She's had a hard time dealing with the loss."

Cody and Brooke were still talking in the living room, their bond and closeness evident. Alex was climbing over Cody's back. Cody reached behind him and pulled Alex around to the front of him. He hooked his big hands at Alex's armpits and held him aloft and kissed his belly. Alex squealed and grabbed fistfuls of Cody's hair. "They've had so much loss in their lives."

"More than their fair share, that's for sure."

Summer's cell phone vibrated in her pocket and then beeped, letting her know she had a text message. "If Mom is texting, she's desperate."

"Now isn't the time to talk about all of this. You need to think about how you really feel and what you want to say to her about what she's done. Decide what you want to do. Whatever you choose, I hope you'll stay. But if you want to go home, know that I'll be coming to see you as often as I can. I'll pretty much make a pest of myself."

She went into his arms. "That's the nicest thing you could have said to me." She held him close because she could. "Meeting you, being here with you, is definitely the highlight of my day."

"Hearing you call me dad has been the highlight of mine. My life, really." He turned her loose.

"I know it's still early, but it's been a long day. I'm tired. I think I'll let Mom stew a bit longer and just go to my room and do what you suggested, think about what I want to do and say to her."

Nate gave her a reluctant nod. "I'm here if you need me."

It was all she needed to hear to know he loved her and that his love ran deep. She walked with him toward the house, but split off and went to the doors that led into the glass foyer and the other side of the house, while he went into the living room across the way.

Her phone was still going off when she entered her pretty bedroom. She ignored it and did something she hardly ever did: she put herself first.

She changed out of her clothes and into a comfortable tank and shorts set, crawled under the covers, settled into the very comfortable bed, and listened to the quiet.

She had so much to think about, it was hard to focus on one thing. The headache pounding away didn't help.

She let all the troublesome stuff fade and focused on the one thing that had gone right today. She had met her father.

He loved her.

He wanted her.

But that wasn't the only amazing thing that happened. She had met Cody.

She'd never met a man like him. She'd never been drawn to anyone the way she was to him. So maybe this upheaval in her life would turn out to be a good thing. And she wanted to share all of this with someone who'd get it. She called Lucy.

Chapter Eleven

*D*o you have any idea what time it is in New York City?" Lucy answered every phone call from Summer the same, because she was usually overseas and when Summer called it was usually the middle of the night, or some ghastly early time in the morning. Lucy was not a morning person. Mostly because she was a night owl.

Plus, Lucy loved to travel, so a lot of times when she answered the phone, she really didn't know what time it was in that time zone and the question was genuine.

Not tonight. It was too early for Lucy to have lost track of time.

"Three hours later than it is in Carmel, California," Summer answered.

"Wait. What are you doing there? Last we spoke about the hotel renovation here, you were in Texas." Lucy waited a breath, then asked the second question she always asked. "What did she do now?"

By "she," Lucy meant Summer's mother.

Instead of going with the bad news, Summer went with the good. "Something amazing happened to me today."

"You met a guy. Finally."

Summer grinned, thinking immediately of Cody, then, of course, her dad. "Yes. Two of them actually. And they're both great. One of them is my father."

"What?" Lucy gasped. "He finally reached out?"

"No. My grandfather set up this ridiculous DNA test thing to match me with my half sister, so that my dad would finally find out about me."

"What? Tell me everything."

Summer gave her a condensed version of the events today.

"That bitch."

It felt really good to have someone in her life who knew her mother like Summer did and understood without Summer having to explain every tiny detail.

"How could she make you think he didn't want you when the whole time he didn't even know you existed? Like . . . what?" Lucy's outrage matched her own. That's why she and Lucy got along so well. They both came from families where they were mostly left to raise themselves.

Lucy's father had been Jessica's third husband. Lucy and her dad spent a lot of time together when Lucy's mom dumped her with him to do whatever she wanted to do, so Summer and Lucy had gotten to know each other very well, and that friendship lasted through the divorce and beyond.

"I know. It's a lot to process."

"How do you feel?"

She wasn't quite sure at this moment. "Stunned. I can't believe I'm here. In his house. I have my own room. I have two sisters."

"I mean . . . I don't know what to say. Congratulations. You have a whole other family. It's what you always wanted. Is he nice?"

"He's great, like I said. Kind. Loving. He's angry about what my mom did, but he seems genuinely happy to see me."

"That's amazing. And you're staying for several weeks. That will piss off Jessica and give you time to get to know all of them."

"That's all I want, to find my place here, so that I can come back whenever I want to see him."

"Well, don't worry about any of the property stuff. I've got it covered. Just focus on being there, being present with all of them. Wow. My mind is totally blown."

Summer appreciated that she wasn't the only one.

"Now tell me about the other guy."

"What other guy?" she hedged, messing with Lucy.

"Come on. You said, two great guys. You don't like guys, so tell me about this one."

Summer couldn't contain the grin. "His name is Cody."

"Love it." Lucy's excitement was infectious.

"He's a lawyer and my dad's business partner."

"Nice, but also complicated."

Summer nodded though Lucy couldn't see her. "Yeah. He lives here, too."

"Like in the same house?"

"It's a huge house. He and his sister live on one side, Nate and his family on the other." She filled Lucy in on Cody's father and how Nate took them in.

"That's tough. And let me guess, he's gorgeous but also nice. He'd have to be a good guy for you to like him."

Summer grinned. "Think Chris Hemsworth but more serious."

"Gah. You know that man is my kryptonite."

Summer chuckled, because, yes, she knew that, but it didn't make the description any less true. "Cody's . . . thoughtful. Honest. Like he actually says what he means."

"Oh, I like that."

"Me too. I've never been so physically attracted to someone. It's like I feel him when he's near."

"I am loving this for you." Lucy sounded positively giddy.

"I don't know how to do this." It had been a long time since Summer had dated anyone seriously.

"Just go with your gut. And for god's sake, give in to temptation. You have been all work, all the time. Have some fun. Open yourself to the possibility of it all."

That was good advice for getting to know Cody and her family. "I will."

"And, Summer . . ."

"Yeah?"

"You deserve good things to happen to you."

"Thank you, Lucy. Right back at you."

"I'm your best friend. I want you to be happy."

"You're my best friend. I want nothing but good times, good wine, and good love in your life, too."

"You know me so well." Amusement filled Lucy's voice, because those were the three things Lucy loved most in life.

"I love you, Luc."

"Love you back, babe."

Summer ended the call, held the phone to her chest, and smiled, feeling lighter and ready to dive into getting to know her family better tomorrow.

Chapter Twelve

Summer didn't sleep well. Her headache dissipated, but still she tossed and turned and tried to ignore all the thoughts circling her head that wouldn't quiet. She woke up early, put on her running clothes, and headed outside.

The morning was cold and gray, the fog misting the air and making it difficult to see out past the pool to the beautiful coast beyond, but she loved it. She liked everything about being here. Especially, as Lucy said, the possibilities this change could bring into her life.

She had pulled out her phone to play her favorite playlist when it rang.

She thought about ignoring her mother again, but decided to get this over with now so she could run off her mad later. No doubt she'd need a few miles, or ten, maybe a hundred, to release the tension from this call.

She tapped the screen but waited for the initial blast of words before she put it to her ear.

"How could you do this to me?" Jessica sobbed to punctuate the inevitable guilt trip. "How could you just leave?"

In the past, Summer would have led with apologies to soothe

her mom and avoid the drama while squashing her own feelings. Now, instead of platitudes, she said what she wanted to say. "You lied to me. Worse, the lie purposely hurt me. You could have come up with something that didn't make me feel unwanted and unloved. You could have said he died. But no, you chose the one thing that would cut deep."

"You kept asking and asking and it just came out. And then I couldn't take it back. Not without explaining. I . . . I just couldn't."

"You wanted to shut me up, and, boy, did that do it."

"I never meant to hurt you."

The anger roiled in Summer's gut. "You never do, but you do it anyway. Do you know how incredibly damaging it was to tell me my own father didn't want me? Do you have any idea how that made me feel? Do you know how I've carried this with me all these years? Of course you don't, because your father has your back no matter what you do. He's there for you, no matter how terribly you behave or screw up. But you can't do that for anyone else, not even me. Your daughter. All you think about is yourself."

"You don't understand how it was for me. I was only eighteen when I met your father. Eighteen, Summer! He changed my whole life when he got me pregnant."

"He didn't do it *to you*. You can't even take responsibility for your own actions."

Her mother huffed, then went on, as if Summer hadn't said a thing. "I'm the one who had to endure the stares and whispers and people talking behind my back about being a pregnant teen. Do you know how it feels to have everyone talking about you, judging you?"

She rolled her eyes. "Yes, I do. They all talk behind my back about you, Mom. It's not like you're discreet about the many men in your life. You go from one to the next and never think about how it looks to others or how it affects me."

"They're just jealous that I've lived my life the way I want. If my relationships have failed, it's none of their business if I try to find someone else to love me. Everyone deserves to be loved."

"Yes, Mom. They do. I deserved to be loved by my father. I deserved to have him in my life. But you took that from me. You took away his chance to be a good father to me."

"He wasn't able to take care of you. He didn't have the financial security I had to offer you."

Summer exploded out of her seat and started pacing beside the pool. "Money or no money, he had a right to be my father. He had a right to be there to see me grow up. I had a right to see him and know him. Why? Why would you keep me from him?"

"Because I didn't want him to take you away from me!"

Summer believed that, but called, "Bullshit. He's a nice man. A good man. One who cares about his wife and children. He'd have wanted me to have both of you. How hard would it have been for you to let me see him a couple of weekends a month, a month or two in the summer, a holiday once in a while? Was that so much to ask? God knows you were gone more than that most of the time, so why not leave me with my dad instead of someone you paid to watch me?"

"That's not fair, Summer. I was always there when you needed me."

"Some of the time," Summer qualified, because her heart wouldn't allow her to not give her mom credit for coming through the times she did. Positive reinforcement. "It might have been nice to have a man in my life who didn't leave and never looked back once he was done with you. None of your exes loved me like I was their child. You know what I learned about men from you? I'm not good enough for them. They leave. They're expendable. They're not worth the effort to make them want to stay. If they don't work out, find a new one."

Her mother sniffled. "Don't be mean."

"I learned it from you." Summer tried to reel in her rage before she said something too terrible to take back.

"You had your grandfather. Look what he's made you into. You practically run that company."

"Again, Mom, not the same."

Jessica cried softly. "I've made mistakes. Lots of them. My greatest hope is that you don't make the same ones. I hope with my whole heart you find a man who loves you more than anything and spends a lifetime building a life and making memories with you."

Funny, Summer had the same wish.

But she didn't let her mom off the hook. "Yet you continue to try to set me up with men I have nothing in common with or even like."

"How would you know? You never give any of them a chance."

"In the beginning I did, but we both know how that turned out." She'd been set up to fail.

"I only want the best for you. I'm your mother. That's my right."

"And Nate Weston is my father. What rights did you allow him? You took them all away by not telling him he had a daughter. Didn't you think he'd want the best for me, too? He's welcomed me into his home and his life without reservation. He loves me."

"He doesn't even know you."

"He's my father! I'm his daughter! That's enough for him. It's enough for me! There doesn't have to be anything else. I love him because he's my father. I love him because he wants to be a part of my life. I love him because I know, no matter what, I can count on him to be there for me. That's the kind of love we all want, Mom. It's the kind of love I have for you. No matter what else happens between us, I love you. I love you despite what you've done. I just don't like you right now."

"Your father and I came from different worlds. I had enough

money to do as I pleased for the rest of my life. Having that kind of money so young can allow you to do stupid things."

"Like run away from home looking for adventure, only to end up pregnant." Summer plunked her ass down on the end of a chaise longue.

"Yes. I loved your father for those few short months. We were happy together and so much in love when we made you. Those are memories I'll never forget. I'll cherish them the rest of my life. Your father will always be special to me because he's your father."

"Mom, I hear you saying the words, but your actions say the opposite. You loved him enough to spend time together and make me. Couldn't you find a little of that love left in your heart to tell him he had a daughter?"

"I was young and scared. I had a brand-new baby. I was so overwhelmed and out of my element trying to take care of you. I just wanted to have you all to myself. I know that sounds selfish. But that's how I felt. Summer, darling, it's complicated. When you have a child of your own, you'll see. Nothing is easy about having a baby and raising them."

"It could have been a little easier if you'd had Dad to help you."

"That would have just made things more complicated."

"Yes, because you were about to be married to Thomas."

"That had nothing to do with it." Her mother's quick defense didn't make the words ring true.

"No? I wonder. You said you left Dad because he wasn't financially sound and you didn't think he could support me. Yet, when you left Dad, you didn't know you were pregnant with me. You told Grandfather you'd changed your mind about going to college. Then, you found out about me a few weeks later. From what I've heard, Thomas came into the picture about that time, too. A nice, sweet man, a few years older than you, who adored you enough to want to raise a baby with you. You had months to tell Dad about me before I was born, but once you met Thomas, the thought of telling Dad went right out the door. I know what you wanted. You wanted to marry Thomas and have the perfect husband, the perfect daughter, the perfect marriage filled with love and happiness."

"Summer, listen to me. It wasn't like that."

Yes, it was. "Don't, Mom. It's like that with all of them. Once you had Thomas in your life, the past was just a dark memory and your future looked so bright. You always tell me to look forward, there's always a light at the end of the tunnel. What you don't realize is that people aren't perfect, love isn't perfect, you have to work at it to make it the best it can be."

"I'm glad you've learned that, darling. It's a lesson I don't seem to take to heart. I'm always looking for the perfect guy and the perfect love."

"They don't exist." Summer pressed the heel of her hand to her head. She had a hard time deciding what hurt more, her head or her heart. "You taught me that. It was a lesson learned the hard way, but one I won't forget."

"Summer, please try to understand."

"I do understand. You don't have a single valid explanation for what you did. As usual, the only person you were thinking about was yourself."

"Summer, please. Come home and we'll talk about this."

"No. I'm staying with Dad. I think it's past time I get to know him and myself a little better. I'm tired, Mom. I'm tired of living my life the way you and Grandfather want. Yesterday really opened my eyes. I saw my life through Dad's eyes, and it's a sad and lonely existence."

"Seriously. You have a great job. You've got a top-notch education, money, and enough real estate to make one of those Kardashians jealous."

Summer sighed heavily. Her mother just didn't get it. Maybe she never would. "Mom, what you don't seem to realize is that none of that matters when I'm alone."

"You have me. You have your grandfather. And if you actually tried to open your heart, you could have any man you want."

"You and Grandfather lied to me my whole life." Summer pressed her hand to her throbbing head and let the tears fall. "Did you know I've spent my whole life thinking that if my own father didn't want me, why would anyone else?" While Summer knew her mother loved her, Jessica didn't always show it, and sometimes she wasn't even nice.

"Oh, Summer, I'm sorry."

The words didn't hold a lot of meaning right now. "It's too late for sorry!"

"Summer, what are you saying? You can't possibly think to stay there with your father indefinitely. You have a life here in Dallas."

"I've spent my whole life trying to be the best I can so that maybe you'd notice me and want to be with me instead of whoever else you were with. I've tried very hard to be what you wanted."

"You're everything I wanted, darling. Always. You're my special girl." Again the words were nice, if only Summer believed Jessica meant them.

"It's all I ever wanted to be, but I never felt special. You never made me feel that way. You lied to me. That lie changed who I might have been into the woman I was yesterday. Today I know the truth. Somehow, I have to figure out who I am now."

"You're the same wonderful woman you've always been."

"Not anymore. I feel like the rug has been pulled out from under me. Everything I thought I knew is based on a lie."

"Please, Summer. Come home. We can work this out."

"I'm staying here. Good-bye, Mom." Summer hung up as her mother yelled protests. Her cell phone rang immediately. Summer turned it off and let the tears stream down her face.

Chapter Thirteen

*C*ody slowed to a walk the second he entered the property along the coastal side. Normally, he'd stop and take a few minutes to enjoy the view. Sometimes he even went down the stairs to the beach. But he thought he saw someone sitting by the pool through the misty morning and headed that way without thinking, like some force was pulling him in that direction.

It all made sense when he got close enough to make out Summer, sitting on the end of the lounge chair dressed in tight black pants, a light blue hoodie, and running shoes, her long dark hair tied in a ponytail.

It didn't take a genius to figure out why she was crying when he spotted the phone in her hand.

He squatted in front of her and put his hand on her knee. "If I'd known you like to run in the morning, I'd have waited for you." He'd be happy to go with her now, except he needed to get to work soon.

It took her a second to wipe her tears and look at him. "How far did you go?"

"Five miles." He could do five more. "Did you sleep well?" He didn't think so, judging by the dark circles under her bloodshot eyes.

She looked tired and defeated. She pressed the back of her hand to her forehead. "I slept some. Mostly, my head kept spinning."

He didn't like the strain in her eyes and voice. "It must be incredibly hard to talk to your mother when she just doesn't get it and never will."

His knees started to ache, so he turned, sat on his ass on the stone patio next to her, knees up, his forearms balanced on them.

She stared off into the distance. "It's been a long time since I cried over something she did."

He believed it. Why cry when the other person didn't care if you hurt or not? "This one deserved a good cry. Feel better?"

"About her? No. Plus I'm embarrassed you caught me looking like a complete ragged mess."

Cody bumped his shoulder against her arm. "You're beautiful no matter what."

Tears gathered in her eyes again. "Don't be nice to me. Not right now. It's just not fair."

He hated that a little bit of kindness undid her all over again. But she'd have to get used to it, because he didn't know how to be any other way when it came to her.

"Get used to me being nothing but nice to you." To prove it to her, he stood, straddled the chair behind her, and slid his palm up her back and massaged the tight muscles in her neck.

She sighed out her pleasure and relaxed as the quiet morning surrounded them and the ocean kept its beat against the beach and rocks in the distance.

"You don't have to do that."

"You've still got that headache. If it means you feel better, I'll sit here all day doing this." He'd cancel all his meetings if it made her happy.

"Even if you freeze your ass off?"

"Even then," he assured her, though the cold was starting to steal the heat from his sweaty body.

Silence wrapped around them as they sat quietly, peacefully. He didn't feel the need to talk.

She seemed content to sit and stare at the pool and gray mist beyond, with him working out the knots in her neck and shoulders.

He'd never experienced a comfortable silence. Not like this.

He liked it. With her. He loved the feel of her, the sweet, intoxicating scent of her, and the way she sat in this moment with him, content to just let it be.

The longer he sat with her, the more reluctant he was to end it and go up to the house where they'd eventually part for the day. It felt too good. It felt so right. And it scared and thrilled him all the while that he felt like he was where he belonged.

Cody leaned in and whispered, "Do you feel it? This thing between us." He thought she did, but he had to hear her say it.

She nodded. "It's unexpected."

"And?"

"Unfamiliar."

"And?"

"Nice. Really nice." She turned and smiled at him.

That simple thing made him feel ten feet tall and so damn happy. He wanted to bask in her sweet grin.

She pressed her lips tight. "I've never felt . . . comfortable with men. I'm always waiting for them to reveal what they actually want from me, once the pleasantries are done."

"If you think that about me, I'll end the suspense, though I think you've found me out already. I want you. It's that simple. I can't explain it. I can't define it. It just is what it is."

She shifted again and looked directly at him.

He regretted having to take his hands off her.

"I don't know what to say to that."

He only wanted to know one thing right now. "Are you open to the possibility of us?"

"I . . ." Her gaze dropped to the pool deck.

He touched his finger to her chin so she'd look at him. "Don't overthink it. Just answer the question."

She took a steadying breath. "Yes. I'm open to . . . whatever this thing is happening between us."

A simple agreement, like her smile, shouldn't make him this damn happy, but it did. They barely knew each other. They hadn't even kissed. Yet just knowing he was going to have the chance to forge a relationship with her eased him in a way that he'd never felt asking anyone else out. Ever.

It floored him.

"But . . ." she added.

He didn't want to hear what came next. "What?"

"I need some time."

He exhaled his relief. "Take all the time you need." She'd had a hell of a time since yesterday. A lot had happened. She hadn't expected to be reunited with her father. Or for the attraction between them to be so intense.

Maybe he needed a minute, too, but it seemed all he could do was lock down her yes to them being more to each other.

"But Summer . . ."

"Yeah."

"Don't push me away. I'm used to getting what I want." Maybe that was too blunt, but it was true.

"Because you go after what you want." She knew that about him already. The admiration in her eyes said she liked that about him. Maybe especially because he wasn't holding back going after her.

He couldn't wait to share more of himself with her. "I can be patient for you. I can go slow. But I don't think I can hold back entirely."

"We've already started, haven't we?"

"Yes. We are off to a really great start."

"I would really like it if you were my friend. And more," she added, a blush brightening her soft cheeks.

"I look forward to you thinking of me as your friend and us becoming much, much more." Maybe that had been the problem all along. He'd never let any other woman that close after Amy. He'd tried so hard to connect with her and it didn't work. Now, with Summer, it felt so easy to open up and ask for what he wanted. Because it mattered to him.

Yeah, he wanted Summer. But he really liked the idea of being friends and lovers.

Nate and Miranda were like that with each other. He admired them as a couple. He thought what they shared was special. Now, he realized the reason they worked so well together was that they were truly friends. And more.

Summer had it exactly right.

So as much as he wanted to kiss her right here, right now, and seal the deal that they were together, he didn't.

He simply decided to spend the next few days getting to know her better and letting her get to know him. "I'd really like to hang out with you today."

She gave a half smile. "But you need to get to work."

He frowned. "I do."

"I'm going to go for my run, then ask my dad to lunch, so maybe I'll see you later."

"I look forward to it." He looked out toward the ocean. The mist had thinned as the sun rose higher in the sky. It would be another beautiful day. "Once you get to the path along the cliff side, go right. You can follow it for several miles until it branches off into a regional park. From there, it goes on for several more miles on different trails. There are maps along the way."

She held up her phone. "Thanks. I found a map and plotted a course."

"Good. Then I won't worry about you getting lost." He stood and held his hand out to her.

She took it and stood next to him.

He held on for a long moment as they stared at each other. He wanted to wrap his arm over her shoulders and draw her close to him. It took a great deal of effort to simply enjoy the feel of her hand in his.

Something drew her attention away from him and up to the second floor of Nate's side of the house.

He followed her gaze to the upstairs windows and spotted Natalie staring out at them from her room.

Summer held up her free hand and waved.

Natalie whipped around, turned her back on them, and stormed off.

Cody's gut tightened with a warning. "I don't understand why she's so upset about you."

"She thinks I'm taking something away from her."

"Nate is your dad, too."

"I think she doesn't want to share *you* with me."

Cody snapped his gaze back to her. "Natalie and I are close. As in sister and brother. We practically grew up together. I look out for her. She looks out for me. After the breakup with Amy, I was torn up and angry. She tries to protect me because of it."

"She doesn't want to see another woman do that to you again."

"I don't want that, either," he admitted.

"I completely understand. It sucks to have someone treat you so callously."

"You're not like that."

"I hope Natalie sees that soon and she and I can be friends, too. But I think you need to be aware that her feelings for you may run deeper than yours do for her."

"That's ridiculous. It's not like that."

Summer shrugged one shoulder and gave him a look. "You know her better than I do."

"Which is why I can tell you, in a day or two, she'll come around and see you the way I do. You're not after anything. All you want is the family you were denied all these years. And me."

She smiled again, and he loved it. "Lawyers. Always so sure of themselves."

"Especially because I know we're on the same page."

She tilted her head. "Promise me you'll always say what you mean."

"You're beautiful and I want to kiss you so damn bad it hurts. How's that?"

The pretty blush came back. "Perfect. It gives me something to look forward to." With that, she squeezed his hand, then turned and walked past the pool toward the ocean, giving him zero opportunity to try to change her mind about waiting for that kiss.

But he'd already decided that her needing time was a good thing for both of them.

Even if he wanted to kick his own ass for not going on instinct and kissing her.

Something to look forward to, indeed.

Chapter Fourteen

Summer ran about two miles out, then stopped and turned back. She didn't have the strength to go on. Her head hurt, so she walked back to her father's place to see if she could catch him before he left for the office.

She spotted the family through the glass doors leading into the kitchen. She hesitated for only a moment before walking in.

Haley shrugged on her backpack and smiled. "I went to your room, looking for you, but you weren't there. I thought maybe you left." Haley looked relieved she hadn't.

"Nope. Still here. I just went for a run."

"Trying to impress Cody?" Natalie asked.

"I run most mornings." Summer smiled at Natalie, hoping to show her sister she wasn't doing anything she wouldn't do at home.

Miranda picked up her keys from the counter. "Did you sleep well?"

"Not really. The room is beautiful. I was just overwhelmed."

Miranda nodded. "Totally understandable, given the circumstances. Please make yourself at home. Breakfast is everyone for themselves around here. There's lots of stuff in the fridge and pantry. Make whatever you want. Add whatever you'd like to the grocery list on the bulletin board in the pantry. Our housekeeper does the shopping every Tuesday. The girls and I will be home around three-thirty. Nate usually gets home by six, though I suspect he'll try to make that earlier since you're here."

"I'll be fine. No one needs to change their schedule or entertain me."

"Can we do something together after I get home from school?" Haley asked.

"Absolutely." Summer wanted to get to know both her sisters, but she'd start with Haley and hope Natalie came around in time. "Natalie, I'd love it if you joined us."

"I'm busy." Natalie didn't even look at her.

Miranda gave Summer a sympathetic look. "Come on, girls, time to go to school."

Haley gave her a wave. Natalie kept her focus on her phone. Miranda touched her on the shoulder as she passed, then kissed Nate good-bye.

Her dad joined her in the kitchen. "It's crazy here in the morning sometimes."

Summer tried to act casual and like she belonged. She went to the coffeepot and took a mug from a hook above it. "Can I pour you a cup?"

"I already had mine while you were on your run."

She sipped the coffee, then turned to him. "I take it you saw me and Cody out back this morning before I left."

"I saw you on the phone first. I assume you spoke to your mom."

"I did. She's unhappy I won't come home." She didn't want to get into all that again, so she changed the subject. "Do you have time to have lunch with me today? I can meet you at your office, maybe get a tour if you have time."

His whole face lit up with joy. "I'd love that. I wanted to clear my calendar for a few days, but we've got this big project going and—"

"It's totally fine. Although I told my grandfather I'd be back in six weeks, I'll be checking in with the office and taking care of things from here. I don't expect you to upend your life just to spend time with me. We'll do that when we're all together. I don't need to be entertained." She sounded like a broken record, but wanted everyone to do what they normally did and include her when appropriate.

Brooke and Alex walked into the kitchen. "Hey, I just wanted to say good morning before I take this one to school."

Alex ran to her and wrapped his arms around her legs. "Hi."

She smiled down at him and rubbed her hand over his back. "Hi. Have a good day at school."

He looked up with big, round eyes. "Can I stay home with you?"

"No," Brooke said. "Aunt Summer has things to do. And you need to learn new things."

Summer stared down at Alex. "You can tell me all about what you learn today when I see you later."

Alex sighed. "Okay." He released her and took his mom's hand.

"Bye." Brooke left with Alex, waving to her and Nate as she turned to go.

Summer focused on her dad. "You've got a houseful."

"That's why I built this place. I wanted everyone together." Her dad's eyes turned thoughtful. "You and Cody looked pretty serious this morning."

Just thinking about Cody made butterflies take flight in her belly. "I like that he's blunt and honest. It feels like things are moving faster than my normal speed." She thought twice about that. "Actually, I don't know my speed, since I don't really date. But, here's the thing. I like him. It's been a long time since I liked a man as anything more than just an acquaintance."

She saw her father's concern and knew he wanted to say something more. "He saw that I was upset about the call with my mom.

He sat with me without bombarding me with questions. He didn't try to fix it or offer me platitudes that everything would be all right. He just wanted to be there with me. No manipulations. No expectations. No wanting something in return." She shrugged and hoped he understood.

"Cody can be a very kind man. He gives all of himself for this family, to each and every one of us. He's reserved with other women, and always polite. He's different around you in a way I can't exactly explain. Though it looked like your conversation was serious, he was all in it with you. Totally focused and present."

"He wanted to know if I felt what he's feeling. And I do. Neither of us can really explain it, but we both want to see what comes of it."

"He expressed as much to me last night."

It eased her to know he'd been just as open with her dad as he'd been with her. But it seemed her dad needed some reassurance as well. "I'm here first and foremost to get to know you and find my place in this family. I asked Cody for some time to settle in. He agreed that we'd take things slow."

"I'm happy to hear it. This has got to be a lot for you to process. I know it is for me, and all I've got to do is be with you. You're in a different state, in an unfamiliar home, away from your family, friends, and work. And there's what's happening between you and Cody."

"It's a lot," she agreed. "But I have a lot of options available to me and a lot of opportunities, too. I'm lucky that way. This is the first time in my life I haven't done what's expected without question. I'm not going to do that anymore."

"I want you to stay here with us because it's what you want, too. I love you, Summer. Your happiness is all that matters."

"It's really nice to know you have my best interests at heart."

"Always."

"Well, I better let you get to work."

Nate pulled out his wallet and handed her a business card. "There's my number and the office address." His gaze narrowed. "I didn't think of it until now, but you don't have a car."

She held up her phone. "I'll use a ride service. No worries. Plus, I think I'll buy a car to keep here for when I visit."

Her dad went still. "Um, I could get you one, if you want."

She shook her head. "It's not necessary. I'm sure Cody told you the money in my trust came from your success. You provided well for me."

"I really hate the thought of having to thank your grandfather," he grumbled.

"In this case, I think he still owes you an apology."

Nate's eyes brightened at that. "Good, because I don't think I could get the words out."

"I won't be thanking him for it, either. But I will meet you for lunch. Around noon?"

"Sounds perfect. I'll see you later." Her dad smiled, then leaned in and kissed her cheek. "I'm looking forward to this."

"Me too." She walked with him to the front door and waved him off, then went to her room to shower and pick the perfect outfit for lunch. And for seeing Cody again.

It felt new and exciting to think about how she looked for someone else. She wanted to impress him. She wanted him to like her.

So far, he did. A lot, it seemed.

And for the first time in a long time, she opened herself up to wanting more.

Chapter Fifteen

Morning didn't pass in hours, but in the number of times Cody thought about Summer. She was a distraction he couldn't afford to indulge in, but his mind didn't seem to want to think about anything else. By his third meeting, it was getting embarrassing to have colleagues and clients clear their throats or call his name to get his attention back on the subject at hand.

After this last meeting, he'd opted to stay in the conference room for a few minutes to clear his head. He had a million things to do today, but all he wanted to do was go home and see her. Before he thought about it, he picked up his cell from the table to call her, then realized he didn't have her number.

Glancing at his watch, he wondered if she'd arrived for lunch with her dad yet.

He grabbed his files and headed for the conference room door as two guys walked side by side down the hallway, engrossed in conversation and not paying attention to who was around them.

"Did you see her?"

"I couldn't miss her. I thought his oldest was in high school. But she's definitely not. She's hot."

The first guy got a certain look in his eyes. "Those legs . . . I'd like to . . ."

"Not finish that sentence and keep your job," Cody said just as they got to the door he stood in, files and phone in hand.

"Mr. Larkin, I . . . uh, didn't see you there," the guy stammered.

Cody recognized both men. They worked in the finance department, but he couldn't place their names at the moment. "If you don't want to spend the next week at the mercy of the human resources department going through their comprehensive sexual harassment seminar, I suggest you choose your words more carefully in the office."

"Yes, sir," both men said, looking properly contrite and nervous about being reprimanded. Cody couldn't have employees talking about any woman that way in the office and thinking it was okay. And he damn well wasn't going to let anyone talk about Summer that way when he was around.

"I suggest the two of you get back to work."

Wisely, they left without another word. Cody headed out of the conference room and upstairs. His day was looking up, Summer was in the building. Now all he had to do was catch up to her before she left with Nate.

Walking off the elevator, he scanned the wide room, disappointed that among all the cubicles and people outside the executive offices, he didn't see the one woman he wanted. And god, how he wanted her. If he was this tied up in knots after a day, he didn't want to know what he'd be like in a week. He hoped she didn't have him on his knees begging.

With that thought in mind, he told himself to take a step back, not let her see just how much she affected him.

Yeah, right. Like she didn't already know.

Brenda, his administrative assistant, looked nervous and rushed as he approached her desk outside his office. Three lights were lit on her phone and she was opening documents on her computer as the printer spit out papers with a steady hum and slide.

"Cody, security just called. The gentlemen from Parkington are on their way up. The contracts are on your desk. I can set you up in the executive conference room if you'd like."

"My office is fine. What are you printing?" He didn't think he'd ever seen the thing spit out so many pages at once.

"Sutherland Industries sent something to Miss Weston. She's using your office." Brenda's eyes darted from him to his open office door and back again. "Nate said she could while he finished his own meeting."

Now he understood what had her so frazzled. He didn't like people in his office without him or Brenda present because of the sensitive information he dealt with. "It's fine. I don't mind if Summer uses my office while she's here. In fact, I wouldn't be surprised if she comes in to work from here from time to time."

"Mr. Sutherland called several times this morning trying to reach her through Nate's office. No one knew anything about her, or her connection to Nate."

Cody understood exactly what Brenda was saying and what she and everyone were wondering about. Nate was going to have to spread the word that he had another daughter.

"She was busy this morning and not answering calls. I'm sure Mr. Sutherland figured the next easiest way to contact her was through her father here at the office." Deciding that was enough information to put out on the grapevine without really saying anything confidential or personal about Nate and Summer, he changed the subject quickly. "Who's holding? Anything I need to take?"

"Actually, that's Miss Weston. She's using all the lines at the moment. Is she a lawyer or businesswoman of some kind? She's been issuing orders and talking nonstop since she went into your office."

"She's Charles Sutherland's granddaughter and his right hand. He wasn't expecting her to take a sudden vacation, so he's probably got some urgent matters to talk to her about while she's out of her office."

"Oh. Well. It's just . . ."

"What?"

"I thought you and the others worked hard. That woman's on a mission."

No doubt. In the little time he'd spent watching her at Sutherland, he'd learned one thing for sure: Summer was exceptionally competent and smart. He had no doubt Charles was feeling her abrupt absence.

"Like I said, she might be here on and off over the next few weeks. You and the others should assist her with anything she needs."

"Of course. The Parkington guys are coming off the elevator. Shall I ask them to wait?"

"Give me a few minutes." He went into his office and closed the door behind him.

Damn, Summer took his breath away. No wonder those two finance guys were talking about her. She looked like a million bucks in that dress.

"Listen to me, Roger. I know my mother is upset. I know this is supposed to be a happy time for her. I'm sure you can understand my perspective in this. I'm the one who's been hurt. She was wrong to do what she did, and now she's going to have to live with the consequences of what she's done."

Cody watched her rub her fingers above her eye in a gesture he was tired of seeing her do. He knew that headache still bothered her. And she was still dealing with her mother through Roger, the newest husband.

"I'm sure the party will be lovely. She'll have no trouble putting together a fabulous spectacle for everyone attending."

Cody walked right up to her as she stood behind his desk, phone to her ear, distress written all over her face. Dropping his files and phone on his desk, he stepped behind her, put his hands on her shoulders, squeezed, and dug his thumbs into the knotted muscles in her neck. It felt like her whole body sighed with relief, so he kept doing it.

"I'm not coming home until I'm ready, Roger." A second later, she added, "She doesn't need me at the party."

Summer continued to listen to what Cody understood was a major guilt trip on Roger's part. It wasn't hard to see why Roger wanted to make his new bride happy, but it was at Summer's expense. Cody didn't like it and wanted to snatch the phone away and hang up.

It was enough already.

Couldn't they accept Nate was her father and she had a right to stay as long as she wanted to get to know him?

"We've got a date for the benefit next Friday," Cody interrupted. His gut tightened when she turned her head and smiled up at him.

"Roger, I have people holding. Tell my mother I'm staying in Carmel with my father. As always, I wish her all the happiness in the world." She hung up with a brisk good-bye and frowned at Cody over her shoulder. "Sorry I took over your office."

"Not a problem. Get rid of those calls so I can have two minutes with you before I boot you out of my office for my next meeting." He kept up the massage and smiled at her. She could stay as long as she wanted as far as he was concerned. In fact, he was happy with her right here beneath his hands.

Working his phone like a pro, she used the intercom to ask his assistant if the printout had finished.

She tapped one of the red lighted lines. "Amanda, I've got the document. I'll go over the proposal and email Charles with my assessment. You've got my Carmel address. Send everything there. You can reach me on my cell. And tell my grandfather I'll pick up, but it better be important." She hung up. "I swear, Cody, I'll be out of your hair in a minute."

Sitting back against his desk, he drew her between his thighs, her back to him. Rubbing at the base of her neck, he said, "Take a breath, Summer." Instead of doing that, she punched the next line on the phone. She did lean into him and relaxed against his thighs as he massaged the tight muscles in her shoulders. He wanted to touch her, but more, he wanted to make her feel better.

"Tony, thanks for holding. I've got the proposal. Give me a couple of days to go over it, assess your figures and the project itself. Charles is very interested in working with your company, but until now the timing and financing haven't worked out and the development ideas haven't lived up to the original idea. I'm interested in your company's take on the execution of the product, keeping in mind the quality standards Sutherland Industries has in place for all its products and how that will impact the proposed production costs and final consumer price." She listened for a moment. "Yes. Absolutely. I'll keep in contact with you. You can reach me on my cell, since I won't be in the office for a few weeks. Charles and I will work over the proposal and have an answer for you next week."

He took the phone from her hand and tossed it onto the cradle and continued massaging the tight muscles in her shoulders and neck. He was concerned about the stress and pressure she was under.

"You need to . . ." Relax, he thought when her cell phone rang, cutting him off.

She answered with a sighed "Hello, Grandfather." She turned to him, standing close, but just out of his reach. "Let me explain what a vacation means . . ." Summer rolled her eyes. "Yes, I realize I left without giving you any notice. Regardless, you've got hundreds of employees at your beck and call. So beckon. Call. Send an email. But quit calling me to take care of every little thing."

Cody smiled. She had a strange sense of humor, and he bet no one besides her would get away with talking to Charles that way.

"I'll take care of the major projects while I'm here. Amanda and Leslie know to contact me when there is . . . No. Other. Choice. So give me some time and space to take care of my personal life."

Summer listened with a frown on her face. "I know I can't avoid Mom forever. She's had twenty-five years of my undivided attention. I think it's time she learned how it feels to come second because of a man."

He didn't like the disgruntled look on her face. "I realize that's petty. But I've earned petty. And selfish. And let's not forget self-indulgent. I come by those things naturally. I think it's time I broke them out and exercised them."

She huffed out her frustration. "Keep this up, Pappy, and I'll get on a plane and find an island that's got a warm beach, cold drinks, and no phones."

Suddenly she relaxed. "I love you, too. But sometimes you make it hard. She makes it near impossible. So give me a break. This time, I'm doing things my way, for me."

A soft grin tilted her lips. "Yes, the lawyer is still around."

She rolled her eyes again. "Not every lawyer can't be trusted. Besides, I like this one. He's honest. And sometimes uncomfortably blunt. Now I have to go. The lawyer wants his office back." She hung up, tilted her head, and stared right at him.

Cody blurted out his first thought. "You're very careful about not being specific about the amount of time you're staying."

"I wouldn't want to overstay my welcome."

"Not possible." He reached for her hand, pulling her closer. The sweet scent of her wrapped around him.

She looked him in the eye. "It's only been a day. You might be sick of me in a week."

"I don't think so." Holding both her hands in front of him, he looked directly at her. Since he was leaning against his desk, they were about eye to eye. "I'd like to spend some time alone with you. That warm beach, cold drinks, and no phones sounds pretty good to me."

As if to punctuate the point that they couldn't do that right now, his assistant's voice came over the intercom, "Cody, the gentlemen from Parkington are waiting. Nate's meeting just let out as well."

Frowning, he shrugged his shoulders and said to Summer, "Would you like to go out to dinner with me on Friday?"

Her lovely smile warmed his heart. "Yes."

He roamed his gaze over her, taking in her pretty blue dress, her sexy curves and gorgeous legs, then back to her beautiful face. "I wish I didn't have to say good-bye, but duty calls. Sounds like your dad is ready to take you to lunch."

"I'm taking him to lunch."

Cody got it. "I know he'll appreciate the gesture." He stood, and though he was reluctant, he tried to let her go, but she stopped him with a squeeze of his hand.

"I don't fall into bed with men I hardly know."

He stilled, hoping she didn't think that was all he wanted. "I never thought you did, or that you would with me, despite the powerful attraction between us. But it is a thrill to know you're thinking about being in my bed."

"So cocky, Counselor."

"More like desperate. Because all I think about is you. Not just in my bed, but in my life." It seemed his heart had taken over speaking for his brain.

"Cody."

"I know. Too much, too soon. So I'll settle for dinner alone with you." And maybe he'd get to share their first kiss.

She did the unexpected and walked right into him, winding

her arms around his neck and hugging him. "Thank you for being patient."

His assistant buzzed him again without saying anything to remind him people were waiting on him. "My assistant is not so patient." He squeezed Summer to him because he loved the feel of her close and thought that maybe she needed a good hug after all she'd been through, then he reluctantly released her.

Her hands slid slowly off his shoulders, like she didn't want to let him go, either. "I'll see you soon."

"Not soon enough." He hit the intercom. "Brenda, send them in."

If he spent any more time alone with Summer, his promise to be patient would go right out the window along with his good intentions.

Chapter Sixteen

Summer stepped away from Cody, putting some distance between them for propriety's sake as her father and their clients came into the office. She didn't like being the center of attention, or the way her dad looked from her to Cody, like they'd been doing something inappropriate in the office.

But Nate's happiness at seeing her didn't diminish, and she gave him a welcoming smile.

Cody walked to his clients and greeted them with a handshake.

Summer looked at her father. "Ready to go, Dad?"

The huge smile on his face warmed her heart. So much pride and appreciation shone in his eyes.

She wished her mother found this kind of joy in simple things.

"I'm ready, if you are."

"Then let's go have a long lunch and get to know each other." She hooked her arm through his.

He put his hand on her arm. "Gentlemen, I'd like to introduce my daughter Summer."

"My apologies for taking up Cody's time and making you wait." She stepped closer to the men and shook their hands. Their smiles and appreciative glances didn't go unnoticed by Cody, or her father, as Nate gave her arm a little tug to move her farther away from the men. "If you'll excuse us, gentlemen. I've got a date with my father."

They left the men to their business and walked out. After Brenda handed her the file folder containing the proposal she'd been waiting for, Summer walked beside her father to the elevator.

They rode the elevator down to the lobby. Her father took her elbow and guided her out the massive glass doors into the warm sunshine. He helped her into the car, went around, and got in beside her. "Where do you want to go?"

"I'll defer to you, since this is your town."

Nate started the car. "There's this great Italian place not far from here. It's my favorite."

"I love Italian," she said with a huge smile. One thing to add to the list of things they had in common.

They parked behind the restaurant and entered through the front. The hostess steered them through the white linen–covered tables to a booth along the windows. The view was of a side courtyard lush with bougainvillea climbing the trellises.

She took her seat and accepted the menu from the hostess. Setting it aside, she studied her father. The strange awkwardness was slowly beginning to dissipate. Soon, she hoped, they'd feel like family. She very much wanted that easy way of knowing someone so intimately that she could let down all her defenses and just be with him. She didn't want to have to guard her words or choose her actions carefully to ensure she didn't make a mistake and tarnish the relationship. When you were family, loved like that, nothing else mattered.

He met her gaze. "What is it?"

"You. Acting like my dad. I like it. I've missed it."

"We missed so much. I wasn't there to give you guidance while you grew up, or the safety and protection of my being there for you over the years. I didn't put a roof over your head, food in your stomach, clothes on your back, or send you to the best schools. Your mother did those things. I didn't have a say in any of it. There's no way to go back and make it right. I can only meet you where you are right now in your life and offer what wisdom I've gained in mine and be there for you when you need me. You're a grown woman. Smart, capable, independent. But I hope that doesn't mean you don't need your dad."

"I need you very much."

He squeezed her hand, let it go, his shoulders relaxed. He sat back in his seat, relief in his eyes. "I think we both agree this is an impossible situation. We're both angry with Jessica for what she did. We both regret missing the details of all those years. It's time we can't get back."

"I've spent so many years wondering about you and how things might have been different for me if you were around."

"If I'd wanted you." He voiced the very thought she'd had for years.

Often, it was the very thing that kept her up at night and filled her dreams. If only he'd wanted her, had been a part of her life, she might not have been so sad, or angry, or alone when Jessica was wrapped up in her own life, Summer just an afterthought. And now she knew. When Jessica had been self-involved and unavailable, Summer could have turned to Nate and found the safety and support she'd needed so desperately at times.

"You did want me. And that's what makes looking back so hard. My mother wasn't always there for me. She knows it and has never made excuses for the way she is."

"No. She just wanted you to accept it and allow it, no matter how it hurt you. I remember well. We often argued because she wasn't willing to change in even the slightest way. She is who she is, and to hell with everyone else." His anger rose again, sending the approaching waiter in another direction.

"That's the motto she lives by. And she's paying for it now. Though I'm sure she thinks she'll come out of this unscathed. I've always been quick to hide my anger and disappointment by acting like nothing happened. I can't do that this time. This isn't the same as not showing up for a ballet recital or a swim competition."

Nate perked up with interest. "You took ballet lessons?"

"From about the age of three to ten. It was fun, but it didn't satisfy my drive or competitive nature. I started swimming when I was nine. By the time I was ten, ballet was too tame. I started winning, and that was it for me. I loved it. The power, the accomplishment, the freedom. I swam all four years of college. Grandfather pushed college despite the fact I wasn't really sure what I wanted to do. It was always expected I would go into business and work beside him. Eventually the company will come to me. I inherited the real estate. I have my trust fund on top of my salary. If I wanted, I could travel and never work a day of my life. Despite all I have, I still felt like I was sliding through life like it was a frozen lake and I couldn't get my feet under me. Every time I tried to stand on my own, family expectations slid me right back to doing what Grandfather and Mom wanted. Swimming was the one thing I had that was mine."

"Were you alone at those swim meets?"

"Not always. Mom came sometimes. Though she was more interested in the fathers and being seen and envied by the other mothers." Giving Nate a wicked smile, she said, "Grandfather would come wearing his suit and tie and looking so out of place. He always seemed to show up just in time to see me swim. Sitting on the bleachers, his fists clenched, waiting for me to come off the block. He never cheered, but when I'd win, he'd pound his fists on his knees once and yell, 'That's my girl.'"

Giggling, she saw her father's smile falter. "It wasn't so bad, Dad."

"I should have been there."

"You would have been. I know that, and it makes it easier. As furious as I am with Grandfather for keeping the secret, and especially for knowing who and where you were all these years and never telling either of us, I can't discount the fact that whenever I needed him, he was there for me. Whether he would have been the same if you were there, I can't say. Maybe it was his guilty conscience. Whatever. All I know is he tried to be the best father figure to me he could be. Where he spoiled and indulged my mother because he was so focused on work, he learned the error of his ways and pushed me to be better than her. I've officially worked at the company since I was sixteen. I learned how the business works from the ground up and how to stand on my own thanks to him. I learned there are more important things in life than getting a man to love you and making sure you never leave empty-handed."

"I won't thank Charles for keeping the secret and what it's cost us." One side of Nate's mouth pinched with his next words. "But I'm glad you at least had him."

"I am what I am because of them." Reaching out, she took his hand again. "I'm also who I am because of you. DNA aside, I spent all those growing-up years trying to be the best I could be, hoping to make you proud."

"For the wrong reasons," he said, not giving an inch on his anger toward her mother. "I am so proud of you." That pride turned to pain in his eyes. "Every time I look at you, I think of something else I don't know, or I missed. I can't get that back. Holding you on my chest as you slept as a baby, or taking you to your first day of school. All the birthdays I missed, cuts and scrapes I didn't get to kiss better, boys I didn't get to run off from the house."

"You could run Cody off if you like," she said, teasing.

"We both know you don't want me to do that."

"Not right now, anyway." She hoped to lighten his mood.

The waiter arrived to take their order. Funny, they ordered the same thing, even though they hadn't discussed what they wanted beforehand.

"Honey, are you not feeling well?" Nate asked.

Realizing she was rubbing at her head again, she answered, "It's just a headache. I get them sometimes when I'm under a great deal of stress."

"If you'd rather go home and rest, we could . . ."

"No. I'm fine." It touched her that he was concerned about her well-being. "Hey, Dad. There's another way to think about all this."

"How's that, sweetheart?"

"There's still a lot for us to look forward to. One day, you'll walk me down the aisle on my wedding day. You'll come to the hospital when your grandchildren are born. As young as we both are, there's still a lot of life left to live for both of us."

"If not for your grandfather's meddling, I might not have ever known you existed." Sighing heavily, he gave in to the moment. "But, yes, we have lots of time to make memories. I'll try to focus on that, rather than everything we've missed. Better?"

"Better."

He eyed her. "So your mother hasn't soured you on the idea of marriage and children?"

"No. I just don't want a marriage that looks like hers. Or that's just a business arrangement. I want it to be real. Like yours and Miranda's seems to be."

"I still look at her sometimes and can't believe how lucky I am that she loves me."

"It shows when you two look at each other."

"Sometimes it's just there between two people."

She immediately thought of her reaction and connection to Cody. Her dad gave her a knowing look, like he'd read her mind.

She didn't say anything and happily accepted her plate of lasagna from the waiter as a distraction. "So, tell me about your side of the family and about the girls. Haley and I are hanging out later when she gets home from school today."

"You and Haley are a lot alike."

"Natalie seems less easygoing and more intense."

"You mean spoiled."

She shook her head. "I didn't mean that. She seems to feel things deeply."

A thoughtful look came over him. "You might be right. I think she hides her true feelings behind her anger and stubbornness. Where Haley wants everyone to be happy, Natalie wants to ensure she gets what she wants and everyone does what she wants. I hope she grows out of it as she gains more independence."

"You should put her to work. Give her a purpose and a sense of accomplishment."

"I've offered to have her work here."

"An offer implies it's optional. I can tell you from experience, I didn't always want to be my grandfather's protégée. Now I see the value in him instilling a work ethic and drive in me."

"I don't know what she'd do there that wouldn't feel like a punishment to her."

"What are her interests?"

"Her friends. Her phone. Shopping. Graduating. All she talks about is the new car she wants as a graduation gift to impress her friends."

"Are you going to get it for her?"

"Yes." He sighed. "The car she drives now is a secondhand starter vehicle. We bought it because we figured as a young driver, she was bound to dent it up a bit. Where I'm practical, Natalie is at an age where appearances matter."

"In high school, everything is about how you look, what you drive, who you're seeing, that kind of superficial stuff."

"I understand that. And I want to make her happy. When she and Haley were very young, I missed a lot of things because I was working to build the business. I regret the time lost. Now that the business is thriving, I make it a point to spend more time with them. And for all of Natalie's complaints about the car, she does take care of it. She drives Haley to school and drops her at friends' houses and stuff, taking some of that off Miranda's plate. So yeah, when she graduates, I'll upgrade her car and pass down the one she's driving to Haley."

"What's Natalie's college focus?"

"Right now, general studies until she figures out what she wants to do."

"You should ask her more about her interests, see if you can get her focused on what she's good at and what job goes with it, then find her a spot in the company to try it out."

"That's brilliant. She's got the whole summer before she attends UC Santa Barbara."

"There's nothing like experience to tell you what you like to do and what you hope you never have to do again."

Her dad nodded.

From that moment on, the conversation was easy. They swapped stories about their past. He filled in her family tree with who was dead and who was still alive. He told her about starting the business with Cody's father, their mission, and the products they developed.

She talked more about her growing-up years.

Before they knew it, three hours had passed.

They said good-bye outside the restaurant. Her dad waited for the rideshare car to arrive and made sure the guy driving was the one on her app. She appreciated his overprotective streak.

She arrived at the house at the same time Natalie and Haley drove in from school in a silver Toyota sedan. She agreed with Natalie on the uncool factor.

Haley came bounding over as soon as Summer exited the car and threw her arms around her. "You're home."

"I just got back from a long lunch with Dad."

Natalie frowned and headed for the front door.

Haley watched her sister go ahead of them.

Summer tried to enlist her little sister's help. "What's it going to take to get her to talk to me?"

"Bribes." Haley's honesty made Summer laugh.

"I see. Well, what should I start with?" Summer wasn't averse to trying to sweeten up her sister with a nice gesture, but if it didn't open the door to them actually getting to know each other . . . Well, she didn't want to appear to be buying her sister's affection. That would only sour Natalie toward her even more.

"She loves the downtown shops. Mom thinks they're overpriced. But Natalie loves to be seen there."

Summer hooked her arm over Haley's shoulder. "I see a shopping trip in our future."

"You mean you'll take me, too?"

"Of course. We'll make it a girls' day this weekend. Once I get a car."

Haley gave her a big grin. "Awesome."

"So, what did you want to do today?"

Summer had a mini panic attack at Haley's answer before she thought, *Why not?*

$\mathcal{H}$aley couldn't believe her big sis wanted to hang out with her for so long. Or that she got Summer to do the TikTok challenge all her friends were doing. And then Summer came up with an even better one and did that with her, too.

After the last crazy dance-off, they fell to their butts on the floor, laughing and trying to catch their breath.

Summer was such a good dancer. "You learned those steps really quickly."

"I used to do ballet. But it's been a long time. And I'm old."

"Not that old."

"I have eleven years on you. I'm dying. You're barely out of breath."

Haley wanted to ask her sister something, but held back.

Summer leaned in close. "What's on your mind? Please don't tell me there's another routine you want to do. That last one was like bouncing on a trampoline with all those hopping and jumping moves."

Haley shook her head. "It's not that."

"What is it? You can ask me anything."

Haley didn't want to hurt her sister's feelings. "It's strange to have you here. I mean, you're my sister, but we didn't grow up together."

"It's strange for me, too. We are sisters. Our DNA tells us that, right?"

"Yeah."

"But being friends is something else. I'd really like to be your friend as well as your sister."

Haley scrunched her lips. "I think we already are."

"Me too," Summer agreed.

Excitement exploded through Haley. "I hope you stay."

"I'll be here for a while. I'm not sure how long. But even if I go back to Texas, we'll keep in touch. We'll talk and text on the phone. I'll come back to visit. Maybe you'll come see me, too."

"I'd like that. I've never been to Texas. Plus I want to see your place. Maybe go to your house in Belize."

Summer looked excited about it, too. "That would be a fun vacation for all of us."

Haley liked that she wanted to be with them. "Give me your phone. I'll put in my number. I'll even log into my TikTok account so you can see the videos we posted and the other stuff I do, since you probably don't want your own account."

Summer handed her the phone. "I totally want to see how many likes you get for it. Plus you'll be able to get in touch with me whenever you want. For anything," she added, letting Haley know it was okay to call just to chat.

"You're really nice."

"You are, too. Thanks for being so welcoming."

Haley glanced at her. "You mean, when Natalie hasn't been."

"I think she's just being cautious."

"She's being a b—brat."

"Nice save on that b-word." Summer patted Haley's knee. "It's okay about Natalie. I burst into her life unannounced and made things complicated for her. She's graduating in a couple of weeks and thought all the attention would be on her. And it will be. In a couple of days, my being here won't seem so novel and everyone will be doing their thing like always and it won't seem so strange that I'm here."

At that moment, Miranda came in. "Dinner's ready."

Summer stood and brushed her dress down her legs. "I meant to come and help you tonight."

Miranda waved that off. "It sounded like you two were having a lot of fun up here."

Haley jumped up with her phone and ran to her mom. "Check this out. Summer did the dance challenge with me." She showed Miranda the video.

"Wow. You two look really great together." Miranda smiled at Summer.

"Haley is a great dancer. We worked out the steps together until we got it just right." Summer looked at her. "I hope your friends like it."

"It's better than anything they did."

"We had fun; that's what counts the most."

Haley thought so, too.

Miranda brushed her hand over Haley's hair. "I'm glad you had fun. It's your turn to set the table."

Haley turned to Summer. "Thank you for hanging out with me today."

"It was my pleasure."

"Wait until I show Dad what we did."

Summer eyed her with a grin. "Next time, I get to pick the activity."

Haley couldn't wait. "What do you want to do?"

Summer tilted her head. "Have you ever played chess?"

"A little bit. It's confusing."

"I'll teach you all my tricks."

Haley frowned. "We used to have a family game night, but we haven't done it in a long time."

Miranda put her hand on Haley's shoulder. "You're right. We should do it again. Maybe on Friday."

Summer frowned. "Oh. Um. Cody and I are going out to dinner that night."

"What?" Natalie asked from behind them.

Summer met Natalie's furious gaze. "Cody asked me to dinner."

"You're going to eat together here, I don't see why you need to go out to do it."

"Natalie, that's none of your business," Miranda said.

Natalie walked away, a disgruntled look on her face.

Haley shrugged. "I think it's nice he likes you."

Summer side-hugged her. "Thank you."

They all walked out of her room and down the hallway toward the stairs with Haley in the lead.

"I'm worried about Natalie," Miranda said to Summer.

"I'm sorry she's upset."

"She's like every teen. She wants to be older than she is. And she thinks she knows everything."

"Still, as a mom, you've got to be worried that my presence here has upset her."

"That's not your fault. I hope she comes to that conclusion soon, because Nate is so happy to have you in his life. Given a little time, I hope we all come together as family."

Haley hit the bottom of the stairs and spotted Cody and Natalie standing close, Cody's hands on her cheeks as he looked into Natalie's eyes.

Summer stopped behind her.

Miranda kept walking toward Cody. "Everything okay?"

Cody turned Natalie's head a little to the right. "I don't see anything. I think you got it." He released Natalie and spoke to her mom. "Nat had something in her eye, but I think it's out." He shrugged and looked past Miranda at Summer. "How was your day?"

Summer smiled at him. "Dad and I had a great lunch. Haley and I danced our butts off. I'm going to help her set the table."

"I'll help, too." Cody looked at Miranda. "Whatever you cooked smells amazing."

Natalie spun around and headed for the kitchen.

They all watched her go.

Mom sighed. "Come on. I made my famous enchiladas and Spanish rice."

"Dad's favorite," Haley said, taking Summer's arm and pulling her to come along.

She did and gave Cody another smile as they passed him.

Haley glanced back and caught the happiness in his eyes when he looked at Summer. She hoped they got together. It would be so cool if her sister married Cody. Then he'd really be their brother by marriage, not just because they were a family joined by a close friendship.

Haley really liked Summer. She wanted her to stay. What better way to get her to stay than for her to be with Cody.

If only Natalie would stay out of it and stop being such a b— brat.

$\mathcal{C}$ody arrived home on Friday with a sense of relief and anticipation. He'd waited practically all week to take Summer out on their date, while simultaneously trying to play it cool, not dominate her time while she was building relationships with her family.

They had started their own routine the past two days. They both rose early and met in the kitchen to grab some water, eat a protein bar, then head out to stretch on the back lawn and go for a run together. He loved that the first time they went together she said, "Don't take this personally, but I like to listen to music and think while I run." He liked to do the same thing. So while they went together, they kept to their preferences and only chatted while they walked to cool down.

She could talk about anything. The movie or show they watched in the evening, work stuff, their interests outside of work, trips they'd taken. It didn't matter. Every little new thing he learned about her made him like her more.

Everything about her appealed to him.

And it scared him a little that it was happening so fast and somehow he could lose it.

Their being under the same roof, having dinner together every night, spending time with the family was beginning to make him feel like he'd known her forever, even though it had been only days.

She used his home office while he was at work. Last night he had gone in there to respond to some emails and grab some paperwork. There she was sitting at his desk, head down as she read some report her grandfather had sent her. She looked so intense and beautiful and just right at his desk.

He'd wanted to go to her, spin her chair toward him, lean down, and finally kiss her. But both of them were wholly aware they weren't alone in the house. Anytime they found themselves alone together for a few minutes, someone interrupted.

He didn't mind so much when it was Alex. Nate and Miranda seemed to be keeping an eye on them. Haley simply wanted Summer's attention, and that was a good thing. But he hated that every time Natalie came to ask about watching their show together he put her off and disappointed her.

And because Cody and Summer weren't alone, every night when they called it a day, they said a regretful good night, the longing they both felt pulling them together, even as they parted and went to their separate rooms. It was all he could do last night to hold back the kiss he wanted and not beg her to share his bed.

He'd seen it in her eyes, she wanted it, too, but in the end she let him walk away and up the stairs to his room alone.

She'd started another habit. Each day she came to the office and had lunch with her dad. He got to see her for a few minutes at the office, but then he let her have her time alone with Nate. And it was paying off. They had grown closer, and Cody was happy for them.

In the evenings, she'd helped Miranda cook dinner. And, man, could she cook. One of the facts he'd learned about her was that she often spent time eating in the kitchen when she was young. Their chef had taken a shine to her and taught her to cook. It was something she both felt pride in and loved. Not to mention the fact that she loved to eat. It was more than fuel for her; it was an experience. One she enjoyed even more sitting at their crowded table.

He parked in the driveway behind Summer's brand-new white Porsche Cayenne. He liked her choice in a vehicle. It had all the power and luxury the brand offered, plus room for her sisters. Natalie had even asked if she could drive it. Summer had jumped at the opportunity to bond with her and took Natalie for a drive along the coast the other night.

He walked in the front door and headed back to the office he now considered theirs, thinking about the night ahead and his plans for dinner and later if things went his way. He couldn't wait to be alone with her. Completely alone, so he could talk to her, look at her, be with her without any interruptions or piles of papers separating them.

The house was quiet, the lights out in the office, but he heard her cell phone ringing and headed that way. She was indispensable to her grandfather; overnight boxes from him had begun to arrive two days ago. And she was a damn hard worker.

She wasn't there, but her cell phone lay on the desk, still ringing. Several overnight packages were left unopened. It wasn't like her to go anywhere without her phone. He picked it up and tapped the screen. Without her code, all he could see was the twenty-three missed calls notification.

A warning went off inside him.

It wasn't like her to ignore her obligations.

He glanced at the desk again and noted the same papers and folders from last night were still there in the exact same spot she'd left them before bed. The only thing that had changed was the addition of the new packages that must have arrived sometime today.

Maybe she'd finally had enough and left her phone and the work for Monday and taken the day off. She was supposed to be on vacation, though she hadn't acted like it since the first day she'd arrived.

Still. Something wasn't right.

He heard something down the hall and dropped his briefcase on a chair and headed to the kitchen. He found Brooke cooking dinner, because Miranda and Nate went out every Friday and Saturday night. Alex sat at the breakfast bar working on his homework. Looked like spelling tonight.

"Have you seen Summer?" He'd check her room next. Maybe she was getting ready for their date.

"I haven't seen her since I got home just after the girls," Brooke said. "I put the boxes that were left on the front porch in your office."

He went behind his nephew and looked over his shoulder. "'Should' is spelled with an OU, not just a U."

"Are you going to take me fishing this weekend?" Alex looked up hopefully at him.

"I'm not sure. I was hoping to spend some time with Aunt Summer." Cody was getting used to thinking of her that way. She was great with Alex. She gave him her attention and her affection, and it did something to his heart to see them together. It made him think of that future he'd once wanted but hadn't thought about in a long time.

Celeste, their housekeeper, walked into the room. "I'll just dust the living room and mop the floor and be out of here soon."

Brooke nodded. "I'll keep Alex off the floor until it's dry. Take your time."

Celeste hesitated. "Miranda told me this morning that you have a guest. She didn't seem well earlier when Natalie brought her back to her room, so I haven't disturbed her."

"Wait. What?" Cody asked, concerned. "What do you mean she wasn't well?"

Celeste's forehead creased into lines of concern. "The girls arrived home from school while I was finishing that side of the house. I was coming to do this side when I met them in the foyer. The woman, she didn't look well. She was stumbling and asking Natalie for help. I offered to assist, but Natalie said she'd deal with it. I left them to do the upstairs here." Celeste bit her lip. "I hope she's okay."

Cody's heart dropped. "Something's not right." He rushed back down the hall to Summer's room and called out, "Summer, I'm coming in." He gave her a second to say no, then opened the door and found her curled in the fetal position on the floor, her arms covering her head like she needed to protect it, a pool of vomit next to her.

Chapter Nineteen

The knock on the door sent a lightning bolt of pain up the back of her head to the front and made the pressure behind her eye pulse in agony. Nausea rolled through her again as the stench of vomit filled her nose. She wanted to get away from it, but moving seemed impossible at the moment.

The door flew open and Cody swore.

The sound of his voice was both a relief and another round of anguish. She curled up even tighter and pressed her arms over her ears as she used her hands to try to hold her head together, like it might shatter at any moment from the enormous pain radiating through her skull on the right side of her head.

She needed to keep the light out of her eyes, the noise from ringing in her ears. Anything and everything that made the pain worse.

"Summer?"

Her name felt like an ax through her head. "Don't talk," she whispered, and tightened her arms around her head.

"Summer, baby, what's wrong?"

"Shut up." She needed him to stop, to go away and let the silence come back. "Too loud. It hurts." Even those few words made her want to scream in agony.

God, she was so tired. Her body was so tense her shoulders ached, her stomach wanted to turn over, and pain radiated throughout her head with each beat of her heart. She tried to breathe with shallow, steady breaths, but even that was an effort.

Cody brushed his hand gently up her arm and whispered, "Sweetheart, tell me what's wrong."

She winced with pain. "Cluster migraine." She grabbed his hand and held on to him. He was an anchor in her sea of agony. She couldn't remember another migraine ever being this bad. Ever since she got here, she'd known the mild headache was warning her to take care of herself, not work too much, get some rest, and not let the stress get to her. But she hadn't listened to the little voice in her head telling her she was setting herself up for this.

"I'll get you some ibuprofen."

"Won't work. Hospital. Narcotics. It's the only thing that will work now." Every word cost her, but she needed the pain meds. Now. "Please," she begged.

Cody thankfully didn't speak, but did what she needed him to do and scooped her up into his arms and carried her out of the room.

"What's wrong?" Brooke asked, making Summer tighten her hold on Cody and bury her face in his neck.

He held her tighter, too. He spoke in a soft whisper. "I'm taking her to the hospital for a very bad migraine. Ask Celeste to clean up the vomit in her room, please. I'll call you later." Cody moved quickly to the foyer. The brighter light made her close her eyes tighter.

"Is she okay?" Haley asked.

Cody didn't speak, just shook his head, brushing her sweaty forehead.

"Are you taking her to the hospital like she asked?"

Cody's whole body went perfectly still. "What?"

Haley mimicked Cody's tone and spoke softly. "She asked Natalie to take her, but Natalie said it was only a headache and not an emergency."

Cody felt Summer trembling, every word adding to her pain, and pressed his cheek to her head. "Haley, you will tell me and your father exactly what happened later. Get the door. Help me get her in the car."

Cody practically ran with her to his car and set her in the front seat. He put the seat belt around her and she curled in on herself, trying to still hold her head and not vomit all over his car. He closed the door with a soft push instead of slamming it. Summer overheard some mumbled words between him and Haley, then he was behind the wheel and started the car. The second the radio came on he shut it off.

Without a word, he put the car in motion, then put his hand on her head and brushed his fingers against her hair. He took it away, and she missed that anchor and wanted it back.

She heard him speaking into his cell phone. "David, man, I need your help. Are you at work?" Cody paused. "Great. I'm bringing in someone with a cluster migraine. She says she needs narcotics. She's in bad shape, man. The light and noise are killing her. She vomited. She's sweating." Cody paused again, then let out a huge sigh of relief. "We'll be there in like ten minutes. Thank you. I owe you." Cody put his hand on her back and rubbed it in circles, but didn't speak again, even though she knew he wanted to offer words of comfort and reassurance.

She appreciated so much that he gave her what she needed most right now. Quiet. His presence. Relief in the way he gently touched her.

A ride when her own sister had refused her.

Cody stopped the car and got out. A second later, he was at her side, unbuckling her, and picking her up again. He used his hip to close the car door, then walked with her. She couldn't see where they were or what was around her with her face pressed into his neck and her hand still holding her head. Not that it did anything but make her feel like she was holding it together in some way.

The noises and people talking around her made it all worse.

She heard doors sliding open and then a man's soft voice. "Over here."

Cody kept moving, then gently set her on a bed. She curled back into a ball.

That same soft voice spoke close to her. "I'm Dr. Underwood. Tell me where it hurts."

She spread her hand over her head. "Always the right side. Behind my eye, too."

"Okay, one to ten, ten being the worst pain you've ever experienced, what's your pain level right now?"

"Nine. Make it stop."

"What if any medication have you taken today?"

She knew they had to go through this routine, but every second of it hurt. "Ibuprofen this morning. I forgot to pack my migraine meds."

Cody filled in the rest for her. "She lives in Texas and is here visiting her dad, Nate. She's had a headache on and off for the last four days, but nothing like this."

"The nurse is going to put in your IV," Dr. Underwood whispered. "I've got the good stuff for you."

Summer went along with the nurse helping her take off her shirt and put on a gown. The nurse attached several monitors on her chest and abdomen, so they could monitor her heart, respiration, and oxygen levels. She didn't even care that Cody and the doctor saw her in her bra. The nurse finally took her arm and poked the needle in, all while Summer kept her hand on her head, eyes closed.

"We'll start with the anti-nausea first, then flush the IV," Dr. Underwood explained. "Second is the migraine meds, then another flush with saline." Everything went quiet while the nurse did that. "Here comes the good stuff, Summer," Dr. Underwood warned her.

And not even five seconds later, she felt the whoosh of the pain meds course into her system. It took another couple of minutes before she sighed out her relief.

"What did you give her?" Cody asked.

"Dilaudid. This called for a heavy-duty painkiller. I also gave her sumatriptan to eliminate the migraine. And I'll make sure she doesn't leave without her regular prescription."

Summer opened her eyes and looked up at Cody. "Thank you for bringing me."

Cody leaned down and pressed his forehead to hers. "Are you okay now?"

"He's got good drugs."

Dr. Underwood chuckled. "You shouldn't have waited this long to get help."

Cody stood and faced his friend. "She tried. I wasn't home."

Dr. Underwood raised a brow at Cody's admission. "I'll get the details on you two later." He put on his stethoscope and pressed it to her chest. "Your heart rate is a little fast." He slid a cuff up her arm and checked her blood pressure. "A little low." He sighed. "All the stress on your body is making the migraine worse." He pulled a paper towel from the dispenser on the wall and blotted the sweat on her brow. "How's your stomach right now?"

"Still queasy."

"The meds will work soon. How about your vision? Are you seeing any flashing lights or halos? Maybe a blind spot?"

"Lights that zigzag through my vision. You're kind of hazy."

"Okay. Are you having any dizziness?"

"Only when I move. I'm tired." She'd had enough. She just wanted to curl back up and go to sleep.

Cody turned to the doctor. "I owe you for getting her in right away."

The doctor shrugged that off. "What are best friends for?"

"Whatever he owes you, I'll double it," she swore.

Dr. Underwood grinned. "I'm going to keep you here for a couple hours, so I know the headache is either gone or we're at least managing your pain until it is. I'll be back in a little while to check on you."

Dr. Underwood slapped Cody on the back. "She'll be okay. You can take her home tonight. A good night's sleep plus the meds should do the trick, but if not, call me."

"Thank you. And seriously, name it, whatever you want for the VIP urgent care, it's yours."

"Same as always, a bottle of top-shelf scotch."

"I'll send you a case," Summer assured him, finally feeling like her head wasn't going to explode.

"I like her, man."

"Thanks, David. This means everything to me."

"Yeah, I can see that. You can take me out for a beer sometime and tell me all about her."

"You got it."

"And maybe bring her and your sister. You know, to get Brooke out of the house and out with friends."

Cody eyed the good doctor. "She could use some adult time."

"How's Alex?"

"A handful, but better. He and Brooke have both found their smiles and happiness again."

"I'm really glad to hear that. I'll be back soon." Dr. Underwood closed the drape to give them some privacy.

Cody pulled a chair over and sat next to Summer.

She turned on her side, making sure she didn't disturb the IV in her arm, rested her head on the pillow, and stared at him. "I'm sorry about our date."

"Don't be. I'm just glad you're okay now."

"It was stupid not to bring my medication. Even stupider not to get a refill here when I knew those headaches weren't going to stop until they escalated to this."

"It's been a hell of a week. I made you pack too fast. If you'd told me you needed something, I would have called David to get it for you."

"It's not your responsibility to take care of me. I knew better and I didn't do anything but ignore it."

"You mean you were too busy holding off your mom, working like a maniac for your grandfather, trying to get to know everyone here, and not having any time for yourself."

She managed a half smile. "Look how well you know me."

Cody leaned in and put his hand on her face. "When I saw you lying on the floor like that in so much pain . . ." His eyes filled with remorse. "I thought something really terrible happened to you. Not that what happened wasn't bad."

"I'm sorry I told you to shut up."

"I understand. The last thing I'd ever want to do is cause you more pain."

"You rescued me."

"Summer," her dad called out.

"She's in here." Cody stood and opened the drape.

Her father and Miranda rushed to her side. "Are you okay?" they asked in unison.

"I'm better. Heavy-duty pain meds are masking the worst of it, and the migraine meds should kick in and stop the headache altogether."

"Why didn't you call one of us, or an ambulance?" her dad asked.

"I couldn't find my phone. I was in so much pain, I couldn't think straight or see very well. I was disoriented and—"

"Tell him the truth," Cody snapped.

Her dad put his hand on Cody's shoulder. "Haley told us what happened. Natalie refused to take you to the hospital. She didn't call me to tell me you needed help. Haley is beside herself, thinking she should have intervened."

"All they had to do was call you, me, or tell Brooke when she got home." Cody didn't hide his anger at all.

Miranda frowned. "We'll talk to the girls and explain the seriousness of what happened."

"Natalie is eighteen," Cody pointed out. "Someone asks you for a ride to the hospital, you take them."

"She thought it was just another headache," Miranda said. She wanted to believe Natalie didn't mean any harm.

Summer knew the truth. Natalie's jealousy had made her dismiss Summer's condition.

"Who asks to go to the hospital for just a headache?" Cody said. "She had to see how much pain Summer was in. They had to shoot her full of narcotics just so she could open her eyes."

Summer reached out and took Cody's hand. "Enough. I'm fine now."

"No, you're not. You're so pale. I can see the exhaustion in your eyes and how much effort it is for you to move."

Summer pressed her lips together, overwhelmed by his emotion and how much this affected him.

"What she did was wrong." Cody said the words to Summer, but they were meant for her dad and Miranda.

"I know. But you can't make her like me."

"But she can still do the right thing," her father added, then looked at Miranda. "We'll deal with her when we get home."

Summer sighed. "I'm sorry I ruined your date night."

Her dad shook his head. "Are you kidding me? You needed me and I wasn't there. Again."

"You didn't know what was happening. It's not your fault. It's mine for not remembering to pack my meds."

"I just wish you would have called me." He glanced at Cody, like she'd called him and not her dad.

"I didn't call anyone. Cody found me on the floor in my room, completely incapacitated by the pain."

Her dad and Cody shared a long look that said so much about how they felt.

"Everyone stop thinking of who to blame and let's just be happy all is well. I'll get some sleep. Tomorrow I'll be back to my usual self," Summer assured them.

The nurse walked in, and everyone remained quiet while she checked Summer's vitals again, noting them in a tablet. "Blood pressure is better. Back soon."

Summer settled into the bed, Cody's hand in hers, her father with his hand on her shoulder. They talked among themselves in low tones until sometime later Dr. Underwood arrived. She'd kept her eyes closed, needing the rest so the drugs could do their job.

"How are you feeling, Summer?" the doctor asked.

"Much better."

"What's your pain level now?"

"One. But that's just some pressure behind my eye."

"Okay. If this flares back up, you let me know. I also want you to follow up with your physician and fill the prescription I called into the pharmacy Cody uses."

"We'll stop and grab it on the way home," Cody assured her.

The doctor patted her leg. "The nurse will remove the monitors and you're free to go home."

"Thank you." Summer gave the doctor a smile.

He left them in a rush, probably to attend to another patient.

She sat up and started pulling the wires off her chest beneath the open-backed gown.

Cody stood. "I'll be back in a minute. I just want to thank David again for getting you in so fast."

"Thank him again for me, too."

Cody leaned down and kissed her on the forehead. "Back in a sec."

She looked at her upset father. "Natalie and I will work things out. It hasn't even been a week. She's still getting used to the idea that I'm her sister and I'm not going anywhere."

Her dad's mouth drew into a tight line. He didn't say anything.

Miranda did. "Thank you for understanding this is difficult for Natalie. While she was wrong in what she did, and I will speak to her about it, she's usually not like this. I've never known her to be mean."

For a split second, Summer caught the disbelief in her dad's eyes at that statement.

Summer didn't blame Miranda for seeing the best in her child. She wished her own mother could do the same for her.

"As I said, I'm fine now. Let's just drop it."

"Natalie will apologize for what she's done," her father announced.

"Why don't you give her a chance to do that on her own, once she sees that the situation was more dire than she thought." *When she blew me off,* Summer wanted to add, but refrained in hopes of keeping things civil and not upsetting her dad more. "After all, I got much worse after I saw her." That was true, though she'd have fared much better if she'd gotten to the hospital sooner.

Cody walked back in with the nurse, who gathered the discarded stickers that had held the monitors on her chest and handed Summer her shirt and discharge papers.

Summer sat forward and had to take a second because her head spun from the pain meds. "I'm good," she assured all of them, especially Cody, who reached to steady her.

Cody held her arm. "I'll help you change."

"We'll wait outside the curtain." Miranda pulled Nate out to the other side.

Cody drew the gown off her arms and she put her shirt on, not making a big deal about him seeing her half naked.

"My car is right out front." Cody held her arm as she scooted off the bed and stood on her own.

"I'm fine."

Cody pulled the curtain aside. "I'll drive her home."

"We'll be right behind you." Her dad went ahead with Miranda.

It only took a couple of minutes to get settled in Cody's car. She took his hand and squeezed it. "Cody, look at me."

He turned to her, frustration and fatigue in his eyes.

"I'm okay. Everything is fine. Except for one thing."

"What?" The concern in his eyes amped up.

"I'm sorry I missed our date."

He squeezed her hand back. "Me too. I'll get us a reservation for tomorrow."

"Sounds good. Can I borrow your phone?"

He pulled it out, unlocked it with his thumbprint, then handed it to her. He didn't ask what she wanted it for and just drove them out of the lot to the pharmacy, through the drive-through pickup line, which thankfully took less than five minutes, and then home.

She made plans to thank him and her dad and stepmom for tonight, hoping that when they arrived at the house everyone would be more relaxed and less inclined to escalate this situation.

It felt like a foolish wish, but she swore to herself she would not be the cause of more strife.

Chapter Twenty

Summer noticed the problem the second they drove up to the house, but it was Cody who asked, "Where's your car?"

She had a good idea.

"Did someone actually steal it right out of the driveway?" Cody cut the engine and opened his door.

Her dad and Miranda must have waited the few extra minutes for them inside their Land Rover. He and Miranda got out and joined Cody.

She reluctantly got out on her side.

"What do you mean, her car is missing?" her dad said.

Summer caught the knowing look that came over Miranda. Their eyes met. Summer didn't say anything.

Another vehicle arrived.

Cody glanced at the Prius. "Who's that?"

"I ordered dinner for everyone, since none of us got to eat." Summer went to the driver and accepted the bag of food. She held it up. "Your favorite, Dad." She'd ordered from the Italian place he loved. "Who's hungry?"

Cody looked at her, perplexed. "Aren't you worried about your car?"

"I'm more worried that the person who took it drives carefully." The car had a lot of horsepower, and speeding on the winding roads in Carmel could be dangerous.

Cody went still, then he slowly turned to her dad. "Natalie took it." Cody fumed and walked toward the house, her dad and Miranda on his tail.

Summer walked in at her leisure, wishing her sister hadn't compounded things.

Somehow, Summer knew, this was going to come back and bite her in the ass. She'd end up paying for Natalie's self-indulgent ways.

She found them all in the kitchen.

Haley rushed at Summer and threw her arms around her. "I'm so glad you're okay."

Summer handed the bag of food off to Cody and held Haley close. She leaned back and cupped Haley's face. "Thank you for worrying about me. You're sweet."

Haley let her go and sat on one of the stools at the breakfast bar next to Cody.

Miranda sighed and stared at her phone. "She's not answering."

"Maybe she's driving and can't use her phone right now," Summer offered, hoping to ease Miranda's mind.

As stunts went, stealing a car and going for a joyride was top ten for teens. Summer wasn't too worried about it. "It's been quite a day. I think I'll go take a quick shower before I have my dinner."

Cody reached for her and took her hand. "I'll come check on you in a few minutes. We'll eat together."

She brushed her fingers along his hard jaw. "I'd like that."

Her dad stepped in front of her before she left the room. "I'm sorry Natalie's acting out like this."

Summer nodded, not saying anything, because what could she

say? Nate and Miranda needed to deal with Natalie. Summer needed time and space to decompress from all that happened and let it go.

Cody spoke up as she walked away. "Natalie is out of line."

"And Nate and I will deal with her without your interference." Miranda's angry, defensive words warned Summer that the mama bear in her would protect her child, even when Natalie was in the wrong. It made Summer feel even more the outsider in this family.

Time, she reminded herself; it would take time for some of them to see her as an equal.

Chapter Twenty-One

Cody didn't mean to get on Miranda's nerves. He simply couldn't hold back his anger. But he could take himself out of the situation and do what he really wanted to do: spend time alone with Summer.

She'd handled herself so well, given what Natalie had done.

He had no doubt Nate and Miranda had a stern lecture in the making for Natalie, so he opened the bag of food Summer had generously ordered for them and pulled out the containers, recognizing immediately that she'd paid attention and knew what they all liked. He left Miranda's pesto pasta with chicken and Nate's lasagna on the counter, along with one loaf of garlic bread. The rest, he kept in the bag. "I'll see you guys later." He rubbed his hand over Haley's back to reassure her as he walked by and headed for the foyer, just as a car's headlights swept across the front of the house. "She's back," he called out.

Nate and Miranda rushed out of the kitchen and caught up to him in the foyer as Natalie opened the front door.

"Cody." Natalie's tone was timid as she eyed him.

He was so angry, he held his tongue, not wanting to say something he'd regret later.

"Young lady, where have you been?" Nate barked out the words.

The nervousness and apprehension in Natalie's eyes turned defiant. "Out with my friends. I told Mom this morning that I was meeting Rebecca and Stacy."

Cody stood there stone cold and still, wanting to hear her explanation for what she'd done and how she was going to play it off like it was no big deal. His mind flashed to seeing Summer lying on the floor next to a pool of vomit, curled up like an infant, holding her pounding head, her face a mask of agony.

"Who said you could take your sister's car?" Nate asked.

"She said I could borrow it. She wasn't using it, so I took it." It amazed him how she could look so innocent.

Nate's usual patience snapped. "She wasn't here because Cody had to rush her to the hospital. They had to shoot her full of narcotics to stop the agonizing pain. She couldn't see straight. She couldn't get herself there on her own. She asked you for help and you didn't do anything."

A plea filled Natalie's eyes as she stared at him, possibly looking for help out of the jam she put herself in, but Cody didn't see half the remorse he expected. "I didn't realize it was that bad."

Cody shook his head at that pathetic excuse and walked away.

Natalie shot forward and grabbed his forearm. "Wait. Don't be mad."

Cody turned and pinned Natalie in his gaze. "You know what I am? Incredibly sad about what Summer went through and how I found her. Your mom and dad didn't see her lying on the floor helpless, but I did, and I will never forget it." He pulled away so Natalie had to release him, turned, and walked away just as Miranda said, "We need to talk," and Natalie huffed out her irritation that her parents weren't going to drop this.

He knew how it felt to do something stupid and have to own

up to it with his dad. But he'd never purposely turned his back on someone in need. Natalie needed to own up to this and do the right thing.

Cody hoped she'd find a way to accept her sister, because Summer was a part of the family now and that would never change.

Chapter Twenty-Two

*M*iranda had never seen Nate so upset and angry at one of their girls. In the past, she was left to handle the discipline and heart-to-hearts on her own because of Nate's busy work schedule. Not that she wasn't also busy with her own job as a Realtor, but her hours were more flexible, and she supposed a lot of that kind of thing fell on moms the most.

She always shared those incidents with Nate. He often circled back to the girls, but by then the issue had already been handled, everyone ready to move on.

In the last five years, Nate had been more present with the girls, but this was the first really big thing he was here for, and Miranda wasn't sure if she should take the lead this time because this involved Nate's daughter Summer.

Miranda needed to tread carefully. She didn't want Natalie to think she was taking sides. She didn't want Nate to think she blamed Summer, though it was Summer's sudden arrival in their lives that was causing Natalie to act out.

Natalie and Haley had their fair share of squabbles, but Natalie had never done something so blatantly hurtful or stolen something that didn't belong to her. Miranda didn't buy that she "borrowed" the car.

Summer had remained neutral. Miranda appreciated that Summer said nothing and allowed her and Nate to deal with Natalie when Summer had every right to express her anger and hurt that Natalie had treated her so poorly.

Nate barely stepped into Natalie's room when he went off. "I can't believe you were so callous and left your sister in that much pain just so you could meet up with your friends."

Natalie gaped at her father. "How was I supposed to know it was that bad?"

Nate eyed her. "She didn't ask to go to the hospital for no reason."

Natalie huffed and scrunched her lips in an angry pout, caught by Nate's logic.

Miranda stepped between Nate and Natalie. "Why did you turn her down?"

Natalie held her arms out wide, then let them drop. "I really didn't think it was that serious." She dropped onto her butt on her bed. "I mean, it wasn't like she was bleeding all over the place and needed 911." Natalie hung her head. "Everyone keeps fawning all over her. All Haley talks about is her. Dad's spending his lunch with her. Cody spends all his free time talking to her. Now he's mad at me." She folded her arms across her chest. "She should have made it clearer *why* she needed to go to the hospital."

Nate's eyes went wide. "If someone asks you to take them to the hospital, you do it."

Natalie gave her dad a *duh* look that only made Nate more agitated.

Miranda tried to understand what her daughter was feeling and why. "Natalie, I understand this situation isn't easy."

"She's a stranger. But you all treat her like she's one of us."

"She is one of us," Nate said, his voice gentle. "She's mine, Nat." The pain mixed with joy in Nate's voice touched Miranda's heart. "Which makes her yours, too."

And hers, too. Miranda really took that in and what it meant.

Summer didn't need Miranda to raise her, but Summer could definitely use a mother who was kind and understanding and supportive.

Miranda sympathized with Summer's situation with her mom and with Nate having missed all of Summer's life up until now. But Natalie was right, they all needed time to get to know each other and adjust to this new reality.

Miranda wanted Summer to feel welcome, but she also wanted Natalie to feel safe and secure with her place in the family. "It's natural that there will be some changes now that Summer has joined the family."

"She *took over* the family," Natalie snapped. "She's practically living here now. She's going to the benefit *with Cody*. She and Haley are best buds, and no one is talking about my graduation and what we're doing to celebrate."

Miranda gave Natalie a sympathetic smile. "The plans for your graduation are all set. We will all be there to celebrate with you. Dinner's at your favorite restaurant. I've ordered your favorite dessert. There will be presents." Miranda hoped that cheered up Natalie.

"But before that happens, you will apologize to your sister," Nate ordered in a calm but definitive tone.

Natalie nodded.

Nate sat next to her and put his hand over hers in her lap. "Please, Nat, give Summer a chance. She wants to be your friend. I'd love it if all my girls got along."

"Okay." Natalie's lackluster agreement made Nate frown.

Miranda wasn't so sure Natalie would give Summer a chance and wondered if there was something more going on here. "Natalie, it sounds like your concerns about Summer don't really have anything to do with how she's treated you."

"She's so very nice." Natalie made it sound like a disingenuous thing.

Miranda held Natalie's gaze. "I appreciate that she is trying to understand that we're all getting used to this and she's taking the time to try to get to know each of us."

"Some of us more than others," Natalie grumbled under her breath.

Miranda's suspicions were confirmed. "Cody seems particularly taken with her."

Natalie's gaze fell away, but not before Miranda saw the hurt in her eyes.

Nate caught it, too. "You and Cody have always been close. That's not going to change."

Miranda wasn't so sure about that, because Cody's interest in Summer was making Natalie jealous, and that could certainly change or even harm their friendship.

She tried to put things into perspective for Natalie. "Cody and Summer are close in age. They have a lot in common and similar life experiences. They're both independent adults with jobs, settled into their professions."

"And what, I'm just a child? I'm eighteen. An adult."

"One who still has her whole life ahead of her, including going off to college and figuring out what comes next. Cody and Summer have already done that, that's why they relate so well to each other."

"I have lots of things in common with Cody."

"That's true," Nate confirmed, gentling his tone. "Which means you probably have things in common with Summer, too."

Natalie pressed her lips tight. "I suppose."

"And since Haley and Cody like her so much, maybe if you gave her a chance, you'd find that you like her, too."

Miranda held back a smirk when Natalie rolled her eyes, caught by her father's logic again.

Nate patted Natalie's knee. "First thing in the morning, I expect you to apologize to her. And since you took her car without permission to see your friends, you're grounded for a week. No going out."

"What? You can't do that. I'm an adult."

Nate shrugged. "We own the car you drive. We pay for the gas. You can use the car to get to and from school."

Miranda agreed with Nate's punishment, but wished they'd had time to discuss this ahead of their talk with Natalie. "You really need to think about what you did today and why. Was it a mistake? Were you dismissive to Summer out of spite? Did you take her car because you thought you could and she wouldn't say anything because she wants you to like her?" Miranda held up her hand to stop Natalie from offering any more excuses or even admitting the truth. "You're responsible for your actions. As an adult, you make your own decisions and suffer the consequences. Summer seems like a very forgiving person. I'm sure she'll give you a second chance. But Natalie, if you keep pushing her away, you might find that she does exactly what you want and you miss out on having another sister who is there for you when you need her. How will you feel if that happens and she becomes close with everyone else in the family, except you? If I were you, I'd feel left out. And I know you don't want that."

Natalie didn't say anything.

Miranda held her daughter's gaze. "Something to think about." She'd learned long ago that kids didn't always act like they were listening, but they heard what she said.

She'd leave it to Natalie to stew on all that happened tonight, all that had been said, and let her come to, hopefully, the right conclusion, so she'd do the right thing in the morning and offer a sincere apology to Summer.

Nate stood to leave with her, but turned back to Natalie. "There's something else I wanted to talk to you about this weekend."

"Now what?" Natalie held her father's gaze, hers filled with hope that this wasn't another lecture.

"Now that you're heading off to college and trying to figure out what you want to do in this next chapter of your life, I thought I could help you decide."

"How?" Natalie remained cautious.

"I want you to work at the company part-time through the summer. You'll earn money that you'll need when you're on your own on campus, plus you can check out the different departments and see if there's anything in tech or business that you find interesting."

Natalie looked skeptical. "Do I have to?"

"Earning your own money means you can spend it however you want, though I hope you'll be responsible and think about your future needs. Plus I really do think it will help you focus on what you want for your future."

Natalie looked to Miranda. "What do you think?"

"I had my first part-time job when I was sixteen. You're lucky you didn't need to work to pay for your car and going out with your friends. You need to learn how to budget your money and live independently. This job will ease you into that before you go to college."

"What if I hate it?"

Nate grinned. "That's why you'll only spend a limited time in each department. A few weeks at most. Unless you find something that you really like and want to learn more."

"Okay," Natalie grudgingly agreed.

Miranda held back her grin and tilted her head toward the door, giving Nate the signal they should leave on a high note. "Good night, Natalie."

"Night."

Nate kissed Nat on the head, then walked out with Miranda. They headed down the hall to their bedroom.

The second Nate closed the door, he said, "Can you believe her?"

"Actually, yes, I can. One day she finds out she has another sister, who none of us knew about, then a couple days later, a stranger is living in her house."

"She's family."

Miranda gave Nate a look he understood all too well.

He conceded. "You're right. I just thought the girls would love to meet her, that they'd both embrace her with open arms."

"Haley is like that. Sweet. Kind. Everyone is a friend. Natalie is more cautious. I don't like what she did, but I can understand from her perspective that Summer is getting all the attention at a time when she thought the focus would be on her. And we keep treating her like a kid when she's grown up and we need to let her make her own decisions and mistakes."

Nate agreed with a nod. "It's hard to let go. It's only been a few days. Things will settle down. It will feel like Summer's always been with us."

Miranda hoped that happened sooner rather than later. There might be a few more growing pains for Natalie yet.

Nate took her hand. "And how are you feeling about all this?"

Miranda wanted to say that everything was fine. "I know you're excited to have her here. From what little I've learned about her, she seems like a very nice, wonderful woman. She's accomplished, smart, and always offering to help."

"But?" Nate held her gaze.

"No 'but.' I see so much of you in her. I know you want to make up for lost time."

"I do. I feel like I owe her that much."

"She's your child. I try to imagine what it feels like for you to find her after twenty-five years have passed. I just can't fathom it."

"I feel a connection to her. I love her. But I don't feel like I know her, the way I know our girls. And I want that."

"I know you do. But it'll take time. And while you're doing that, I need you to remember that our girls need you, too."

"I know that."

"And yet here we are, with Natalie accusing us of favoring Summer."

"Isn't that how it sometimes goes? One child needs you more at times for whatever reason, so you give them the attention they deserve and need. That doesn't mean you don't still love the other child and spend time with them. It's like a marriage. It's not fifty-fifty all the time. And I know I've been guilty of leaving you with eighty percent of the family stuff while I focused on work. I know it's not fair to you. I know I have making up to do."

They'd had this discussion before when Miranda had expressed her feelings about Nate neglecting her and taking her for granted. They made it a point now to talk about things and to do more things together. She appreciated that Nate, blinded by his passion for his work, opened his eyes when she needed him to see that the small things he didn't do were adding up to a big problem in their marriage. He adjusted and made it a point to fix things because he loved her and didn't want to lose her. He didn't just say those things; he'd proved it by changing his behavior and doing what she needed him to do to make her feel like she mattered.

"Natalie is letting us know she needs reassurance that she's still equal in our eyes. Yes, Summer deserves and needs our special attention now because we want her to feel like a real part of the family. But we also need to let Natalie know what's happening in her life is important, too."

"Of course it is. I'm excited that she'll be graduating and going off to college. At the same time, I can't believe she's grown up so fast."

"Then let's make sure she knows that we want to celebrate her accomplishments and Summer isn't going to overshadow that or take away from what we have planned."

"Absolutely. I hope tomorrow they'll work it out." Nate gave her a narrow-eyed look. "But right now, I'd like to show my appreciation to my beautiful wife for being so understanding and welcoming to my daughter and also just for being the wonderful woman you are."

Miranda grinned. "Oh, yeah? And how are you going to do that?"

"I'm going to start with my hands, then my mouth, then I'm going to make love to you until you moan my name."

They reached for each other. This was the part she liked most about their marriage. Yes, the great sex, but more than that was that they nurtured the intimacy between them. It had kept their connection and the love between them strong all these years.

She hoped that no matter what trials and tribulations came their way, they'd always have this and the trust and love they'd built between them.

Chapter Twenty-Three

Cody knocked on Summer's door without toppling the tray of food he'd reheated in the kitchen. She didn't answer, so he cracked the door open and called out, "Summer, it's me."

"I'll be out in just a sec." She was still in the bathroom.

"I'll be on the patio outside your room."

"Okay."

He went out the sliding door and set the tray on the table next to the lounge chair. He pulled the cushioned rocking chair over and sat, letting the sound of the waterfall in the small pond and the quiet night calm him.

"Hey." Summer stood in the doorway wearing a pair of black yoga pants and socks, a pink T-shirt, and a black cardigan. "I feel underdressed for this patio dinner."

He realized he was still wearing his suit. He hooked his fingers over the knot in his tie, pulled it loose, and undid the top button on his shirt. He held his hand out to her.

She took it, and he pulled her around in front of him, then tugged her hand so she'd take the hint and sit on his lap. She settled on his thigh and leaned back into him as he wrapped his arms around her and held her close.

"Are you okay?"

"I should be asking you that." He hugged her to him, a need deep inside him wanting to comfort and erase all the bad from today.

She rubbed her head against his. "I like this."

He held her tighter.

She snuggled into him. "What's your favorite thing to do when you have nothing to do?"

"What?" He hadn't anticipated the odd question.

"I'm changing the subject. Right now, I'm more interested in *you* than anything else."

He didn't know what to do with the way that hit him with so much emotion, so he went with honesty. "These days, all I want to do is spend time with you."

"That's the nicest thing you've said to me." She shifted on his lap, cupped his face, and kissed him softly, her eyes locked with his. The soft press of her lips to his wasn't nearly enough, but the warmth and emotion she packed into it told him everything he needed to know.

She cared about him.

She wanted him.

This was just the beginning.

She broke the kiss, but remained close, her eyes locked with his. "Thank you for taking care of me."

"I can't stand it when you're not smiling."

"That's very sweet."

"I don't get why Natalie would do something so dismissive."

Summer pressed her lips tight, then her stomach rumbled. "Let's forget it and eat."

"Your discharge papers said not to eat until tomorrow and to drink a lot of water."

"I'm starving. They gave me anti-nausea meds. I'll take my chances."

He gently helped her up, even though he'd like nothing better than to keep kissing her.

She shifted and sat on the lounge chair next to him.

He pulled the top off her food and handed her the container along with a fork, then grabbed his own food.

She glanced at the garden and the lights strung overhead and along the privacy fence surrounding the courtyard, then her gaze settled on him again. "This is really nice."

He liked it, too. "Not the five-star dining I had planned. But this is better. I have you all to myself."

She chewed a bit of her food, then said, "I don't need a fancy restaurant. I like casual and intimate."

"We can do whatever we want."

They both dove into the food and let the quiet, cool night surround them.

Halfway through his food, he felt better. His anger had dissipated just being with her. "Thank you for thinking of getting everyone something to eat. You're always thinking of others."

"I try." She shrugged a shoulder. "And I wanted to do something nice for all of you. I appreciated having you there with me." Because if she'd been home, she'd have been alone. Of course, she'd have had her meds, too, and this wouldn't have happened.

Still, he hated thinking about all the nights she spent alone.

"Have you ended up in the hospital often with those migraines?"

"A couple of times." She went quiet, then changed the subject again. "You obviously like the ocean. You live here. So . . . road trip or overseas destination?"

He went with the roundabout that took them back to getting to know each other better. "Either one. My dad used to take me and Brooke camping and fishing all the time when we were young. I've traveled to several countries for work. It's interesting to see new places and experience different cultures."

"If you could go anywhere in the world, where would you go?"

That was easy. "Anywhere with you."

She smiled, and he felt that connection between them amplify. "I'll let you pick. Where would *we* go?"

He liked that *we*. "New Zealand. All the beauty of Australia, none of the deadly creatures."

She laughed. "Sounds good. I've never been there."

"Where's your favorite place to visit?"

"Italy. And Spain. I'd like to go back to both and see more."

"I've never been to either of those. You could show me what you like about them, then we can explore more of them together."

"Sounds like a plan." She broke off a piece of garlic bread and handed it to him. "Favorite thing to do on vacation?"

"The usual. Explore. Eat. Find a good spot to do nothing for a while. Relax and not worry about work or anything else." He thought about spending days doing all those things somewhere else with her, and the nights wrapped around her between the sheets. That's a vacation he couldn't wait to take.

"That's what I like to do, too. Though I haven't gone anywhere in a few years."

"Then we should plan something." Normally, work consumed his life, too, but he'd go anywhere, anytime with her. And didn't that tell him a lot about the feelings stirring inside him?

Summer frowned. "My grandfather is already having a stroke over me being gone the next few weeks. A trip would really send him over the edge."

"When will it be okay for you to live your life the way you want to live it?"

She went still, and he thought maybe he'd gone too far.

"When I stop worrying about what he and my mom want me to do for them." Sadness filled her eyes. "Things are even more complicated with my dad and his family."

"You mean, *your* family."

Her earnest gaze met his. "I feel like I'm getting closer to him. When he abandoned his plans with Miranda and they showed up at the hospital . . . It really meant a lot to me. Haley is easy. We have a lot in common. She's so open to having me here."

"Miranda wants to protect her kids and Nate from any upset." Cody had seen the wary way Miranda watched everything unfolding.

"She's the kind of mom mine isn't. And I get it. They're her heart. She's only truly happy if all of them are."

"And Natalie is unhappy and making waves, making it hard for you to fit in."

"I sometimes feel like I'll never really fit anywhere."

He wanted her to believe she fit here, with him. "You and I together feels so right that I have a hard time believing and trusting in it." He figured she could relate to that.

"You're afraid I'll disappoint you."

He shook his head, even though he knew that was part of it, but focused on what was more important to him. "I just want it to be what I want it to be." The picture in his head. The feeling in his heart matched by hers.

"I totally understand that and feel the same way. So we'll keep things real and honest and see where that takes us."

"I hope it leads to more time together and another kiss tonight." Her cheeks pinked and she leaned in.

He met her halfway and kissed her softly, tasting the garlic and tomato sauce from her dinner. He wanted to dive in for more, but now wasn't the time. Not after the day she had. But one kiss led to two, led to a third before he pulled back and smiled at her. "I think we're getting good at that."

Her soft, sweet smile warmed his heart. "I could definitely get used to that with you."

"It's starting to feel like a craving I can't deny."

She kissed him softly, then put her hand on his face and looked deep into his eyes. "You are so unexpected."

"I like that you feel that way. It seems to me your life has been one way for far too long. I'm happy to change that for you, so you'll be looking for good things to happen and not always thinking the worst is coming."

"That has become a bad habit of mine."

He wanted to stay longer, but the fatigue in her eyes told him she needed some rest. "How are you feeling?"

"The pain meds are wearing off. The headache is gone. I feel drained."

He stacked all the dishes on the tray, then stood. He held out his hand to her.

She took it and stood with him.

He brushed a stray strand of hair behind her ear. "Get some rest. I'll see you first thing in the morning."

"I'd like that."

He cupped her face and kissed her, long and deep, then kissed her on the forehead. "I don't want to let you go, but . . ." He left it hanging because they both knew he wasn't staying. Tonight wasn't the night. But soon. He hoped. Because having this gorgeous, sweet, kind, and giving woman so close made him want and need like nothing he'd ever felt.

She looked up at him with her beautiful blue eyes. "Good night, Cody."

He brushed his lips to hers one more time, then reluctantly released her, grabbed the tray, and walked with her back into her room, then out her door.

She gave him one last look, then closed the door softly.

He missed her already, but hoped she got a good night's sleep so they could do something together tomorrow.

He wanted to hold on to the memories of tonight, the feelings that overwhelmed him when he kissed Summer, and the anticipation he had to see her again in the morning.

And then he spotted Natalie waiting for him on the stairs leading up to his room and the anger returned.

Chapter Twenty-Four

*N*atalie released a relieved breath as Cody walked out of Summer's room with the dinner tray. He didn't kiss her good night. He hadn't stayed the night in her room.

Thank god!

"You should be in bed." Cody walked past her toward the kitchen.

She frowned, stood, and scrambled down the three steps to catch up to him. "I'm not a child with a bedtime." Why couldn't her parents, and especially Cody, see that she'd grown up?

Cody made some dismissive noise. "You want to be treated like an adult, then act like it."

She trotted along behind him. "I am. I'm here to make things right between us."

Cody set the tray on the counter by the sink, then slowly turned to her. Something in the way he looked at her didn't bode well. "And how do you plan to do that?"

"By apologizing for upsetting you. I'm so sorry, Cody. I made a mistake. Summer had a headache. At the time, I didn't understand how serious that could be. Now I do. I will apologize to her in the morning."

"So she can wait, but I can't."

"Yes, because our relationship means everything to me. There's never been any anger between us. I don't want there to be now because of her." She tried not to make it sound like she blamed Summer, when in reality, she did. Without Summer here, everything would be fine. Normal. The way it used to be.

Cody folded his arms over his chest. God, he looked good tonight with his shirt sleeves rolled up, his tie loose, his hair perfect. "Why can't you try to get along with her? All she wants to do is get to know you and everyone else here."

Especially you.

All anyone in the house talked about was Summer. Her dad, Haley, and especially Cody went out of their way to spend time with her.

They all thought Summer was perfect and they sympathized with her sad life.

Well, that life looked pretty good to Natalie.

Summer had money to buy whatever she wanted, homes around the world when she wanted to travel. She had a good job and the looks to get any man she wanted, even if she preferred to be alone. At least it seemed that way until she locked on to Cody and used his sympathy to reel him in.

Natalie wasn't giving him up so easily. "You're right. I've been skeptical of her. I mean, she could have found Dad anytime she wanted to, but she didn't."

"You know why."

"If it was me, I'd do anything to meet my father, even if it was just to tell him how shitty it was to leave me."

"It sounds easy, doesn't it? You can't imagine being left or dismissed so callously. You have no idea what it's like to have someone be that cruel to you. Summer knew that kind of hurt all too well, even as a small child. While you were here, surrounded by your family and me and Brooke, every holiday and birthday and special and ordinary day celebrated and enjoyed without a second thought about us being here, Summer believed her father didn't want to share any of that with her. Summer didn't know when her mother would come or go, who'd be with her for her birthday or Christmas, or if she'd be alone with the staff."

Yeah, that sucked for her. "You're right. I don't know how that feels, because we are so close. But right now, it feels like she's changing things here."

Cody nodded. "She has. But you're the only one who thinks that's a bad thing, instead of seeing that you have another sister who wants to be a part of your life and be there for you always. She's that kind of person. I don't understand why you can't see it."

"I simply want to take my time to watch and listen and learn more about her. I want to know that she's here for the right reasons. I don't want Dad or anyone else to get hurt by her. I don't want our family messed up because she doesn't know how to belong to one."

Cody's arms loosened and dropped. "She's trying her best to fit in."

"I feel like she's been rather pushy with me."

"Because you've been so resistant."

"She should respect that I need time to adjust to this new normal for us."

"Then you should do that without taking advantage of the perks of having a big sister with a fancy car you can *borrow* to show off to your friends while you turn your back on her when she needs help."

She pressed her lips tight. He had her there. "I handled things badly tonight because I had plans and didn't want to change them because of her. I won't make the same mistake twice. I hope she'll understand I didn't do it out of malice."

Cody eyed her, not really buying it.

She kept her expression apologetic, hoping he'd give her the benefit of the doubt, even if she didn't deserve it. "Did it ever occur to you that I'm looking out for you, too, by being hesitant to accept her at face value?"

He planted his hands on the counter on either side of him and leaned back, the muscles in his forearms cording. "I don't need you to protect me."

"You're my friend." More than that, really, but saying that to him felt like a big step, and her stomach knotted and the words wouldn't come, so she said something close to what she wished she could say. "You're one of the most important people in my life." That got her a warm smile. "Of course I want you to always be happy."

"Thank you, Nat. I appreciate it. So cut your sister some slack. Show her the girl I know, and you'll be friends with her, too."

Natalie cringed. How could he still think of her as just a girl? She'd have to prove she'd grown up.

"I'll speak to Summer in the morning. Hopefully, we can put this behind us." And if Summer didn't want to do that, well, she'd look like the bad guy.

All Natalie had to do was get along with Summer for a few weeks. Then Summer would go back to Texas and everything would be normal again.

She'd have to endure birthdays and holidays when Summer visited, but Summer would always be just passing through on her way back to her life in Texas.

If Cody didn't see that now, he would in time.

Cody might be fascinated with Summer now, but that would wane when time and distance kept them apart.

And Natalie was here and always by his side.

Chapter Twenty-Five

Summer woke up early, refreshed and feeling like herself. No headache. No lingering fatigue. She remained angry about Natalie's behavior, but she'd deal with that later.

After getting ready for the day and grabbing a light breakfast and some much-needed coffee, she sent off the final email to her grandfather about the proposal she'd been working on, then picked up her cell phone and called him. Even on Saturday he got up early, so she had no doubt he'd seen the email come in.

"Hello, Ladybug. How are you this morning?"

She appreciated so much that he didn't dive into the work he'd wanted her to finish yesterday but couldn't because of her migraine. "Better."

"What does that mean?" he asked, concerned.

"One of my headaches turned into a full-blown migraine yesterday. I didn't have my meds, so I ended up in the hospital last night."

"Why didn't you call me?"

"What could you do? You're in Texas." She briefly explained what happened with Cody finding her and taking her to see his buddy at the hospital. "The meds worked. Everything is fine now."

"And the doctor there gave you a prescription so this won't happen again while you're gone?" He didn't put any censure into his words, just concern for her.

"Yes, Pappy. It's a mistake I won't soon forget."

"You're not telling me something. What is it?" he demanded to know. "I thought things were going well with Nate."

"They are. I just wish everyone was happy I'm here." She didn't have to hide her disappointment with him.

"Who's not happy about you being there? Nate's wife?"

"Miranda is very nice. Haley is everything I ever wanted in a sister. But Natalie . . . she's a tough one."

"People don't always get along."

"It's more than that. She won't even give me a chance."

"Then it's her loss."

She smiled because that was so her grandfather, and she missed his direct and to-the-point conclusions. He didn't spend time worrying about other people's opinions of him. He didn't need to be liked. He simply said what he meant and went after what he wanted. Never in a mean way. Just with purpose.

And for her, he could be endearingly kind and soft. In his way.

"I just hoped . . ."

"The perfect family doesn't exist, Ladybug. Everyone has problems and squabbles. Just because you're family doesn't mean you have to like someone. I don't need to remind you of how you feel about your mother."

She rolled her eyes. "No, you don't."

"You can't make Natalie like you. Focus on your other relationships. Strengthen those bonds. Maybe she'll come around given some time and space."

"That was my thought, too."

"Great minds . . ."

She loved the praise of being compared to him. "What are you doing today?"

"Golfing with a friend and avoiding your mother."

She chuckled. "So your usual Saturday."

"Except I won't be having dinner with you," he grumbled.

That made her smile. "So you miss me already?"

"I hoped things would go well there and you'd be home by now, keeping the machine running in top form."

"I'm sure Sutherland Industries is doing just fine without me."

"Yeah, well, I'm not. I turn around ten times a day to say something to you and you're not there." The sadness in his gruff voice warmed her heart, but there was something else that worried her.

"Pappy, are you okay?"

"I thought doing this would make you happy, but you're not and that worries me."

"Why?"

"Because you deserve to be happy, and I hoped this would give you a sense of belonging and joy that I've wanted for you for a long time."

"For the most part, everything is fine. I have no doubt Natalie and I will come to some sort of understanding and peace between us." She thought of what had brought her happiness. Actually who. "I had a really wonderful dinner with Cody last night on my private patio with strung lights and the stars overhead. We talked. I kissed him." She didn't know how to convey to her grandfather how something so normal felt so monumental.

"*You* kissed *him*. Well, now, that's big. That's initiative. Keep it up."

"Kissing him, or going after what I want?"

"One will get you the other if you do it right," her grandfather said with humor in his voice.

"I'm scared," she admitted.

"That means it matters. But it can't turn into what you want unless you put in the effort."

"For the first time in a long time, I am."

"That's what I want to hear. Do the same with your sister and see where it takes you."

"I will."

"You've got this, Ladybug." He sounded so sure. "It will all work out."

Cody walked into the office and didn't hesitate to come around his desk, lean down, and kiss her on the head. "Morning."

She smiled up at him and said into the phone, "You know, Granddad, I think you might be right."

"Always am," he said with all his Sutherland confidence, and hung up on her.

She laid her phone on the desk, stood, grabbed a handful of Cody's sweaty T-shirt, and pulled him down for a soft kiss. "Morning."

He searched her eyes. "You look rested."

She'd bowed out of their run this morning in favor of calling her grandfather and giving her body a rest after her ordeal yesterday. "I slept thanks to the meds your doctor friend gave me."

"Good. I thought maybe we could hang out today, take things easy, maybe go for a walk on the beach later."

"I'd like that."

Cody grinned. "Looking forward to it. I'll go shower."

"Summer," Natalie called from the doorway. "Can we talk?"

"Yes. Come in." Summer kept her voice neutral, not wanting to discourage Natalie or make her think she was off the hook for what she'd done.

Cody brushed his hand down her arm. "I'll see you soon." He walked out past Natalie without a word and barely a look.

Natalie watched him walk away before turning back to her.

Summer waved her hand out toward the extra chair in front of the desk and took her seat behind it.

"It's strange. Usually Cody's the one in here all the time. But lately, it seems you're always in here."

"My grandfather has trouble understanding that most people don't work on their vacations."

Natalie sat and stared at her. "He relies on you."

"Very much. Yes. You're a little like him."

Natalie cocked a brow. "How so?"

"You make me earn everything. My place here. A relationship with you. Your trust. The others were happy to let me in. You wish I'd never come at all." Summer wanted to put it out there and see if Natalie was brave enough to admit it.

"You've known about Dad your whole life and you did nothing about it."

"And that makes you angry. Why? Because I should have done something? Or because it hurt *our* father that he was kept in the dark?"

"Both."

"Thank you for the honesty. I just wish you understood things from my perspective."

"You thought he didn't want you, but you didn't confront him about it." Natalie had probably never had to put herself out there like that.

"If that had been true, that he didn't want me in his life, what would have been the point of demanding that he see me? So he could say it to my face?"

Natalie shrugged that off.

Summer couldn't make her understand something that seemed so foreign to her. So she stuck to their relationship. "You've made it very clear you don't like me and you don't want me here. It hurts my feelings and makes me sad, because I really want us to be close. But I won't force myself on you. That would only make you dislike me more. But it also seems that you're annoyed when I don't make an attempt. I'm good for some things, it seems. I mean, you wanted to impress your friends, so you stole my car."

"You said I could borrow it."

Summer tilted her head. "You spend an awful lot of time trying to get everyone to see that you're a grown-up, but you act like a child."

Natalie's eyes filled with rage.

Summer knew the truth hurt. "I get it. You pout, they all pay attention. You're upset, they all try to make you feel better. And because it works for you, you use it to your advantage." Her mother was the same way, though to the extreme. She hoped her sister learned a better way before she found herself without any real friends. "You know you should have asked to use the car. Instead, you went into my room while I was at the hospital, took the keys, and left without anyone knowing what you did."

"I'm sure you can't wait to tell them."

"We're not kids, Natalie. I'm not tattling to your parents. I'm talking to *you*. Directly. Honestly. Like adults."

"It feels like you think we're going to be this close family unit just like that."

"We are family. But the rest . . . that's why I'm staying here, so we can find our way to being friends. But we both have to want it."

"I'm not against it. I'm just . . ." Natalie couldn't seem to come up with the right word.

"Resistant" came to Summer's mind. "I get it. I'm the outsider. But, Natalie, I want to be a part of your life. You're going to be busy with college soon. This is our chance to build a solid foundation. I'd love to visit you at school, have you come see me in Texas, maybe go on vacations together. I don't want our relationship to be two strangers meeting for holidays and birthdays. We didn't grow up together, so we don't share history. But I'd like to hear your stories and make memories with you, too, because I'm not going anywhere. I am your sister. What we make of that is up to you, because I'm all in."

Natalie took a few seconds before she sighed. "Okay. I'll stop . . . putting you off and try the whole friend-sister thing."

"Thank you. Now, you did something wrong, and you need to make it right."

"I came here to apologize."

"Great. I'm happy to hear it." Summer waited, knowing Natalie meant for the sentiment of her statement to be accepted as the apology. But Summer expected more from Natalie. She refused to let her off the hook so easily. Not the way the rest of them did.

Natalie pressed her lips tight, then sighed again like only teenagers could do when it felt like the world was against you and you had to do something you didn't want to do, but it was expected, so you grudgingly complied. "I'm sorry I didn't take you to the hospital when you asked." She scrunched her lips. "I really didn't know it was that bad. Seeing Cody so upset about it . . . I guess it finally sank in that you really did need help."

Summer understood all too well that Cody's anger and upset impacted Natalie more than Summer's suffering, but let it go in favor of getting Natalie to acknowledge what she'd done.

"Yes, I took the car without asking. I won't do it again. And I hope you will let me borrow it, because it's a really awesome car."

Summer held back a grin and nodded that she'd let Natalie borrow it again.

"Because of all this, Dad says I need to learn some responsibility. He's making me work at the company until I leave for college."

"It's a chance for you to try something new."

Natalie narrowed her gaze. "I knew you had something to do with this. You were forced to work with your grandfather, now I have to work with my dad."

"See it as an opportunity to show everyone what an adult you are by earning your own money. You never know, you might discover you love working in one of the departments."

"I doubt it."

"There are a lot of people who would love a paid internship at Dad's company. It'll look good on your résumé when you do find what you want to do."

"Not work there."

"Dad is going to bounce you around from one department to the other. Take advantage of that. Ask questions about what people do for the company. How does it all fit together? What feels like fun versus something you dread doing?"

"All of it."

"How would you know?" Summer shot back. "All I'm saying is, give it a chance."

"Like you want me to do with you."

"Exactly. Plus, if you do a good job, it's a way for you to show off and be a part of what Dad and Cody work so hard on every day." Summer knew mentioning Cody would perk Natalie right up and spark her desire to prove herself to him.

Maybe it wasn't right to use Natalie's crush, but Summer hoped the confidence Natalie gained from this would help her see that she could accomplish anything and that she had bigger and brighter things in her future.

"I guess it won't be so bad working there part-time over the summer." *With Cody*, Summer heard without Natalie actually saying it. Natalie stood. "So we're good?"

"You tell me."

Natalie studied her a moment, then nodded. "We're good."

Summer wished for more enthusiasm, but took what she could get. "If you need help studying for your math final, I'm happy to help."

Natalie rolled her eyes. "I'll be lucky to pass that class."

"With my help, I guarantee you will."

"I'll let you know." Natalie walked out of the office and headed back to the other side of the house.

Cody popped his head in a moment later, unshowered and still wearing his running clothes. "That went well."

"Eavesdropping, Counselor. Really?"

Cody glanced over his shoulder to be sure Natalie had left and they were alone. "Just making sure she didn't make things worse."

"She knows she's in trouble and doesn't want her parents, or *you*, on her case anymore, so she said what she needed to say to get everyone off her back."

Cody leaned his shoulder against the door frame. "Let's hope this is the end of the snubbing and she accepts you now."

"We'll see." Time would tell.

"I think this was a wake-up call for her."

Summer piled her folders and papers and moved them to the unused credenza, clearing off the desk the way Cody preferred. "She's at that age where she wants to be seen as an adult, fully capable of making her own decisions and being responsible for herself. But she also wants to have all the benefits of being a carefree teen who has parents who take care of everything for her."

"I miss those days sometimes."

Summer chuckled. "I was always more the parent in my relationship with my mom. I felt like I had to always be responsible."

"No rebellious teen stories to tell?"

She shook her head. "I always did what was expected of me. I went along. I pushed away my feelings in favor of keeping the peace or making others happy."

Cody frowned. "You've been unhappy a long time."

"That's why I came here. I did this for me." She stared at him. "It meant a lot to me . . . what you did yesterday. Dinner last night . . . I loved it, just the two of us."

"I liked it, too."

"As first dates go, that was the best one I've ever had. The kiss, too."

His eyes heated with desire. "That was my favorite part."

"Mine, too."

Cody took a step toward her, the intent to kiss her again clear in his eyes.

Alex ran in and grabbed his hand. "Can we go build sandcastles on the beach? Pleeease."

Cody stared at her for one long moment, then looked down at his nephew. "Where's your mom?"

"On the phone." Alex's upper body went lax. "Please."

Summer stood. "Your uncle needs a shower. But I'll take you." She glanced at Cody. "If that's all right."

"Of course it is. I'll meet you down there in twenty minutes."

Summer held her hand out to Alex. "I bet we can build a huge sandcastle before he gets there." She walked out of the office with Alex.

Cody followed behind them. "His pails and shovels are on the back patio."

"Don't forget to tell Brooke he's with me."

Cody touched her arm to get her to stop. "I will. But first . . ." He cupped her face and kissed her softly. "Good morning."

"Good morning." She managed to say it back even though he'd completely scrambled her brain with that sweet kiss that packed a punch of lust.

Cody grinned, then headed upstairs.

Alex looked up at her. "Are you his girlfriend now?"

She didn't know how to answer that. At what point did that become true?

"We like each other a lot." She thought about it some more. "I'd like to be his girlfriend," she admitted.

"They barely know each other," Natalie said, coming up behind them in the living room.

Summer turned to her. "You're back."

Natalie gave her a *duh* look. "Brooke texted and asked if I'd take Alex down to the beach."

"Great. We'll all go together."

"If you've got him . . ." Natalie backed up a step.

"I do. And Cody will be joining us shortly."

Natalie started moving forward again. "Well, let's go get set up."

Summer let Natalie take the lead and shook her head.

Maybe Cody was the way in to getting to know her sister better and spending more time with her.

Chapter Twenty-Six

Summer laughed when Alex put his hands up like claws, roared, and stomped the sandcastle Natalie had just finished making with him.

"Hey," Natalie grumbled. "It took forever to get that second story to stay up." Suddenly Natalie's frown turned upside down. The brilliant smile could mean only one thing. "You made it."

Summer turned to smile at Cody as he made his way across the sand to them. She put her hand to her forehead to keep the sun out of her eyes, which gave her a great view of him in a simple heather gray tee and black shorts, bare feet, and a sweet smile for her.

Cody dropped down beside her, leaned in, and kissed her cheek.

"See. Girlfriend," Alex announced.

Natalie went quiet.

Cody took it in stride without comment. "I thought we were building castles, not destroying them."

"I bet I can build a bigger one than you," Natalie challenged him. "You're on."

Cody put his hand on Summer's thigh. "You in?"

Summer put her hand over his. "Absolutely."

They spread out on the beach, each of them working on their castle. Alex teamed up with Cody.

Summer had to admit, Cody took the game seriously and had the water-to-sand ratio down. Before she knew it, he had built a four-tower castle with a moat.

Natalie had obviously learned from her idol. Her castle resembled Cody's, though Natalie had added some details to hers. Using a stick, she drew a stone pattern into the walls and used seashells to decorate the roofs.

Summer kept hers basic, taking more pleasure in watching Cody and Alex create theirs. She loved seeing Cody with his nephew. He obviously adored the boy. He'd be a good father one day, one who'd stick around for his kids and make sure they knew every day that they were loved.

He was the kind of man she wanted in her life.

Just as she had that thought and a smile spread across her face, she caught Natalie's eye. Her sister didn't look too happy about the way Summer was looking at Cody.

Summer couldn't help it. The attraction was too strong. The need inside her to finally be with someone who saw her for who she was, was too great to ignore.

She tried to appease Natalie in some way. "I think you made the prettiest castle."

"Ours is the biggest," Alex announced.

"It sure is," Cody agreed. "But Aunt Summer is right. Natalie has the magic touch. Nice job, Nat."

Natalie's cheeks pinked. Her smile brightened her whole face. "Thank you. I learned from the best."

"The student surpassed the teacher." Cody checked his watch. "It's time for lunch."

Summer hadn't realized how long they'd been at it.

Alex groaned. "Just a little while longer."

Cody shook his head. "Your mom said you're going to Brian's this afternoon. You need to eat and get your tennis racket."

Alex rolled his eyes. "I hate tennis."

Cody started picking up the shovels and different-shaped pails. "Your mom and her friend like to play. Do it for her."

"Okay." Alex said it like he was suffering the worst fate.

Summer grabbed the towel she'd been sitting on and folded it.

Natalie picked up her pail and shovel and pocketed one of the larger shells she'd found.

They all headed back toward the cliff stairs, Alex in the lead, followed by Natalie, then Summer and Cody.

He put his hand to her back as they made the steep climb.

She glanced up at him. "That was a lot of fun."

He smiled down at her. "Always is. We should take a walk on the beach later tonight."

"I'd like that."

He slid his hand up her back to her shoulder. "Then it's a date."

She smiled, but noticed the frown Natalie shot down to her.

They made it to the path at the top and started back toward the house, making their way across the expansive lawn toward the pool.

Suddenly, Natalie tripped and fell to her side, hitting her hip on the grass as she reached for her ankle. "Ouch. Stupid squirrel hole."

There were dozens around them.

Cody dropped the stacked pails and shovels and bent next to Natalie. He took her foot in his hands and examined her ankle, gently pressing his fingers into it. "Does that hurt?"

Natalie hissed in pain. "Yes."

Cody met Natalie's gaze. "You're such a klutz. I tell you all the time to watch where you're walking out here."

They had all been careful about where they stepped. It seemed odd that Natalie would walk into such a big, obvious hole.

Perhaps Natalie had gotten distracted.

Like the many times she'd side-eyed Summer and Cody walking just a few steps behind her, Cody holding Summer's hand.

Cody looked up at Summer. "Mind grabbing that stuff? I'll carry her up to the house and we'll put ice on that ankle."

Natalie immediately put her arms around Cody's neck as he picked her up like she weighed nothing. Natalie even put her head on his shoulder.

Summer studied her sister.

The affection between Cody and Natalie was real, as she'd expect from two people who'd practically grown up together. But that was the thing. Cody was a grown man in his late twenties. Natalie had just recently turned eighteen and had all those teenage hormones and a gorgeous man living in close proximity.

Summer hoped Natalie realized sooner rather than later that Cody didn't return her feelings. From the outside looking in, it seemed to Summer that Cody saw Natalie as a sister.

What a crushing blow that could be for a young woman like Natalie.

Summer would have to be mindful of it and not flaunt her budding relationship with Cody. But eventually, if it hadn't sunk in yet, Natalie would see that what Summer and Cody shared was real and getting serious.

Summer and Alex returned the beach supplies to the back door of the Larkin side of the house, then walked across the courtyard to the Weston side and into the kitchen, where Cody had set Natalie on a chair. He had his head inside the freezer. Natalie was staring at his backside.

Summer announced her presence by clearing her throat. "How's the ankle feel now?"

"Sore," Natalie said immediately.

Cody finished filling a plastic bag with ice, brought it over, and gently picked up Natalie's foot and placed it on the opposite chair, then laid the ice over her ankle. "Leave this on for about ten to fifteen minutes. Hopefully you just have a slight sprain and it will be better in a day or so."

Miranda walked in and gasped. "What's happened?" Her gaze shot to Summer.

"We were walking back from the beach and Natalie accidentally stepped in a squirrel hole. I don't think it's serious. Cody carried her back to the house."

Miranda's gaze went from Cody to Natalie, and a knowing look came into her eyes, but it was gone so fast that Summer wondered if she'd seen it at all. "I see. Well, you'll have to try to stay off of it for a little while. Which will give you plenty of time to study for finals."

"I was hoping Cody and I could watch a couple episodes of our show." Natalie turned puppy dog eyes on Cody. "You promised we would soon, but you're always busy. I'm dying to find out what's happening."

Cody glanced at Summer.

She caught the concern in Miranda's eyes and Natalie's rapt attention on Summer, a look of hope that Summer didn't ruin this for her, and a dare to do just that and see what happened. "I have a call to return and dozens of emails." That's what came out of her mouth. Inside, she'd hoped to invite Cody out to lunch, somewhere they could be alone and spend time talking and getting to know each other better.

Cody frowned. "It's Saturday. After the day you had yesterday, take a break."

"I did this morning. I will later."

"Right," Cody agreed. "We have plans."

"I remember. I'll see you soon." She turned to Natalie. "I hope that ankle feels better soon."

Natalie nodded, then immediately shifted her focus to Cody. "Will you help me to the couch?"

Cody stepped right in to help her up on her good leg, then he scooped her up in his arms and carried her out of the kitchen to the living room.

Alex followed.

Summer hung back with Miranda.

"Are you feeling better today?" Miranda went to the fridge and pulled out the fixings for sandwiches.

"I am. Thank you."

"It made Nate feel good to be there for you. I'm glad what happened to you wasn't serious. Though I bet it felt that way in the moment."

"My migraines are no joke. Thank god for medication."

"I haven't seen Cody upset like that in a long time. I'm glad he and Natalie worked things out. Looks like you both did, too."

"Natalie apologized this morning."

"I don't know what got into her."

"She's jealous." Summer pointed out the obvious, knowing Miranda saw what Summer saw when it came to Natalie's feelings about Cody. "But I hope in time Natalie will see that I'm not taking something away from her."

Miranda nodded. "It's a strange time, that transition from graduating high school and becoming an adult and starting the next phase of your life."

"Exactly. The things you thought you wanted when you were young you see differently as your world expands."

Miranda grinned. "Yes. I hope she sees all the possibilities ahead of her come the fall when she's at a new place with new people."

Away from Cody.

"I'm sure she will. But right now, she's just trying to get through these last two weeks of school and a summer working at the company before she tackles the next new thing."

Relief filled Miranda's steady gaze. "Thank you for understanding that not everything comes easy for her."

"This can't be easy for you, either. I imagine you were just as shocked as everyone else to discover your husband had another daughter. You only had a couple of days to come to terms with it before I showed up and disrupted your lives." Summer wondered exactly how Miranda felt about the entire situation. Miranda had been kind, but she'd been keeping her feelings very close.

Miranda gave a nervous laugh. "I thought after all these years of marriage Nate couldn't surprise me with anything. Oh, sure, little things, but something like that . . ." Miranda shook her head and pulled out a loaf of bread. "I love him just as much today as when I fell in love with him all those years ago. So it was easy to sympathize and be angry on his behalf that your mother kept you from him. That wasn't fair. He's a good man. A good father."

Summer appreciated the anger that backed up those words. "There is no excuse for what she did."

"I think about what you've told us about her, your life, and I think, *What a shame.* This all could have been different if you'd been a part of his life all this time."

"I'd have had a family. Well, one that looked like the one I always wanted."

"You have it now." Miranda said it like she meant it, but there was some hesitation, too.

"It kind of feels like I have to earn it, because I haven't been a part of it all these years. Everyone has their spot. Everyone knows each other's history. You all feel like a family."

"It's barely been a week. Give it time."

"I am. I will."

"Nate feels like he missed everything with you, so when we talk about doing something for the girls now, it's like another blow to his heart that he didn't do anything for you along the way."

"I appreciate the sentiment. I know he means it. And let's face it, I'm an adult, fully capable of taking care of myself. It's okay for things to be different between us because of that. I'll remind him of that when I see him next."

"Maybe that will ease his guilt."

"I hope so."

Miranda spread mayonnaise over the bread and set the knife down. "And Summer . . ."

She held Miranda's serious gaze. "Yes?"

"For what it's worth, I'm glad you and Nate finally connected. It's never too late. But I wish, like you, it had been sooner. Maybe it would have been easier for Natalie. But she'll come around."

"I feel like if I had more history with all of you, it wouldn't feel like I'm visiting."

"You're not. You're home."

Summer took a chance, closed the distance between them, and found Miranda already spreading her arms wide to accept the hug Summer wanted to give her. "Thank you for saying that."

"It's true." Miranda gave her a squeeze, then let her go and smiled.

"Well . . ." Summer often felt awkward after displays of affection because they had been few and far between. "Um, I guess I'll go make my call."

"See you later." Miranda went back to making the sandwich with a knowing grin.

Yes, Summer was retreating, but with a full heart, knowing she'd gotten a step closer to what she really wanted: belonging.

$\mathcal{N}$atalie walked out of the dressing room at the boutique Summer suggested for dress shopping for the upcoming benefit. Her mom had wanted to take her and Haley to the store where they bought Natalie's prom dress. Natalie had begged for something more chic.

"Absolutely not," her mom said the second she spotted Natalie in the black gown with the spaghetti straps, deep plunging neckline, and slit all the way up to her hip bone, showing off a lot of leg.

Summer put a hand on Miranda's shoulder and stood. "You definitely have all the assets for that killer dress."

Natalie appreciated the compliment.

"But . . ." Summer came to her, put her hands on Natalie's shoulders, and turned her toward the mirror. They locked eyes in the glass. "What does this dress say about you?"

That I'm sexy as hell. "That I'm not a kid anymore."

"You've got all the curves to back it up," Summer agreed. "But— and maybe I'm wrong—you look hesitant, like this dress is outside your comfort zone."

What Summer was saying kind of made sense. "This dress is killer."

"It is. But do you feel confident in it?"

Natalie studied herself in the mirror with a critical eye and realized she kept her hand at the slit of the dress on her thigh, trying to make sure it stayed in place and didn't show too much. She also had to stop herself from tugging at the top again to keep from spilling out of it.

She didn't feel self-assured; she felt exposed.

Summer made a suggestion. "Try on the dress I hung outside your dressing room. I want you to see the difference, not just in how you look, but in how you feel. If I'm wrong, then you argue with your mom about which dress you'll get." Summer gave her a teasing smile.

Natalie went back to the dressing room and saw the dress Summer had left hanging there. It wasn't one she would have picked, but Natalie went in to try it on anyway.

Through the thin door she overheard Summer and Miranda gushing over Haley's dress.

"That color is perfect on you," Miranda said.

"I love it." Excitement filled Haley's voice. "Summer, you were so right." Haley loved bright colors, and Summer had picked a pretty lilac-colored dress to offset Haley's dark hair and darker blue eyes. Natalie bet it looked great on her.

The dress Natalie slipped on wasn't black, like she wanted, but midnight blue. The second she saw the color against her skin and lighter blue eyes, she loved it.

She hadn't been sure about the scoop neck or cap sleeves, but the second she zipped up the dress and the bodice hugged her breasts and pushed them up slightly, she got the sexy vibe she wanted. Especially how the dress draped from the nipped-in center just below her breasts, down to her knees. The dress didn't cling. It skimmed her curves. And the slit on the side to mid-thigh added just enough sexy.

A pair of shoes appeared over the top of the door.

"Try these," Summer called out.

She took the gorgeous strappy silver heels that weren't too high or too low. She'd be comfortable in them, without feeling like she was teetering on stilts.

Sure enough, they fit great and made her legs look amazing. She'd have to remember to favor her *sprained* ankle a little longer.

She didn't want to give credit to Summer for pulling this together, but the woman knew what she was doing when it came to looking good in a dress.

Natalie stepped out.

Haley was by the shoes with Miranda, picking out something.

Summer clasped her hands together and held them up at her chest. "Oh. My. God. Stunning." She smiled so big her cheeks went pink. "Do you like it?"

Natalie turned to the larger mirror and stared at herself, surprised by the difference in how she looked in the two dresses. This one made her feel sexy, but in a different way.

"You look confident and so grown up," Miranda said.

She turned to her mom. "Do you mean that?"

Miranda nodded, her eyes a bit misty. "I can see it." She took a sweeping look from Natalie's head to her feet and back up again. "It's perfect. You're so lovely. How did you grow up so fast?"

Natalie wiped away a tear, then turned to Summer. "Thank you."

"You're welcome. If my mom taught me anything, it's how to pick a dress."

Miranda glanced at Summer. "You've got a great eye."

"Years of shopping practice with my mom. It's the one thing we did together the most."

Miranda took Summer's hand. "I'm so glad we got to do this together."

Summer's eyes shone with unshed tears. "Me too. Thank you for letting me tag along."

"We wanted you here," Haley said, holding up a pair of black flats with satin trim in one hand and a pair of silver ones in the other. "Which ones?"

Miranda looked at Summer. "I think you can find her something more suited to the young lady she is today, not the little girl she used to be."

Summer went to the shoe display and chose a pair of silver kitten-heel pumps that had a heel strap and cutouts on both sides of the pointed toe. A rhinestone daisy adorned the top of each shoe. "Sophisticated and cute."

"Those are the ones I wanted, but Mom always makes me get flats."

"Not this time," Miranda said. "Those are so you."

Haley snatched them from Summer's hand and put them on. She shifted her feet this way and that way, admiring them.

Natalie's heart warmed watching her sister, so happy and excited about the shoes.

Natalie wasn't the only one who'd grown up. Haley wasn't so little anymore, either.

It had been strange to see her sister on campus this past year after not being at the same school for three years because of their age difference. Natalie would see Haley with her friends, hanging out on the quad at lunch, and passing in the halls. Natalie had made it clear she didn't have time for her little sister when she was with her friends.

How stupid was that? Haley was fun to hang out with, and all of Natalie's friends liked Haley.

Natalie caught Summer staring at her instead of Haley, with a soft grin on her face and eyes that held approval and understanding. "You're both beautiful and so special."

Miranda hugged Summer, then stepped back, choked up. "All of you are."

Natalie hadn't appreciated her mother enough. "Dad's going to keel over when he sees you in your dress."

Haley tilted her head. "Summer, are you sure you don't want to get a new dress?"

"I brought one of my favorites especially for the event."

"Because Cody wanted you to go with him." Haley grinned, obviously loving what was happening between the two.

Natalie tried to tamp down her own feelings, but the harder she tried, the angrier she got. Sometimes when she saw them together, she wanted to scream at Summer to just leave.

Cody was completely wrapped up in her. Just like he'd been with Amy.

That ended in disaster and Cody turning into someone she'd hardly recognized. He'd been sullen and sad and withdrawn from everyone for weeks. He didn't want to talk to anyone. Including her. Brooke had been living with her husband at the time and had to come to the house at Dad's request, because he was so worried about Cody.

But it was Natalie who finally snapped him out of it. It hadn't even really been that hard. She'd simply said all the things she'd hated about Amy and how that woman treated Cody. He deserved better.

A week later, he hadn't come home straight from work like normal. Her dad had mentioned to her mom that he had a date.

Natalie waited up, sighing with relief when he returned near midnight. Alone. The next morning, he'd seemed . . . not happy, but more like his old self.

It didn't bother her that he saw other women. He never brought any of them home. They didn't mean anything to him.

Until Summer.

He didn't act with Summer the way he had with Amy. This was different. More intense. It was like he needed to be near her all the time. Natalie saw it in the way he stared at Summer, got up to fetch her whatever she wanted. A glass of water. A sweater from her room so she wouldn't catch a chill when they sat out back. Little things.

But Natalie saw how those little things added up to them growing closer together.

Like the way they sat next to each other at dinner each night. The accidental brushes of their hands when passing the food turned into handholding and leaning into each other when they spoke.

"Are you different around him?" Natalie blurted out the question without thinking.

Her mother's gaze sharpened on her. A sure sign her mom didn't think the question appropriate.

Summer took it in stride. "I suppose I am. He called me out on the way I dismissed him at first because that's what I did with most men. I liked that he wanted me to pay attention to him. He practically dared me. But he's not a man to be overlooked. His intellect and insight are sharp and intriguing. But it was the way he talked about his mom, his sister, and all of you that really touched me. He cares so deeply for the ones he loves and he doesn't mind showing it. It's in the way he jumped to help you when you twisted your ankle, and watched TV with you just to be sure you were okay, and offered to get you anything while you were incapacitated. He shows it in all the little things he does for everyone around him."

"He texted me a picture of a bunny this morning because he knows I love them," Haley said, making Natalie realize she wasn't the only one Cody did things like that for.

Miranda added, "Whenever he stops by the store to pick up groceries for their kitchen, he always calls to ask if I need anything, even though he knows Celeste does the shopping each week. Every Mother's Day, he brings me a huge bouquet of flowers. My birthday, too. But the Mother's Day one gets me every time."

"We should do something nice for him." Natalie thought about what he'd like. "That really cool bar he loves is right down the street. We should get him a bottle of that whiskey he likes. It's the bar's label. I forget what it is, but I'll know it when I see it."

Her mom lifted a shoulder. "That's a really nice gesture, Natalie. I'll run in and get one." Her mom looked so pleased that Natalie had thought of it.

Natalie couldn't wait to see Cody's face.

Summer picked up the shoeboxes. "You two need to change, so we can get home and surprise Cody."

Natalie went into her dressing room and took off the dress and shoes, pulling on her other clothes and meeting everyone by the cash register.

Her mom slipped Natalie's dress into the garment bag the boutique provided to customers. Haley stood nearby with the shoes.

Summer held a bag with the boutique's label on it.

"What did you get?"

"Oh, just a little something for Cody."

Natalie wondered what, but didn't ask, because she knew he was going to like Natalie's surprise the most. Still, what could Summer have possibly gotten him at the high-end clothing store?

Nothing he probably didn't already have in his wardrobe.

They arrived home and found Cody sitting in the backyard with Nate, having a beer on the patio by the pool.

Nate got up to greet Miranda with a kiss.

Cody stood and brushed his hand down Summer's arm. "How was your day?"

"Really good. I got to spend time with Miranda and my sisters."

Natalie stepped in between them and held up the bag from the bar Cody loved.

"What's this?" he asked.

"For you. I know this is your favorite."

Cody peeked into the bag, grinned, then pulled out the bottle. "Thank you. It is my favorite. But how did *you* get this?"

Miranda spoke up. "It was Natalie's idea, but it's from all of us because you're always so good to us."

Cody's eyes went soft, and his shoulders went lax. "Really. That's so nice. I appreciate it."

"We appreciate you," Miranda added.

Cody sighed and said to Mom, "You are always there for me." He looked at Natalie again. "You're the best, Nat. Thanks." He turned to Haley. "And you, you always make me smile." He looked at Summer. "You . . . you make me believe what I thought I'd never find is right in front of me."

Natalie couldn't believe he'd say something so . . . so . . . What the . . . How could he say that to her?

Summer held up whatever she'd bought at the boutique. "I got you something, too."

Cody's smile turned megawatt. "Really? If I'd known we were doing gifts, I'd have gotten you something."

What?

Natalie's head felt like it might explode.

"It's just a little something for our date."

Cody pulled out the simple silk tie and grinned like he'd been given something that he didn't have several dozen of and wore every day. "It's the exact same color as your dress."

Summer blushed. "Maybe it's a little cutesy to match, but . . . I don't know, I saw it and thought, why not?"

Cody took a step closer to Summer. "Everyone will see that we match and know you're with me."

"I know. That was kinda the point. You know, because your sister said otherwise all those women would be after you."

"The only woman I see is you."

The look they shared could steam up the windows even though they were outside.

Natalie turned and walked back to the house.

No one really noticed. They were all talking about how sweet it was that Summer got him the tie. Haley and Mom were telling Dad and Cody about their dresses.

They all talked about how they couldn't wait for the charity event.

Yeah, well, Natalie had been excited about it right up until Summer ruined her surprise for Cody with one of her own.

Still, she'd show Cody that she really was *the best*, as he put it.

When he saw her in her dress, he'd see what Mom and Summer had seen.

She was all grown up and ready to take the next step into adulthood. And everything that came with it. Including a real relationship with the guy she wanted more than anything.

Chapter Twenty-Eight

Summer walked into her dad's office holding a takeout bag of Chinese food, since he didn't have a lot of time today to go out to eat. She'd take what time he did have to share a meal and some conversation before his next meeting.

Her dad stood and greeted her with a kiss on the cheek before he rubbed his hands together. "Please tell me they had those amazing pot stickers."

"I got two orders, plus the moo shu pork, extra plum sauce."

She set the bag on his desk and pulled out the containers while he went around to take his seat. "Are you having a good day?"

"I am. Cody's not."

"Why?" Concern made her gut tight. "Is everything okay?"

Her dad waved it away. "He's been watching this company we've wanted to buy for a long time. They recently had a management shake-up and now the company's stock is down. Cody wants to swoop in and buy it now, but we don't have the equity or leverage to do it at this time. Not without putting our financials in jeopardy." Nate opened his chopsticks and picked up a pot sticker. "I wish we could do it." Her dad popped the pot sticker into his mouth and chewed, a thoughtful look coming over him. "The company is in Austin."

"Really? Tell me more."

The more her father told her, the more she wanted to know, because this could be an opportunity she didn't want to pass up. A chance that could bring her and Cody closer together.

$\mathcal{N}$atalie sat back in the chair at her desk and stared at the page filled with math equations. All of them solved correctly, thanks to Summer.

"You've got this, Natalie. You're going to ace that test."

Thanks to you, she silently acknowledged.

She hadn't been thrilled about asking for Summer's help. She thought her big sister would think she was stupid. Math sometimes didn't compute for her. But Summer had worked with her, going step by step through the problems, and actually explaining it in a way that made sense.

And maybe Summer deserved some credit for that. "I couldn't have gotten this far along without your help."

"Do you feel ready for the test? If you want to practice a bit more, we can keep working on it."

Natalie shook her head. "No, I think I've got it now."

"Great. I'm so glad I could help." Summer stood and stretched her back, staring out the windows at the backyard. "You have a great view from here. I love those huge oaks."

Natalie did, too. "First thing in the morning, the mist and sunlight coming through the trees is gorgeous. Each day, it's a little different." Natalie stared out at the trees. "Most mornings, there's a herd of deer that come through here."

Summer smiled. "I see them on my runs. A big family of them. Not to mention the squirrels that scamper everywhere and up the trees."

"I've photographed them," Natalie admitted.

"I've seen them. I follow your Instagram account."

Natalie had cringed at first that her sister started following her. But then Summer would leave comments. Nice things, like, "Gorgeous! Great hair day!" when Natalie posted an early morning pic of her before she got ready for school and her hair was a tangled mess. "Cute cuddles!" for the picture of two bunnies next to each other, their heads turned, noses touching.

But the comment she liked the most was the one Summer left on a picture Natalie had taken of storm clouds off the coast and over the ocean. She'd commented simply, "Exceptional!"

"You post the most beautiful pictures."

Natalie tilted her head. "You really like them?"

Summer grinned and nodded, pride in her eyes. "Everything you shoot is amazing. You should use that talent more often. You could probably start your own business and make some money on the side while you're at college."

Wonder and appreciation filled Natalie's eyes. "You really think so?"

Summer gave a firm nod. "Absolutely. Why not? In fact, you should take photographs for the company and work with the marketing and web design team at W. L. Robotics. I know you haven't thought about what you want to study at school, but photography and marketing would use your two talents."

"Two?" Natalie asked.

"You're really smart, Natalie. You see how to get people interested in things through advertising. You're always talking about the stuff you see on social media and TV. What you like. What you don't. You see things in a way others don't always see them. You could be a real asset to the company, or any company's marketing department."

"I never thought about it," Natalie confessed.

"You should. You can add real value to the company your father and Cody built. You have all the talent to do something you enjoy that doesn't feel like work to you. I could even see you working for an ad agency."

Natalie sat there stunned.

Summer went even further. "There are lots of possibilities to use your love of photography. You just have to find the one you like best and go for it."

"Don't you think Dad wants me to study business or engineering and work for the company?"

"Did he ever say that to you?" Summer didn't think so.

"No. Not really. It's the family business. Cody works there. Brooke, too."

"From what I've learned, they chose to work there. It was a way for them to carry on their dad's work. But that doesn't mean you have to, unless you want to, too."

Natalie had never considered that she had anything to offer a robotics company. But now . . . Yeah, it might be nice to be a part of the family business. Or maybe an ad agency where she got to work on lots of different products. Maybe even do fashion shoots.

Summer touched her shoulder. "I see the wheels are turning. Whatever you want to do or be, you can do it. All you have to do is try. And if it turns out you find you like something else more, you can do that, too. Not everyone knows exactly what they want to be when they grow up. Some people have to try lots of different things before they find it."

Natalie stared at Summer. "You were born into your position."

Summer laughed under her breath. "I suppose I was. Most of

the time, I like it. I like knowing that I'm carrying on something my grandfather built. I want to make him proud."

"Even though he kept a big secret from you?"

"The reasons he did are complicated and layered. I'm angry that he did it, but I also see that some of the reasons why he did it are valid and could have made my life, and Dad's, and by extension yours, worse in some ways."

"Because your mother would have caused trouble."

"She can be incredibly selfish and shortsighted. She doesn't foresee how her actions affect others negatively."

"She likes to get what she wants."

Summer nodded. "Yes."

"It seems like you've got everything. Money. Houses. Your own business."

"I have a lot of stuff," Summer agreed. "But the more stuff you have, at least for me, the more you see what really matters. I didn't wish for ponies and parties and clothes when I was young. I wanted my dad. I wanted someone who put me first. I wanted to matter to someone."

An alarm went off on Summer's phone. She pulled it out and checked it. "Time to help your mom make dinner."

"Do you miss having a personal chef?"

Summer shook her head. "Not even a little bit. I love hanging out with your mom, talking about her day. She tells the best stories about why people love and hate the homes she shows them. Oh, and some of the god-awful decorating things in the houses. Some of the photos she's shown me make me cringe. But also laugh."

"I'll come down and help you guys, I guess."

"I'd love that." Summer headed for the door. "Careful on the stairs with your sore ankle."

That made Natalie wince, because her ankle was fine.

And maybe Summer wasn't so bad after all.

Still, she'd watch and see what happened over the next few weeks.

Chapter Thirty

Summer slowed her run to a jog, then walked when Cody stopped up ahead of her. She didn't mind that he ran faster than she did and left her behind. She liked that he did his thing and got his workout in without worrying about whether she could keep up. It wasn't a competition, but something they enjoyed doing together, even if they ran their own miles at their own pace. His speed made her try harder most mornings, and she'd improved her mile time. But she wondered why he'd suddenly stopped.

"Did you get a cramp?"

He shook his head and took a couple of deep breaths, trying to lower his heart rate, just like her. "I hoped we could talk before I have to leave for work."

His words didn't make her worry. They made her feel like he missed her.

"It feels like we haven't gotten more than a moment here or there to really spend any time alone together since last Saturday."

Cody's gaze filled with remorse. "I wanted to spend last weekend with you, but things got hectic with Natalie twisting her ankle, Haley and you spending Sunday together at the movies and out shopping." Cody sighed out his frustration, because there was more that kept them apart.

Brooke had fallen ill with a bad cold and Cody had stepped in to take care of Alex and keep him occupied while Brooke rested. Natalie had been all too happy to help out, too, while also playing up her injury.

Summer didn't mind that the two of them worked together to keep Alex occupied. It's what family did. But it felt a little contrived when Natalie suggested that Summer take Haley to see the movie she was dying to see. Summer couldn't turn down her little sister. She and Cody had both shared a look of disappointment that she wouldn't be the one with him and Alex on Sunday.

And once the workweek started, Cody was at the office early and home at dinnertime where everyone came together, leaving them little time alone because Cody seemed determined to make sure she spent time with the family. She appreciated it. But it also felt like they were becoming good friends while the passion they sparked with those few kisses they'd shared flamed out.

She loved the shopping trip with Miranda and the girls during the week. Cody had been so happy and surprised by her gift.

But again, they'd kept their affection for each other to simple words and longing-filled looks.

Tonight was the charity benefit. She couldn't wait to attend with Cody and her family. Mostly, she hoped tonight would be the start of a very good weekend with her and Cody growing even closer and reigniting the flame between them.

"I don't know what's been happening lately," Cody confessed. "Every time I think I'm going to have you all to myself, someone else is with you or wants your attention." He raked his fingers through his sweaty golden hair. "It's getting really hard not to show how infuriating it is to wait my turn."

She gaped at him. "I had no idea you felt that way."

"I get that you want to get to know all of them. I think it's great that you're teaching Nate and Haley how to play chess, that you and Nate sometimes take a walk and talk about the years you missed together, that you help Miranda cook dinner most nights. Natalie even asked for help with her math final. You and Brooke have started having coffee in the morning together while I get ready for work."

She'd tried to find ways to spend time alone with each of them as well as together in hopes of building the bonds between them faster. "I'm sorry if I've made you feel like I've left you out."

"That's just it, you don't. We have our morning runs together. We talk at dinner. I love it when we share the office at night when we're both trying to get something done."

"But that's not the same as the dinner dates that never happened."

"Life got in the way. I get that. But what I don't like is that every time I even get close to you, someone interrupts. I don't know if it's Nate trying to keep us apart, your sisters, the universe, or what. All I know is that I can't take it anymore." He stepped close, cupped her face, and kissed her like he needed it to breathe again.

She felt every bit of his frustration and hunger and matched it with her own until the kiss turned into an embrace.

Cody broke the kiss and stared down at her, his blue-gray eyes filled with determination. "If we didn't have the charity thing tonight, I'd steal you away and take you somewhere we can be alone."

Summer loved that idea, but didn't get a chance to say that to him when she spotted her sisters coming across the expansive yard at the back of the house, Haley with a wide lead. "Looks like we have company."

Cody sighed.

She understood his frustration. She wanted to finish this conversation and reassure him. "I'm sorry I haven't made it clear that you have my full attention. I don't have a lot of experience with relationships. I'm sorry if I haven't given you what you need."

"It's not that." He raked his fingers through his hair again. "I've been trying to give you the time you need with our family. That's important. It's why you're here. It's just . . ." Cody sighed again. "I am well aware of everyone in the house watching us. It makes me feel like I'm doing something wrong, even though I know this isn't."

She was starting to understand. "I feel like we've both been cautious about any public displays of affection." She caught herself all the time reaching for him or wanting to kiss him and stopped herself so no one else was uncomfortable.

"If feels like we're hiding how we feel about each other. And we're doing it so well, we haven't been able to express ourselves even to each other."

"Our relationship affects others."

"It shouldn't. But I know it does. Neither of us are acting on what we want to do and say because we're concerned about them."

"What do you want to say to me?"

"That I've never wanted anyone more than I want you. You're in the house, but you're not with me. And I want you to be. In every way *with me*."

"I want that, too."

"Then can we stop acting like teenagers who live with our parents and have to sneak around, and just be together?"

She thought about Natalie.

"Stop thinking about them," Cody grumbled. "Do what you want to do because it's what you want." He held her gaze, his earnest and hopeful. "Unless it's not."

She stepped close to him and put her hands on his chest. "That's not it at all."

"If they want us to be happy, then they'll be happy to see us happy together. Right? Or at least they should. And if they don't feel that way, that's about them, not us."

"You make a strong case, Counselor."

"I shouldn't have to make a case," he griped. "But I understand these circumstances are out of the ordinary."

"I accept this no-holds-barred relationship agreement." To prove it, she went up on tiptoe and kissed him like no one was watching. Except she knew all too well that Haley stopped short and stared at them, with Natalie not so far away that she didn't see everything, too.

Summer closed her eyes and gave herself over to the kiss and the sizzling passion that exploded between her and Cody. His arms wrapped around her waist, and he pulled her close and held on tight. His lips moved over hers, his tongue diving deep into her mouth. They lost themselves in the moment, and Summer didn't think but let all the warm and sultry feelings rushing through her take hold.

Then Haley snapped them out of it. "I knew it!"

Cody broke the kiss and stared over at Haley like he'd forgotten she was coming, but he didn't let Summer go. Not even a millimeter separated them.

"Finally." Haley beamed. "I knew you two liked each other, but then it seemed like you weren't going to do anything about it."

Cody brushed his thumb along the side of Summer's face and stared into her eyes. "Not anymore. Never again."

"If you two get married, Cody will actually be my brother then, right?"

Cody suppressed a grin. "Maybe. Someday."

The way he said it made her think that "someday" wiped out that "maybe."

And though it was early days, thoughts of a future with him bloomed so real and crystal-clear that a sense of wonder and anticipation swept through her. She kissed Cody again, just a brush of her lips to his, because she wanted to.

He leaned down and put his forehead to hers. "That's better."

She put her hand on his face. "I like it, too."

Cody stood tall and took her hand.

Shock widened Natalie's eyes. "What's going on with you two?"

Cody didn't hesitate to answer. "We're together."

Natalie went still.

Haley grinned so big her cheeks squished up her eyes. "She's his girlfriend now. Officially."

This time, unlike when Alex had talked about her being Cody's girlfriend, he didn't hesitate to confirm it. "Yes."

Butterflies and joy exploded inside Summer.

Natalie questioned Cody. "But you said you didn't want another committed relationship."

Cody shook his head. "I said I wouldn't go into another one unless it felt right."

"And this does?" Natalie asked, making Cody narrow his gaze on her.

"From the moment I met her."

"But you two have been acting like you're just friends." Natalie seemed completely confused.

"That's how relationships start. You spend time with someone, getting to know and trust them, then things change. There's always an attraction that draws two people together. In our case, we held on to the attraction but focused on the other stuff because of the situation with Summer getting to know Nate and you guys."

"And now, what? You're sleeping together?" Natalie looked aghast.

Haley's mouth dropped open. "You can't ask that."

Natalie held her arms out and let them drop. "Why not?"

"That's personal," Haley said.

"It's private," Cody corrected her. "As in, none of your business."

"It is when we all live together," Natalie pointed out.

Cody raised a brow. "Would you ask your parents about them sleeping together?"

"Gross," Natalie and Haley said in unison.

"What Summer and I do, where we are in our relationship, and where we want to take it is our business. It's between us. No one else gets a say in what we want for ourselves."

Summer put her hand on Cody's forearm. "Girls—"

"I'm not a girl," Natalie snapped. "I'm an adult."

"You're right. I didn't mean anything by that," Summer assured Natalie. "Cody and I want to spend more time together. That doesn't mean we don't want to spend time with you. But it does mean that our relationship is a priority to us because we're both happiest when we're with each other."

"Until you leave," Natalie pointed out.

Summer sighed, not knowing how to address that comment and wondering if that's what had been bothering Natalie all along, that Summer was only here temporarily, so why take the time to get to know her if all she was going to do was leave?

Cody had to wonder how they were going to make this work. Her leaving had to be on his mind and causing him anxiety, too.

She didn't want them to feel like leaving was easy, or in any way permanent.

She just didn't know how to be what everyone wanted her to be for them when she was pulled in two directions. She needed to take a good look at her life and what she wanted for her future and how she was going to make it happen.

Cody eyed Summer. "Natalie, you're right. Summer's life is based in Texas, but that doesn't mean she can't make room for us here. Or that we can't be there with her sometimes, too."

Summer appreciated that Cody understood her predicament.

"She's going to take you away from us." Natalie folded her arms over her chest, looking angry, but sadness and hurt filled her eyes.

Cody went to her and put his hands on her shoulders. "That's not true, Nat. I love you guys. My home is here. My work is here. But none of that means Summer and I can't be together."

"She'll leave and you'll be hurt again."

Cody looked Natalie directly in the eye. "I know you're looking out for me. You always do. I appreciate it so much. But every relationship is a risk when you put your heart on the line. But if you never do, you'll always end up alone."

"What happens if you get hurt?" Natalie glanced at Summer. "I'm not saying you'll do it on purpose, it's just, I don't see how you two can make this work."

Summer appreciated that Natalie gave her the benefit of the doubt, though maybe that was more for Cody's benefit. "If it's worth holding on to for both of us, then there will have to be some compromise and change." The second she said that last word, she understood Natalie better.

Natalie saw change as a bad thing because she'd had a good life here with her family. Everyone lived together in harmony.

But the thought of Cody being with Summer . . . that felt like Cody leaving her for Summer. And if he actually went with her to Texas, that was not just someone leaving, but Cody picking her over Natalie. For a young woman who adored him, that would feel like a massive blow.

Summer didn't know how to reassure her sister that Cody would always love Natalie no matter what.

Cody tried instead. "This is what happens in families, Nat. We grow up. We go our separate ways. But we are always connected. You and Haley will eventually do the same. You'll go off to college, find someone you want to spend your life with, you'll move on."

"But half the house is yours. You don't need to go anywhere."

"What if I want to be somewhere else, with someone else, because that's what makes me happy?"

Summer burst with joy hearing that.

It probably felt like a blow to Natalie. "I don't want this," Natalie admitted. "I thought we'd all be in the house forever. That's why Dad built it. For all of us."

"When we were all young, that worked for us. Now, things are changing. That's what happens as we get older and want different things. Just like when Brooke got married and moved in with her husband."

Natalie pressed her lips tight. "This is never going to work. You two have separate lives."

Cody dropped his hands. "Maybe when you meet someone you really, really care about and want to be with, you'll see that you'll do anything to make that happen."

Natalie stared up at Cody like he was her everything.

Summer knew just how she felt, because that feeling was growing stronger inside Summer every day when it came to this wonderful man. And while she'd settled in here with everyone, especially Cody, time was running out on her vacation and she'd have to figure out how to balance work, life, and relationships in a whole new way.

What she knew for sure: she didn't want her life to go back to the way it used to be. All work. A lonely condo. Eating meals alone. No one there to share her days and nights.

God, how she wanted more. A partner. A friend. A lover.

She looked up at Cody and smiled, because he made her believe they could be everything to each other despite the obstacles.

$\mathcal{C}$ody hadn't expected the morning to go like this. He thought he and Summer would go for their run, then he'd talk to her about taking their relationship to the next level. He was tired of their being so close and still too far away from each other.

Maybe he was taking things faster than he should, but Summer would return to Texas sooner rather than later. He didn't want to focus on how difficult it could be for the two of them living apart. Instead, he tried to remain focused on building the foundation, so they could sustain the relationship.

Natalie somehow managed to say out loud all the reservations he had in his head, but he tried to push them aside.

He'd gotten a glimpse of what it would be like living with Summer. He loved coming home from the office, finding her in the kitchen with Miranda cooking dinner. Later, after they all sat down together and talked about their day, he'd steal time alone with her. He also loved seeing her with her sisters, strengthening their bonds.

Summer and Haley, they were already a match.

And Natalie, for all her reservations, was subtly showing signs of warming up to her. He caught the way Natalie eyed Summer and paid attention to what she said and wore. He thought it cute that Natalie had been slowly changing what she wore from jeans and T-shirts to outfits carefully picked to look put together. She was growing up before his eyes.

Haley had taken some cues from Summer, too. Mostly she and Summer watched videos on how to style hair and apply makeup. Then the two would do makeovers. It was girly, but so fun to see.

The girls were benefiting from having a big sister who took the time to do things with them and encourage them. Natalie might not think so, but it was true.

Natalie had never thought to use her love of photography for anything but a hobby she enjoyed. Now the wheels were turning and her future looked more focused.

If anyone else in the house had steered her in that direction, he didn't think Natalie would have taken it so seriously.

He found himself staring at the house, wondering how he and Summer could join their lives. It would take effort, sacrifice, and a hell of a lot of compromise.

Summer glanced up at him. "You're thinking about me going home."

He shook his head. "This is your home, too. I'm hoping that the next time you come back, it's to be with me. Up there." He notched his chin up toward his bedroom.

"I've heard you have the best view," she teased, because he'd boasted about it.

"I thought you two were—" Natalie cut that short, leaving off the sleeping-together part, thank god.

Cody didn't even look at her. "My room has a coastal vibe. Light woods, soft blues and greens for color." He glanced down at Summer. "I really loved your room at the condo. It felt so tranquil. Like my place, but a little different. I guess that was the feminine touches you added to your space. I'd like that here. We should go out and get some plants. They made your condo feel like you'd brought the outside in. I bet we can make the room feel like that."

Summer grinned. "I'd love to do that with you."

Cody took Summer's hand. "I need to get to work. Walk with me back to the house."

He and Summer walked ahead, Natalie and Haley following along, though they hung back a bit, giving Cody a chance to speak to Summer in relative privacy. "About you going back to Texas . . ."

Summer glanced up at him. "I have a life there. People are counting on me."

"Your grandfather."

"Yes. And others at the company. I'm good at my job. While work has worn on me lately because it's all I really have, I do enjoy it. I feel a sense of accomplishment and pride in working beside my grandfather. I'm sure you feel the same way about working with Nate and carrying on your father's legacy."

Cody sighed. He couldn't argue with that at all. But he wondered how they were going to sustain a relationship in the long run without making some changes.

Summer squeezed his hand. "We will find a way. I've been focused on building relationships here, not on what comes next. We'll come up with a plan together."

They didn't have the time right now to discuss it further. "I know this is new for us. I just don't want to see it end when the six weeks is up and you leave."

Summer nodded her agreement, but didn't add anything more to the conversation. That worried him.

"I'm looking forward to the charity event tonight." Her sweet smile told him she meant it.

They crossed the backyard and entered the house through the living room entrance on his side of the house. "I am, too. I'll be home to change and pick you up around six."

"I'll be ready." She turned into him and put her hands on his chest. Her gaze filled with understanding and concern. "About what we talked about earlier . . ."

He'd like to take her up to his room right now and show her how much he wanted her to stay, even though he knew that wasn't as easy as it sounded. He'd have to figure out a way to arrange his schedule so he could be with her.

He really wanted them to have the kind of relationship that lasted.

He wanted what his parents hadn't been able to pull off, but Nate and Miranda had managed to do by working together and putting their relationship first.

Yes, he and Summer both loved their work, but the job wasn't enough to make them happy. They could get that by being together and sharing a life.

"Summer, there is no question I want you. I feel how much you want me." He pulled her snug against him, and she slipped her hands around his sides and up his back.

"I do." She bit the corner of her lip, then sighed. "I think we've both been cautious and taking this slow because of our bad experiences. You've told me that the encounters you've had recently were nothing more than fun. And I get that. But it also tells me that you haven't asked for more between us until now because it means something to you."

She held his gaze. "I want to let go and not be afraid."

"I'm right there with you." Cody crushed Summer against him and took her mouth in a searing kiss as he backed her into the glass window that overlooked the garden and pool, and he lost himself in her.

aley stopped short when she and Natalie found Cody and Summer kissing. They were so lost in each other, they didn't notice the two sisters standing twenty feet away. Haley was happy that they were together.

Natalie's perpetual frown said she wasn't.

"Why are you so mad at Summer all the time?" Haley asked her.

"Don't you see what's happening?"

Haley didn't need to ogle them again to know what was going on. Her cheeks flushed just thinking about the kissing. "They're adults. They're seeing each other. Cody hasn't been with anyone in a long time."

"Amy crushed his heart. Summer is about to do the same."

Haley shook her head. "No, she's not. She likes him."

"That doesn't change the fact that she's leaving in a month."

"That doesn't mean they won't stay together."

"It will end." Natalie seemed so sure.

"Maybe he'll move to be with her," Haley shot back, not liking how Natalie made everything seem dire.

Natalie gasped. "That is not going to happen."

Haley held her hands out. "Well, she can't run a billion-dollar business from here when the company is based in Texas."

"What about Cody's work? Is he just supposed to give it up for her?"

"Maybe. If that's what he wants." Haley shrugged. "I don't know. They'll figure it out."

"That's the thing, dummy, there is no working it out when they live in different states. They'll try for a while, then it will implode. Cody will be devastated again. Better they let this thing go now, rather than drag it out."

Haley quickly glanced at the couple. Summer held on to Cody like she never wanted to let him go. Cody kissed her like he didn't want to ever stop. Seeing the two locked together like that, it was clear they wanted to be together.

Haley looked away, feeling like a creeper spying on them. "It's none of our business. They obviously want to try, so let them. Summer will be back to visit Dad and us and be with Cody as often as she can."

"He needs someone who will be here for him always. What if Summer meets someone new there and Cody doesn't know about it?"

"She's not like that," Haley defended Summer.

"How do you know?"

"Because she's nice. She cares about him. And us." Haley held her hands up. "She wants to spend more time here." Her hands dropped, like that was the end of the story.

"Uh-huh. Until she doesn't, because she's too busy."

Haley shook her head. "Why do you always have to be so negative about everything?"

Natalie's head snapped back and she got all defensive. "I'm not."

"Yes. You are. Nothing is ever good enough. Cody likes her. Maybe he even loves her."

Natalie cringed. "No, he doesn't."

"How do you know?"

Disbelief filled Natalie's eyes. "It's been like two weeks."

"I saw it the second he got out of the car that first day with her. He couldn't take his eyes off her. He hasn't since she got here. The first thing he does when he gets up in the morning is look for her. Same when he gets home each night. I overheard them talking earlier. He wants more with her."

"He said that?" Natalie paled.

"Yes."

Cody suddenly broke the kiss, planted his hands on the glass, and stared down at Summer, his chest moving like he was breathing hard. They shared some words and a long look, then separated and walked down the hall toward the stairs.

Cody brushed his hand over Summer's hair, said something that made her smile, then he went up and she went to her room.

Natalie sighed with relief.

"You're so jealous," Haley accused.

"What? No, I'm not."

"Liar. You've always treated Cody like he's yours. You hated it every time he and I did something together without you."

"I just wanted to be included."

"You wanted him all to yourself. I've heard you and your friends talking about him. You all think he's hot. You talk about him like you two share this close relationship."

"Because we do. Cody and I do a lot of things together."

Haley conceded that with a nod. "But that's not the same as what he has with Summer, even if you make it seem like it is."

"You don't know anything. You're just a child." Natalie stormed off, walking into the kitchen, dismissing whatever their mom said to her, and running for the stairs so she could go up to her room and blast her music and sulk like a master.

Haley shook her head and followed her sister's path into the kitchen.

"What was that about?" their mom asked.

"Just because you want something to be one way doesn't mean it is that way."

Her mom's eyebrow shot up. "What does that mean?"

Haley rolled her eyes. "Natalie is . . . Natalie."

"Well, that explains it." The sarcasm came with a mom look. "Is this about Summer?"

"Yes. But also no. Summer didn't do anything, but Natalie always acts like she did."

"Natalie is having some growing pains. Life is changing for her. She's graduating soon and facing college. A whole new experience where she'll be going it alone without all her friends around her. It's hard to realize you're going in different directions and it won't be like it's always been. It's the same thing with Summer. Home and family are different now because Summer has been added to the family. Natalie isn't the oldest anymore. Summer is the new thing in the house and everyone is giving her attention."

"Cody is giving her a lot of attention."

Her mother's lips pressed tight.

Haley felt a lecture coming on.

"They're getting close. And that scares Natalie, too, because she doesn't want to lose him."

Haley rolled her eyes. "He's family. You can't lose family."

"Yes, you can. People drift apart all the time. Natalie doesn't want that to happen."

Haley suspected Natalie wanted to be in Summer's place with Cody, even though that seemed absurd. "Things change. It's up to you to make the best of it. That's what you always tell us."

One side of Miranda's lips drew back. "Your sister has a hard time doing that. You see the good, the possibilities. She sees what could go wrong, and that makes it hard for her to see in the moment all that goes right."

"I just wish she was happy instead of always so upset about nothing."

"It's not nothing to her," her mother pointed out.

Haley rolled her eyes again. "I hope she's not like this tonight at the party."

"You and me both," Miranda admitted with a sly smile. She held her arms out wide.

Haley went in for a hug.

Miranda kissed her on the head. "You keep being sunshine and joy, my sweet girl. Don't worry about your sister. She'll find her way. Everyone does, eventually."

"I just hope it's before she really messes things up with Summer."

Her mother squeezed her tight. "Summer seems to have a lot of patience when it comes to Natalie."

"Probably because she's had to deal with her mom all these years."

"I suppose so. That's why I'm not worried. Summer will find her way past Natalie's defenses eventually. I wouldn't be surprised if Natalie learned to be a little more like Summer in the long run."

"It's easy to see why Cody likes her."

"I hope the two of them figure things out, too. I'd hate to see their relationship fall apart and that having an effect on the family."

Haley stepped away from her mom. "Why can't things be easier?"

"Then we wouldn't grow and learn."

Haley shrugged. "I guess so."

Haley grabbed a packet of Pop-Tarts from the pantry, looked at the clock. "I'll go grab my stuff and rattle Natalie's cage. We're going to be late for school."

She dashed off, wishing Summer had grown up with them. Then everything would be different. It would all feel normal.

She stepped up to her sister's door and said under her breath, "I can't wait until everything is normal again." She knocked, knowing as long as things were changing, everything would feel unsettled.

And that would only rile Natalie more.

Chapter Thirty-Three

That evening, Summer met her sisters in the glass-enclosed foyer. She put her hand to her mouth and stared at them. "You guys look amazing." She'd finished Haley's updo an hour ago, keeping it young and fresh with several braids and twists to make it fun.

Natalie did her own hair, curling the long locks into chunky waves. She'd done a small twist just above her right ear, pinning back a section with a pretty crystal clip.

"Natalie, your hair. So sophisticated. I love it," Summer gushed.

Natalie did a little sweep with her arm, showing off the dress, her heels, and a lot of leg. "Your hair looks really cool."

Summer had gone with a similar updo like Haley's without the braids and more twists in her hair, giving it a sleek and sophisticated look.

Natalie eyed Summer's dress. "It's the perfect color on you. And the fit . . ." Natalie looked at her own dress, very similarly cut to Summer's. "It's perfect."

"Not too much. Not too dowdy."

Natalie raised a brow at that term.

"Sorry, I sometimes sound like my grandfather."

"Oh, wow. Look at you." Miranda joined them in the foyer, her gaze sweeping over all of them. "So beautiful." She waved for them to gather together. "I need a picture."

Natalie handed over her phone. "Remember what I told you."

"I know. Not too far away. Center everyone."

Summer stood between her two sisters and hooked her arms around their waists, joy and a riot of other emotions getting to her that this was her family. They were going out for a special occasion and taking photos to remember the moment. So ordinary. So normal. So not something she'd done growing up. Her mother had always been the center of attention.

Miranda got into position. "Say, 'Sisters.'"

"Sisters," they said in unison. Haley's much more exuberant than Natalie's but at least she agreed to the picture.

"Wait," Natalie said before her mom handed back the phone. "One more. Can you frame the bottom of the dresses and our shoes?" Natalie looked at Summer and Haley. "Pose those toes."

Summer stood on one foot and picked up her other heel to show off the straps on her silver heels. Haley put one foot out to show off her shoe's cutouts. Natalie mimicked Haley's pose but with the opposite foot to make the picture more uniform.

Miranda snapped the pic and showed it to them.

Natalie nodded. "Perfect. Thank you."

"I wish I got the memo on the silver shoes." Miranda stared down at her beautiful black pumps, which were dotted with pearls.

Summer loved them. "Those are perfect with that beautiful gown." The black dress had long split sleeves with pearl closures at her wrists.

"I agree," her dad said, joining them. "You're stunning."

Miranda blushed. "You said 'beautiful' upstairs."

"I'll add 'gorgeous' to the list."

Summer sighed and grinned at them. Her heart melted when her dad kissed Miranda, who didn't even hesitate or balk because she didn't want to mess up her makeup. Their kiss wasn't some quick peck, but a soft press that lingered for an endearing moment, their love filling the room.

Suddenly, Cody slipped up beside her, slid his hand up the back of her neck, drew her close, and kissed her just the way her dad had kissed his beloved wife.

Time stopped.

All she knew was him.

She'd never felt so cherished and desired in her whole life.

Cody slowed the kiss, brushing his lips to hers in a soft sweep. Every nerve in her body sparked to life with awareness and a feeling of such contentment she sighed against his lips.

"You take my breath away," he whispered, pressing his forehead to hers.

Their gazes locked and she saw reflected back to her all the adoration she felt for him.

Was this love? Was this how it felt?

Giddy, calm, desperate, content, joyful, amorous, all that rolled into one and so much more.

She took a half step back to take him in. The black suit, the crisp white dress shirt, and the tie she'd bought him made him look like a cover model for *GQ*. She grinned up at him. "Every time I look at you . . . You're just so handsome tonight. Wow."

His smile brightened. "And I have the most beautiful date." He took her hand from his chest, brought it to his lips, and kissed the back of it. "I knew that dress would look spectacular on you."

"You picked it?" Natalie asked.

Cody sharply glanced up, looking like he'd forgotten they had an audience. "Wow. Look at you, Nat. So pretty and grown up."

Natalie blushed. "Thank you."

Haley showed off her dress.

Cody noticed right away. "And you, Haley, perfect. Your hair is super cool. And the heels . . ."

Haley beamed. "Summer picked them out. We all match." Haley indicated her, Natalie's, and Summer's shoes.

Cody glanced at Summer, understanding she'd done this to connect with her sisters, then looked back at Natalie and Haley. "Four beautiful Weston women."

"All my girls," Dad said, holding Miranda to his side with one arm around her waist.

"All we're missing is—"

"Me," Brooke interrupted her brother, walking into the foyer. "Alex is all set up with the sitter. Looks like we're ready to go."

Nate waved his hand toward the door. "Let's go."

Haley walked out first, followed by her parents.

Natalie hung back and waited for Summer and Cody. "Can I hitch a ride with you?" she asked him.

"Not tonight," Cody said. "We're taking my car. Only room for two."

"What about Brooke?" Natalie asked.

"I'm going with you in Miranda's Escalade." Brooke hooked her arm through Natalie's. "Shall we?"

Cody took Summer's hand and held her back. He didn't say anything until Natalie and Brooke were out of earshot. "About tonight . . ."

She looked up at him. "Yes," she prompted.

"I can't wait to go to this thing with you, but later . . . I booked us a room at a hotel down the street from the event."

"Perfect." She couldn't contain her excitement or smile.

He exhaled a heavy breath. "Are you sure?"

"That I want to be alone with you, away from everyone and everything, and feel you touch me, and wake up with you? Yeah. I'm more than sure." She couldn't wait.

"Good. Me too. And I'm glad you're okay with a hotel this time, because I want it to be just us. You know?"

"I do."

Her dad honked once to let them know he was leaving, then drove away.

She and Cody were still standing in the open front door.

He slipped his hand up the side of her neck. "I wanted to do something special for you."

She grinned. "I'm looking forward to it."

His eyes blazed with heat and he kissed her softly. "It's going to be the perfect night."

ody walked into the benefit with Summer's hand in his, feeling like the luckiest man alive. While he anticipated the night ahead, he tried to stay in the here and now and enjoy this time with her, the family, friends, and acquaintances seeing them together as a couple.

It had been a long time since he'd wanted to be linked to someone like this.

He wanted everyone in the room to know Summer was with him.

Thoughts of what happened with Amy circled his mind. He remembered how everyone treated him after he caught her cheating. They felt sorry for him. They said good riddance. At the time, and maybe still, he felt like he'd been played as a chump.

Summer would never do that to him.

Their relationship was just getting to the good stuff.

"Cody, what's wrong?" Summer slipped her hand free of his and stepped back.

He quickly took her hand again and stepped into her. "Nothing is wrong. I'm with you."

She studied his face.

He tried to explain. "I don't know how to explain it. Everything seems so easy with you."

"And sometimes it doesn't," she finished his thought.

"Yes." He wanted to be honest, so they could figure this out together.

"I feel the same way. We talked a little about that earlier today. It's a conversation we'll continue." She put her free hand on his chest and smoothed her fingers down the tie she'd bought him to match her dress. He loved that she'd thought of it, that she wanted that connection visual for all to see. "But tonight, can we just be everything we want to be to each other and enjoy ourselves?"

She'd never had this. A man with her for one of these things, who wanted to be with her because he cared about her. She'd been used as a representative of Sutherland Industries and a pawn in her mother's matchmaking plots that had ulterior motives all over them.

He could be everything she ever wanted and more. "Let's get a drink and mingle."

Summer's smile brightened. "Excellent idea."

Just as they stepped away, Brooke caught them. "Where are you two going?"

"The bar." Cody didn't mind having his sister around most of the time, but right now, he wanted to be with only one woman.

"You made it," Summer suddenly said, looking past Brooke to Cody's buddy. "Dr. Underwood, I'm so happy to see you again."

"Under better circumstances this time." David gave Summer a hug. "Thanks for the invitation."

Summer nodded. "My pleasure."

Cody looked from Summer to his best friend. "How did this happen?"

David took the lead. "Summer promised a case of top-shelf scotch to thank me for treating her at the hospital for her migraine."

"I sent you a bottle," Cody reminded him.

"I got that, too. But her thank-you came with an invitation for tonight's event."

Summer looked up at Cody. "You said you two don't get together enough. I thought this would be a great opportunity to be with friends."

David reached for Brooke's hand, leaned in, and kissed her on the cheek. "It's good to see you. You look absolutely stunning tonight. Then again, you're always gorgeous."

If Cody wasn't mistaken, his sister hadn't stopped staring at David since the moment he walked in. And she didn't let his hand go until she noticed Cody staring at her.

David took it in stride. "So, is it the four of us?"

Cody shook his head, noting the immediate disappointment in his friend's eyes. "Nate, Miranda, and the girls are here, too."

David perked up. "Oh. Nice." He turned to Brooke. "Can I get you a drink?"

Brooke blushed. "Um, uh, we were all just going to do that."

"Fantastic. You can fill me in on how Alex is doing, what the little guy is into now, everything."

Brooke hesitated for a second. "It's been a long time, hasn't it?"

"Yes. Too long." David held Brooke's gaze for a long moment.

Summer squeezed Cody's hand and tugged to get him moving. He hoped his sister and David followed along.

Summer leaned into him. "I think he's been pining after your sister for a long time."

"What even made you think he'd want to come and see her tonight?"

"He asked about her when you took me to the hospital."

Cody had forgotten that; he'd been so focused on Summer. "You were in so much pain. How did you remember?"

"When I see someone who so obviously likes someone else and it's genuine, I kind of feel . . ."

"What?"

"Envious."

He put his arm around her and drew her close. "Oh, sweetheart, lots of people care about you. Especially me."

"I know." She pressed her head into his shoulder, then they kept walking through the thickening crowd to the bar. "Anyway, you two seemed so close. It felt to me like you missed hanging out with him. You both have busy schedules. So I thought why not get him a ticket, have him join us here, and see what happens."

"I don't know if Brooke is ready."

"Sometimes all you need is someone to tell you you are."

"Is that what happened with us after I wouldn't let you dismiss me?"

"You made it so I couldn't stop thinking about you, so I opened the door to possibility."

"After what Brooke's been through, losing her husband . . . I want her to find the kind of happiness she had with him."

"Even if it's with your best friend?"

"I don't think you pick the one you fall for, so much as it just happens because it's meant to be."

Summer raised a brow and smiled. "That's very romantic."

"You don't believe that?"

"Actually, I do. I've seen my mother try to force it. That never works. But I also believe you have to nurture that chemistry and the relationship. It doesn't just grow on its own."

"It's like the big bang. You meet someone, sparks fly, and there's a pull that brings you together. Then it's all about creating the universe of your relationship together."

"Yes." She turned into him, her hands on his arms. "I am definitely drawn to you. Now, we're working on pulling things together so we stay together."

He kissed her softly right there in the middle of the hotel ballroom.

Brooke and David caught up to them.

"Do they do this a lot?" David asked.

"Not enough, if you ask me," Brooke replied. "You never know when you'll lose the one you love, so you should kiss him all you want now."

Summer nodded. "Don't mind if I do." She kissed him again.

It took Cody just a split second to switch from feeling incredibly sad for his sister to falling into the kiss Summer laid on him, a kiss that made him want to drag her home and into bed.

"Let's get a drink, David. You can catch me up and tell me how you went from cute geeky resident to hot doctor."

"Oh, that's easy. Instead of four hours of sleep a night, I get six. And I was always hot; you just had your gaze in a different direction."

"Well, tonight I'm looking at you." Brooke's words drifted off as they walked away.

Cody held Summer close, the two of them staring after David and Brooke. "What just happened?"

"Your sister decided she doesn't want to be alone anymore."

"I have to say, I never saw that coming."

"What? Your sister coming out of her grief and being with someone new?"

"No. David and her. We've all known each other . . . forever."

"Sometimes it's comforting to make a change with someone you know, who knows you. Brooke loved and lost and suffered the grief of that. She's lonely. He's a friend with the potential to be more. Maybe it works. Maybe it doesn't. But this is a step out of Brooke's past and into a new future without the man she lost."

"She's come a long way this past year. I just want her to be happy." Cody stared at his sister with David. They stood close, talking, smiling at each other. Brooke let out a burst of laughter and put her hand on David's forearm. David stared at Brooke and smiled, laughing with her, but the light in his eyes: pure adoration. "They look good together."

"Like us?" Summer asked.

He met her earnest gaze. "Yes. Like us." He didn't know why she asked.

"Summer," someone called out.

She turned in the direction of the voice, gasped, smiled, then released his hand and rushed toward another man, throwing her arms around him and hugging him close. The guy picked her up off her feet, squeezed her tight, then set her down, took her hands, held them out, and looked her up and down. "Gorgeous."

Something wild inside Cody came alive.

He took a step to get Summer back, but Natalie caught his arm and held him still.

"She has a whole other life you know little about. And apparently other men."

Cody pulled his arm free, not liking the implied notion that Summer wasn't committed to him. And then he thought about how they'd been holding back with each other. How he'd thought Amy had been doing the same thing, then found out why.

But this wasn't the same.

Whoever she was talking to wasn't who Summer wanted to be with. Cody held that special spot in her life.

He didn't take his eyes off Summer, smiling and chatting with her friend, and spoke to Natalie. "She's with me, Natalie. I know that. That's all that matters. Whoever that is, is just a friend. From what I know, she doesn't have many close ones." He turned to her then. "And you can stop pointing out that she has a life and home in Texas with her grandfather. Just like we've talked about our relationship, we'll talk about what comes next and figure it out."

"I just want you to be happy, Cody." The earnest look in Natalie's eyes touched him.

He'd just thought the same thing about his sister. "I am happy with her."

"Even though you know things are going to get really hard soon?"

He thought about what his sister said about using the time you had wisely because you never knew when someone's time ran out. "Hard doesn't mean impossible. And I'm happier with her than without her."

He walked away from Natalie.

Summer saw him coming and held her hand out to him.

He took it and smiled at her friend. "Hi. I'm Cody Larkin."

"Summer's boyfriend," the man said. "She just told me. I'm so happy for the two of you. I can't tell you the number of times I've implored her to be happy. And look, she is."

Summer grinned and shook her head. "Cody, this is my very good friend from college, Miles."

Cody shook the man's hand. "You two have known each other awhile."

"She saved my life."

Cody stared at Summer. "You did?"

"Miles was in one of my classes. Everyone was walking out of the building. He was in front of me. Suddenly, he yelped, then dropped to his knees. He was holding his arm and gasping for breath. I didn't really know what happened, but I went to him to be sure he was okay. He'd begun to panic and tried to open his backpack, but his fingers wouldn't work. His face had turned bright red."

"Long story short, I'm allergic to bee stings. Summer found my EpiPen, jabbed it in my outer thigh, called an ambulance, and saved my life."

"We've been good friends ever since. I was his maid of honor at his wedding." Summer glanced around. "Where is Silas?"

"Back in Texas. I'm out here on business. All alone. How long are you staying out here?"

"A few more weeks, then eventually I'll have to go home and face my mother."

Miles rolled his eyes. "What did she do this time?" Miles glanced at Cody, then pinned Summer in his gaze. "Because if she did this"—he waved his hand up and down to indicate Cody— "you should kiss her feet. He's gorgeous."

Summer laughed. "I guess you could say my mother brought us together, but not how you think. Remember how I told you my father wanted nothing to do with me?"

Miles frowned. "Yes. His loss."

Summer shook her head. "No, my mother's scheming. He didn't know I existed at all."

"Well, damn. I'm so sorry."

"Yeah. My father and his family live here in Carmel. Cody is my father's business partner. He came to Texas to bring me home."

Miles gave Cody an appreciative look. "I like you even more. She needs someone to stop her mother from poking at her all the time."

"Summer can hold her own, but I'm happy to be the one she turns to when it all gets to be too much." Because that's how they'd come together. That's what he wanted to be for her always.

"Keep him," Miles implored Summer. "There aren't many like him. I know. It took years for me to find Silas."

The waiters began to serve dinner.

"We should get our drinks and find our table." Cody held his hand out to Miles. "Nice to meet you. I look forward to seeing you soon."

"Me too." Miles hugged Summer. "Brunch, lunch, dinner, drinks, something, yes?"

"Yes."

"Good. Call, text, send a DM, whatever, but let's make it happen." With that, Miles fell in with the crowd making their way to the numbered tables.

Cody wrapped his arm around Summer's waist. "I like your friend."

"He's a good guy. And really smart. He helped me in some of my classes."

"And what did you do for him? Besides save his life." Because Cody knew something else had bonded them for life.

"While his parents knew from Miles's early years on that he was gay, they preferred he didn't advertise or flaunt it. They were afraid for him. They didn't want people to ridicule him or treat him differently than others."

"Or worse," Cody guessed.

"Yes. But when Miles announced his engagement to Silas, his parents were happy for him, but also taken aback by the comments their friends made to them. They withdrew from participating in the wedding preparations."

"I'm guessing not just physically, but financially."

Summer nodded. "I own a lot of beautiful properties. So I offered one to them for free."

"Which one?"

"A beautiful home in Italy surrounded by vineyards."

"You own a winery?"

She shook her head. "No. I lease the land to a vintner, who makes delicious wine. In particular, a really lovely peach wine for me."

"I didn't know you liked that. Go on."

"Miles really wanted his family to be there, but things had become very strained. Silas's whole family was there, so Miles tried to balance things out with close friends."

"But you knew that wasn't enough for him."

"I knew what it was like to feel insignificant on an important day in your life."

His heart withered at that thought. "Summer."

"I know. You don't have to say it. Anyway, I didn't want him to feel that way and for his day to be tarnished in any way, so I intervened."

"You called his parents."

"I did. And I got them on a plane and to the wedding on time. Miles . . . he was floored. It made that day and their relationship better."

"What did you say to make them come?"

"I told them how I felt every time my mother disappointed me, how it chipped away at my heart and soul. I told them if they loved their son and only wanted him to be happy, then he could only truly be that on his big day if they were there to see that all they feared wasn't going to stop Miles from being the kind of happy he deserved to be. They cried when they watched their son marry, because everyone saw the joy and excitement Miles and Silas couldn't contain, the love they had for each other. Miles's parents saw and felt it. And when there's that kind of love, that changes everything."

He couldn't help but feel it inside him when he looked at her. "You're right. It changes everything." He pulled her close and kissed her, hoping the kiss made her feel all the things he didn't know how to say.

They'd shared so many now, but this one mattered more than all the others. Because this was the moment he knew there was no turning back, no stopping the inevitable, no protecting his heart anymore. It was hers.

Chapter Thirty-Five

Summer enjoyed the charity benefit more than she expected. She'd been to so many over the years, but that had been at her mother's or grandfather's bidding. Always for show. Always to talk business. And sometimes to get through her mother's awkward fix-ups.

This time, however, she was simply here to enjoy the time with her family.

And the big bonus: being with Cody.

Something changed after they spoke to her friend Miles. She didn't know exactly what, but it was as if Cody let down all the walls. He seemed more relaxed and . . . just himself.

She liked it. A lot. It allowed her to rest easy in the fact they were together and all was right.

At least right now. Summer grinned at him as he caught her eye while dancing with Natalie.

Her sister had to be in heaven.

Summer knew, because that's how she felt when they'd danced together.

Natalie continued to be a concern. Yes, they'd gotten closer, but it felt like Cody was a barrier to them truly being friends.

Summer hoped that one day soon Natalie would realize that her crush would not be reciprocated. It would be a hard blow, one that would take time to heal. But that would open the door for Natalie to find someone who felt about her the way she felt about them. And she was going away to college, where she'd have the chance to meet so many different people.

"May I have this dance?"

Summer's heart swelled. She took her dad's hand, stood, and walked to the dance floor with him. She glanced back to the table and found Miranda smiling at them.

It felt so good and so right to step into his embrace and sway to the music.

She looked up at him. "You and Miranda make such a lovely couple. It's so easy to see why you two have been married so long."

"There's a lot of love. I can't tell you how much I've enjoyed having you here these last two weeks."

Her heart burst with joy. "I feel the same way."

"I'm really starting to feel like I know you. Having you at the house, meeting you for our lunches, seeing you at dinner . . . it's starting to feel like you've always been here. But I haven't forgotten what your mother cost us."

"Dad."

"Yes, sweetheart?"

"Can we just do this? It's my first father-daughter dance."

Her dad let out a sigh. "I'm sorry, honey. Yes. We can dance." He kissed her on the forehead, then twirled her around, making her giggle. "There you go. I put the smile back on your pretty face." Her dad looked past her shoulder. "He makes you happy, doesn't he?"

She didn't need a name to know who he was talking about. "He knows me. He picked me. I know those things seem simple."

"They're not. Not when it comes to real relationships. They matter."

"Especially to the girl who thought she wasn't enough."

"Does he make you feel that you are?"

"Yes. And then he asks me to be more to him because he won't settle for anything less than all of me. I think that's probably the best thing about him."

"You deserve to be treated like you matter more than anything."

"It's a unique experience for me."

"Not anymore. Because that's how I feel about you."

Right there in the middle of the dance floor, she stopped moving and just hugged him. "Thanks, Dad."

Nate held her close until the song ended.

"Mind if I cut in?" Cody's deep voice resonated through her, just like the first time they'd spoken. Just like it did every time she heard his voice. And just like all those times, she wanted to be closer to him.

Her dad stepped back and met Cody's gaze. "You two make a really good couple." With that, her dad walked toward their table and Miranda.

Cody watched him leave, a dumbfounded and relieved look on his face. "Did I miss something?"

"I think my dad just gave us his blessing."

One eyebrow shot up. "I thought he was okay with us seeing each other before tonight."

She went into his arms and resumed the dance so they weren't the only ones standing still while everyone else enjoyed the slow song. "He was. But even if he wasn't, I'd still want to be with you because it's my choice. But him saying that to you, to us, it makes me feel even more like his daughter."

Cody glanced to the side where Brooke and David were dancing together. "They haven't left each other's side all night."

"I have to admit, I was a bit jealous when you danced with my sister."

Cody's head whipped back toward her. "What?"

She chuckled. "I'm kidding." She glanced at Brooke. "They look like they're having a good time. Brooke is smiling and laughing and enjoying herself. You've mentioned how remote and despondent she was after losing her husband. I have to think seeing her like this tonight feels good."

"It does. I just never saw this coming. My sister and my best friend."

"I never saw you coming, and look how well it's turning out."

Cody pressed his forehead to hers. "Damn good."

She kissed him on the dance floor in front of everyone. It didn't surprise her to hear Miles's signature whistle come from nearby.

An hour later, and after several rounds of conversation with people Cody knew and introduced her to, Summer was ready for another dance, or to get out of there. Either way, she wanted some quiet time with him.

She'd never been great in large crowds. The noise, the conversations, the expectations always drained her.

While she loved standing at Cody's side, his hand always at her waist, his introducing her as his girlfriend and talking her up to the people who mattered to him, she was ready to have him all to herself.

Brooke and David approached them.

Cody finished a conversation about some upcoming contract with a business partner. "We'll talk more about this on Monday."

Trevor nodded. "Sounds good." He turned to Summer. "Really good to meet you. I'm anxious to check out that Sutherland Industries subsidiary you told me about and see if we can do business."

"If you have any questions, you can get my business information through Cody and give me a call." She nodded her good-bye to the man and sighed.

"You sound like you're ready to go." Cody squeezed her hip.

Brooke stepped closer to them. "Hey, you two, we're headed over to the hotel bar for a nightcap. Want to join?"

Cody shook his head. "Sorry. We have our own plans tonight."

David didn't look at all disappointed that Cody had declined the invitation.

Brooke glanced at their table in the distance where Nate and Miranda stood, talking to another couple. Haley and Natalie sat at the table, empty dessert plates in front of them. Both girls looked bored out of their minds.

Natalie stared back at Summer, then her gaze went to and stayed on Cody as usual.

Brooke turned back to Cody. "David offered to drive me home after drinks, so I'll let Nate know they can go on without me. Want me to say good-bye for you two?"

"Yes. That'd be great. Maybe I can sneak out of here with Summer before anyone else stops us."

David smiled at her. "It was really good to see you again. Even better to see this one"—he cocked his head toward Cody—"attached to you, smiling and having a good time."

Cody shook David's hand. "See she gets home safe. We'll catch up again soon."

David nodded. "Sounds good."

Cody took her hand. They walked out at an angle from the Weston table toward the ballroom doors.

Summer caught Natalie and Haley's stares as they went. She gave them a wave.

Haley waved back. Natalie turned away.

Summer hated that her relationship with Cody upset Natalie, but she wanted to be alone with him as much as he seemed to want to be with him. He walked her through the hotel lobby like they were on the march to be first in line for his favorite rock band concert and he wanted to be in the front row.

The valet stopped Cody's car in front of them. Cody opened the passenger door for her, but before she got in, he turned her to him. "Last chance. Where am I taking you?"

She answered with the only place she wanted to be with him right now. "To bed."

The intensity in his eyes changed to a smoldering heat and conveyed a promise of what was to come. "That's what I wanted to hear."

"With you is where I always want to be."

Chapter Thirty-Six

Natalie leaned to the side in the back seat and stared out the car's windshield as they pulled into the driveway and Dad opened the garage. "Cody's car isn't here."

"Maybe they stayed to have drinks with Brooke and David," Haley said.

Natalie didn't think so. "They left before Brooke told us David would bring her home later."

Her mom and dad turned to each other and shared a look before her dad said, "I'm sure you'll see them in the morning."

Everyone got out of the car and went into the house.

The clock on her phone read ten twenty-two. No one bothered to turn on lights downstairs as they went up to get ready for bed.

"Sleep well, girls," their mom called out as she and their dad headed down the hall.

Haley went into her room and closed the door.

Natalie went to her room and right to the windows that over-looked the pool and looked into Cody's room across the way. She stared through the darkness to his empty bed and wondered where they had gone.

When would they be back? What were they doing?

Well, she didn't have to think too hard about that one. Her heart sank. A tear slipped down her cheek. All she could do was imagine them alone in a room.

Together.

In bed.

She wondered if he'd leave with Summer and if she'd lost him.

Chapter Thirty-Seven

Summer gasped in surprise when she walked into the beautiful hotel suite to a fire blazing in the hearth, candles lit on the nightstands, rose petals strewn across the bed, a bottle of wine chilling in an ice bucket, and with a lovely charcuterie board with grapes, strawberries, kiwi, and chocolates sitting on the dresser. "Cody, this is really beautiful."

Cody turned to her. "I wanted a place that felt like it could be ours." He'd put a lot of thought into picking the right hotel.

He pulled the wine bottle from the ice bucket, checked out the label, and held it up. "Want some?"

She shook her head and pulled off one heel, dropping it next to her on the floor. "There's only one thing I want." She took off her other shoe, discarding it like the other.

"I want to take off that dress. Slowly." Cody hooked his fingers in his tie, pulled it loose, then up and over his head. He tossed it on the upholstered bench at the end of the bed.

She grinned, unable to take her eyes off him.

He shucked off his jacket and tossed it over the tie. He toed off his shoes next, then pulled his dress shirt free of his pants and undid the cuffs. "I don't plan on leaving this room until I know every single place on your body that makes you hum."

Oh, she was already revved up and anxious to get her hands on him.

Cody pulled his wallet from his back pocket, held up a couple of condoms, then tossed them on the bed near the plump pillows. His wallet landed on his jacket.

She took a step toward him. "You should know, I appreciate the protection, but I also have an IUD."

He gave her a firm nod. "Anything else you want me to know?"

She appreciated that he not only asked but waited patiently for her answer. "I haven't done this in a while, but that doesn't mean I want you to hold back."

"I have every intention of letting go with you, and making sure you feel you can do the same."

"I really want to see you take that shirt off."

He obliged, not by unbuttoning it, but by pulling the thing over his head, off his arms, and tossing it. Muscles rippled as he moved. His arms, chest, and stomach were all sculpted to perfection and tanned by the sun.

She went on impulse, closing the distance between them, sliding her hands up his abdomen, over his pecs, and back down again, all that smooth, warm skin against hers. "Cody," she said without taking her eyes off her hands moving over him.

"Yeah."

"I'm overdressed now."

That's all it took to unleash him. He came at her with purpose and hunger in his eyes. Her dress didn't stand a chance. Zipper down, he simply pushed it off her shoulders to puddle on the floor, forgotten. He paused for one brief moment, his gaze enthralled by her curves encased in nothing but scraps of barely there cranberry-colored lace.

His upper body dipped low as he scooped her up with his hands on the backs of her thighs. Her feet left the floor and her breasts pressed to his chest. His hungry mouth took hers in a searing kiss.

She wrapped her arms around his neck and held on as he took the few steps to the bed and laid her out on the cool sheets. His golden hair glinted in the firelight dancing against the walls. His body pressed down on hers, the warmth of his skin meeting her hard-tipped breasts. His mouth took hers in another scorching kiss as her thighs cradled his hips between her legs.

With others she'd gone along in a purposeful way to get to the ultimate climax that always seemed to fall into the that-was-nice category. With Cody, she couldn't help but feel everything. His hands on her body. His mouth trailing kisses down her neck. His warmth surrounding her. His tongue licking along the edge of her lace bra, then right over her peaked nipple, sending a wave of heat through her body and bolting to where his thick, hard length pressed against her sensitive folds.

She wanted him inside her, filling her.

She raked her fingers into his silky hair and held him to her breast, even as she asked for more with just his name. "Cody."

She rocked her hips against his erection, needing the pressure and wanting so much more.

Cody wanted more, too, and pulled the bra cup off her breast, releasing it from the confines, only to take her nipple into his mouth so he could suck and lave at it.

Every sigh and moan she let loose made him work her breast even more, so she'd do it again. His hand slipped up her back to the clasp. He released it and pulled the bra off her, only to take her other breast into his mouth. The sensation of his mouth on her brought a gasp, then a sigh as he circled his tongue around her nipple.

She couldn't touch him enough, or get to all she wanted to ex-plore. The muscles in his back were tense against her fingers as she rubbed them up and down the length of his spine. His shoulders were wide and led her fingertips to toned biceps and corded forearms. Then her hands were back on his head, holding him close as she arched up, offering him the breasts he seemed to like so much.

It felt so good. But she still wanted more. She wanted to touch and taste him. She wanted to give him the same kind of mind-blowing pleasure he gave her.

Cody had his own ideas and trailed kisses down her stomach, then he sat up, hooked his fingers in the top of her panties, and pulled. She brought her legs up as he slipped the panties off her legs and feet. She didn't know where they ended up, but his hands were sliding up her calves, over her knees, along her thighs, his thumbs rubbing against her soft folds as he bent and pressed a kiss to her belly again.

She met his gaze as he brushed his chin against her navel and looked up at her. "Now you're overdressed."

"I really like this view."

She bet he did as he stared up at her, her breasts pink-tipped and aching for his mouth again.

"I'd really like you." She hoped he got her meaning.

In one fluid motion, he slipped off the bed, undid his pants, pushed them, along with his boxer briefs, right off. The socks were gone in a second. He stood before her, his erection standing proud, all those sculpted muscles on display, and an endearing and passion-filled look on his face. "God, you're beautiful."

She hadn't expected the compliment, or the sincerity and heat in his eyes. It touched her so deeply when they were together like this, the firelight cocooning them in a soft glow, them finally alone together, swept up in the moment and anticipation.

She held her hand out to him.

He bent, his hands planted on the bed, and kissed her as he eased the rest of his body down beside her. His hand rested on her belly, then stroked down one thigh, up the other, and his fingers dipped between her legs, brushing softly over her wet folds, stroking as she rocked her hips and rubbed herself against those questing fingertips. One long finger sank deep inside her, then two. The kiss they shared matched the slide of his fingers in and out of her as their tongues mimicked the slow, sweet motion.

Summer was the one who grabbed the condom and tore it open.

The moment they broke the sultry kiss, he dipped his head and took her breast into his mouth again. She turned toward him, her leg over his, his fingers still playing with her wet core.

"Cody."

"Hmm," he hummed against her breast in answer.

"I've never gotten to be on top." She wanted to try it with him. She wanted to watch him make love to her.

Without warning, he let her breast loose and slid his arm around her back. The other hand went to her ass; then he rolled onto his back, taking her with him. She found herself lying down the length of him, their bodies rubbing against each other's. "You can have whatever you want, sweetheart." Cody kissed her again, wrapping his arms around her, rocking his hard cock against her belly.

She completely forgot the condom and straddled him. The head of his dick hit her entrance, sending a wave of need through her, and she sank down on him in one fluid motion, filling herself up, finally feeling the full breadth of the connection between them.

"You feel so damn good," he growled.

She moved, wanting so badly to make him feel the way he made her feel. The glide of him as she rose up, then the plunge of him inside her as she sank back down. The sigh that came out of him, the way his hands clamped onto her hips, the way he let her set the pace and rock and roll and move over him . . . Nothing had ever felt like this.

And then he raised up and took her breast into his mouth, sucking and sliding his tongue over her nipple. She leaned into him and felt the urgency in his body as he pumped his hips and she moved hers in concert. The ripples of pleasure turned into waves that built into a storm until her inner muscles contracted around his hard length and pure pleasure shot through her. Cody let loose her breast, pressed his head back into the pillow, his hands tight on her hips as he held her down on him and his cock pulsed inside her.

The sounds he made . . . the feel of him inside her . . . the way he made her feel, that this was truly two people coming together for each other, sent her over the edge again. And though Cody had finished, he thrust into her again and again, riding out the contractions, until she went limp on top of him.

He held her close, his arms around her, his lips pressed to her forehead, her face in his neck, their breaths slowly getting back to normal. "It's never been like that," he whispered.

"For me, either."

"Any other ways you want to try out, because if it goes as well as that, I'm in."

She smiled, knowing he'd feel it against his skin. "It was always one way. Their way. It never felt like it was about me. Or us. With you, it does."

His arms tightened around her. His lips pressed one kiss and then another on her forehead, before he cupped her face in one big, warm hand and tilted her face up to look at him. "All I've wanted is for this relationship to be about us. So no more worrying about everyone else. Let's focus on what *we* want. For me, that's you."

"I've never had anything like this. I don't want to lose it. And I know we have some challenges ahead."

"We'll face them together."

"Do you remember what you said about our relationship the night you brought me home from the hospital and we kissed for the first time?"

It took Cody a second to respond. "That I want this to be what I want it to be."

"Yes. I think about that all the time. And you're right, we'll make it what we want by focusing on us and being together."

Cody hugged her close. "I like us, like this."

"Me too." So much so that the thought of not spending *all* their nights together made her miss him already.

"Don't do that," he whispered.

"What?"

"Worry about what's ahead. We'll figure it out. Tonight, let's not think about anything and just feel." To that end, he slid his hands down over her ass and squeezed, then started the seduction into lovemaking all over again.

By the time they settled into sleep, his arm around her, his face in her hair, they were completely connected. The memory of them was a sweet dream turned into reality when he woke her before dawn with sweet kisses and his body filling hers once more.

What a way to start the day.

$\mathcal{C}$ody was still thinking about how he'd made love to Summer this morning. The sweet sounds she made when he snuggled up behind her, her rump against his aching cock, one of his hands between her legs, the other cupped around one perfect breast. The smell of her still lingered in his nose. The echo of her body moving against his still rippled over his skin.

He loved being with her.

All they had to do was figure out the rest of their lives and what that looked like, so they were never apart.

He walked into his kitchen with her hand in his and stopped short when he found David downing a glass of water at the sink, his back to them.

The man was fully clothed in the suit he'd worn last night, now wrinkled, his hair a mess, a five o'clock shadow darkening his jaw. All of which said he'd spent the night here.

"Good morning," Summer said.

Cody wasn't sure what to say to his friend, who'd apparently slept with his sister last night.

David jumped and spun around to face them. His eyes went wide when he spotted Cody, then guilt replaced the surprise. "Uh.

Morning." David glanced at the still more dark than light outside the windows.

Yeah, Cody and Summer were sneaking into the house, while David looked to be about to sneak out of it before anyone was up and on to them.

"Did you two have a good night?" David asked, catching on that Cody and Summer were also still in their outfits from last night.

"We did," Summer said, no hesitation or reserve in her cheery mood.

His sister walked into the room wearing a silky robe. She didn't hesitate when she spotted him and Summer and went to David, sliding her arm around his waist and leaning into him. "I'll walk you out."

David looked down at her, a look of pure adoration in his eyes. "You don't have to do that."

"I want to."

David brushed his fingers along Brooke's cheek. "I'd like that." He looked up and held Cody's gaze. "Are we cool?"

Cody looked at his sister and knew the answer before he even asked the question. "Are you happy?"

She nodded.

He looked back at David. "I'm happy for you both then."

David held out his hand.

Cody took it and shook.

"Thanks, man. That means a lot. You won't ever have to ask her that again, because you'll know she is. I'll make sure of it."

Cody hooked his arm around Summer and pulled her close. "We should all go out soon."

"It's a date," David said, then checked the microwave clock. "I have to go. I have a shift in an hour." He kissed Brooke like he wouldn't see her for a week, then grinned. "Stay inside where it's warm. I'll call you later." He kissed her one last time, gave her a look that said all too clearly he didn't want to leave, but left anyway.

Cody eyed his sister. "So . . ."

"So, what?" Brooke poured a cup of coffee, handed it to Summer, then poured one for him, then finally for herself.

Cody stared at his sister. "He's right. I didn't have to ask. I see it in your eyes."

"I'm ready to move on," Brooke said simply. "David and I have known each other a long time. There's always been the hint of something there." She shrugged one shoulder. "Before, I'd say it was more on his part than mine. Last night . . . it was so easy to talk to him, to be with him. It felt more than right. It felt inevitable."

Cody knew just how she felt. "I mean it, sis, I'm happy for you."

Brooke eyed him and Summer over her steaming mug. "I'm happy you two finally stopped circling each other and went for it."

"We were taking our time," he defended himself.

"You got burned in the past. You don't want that to happen again. She's complicated for you because of Nate and the family. Summer's wanted someone who is really hers for a long time. She was patient enough to wait for you to stop stalling."

Summer shook her head. "I didn't think that," she assured him.

Brooke rolled her eyes. "Maybe not. But that's what he did. And now you two are together. I hope it stays that way."

"Is that what you're hoping will happen with David?" he asked.

"I don't have time to play around, nor can I when I have Alex to think about. He misses his dad. He deserves to have a good one. I think David could be good for both of us. Enough that I'm willing to take a chance and go all in. Like you finally did."

The soft taunt wasn't lost on him. "We've had some difficult and lonely times, you and me."

Brooke nodded.

"I think it's time we created the family and home we want."

"Now you're thinking right." Brooke gave him a nod of approval, then turned her gaze to Summer. "You're good for him. I'm so happy you came and we get to be friends. Maybe soon, we'll be more."

"I can never have too many sisters." Summer went to Brooke and hugged her.

Cody knew the two had grown close over the past couple weeks. This proved it.

And thinking past today and tomorrow and onward, he saw the family and life he wanted, and thought it looked damn good and happy. Him with Summer. Brooke with David. All of them more than friends. A family.

All he had to do was figure out the obstacles and make it happen.

Chapter Thirty-Nine

$\mathcal{D}$o you have any idea what time it is in Belize?" Lucy sounded wide awake. And she should be. It was the middle of the afternoon.

"It's two sixteen there. You're only two hours ahead of me."

"Are you having lunch?" Lucy asked.

"Actually, yes." Summer bit into a strawberry. She was out on the patio off her room, enjoying the fountain and flowers while Cody gave Alex a swimming lesson in the pool.

She bet Natalie had already found her way out there, too.

"Are you at my place?"

"Yes." Lucy sighed dramatically. "I needed an escape from grumpy interior decorators who know nothing about French contemporary design and show me nothing but abstract art," Lucy grumbled. "Your New York hotel will be chic, sophisticated, and lovely if I have to scream my lungs out to get it."

She hated that Lucy was upset. "Why not just hire another decorator? Or do it yourself? You know what you like and what will work." She trusted Lucy implicitly.

"Of course I do. I just want the person who promised me one thing to deliver it, instead of thinking they know better than me. Isn't the customer always right?"

"Absolutely. Especially when we're paying a fortune for this renovation. If it's ready in time, maybe I'll take Natalie and Haley to New York before Christmas to shop for the holidays."

"I bet they'd love that. How was the benefit last night?"

"Wonderful. I danced with my dad, met a bunch of Cody's friends, and I even ran into Miles."

"Small world. That's lovely. I bet being with your dad really made your night."

"It did. And then Cody really made my night."

"Do tell. And don't forget the details."

Summer grinned. "We snuck away for an intimate night alone. He got us this amazing hotel room with a fireplace." Summer got lost in the memory of their first night together.

"And?"

"It was everything I didn't know it could be."

"When it's the right person, it's magic."

"I want the New York hotel rooms to feel romantic." Maybe she'd take Cody to the cute little boutique hotel instead of her sisters.

"I'm trying."

"I know you are."

"So you and Cody, it's the real deal now."

"We still have some things to work out. But I have a plan."

"Of course you do. And how are you going to blend your two lives?"

Summer thought of the conversations she'd had with her dad this past week. "I'm going to make us partners." She laid out her surprise for Cody to Lucy.

"That's amazing. Do you think he'll go for it?"

"It's something he's wanted for a long time." She hoped he didn't mind that she'd made it happen without his input. "My dad wants us both to be happy. He thinks Cody will be thrilled."

"You sound really happy about your dad."

"We're getting so close."

"And how are things with your sisters?"

"Haley and I continue to just have fun together. Natalie, though . . ."

"She still pushing you away?"

"Sometimes. Other times, like when we shopped for dresses and I helped her with her homework, I feel like we really connect. Going to the benefit with everyone last night, I truly felt like a part of the family."

"I'm so happy for you. It sounds like you're finding your place there and you'll have Cody when it's time for you to return to Texas."

"I just hope it all works out."

"It will." Lucy paused, then asked, "Have you spoken to Jessica?"

"No. I'm focused on being here."

Cody walked out onto the patio, stole a strawberry off her plate, kissed her on the forehead, then picked up her feet, straddled the lounge chair facing her, and set her feet on his thigh. He looked so damn good in nothing but swim shorts, his hair wet and tousled, his chest bare.

"Hey, Lucy, I've gotta go."

"He's there, isn't he?"

"In the flesh. A lot of it."

"I want pictures of you two."

Cody stared at her, his gaze dipping to her mouth, then her breasts swelling over the top of her tank top. That look could set fire to her clothes.

"I'll send them soon. Love you, Luc."

"Love you back, babe."

Summer set her phone on the little table beside her.

"How's your sister?"

She loved that he understood Lucy was the sister of her heart.

"She's disgruntled about the decorator she hired for the New York hotel we're renovating, so she's taking a time-out at my Belize house."

"Nice. I'd love to see it sometime."

"I'd like to see more of you." She roamed her gaze over all his bare skin and sculpted muscles.

Cody shifted one of her legs to the other side of him, reached forward, took her by the hips, and pulled her up onto his lap so she was straddling him. "I came to get you because everyone wants to go for a hike."

"Then you better hurry up and give me what I want, so we don't keep them waiting."

He slid his hands up her sides, his thumbs brushing the underside of her breasts. "And what do you want?"

"You."

Cody dove in for a searing kiss. The man knew how to be quick and thorough. They made it out to meet everyone for the hike only a few minutes late, but very satisfied and happy.

Chapter Forty

Summer and Cody walked into the restaurant behind her family, Natalie in the lead, still wearing her cap and gown over a pretty cranberry-colored dress, her diploma in her hand and a brilliant smile on her face.

The graduation ceremony had lasted an hour and a half. They all cheered when Natalie walked across the stage to receive her diploma. Alex had even colored a sign with Natalie's name on it, so she'd know where they were sitting and could wave at them.

It was a perfect family outing, one Summer hadn't experienced growing up as an only child. Her mother, grandfather, and great-uncle had attended her high school graduation, of course, cheering for her, but also ready for her to hurry up and finish college so she could rule the Sutherland empire one day.

Cody squeezed Summer's hand to get her attention. "Are you okay?"

"I'm fine."

Cody didn't buy it. "What did your mother say in the last message?"

"I don't know. I've stopped listening to them." Her mother had become desperate to hear what was going on in Carmel, when she'd be home, and what was taking so long for Summer to forgive what her mother had done.

The apologies had dried up.

Summer was expected to move on as she'd always done in the past, no matter how much her mother had hurt her. But this time, she didn't know if she could forgive what her mother had done. She certainly knew she couldn't ever let it go completely, even if she did come to terms with it somehow.

Cody held the chair out for her as everyone took a seat at the long table. "You need to tell her how you feel and what you want."

"She doesn't care about how I feel or what I want."

Miranda eyed her. "Your mother again?"

Summer waved it off. "It's nothing. We're here to celebrate Natalie." She plopped a gift bag in front of Natalie, who sat across from Cody.

Brooke sat Alex next to Summer and took the seat on the other side of him. She handed a wrapped package to Nate. It got passed down to Natalie.

Cody put his hand on Summer's thigh and leaned in. "We need to start talking about what happens next."

"Later." Summer notched her chin up toward Natalie. "Open it. It's from Cody and me."

Natalie's bright smile dimmed a bit at that, but then she plucked out the tissue paper and pulled out the small velvet box. Her eyes shot up to Cody, then back down at the box. She opened it slowly, her eyes going wide at the surprise inside. "Thank you, Cody." It took her a second to shift her gaze from the object of her true affection to Summer. "Thank you."

"I hope you like it. It's your school colors." She and Cody had picked out the ring together. Two round white topazes flanked the larger oval garnet in the center.

Nate leaned over and looked at it. "That's a very special gift."

Summer hoped Natalie liked it. "Try it on. See if it fits."

"If not, I can have the jeweler size it," Cody informed her.

Natalie slipped it on and stared at it. "It's perfect."

Miranda leaned into Nate, to get a better look. "Honey, it goes on your other hand."

Summer didn't want to say anything about Natalie putting it on her left hand like an engagement ring.

Natalie slipped it off and switched it to her other hand, where the ring actually fit a bit better. She held up her hand to Cody, who grinned at her.

"Now the one from us," Alex exclaimed, wiggling in his seat.

Natalie unwrapped the small box and opened the lid. Her smile grew even bigger.

"We coordinated," Brooke explained.

Natalie held up the oval garnet stud earrings. "A matched set."

"They go with your dress, too," Haley pointed out.

"Thank you, Alex and Brooke. I love them." Natalie looked expectantly at her parents.

"You'll get your gift when we get home."

Natalie's gaze dropped and a knowing smile came to her lips. She'd been talking about getting a new car since Summer arrived. She barely suppressed her excitement all through dinner and dessert.

When they left the restaurant, Cody and Summer made sure they left first out of the parking lot, while her dad and Miranda stalled by carrying on a conversation with Brooke by the car, irking Natalie, Summer was sure.

But she and Cody arrived home with just enough time to pull the brand-new BMW out of the garage and stick the over-the-top, too-big-for-one-person-to-handle bow on top of it.

When Nate pulled into the driveway, he'd barely stopped the car before Natalie jumped out and ran for her present, screaming, "You got it for me!"

Summer had never seen her sister so happy.

Cody held the keys out to her. "I guess you'll be attending your friend's graduation party tonight in style."

Natalie snatched the keys, eyes bright with delight, and ran for the driver's side.

Cody opened the passenger door, sat in the seat, but kept one leg out the door. "Take a minute to enjoy this and figure out where all the gadgets are and how they work."

Nate and Miranda went to the driver's side and stared in at their daughter.

Miranda tapped on the window and waited for Natalie to put it down. "Do you love it?"

"Yes. Thank you. Thank you so much." Natalie's eyes were bright with enthusiasm and sheer joy.

Their dad nodded. "You need to take care of it."

"I will," Natalie swore, not looking at him, but fiddling with the radio until she paired her phone with it and put on one of her favorite playlists. "It works. Yes!" She turned to Cody. "Let's go for a drive."

Haley stood next to Cody. "Can I go with you?"

Cody climbed out, put the seat forward, and let Haley slip into the back seat. He turned to Summer. "Come with us."

They'd promised each other they wouldn't let anyone come between them, so Summer ignored Natalie's disappointment when she nodded yes and climbed in back with Haley.

"Be careful," Miranda said.

Natalie hit the gas, throwing her and Haley back into their seats and scrambling for their seat belts, while Cody reached over, put his hand on Natalie's arm, and warned, "Slow down, Danica Patrick. You don't want to wreck it your first time out."

Natalie turned left on the main road and grinned. "Not a chance. This baby is mine."

Cody hung on to the oh-shit handle above his head and grinned.

Summer enjoyed watching Natalie drive, her excitement and glee so palpable in the car.

Cody turned to the back seat. "What do you think, Haley? You want something like this when you graduate?"

Haley shook her head. "I want a Jeep with big tires and four-wheel drive, so I can take it to the beach, or up to the snow. It can go anywhere."

"I have one at my Wyoming house. I love to take it on the back roads. It's so pretty there."

"I want to go," Haley exclaimed.

"We'll do it, then."

Haley's grin grew wider. "When? This summer?"

Natalie met Haley's eyes in the rearview mirror. "Probably not going to happen. She's leaving soon," Natalie reminded her. "Summer is expected back at work now that the whole family reunion is done."

"That doesn't mean we can't plan a trip, even if it's just a long weekend," Summer assured Haley, really liking the idea of them going to the Wyoming house. "You'd love it there. It's so pretty with all the trees and land. The property has this beautiful lake and a creek with lots of fish."

It wasn't lost on Summer that Cody had gone quiet on her.

Neither of them liked talking about her returning to Texas, but that talk was coming, sooner rather than later.

Natalie took a sharp turn a bit too fast.

"Slow down," Cody warned.

"When is everyone going to accept that she's not staying?"

Cody shifted in his seat. "At the next light, turn back for home."

Natalie sighed, but did what Cody said.

The ride back was quiet, but when they turned into the long

driveway, Haley touched her hand. "Anytime you want to go to Wyoming, or anywhere, I want to go, too."

Summer reached for her sister and pulled her into her side for a hug. She kissed Haley on the head. "I'd go anywhere with you, too."

Natalie parked next to Cody's Porsche. They exited the front.

Haley touched Summer's arm before she got out. "Natalie is . . ." It seemed she didn't know how to finish that statement. "She wants Cody to be happy. Just not with you."

Summer wished it was different, but Haley had it right. "She loves Cody."

"I love him, too," Haley admitted. "But I think there are different kinds of love."

"That's very true. And when you love, you risk getting hurt."

"But it's worth it, right? To be loved the way Cody loves you and you love him."

They hadn't said the words to each other, but she felt it for him and knew it was returned. "Yes. Love is a connection. Everyone wants to feel and know they matter to someone. It makes all the difference sometimes. Being alone is lonely."

"I think Cody's been lonely for a long time. Brooke, too, because she lost her husband. But she looked happy with David."

"He's a connection she needed."

"If you're ever lonely, you can come see me or call me."

Tears gathered in Summer's eyes. "Thank you. That makes me feel very special. And you will always have me, too. No matter how far away I might be, I will always be there for you."

Cody leaned into the car, his eyes narrowing when he saw her expression. "Is everything okay?"

"I was just having a heart-to-heart with my sister." Summer turned to Haley. "I love you."

"I love you, too." Haley smiled, then got out on her side.

Summer took Cody's hand and stepped out on hers.

Natalie eyed her and Haley. "What was that all about?"

"Just talking about boys," Haley said, and walked up to the house, passing her parents as they came out to see Natalie again.

Natalie stared after her sister. "Are you seeing someone?"

Haley shrugged without turning, leaving all of them guessing, and Summer was impressed with how she told the truth, sort of, without giving specifics.

Cody hooked his arm around Summer's shoulders and smiled at Natalie. "Have fun at your party tonight."

Natalie's smile couldn't get any brighter. "I can't wait to show everyone my new car."

Nate pulled Natalie into a hug. "Be careful. Since you're driving, I expect you to be responsible at the party. No drinking."

Natalie pulled out of the hug. "I'm good, Dad. Stop worrying."

Miranda hugged Natalie, too. "I know you'll do the right thing. Congratulations, sweetheart. We are so proud of you."

"So proud," Nate echoed.

Natalie rushed back to the driver's side and slipped into the car, honking once and waving out the window as she left.

Nate looked at Summer. "I can't believe I have two full-grown daughters now."

Summer grinned. "One to go."

They all walked to the house. Inside the glass foyer, she and Cody headed right, both of them saying good night to Nate and Miranda.

Cody kept Summer going up the stairs to his room. The first thing he did, like every night they came up here, was to close the drapes along the tall, wide windows that overlooked the pool and the other side of the house. They didn't need any prying eyes on them when they were alone up here.

"I'm going to ask my dad if there's an office I can use at the company."

Cody turned to her. "You can use mine whenever you like."

She shook her head. "That's not going to work for the long term. If I'm on a call, or you are, we'll be distracting the other. Plus we need our own space to do our jobs."

Cody stood very still. "Does this mean you're going to work from here full-time?"

"No."

Cody deflated. "What are you saying then?"

"That we need to find a compromise."

"Do you actually want to run Sutherland Industries?"

"It's what I've been raised and educated to do."

One side of Cody's mouth drew back. "That doesn't answer my question."

"Well, that's my answer. I'm good at it. I appreciate what my grandfather has done for me all these years. I believe in the company and what we do there. It feels like it's mine." That was the first time she really admitted it and felt it in her heart.

"And you don't want to give it up. It's okay to say that," he assured her.

She appreciated that he understood she was trying not to make it sound like she was choosing work over him. "I don't want it to be the thing that comes between us, so I'm trying to find a way."

"I suppose I'll need an office at Sutherland Industries then."

She stared at him, completely taken aback. "Why?" She hoped he gave her the answer she wanted so badly that she held her breath and waited.

"Because I don't want to be away from you. If you're there. I'll be there. If you're here. I'll be here."

"Can you do that?"

"I own a quarter of the company. I can do whatever the hell I want." Cody came to her, cupping her face and looking her right in the eye. "Maybe it won't always work out and I'll have to be here for something when you have to be there, but we'll promise each other, right here, right now, we will spend more days together than we ever spend apart."

"I promise."

"I promise, too. And I know it hasn't been easy these last few weeks, working from here when your grandfather can't do something without your input."

"I think he misses me, and this is his way of staying connected to me."

"I get that. And I know your mom's been a whole other drama. I'm not sure how I'm going to get past what she did to you and Nate, but for you, I'll always try to be civil."

"Thank you, Counselor."

Cody grinned. "We can make this work."

"I'm also going to hire a personal assistant to free up some of our time."

He raised a brow. "Our?"

"You know, to take care of things for us, so we have more time together."

Cody nodded. "Actually, I like that idea. Especially if we're going to be traveling back and forth between states." Cody kissed her softly. "I've had ideas circling my head about how this will look for us."

"But you didn't want to bring it up, and I didn't say anything, either, because we wanted to stay in our bubble where this is our life."

"The truth . . . I was afraid you'd ask me to come to Texas with you and I wasn't ready to give you an answer."

"Because your life is here and you don't want to give it up. I'd never ask you to do that."

"You're going to run Sutherland Industries one day. I can be a lawyer anywhere. Even at your company."

"But that's not *your* company. That's not the legacy you're carrying on from your father. I understand that sentiment and how important it is to have that connection and history and want to build on it."

"I know you do, it's just . . . I didn't expect this."

"What?"

"Us."

"And?"

"I don't want to lose you to time and distance or anything else."

"Then we won't let it happen."

Cody kissed her like a promise and prayer, pouring all of his emotion into it, letting her know how much he wanted to hold on to her.

She felt the same way and kissed him back with all her desire to love him and be loved by him, to show him the connection was real and vibrant and not going anywhere.

And just like every night of the past week, they ended up stripping away their clothes from each other, laying their hearts bare, and falling into bed, locked in an intimate embrace, making love. Every touch, sigh, moan, and whispered endearment was a sign of how much they needed and wanted each other. And when the passion overflowed and they lay in each other's arms in the dark and quiet of the night, they slept, content to be close and loved and connected, not alone, but as one.

Summer had never known such bliss. She wanted to feel like this every day for the rest of her life.

She understood why her mother chased this feeling, this bond. Summer didn't think about losing it, she thought about how to hold on to it. It wouldn't be easy, the life they were building together, but it would be so worth it to be this happy wrapped up in Cody's love.

All they had to do was figure out the logistics, because in her mind, the love was real and binding, and more important than where she did her work was whom she was with.

• • •

Summer lifted her head from Cody's chest, her mind not wholly online. She heard the noise, but couldn't quite place it until Cody's phone lit up again with the trilling ringtone. She made a grab for it on the bedside table just as Cody's eyes popped open.

She handed him the phone. "It's yours."

Cody grumbled and tapped the screen. "Hello," he said groggily. "Nat, is that you?"

Summer sat up and brushed her hair back over her shoulder.

Cody put his hand on her leg. "Yeah. I'll come get you right now. Stay put. Drop me a pin so I have the address." Cody's phone pinged with the location he needed. "Do not get in your car. I'll be there in like ten minutes." Cody hung up, dropped the phone on his chest, and rubbed both hands over his face.

Summer glanced at the clock next to the bed. Three forty-seven. "She should have been home by two."

"She's drunk." Cody threw off the covers and rolled out of bed.

Summer did the same and slid into her dress as Cody grabbed sweats and a T-shirt behind her. "I'll go to my room and put on something warmer."

"No, sweetheart, stay here. I've got this."

"Someone needs to drive her car back here."

"I'll drive her back later in the morning to get it."

"I'm up. I'm going with you." Summer left his room, went to hers, and put on a pair of comfy leggings and a soft sweater to keep her warm, along with socks and shoes, then went to the kitchen, found a plastic bowl, and met Cody as he came down the stairs.

"What's that for?"

"In case she gets sick in the car."

Cody winced. "Good thinking."

"We'll take my car, then you can drive hers home."

Cody nodded, then stepped close and kissed her on the forehead. "Thanks for coming with me."

"She's my sister."

"Yeah. But she called me."

"Has she done this before?"

They left the house and got into her car.

"Not because she was drunk. A couple times when she went somewhere with friends and got stuck because she wanted to come home earlier than them. And a couple times when her friends were intoxicated or whatever and she didn't want to get in the car with them. Which resulted in me getting all of them home safely."

"She's lucky to have you."

"I'm easier than calling her parents."

They found Natalie and a couple of friends leaning against her car outside a home that had a long driveway filled with other cars.

Summer stopped the car and Cody got out, leaving his door open.

"What's she doing here? Were you two together when I called?" Natalie slurred her words and looked disgruntled.

Summer dismissed it.

Cody gently took her by the arm. "We're here to take you home. Give me your keys."

"Why?"

"Because I'm driving your car home."

"I'll go with you."

"I think it's best you go with your sister. I'll drive your friends home."

The friends were already stumbling to get into the back seat of Natalie's car.

"I'm coming with you."

"There's not enough room for you and your friends. Get in Summer's car." Cody nudged her toward the open door.

"You're being so bossy."

"I want to get you and your friends home safely."

Natalie finally climbed into the car seat. "Fine. I'll go. Sorry if I messed up you sleeping with *her*."

Cody pulled the seat belt around Natalie and locked it. "Nat. Be quiet. Go home and sleep this off."

"You could come with me."

Summer didn't like what her sister was saying, but she also understood she was drunk and not thinking clearly.

Cody slammed the door without another word.

Summer didn't wait. She backed out down the drive, turned onto the street, and headed home.

Natalie fiddled with the radio, but fell back in her seat when they hit a curve. She reached out and put her hand on the dash to steady herself.

"If you feel sick, there's a bowl at your feet."

"Don't want me messing up your precious car," Natalie grumbled.

"I'd rather you didn't."

"I'd rather you left Cody alone." Natalie turned sideways in the seat. "Why are you still here?"

"Apparently to rescue my drunk sister." Summer tried to focus on Natalie. "You did the right thing tonight, calling Cody to come and get you."

"Yeah, you'll probably just tattle to my mom and dad that I got wasted."

Summer shook her head. "No, I won't. Because even though you shouldn't have been drinking, you behaved responsibly when you called for a ride. You were thinking about yourself, your friends, and anyone else out on the roads tonight you could have hurt if you had gotten behind the wheel."

"Yay for me." Natalie leaned her head into the headrest and closed her eyes.

"It's not always easy to ask for help, especially when you did something you shouldn't."

"It's not like I drink all the time."

"I never said you did. But you had reason to celebrate tonight. I get that. I hope you had fun."

"Would have been better if Cody was there with me."

Summer thought a reminder of the differences between Natalie and Cody might help. Probably not, but she went with it anyway. "Cody would be out of place at a high school party. He'd feel like the weird old guy."

"Hanging with a bunch of kids," Natalie spat out. "That's what you mean."

"That's reality, Natalie. Cody is a grown man with ten years of life experience on you. So, yes, it would be weird for him to be hanging out with a bunch of seventeen- and eighteen-year-olds, who aren't old enough to drink."

Natalie folded her arms over her chest. "I'm old enough to vote. I can do what I want."

"You don't know how glad I am that you did the responsible thing tonight."

"Whatever."

Summer parked the car in the driveway, got out, went around the car, opened the passenger door, and helped Natalie out. She wrapped her arm around her sister's waist and helped her into the house and up to her room.

Natalie stared out the window toward Cody's side of the house. "When you leave, I'm the one who will make him happy again."

Summer helped Natalie to the bed and sat her down on it. She pulled off Natalie's shoes, then unzipped the dress down her back. "Can you get ready for bed, or do you need help?"

Natalie shooed her away with her hands.

Summer went into the bathroom and filled a glass with water. When she went back into the bedroom, Natalie had left her dress puddled on the floor, along with her bra. She'd pulled on a T-shirt and curled up in bed under the covers.

"The room is spinning."

"I bet. I'll leave the water here for you. Drink it all as soon as you can to help with the dehydration. You'll probably have a headache in the morning."

"I have one standing in front of me." Natalie giggled to herself.

Summer dismissed it. "I'll check on you in the morning."

"Why do you have to always be so nice." The words were slurred by booze and sleep.

"Because I care about you."

"Hmm."

Summer left Natalie and walked back to the other side of the house and up to Cody's room, where she took off most of her clothes and slipped back into his bed. She was just about to fall asleep when she heard Cody come in, undress, and slide into bed beside her. She snuggled into his side. "It's a good thing you did tonight."

"I'm just happy she's safe." Cody pulled her closer to him. "Was everything okay when you got her home?"

"Fine. She just wanted you instead of me."

"I don't know why. I'd pick you every time." He kissed her on the head, making her feel loved and cherished and like she was with the right person for all the right reasons. And she didn't want to lose this.

She also felt that maybe Natalie did see that Summer was trying to be the sister Natalie deserved. One who showed up when she needed a ride, didn't bust her to her parents for underage drinking when she did the responsible thing and didn't get behind the wheel. Though Nate and Miranda would probably like to know their daughter did the right thing.

Summer hoped tomorrow Natalie saw her more like a sister who helped than one who stood between her and her crush.

Chapter Forty-One

So the guy comes into emergency high, a huge cut on his thigh that he has no idea how it happened, but he's totally paranoid he's going to get busted. The nurse leaves him to grab a doctor to stitch the wound. He decides instead of making a break for it by simply walking out of the curtained area, he'll just climb into the ceiling and crawl his way out. Of course, the drop ceiling gives way and the guy ends up on the floor at the foot of the bed with a broken arm. It's completely bent in the wrong direction. When the nurse rushes back to him, he looks at her and says, 'I can't fly.'"

Summer, Brooke, and Cody all broke up laughing and shaking their heads at David's absurd story.

Cody took a sip of his beer. "It could have been worse."

David held up his glass. "We're about to eat, so I'll keep the stories about the things people put inside them to myself."

"Oh, no." Summer cringed. "I don't want to know."

Brooke grinned. "You really don't. The stories I've heard over the last two weeks make me think people just don't think things through."

David squeezed Brooke's thigh. "Honey, the sad thing is most of them aren't even drunk or stoned."

The sweet smile on Summer's face told Cody that she saw what he saw between Brooke and David. They'd become very close.

After another long week, Cody appreciated this time to be with Summer, his sister, and David. Good conversation, laughs, drinks, food, and fun. He couldn't ask for more.

And this place was one of his favorite local restaurants. He hadn't been here in a while, but liked the idea of sharing some of his favorite haunts with Summer.

Which made him think of going to Texas with her and experiencing the things and places she liked.

In fact, they had a double date set up with Miles and Silas in a couple of weeks.

"So are you all moved into the office Cody set up for you?" Brooke asked.

"No. Unfortunately it turned out that no one used that space because the air conditioner didn't work, so Cody got maintenance in to check on it. Apparently during some other work, the ducting was detached from the system, so they're repairing it."

"It's not the ideal office anyway," Cody grumbled. "I want her up on my floor."

Brooke put her elbow on the table, chin in her hand, and grinned at him. "Of course you do."

"She's an executive. She'll need an assistant. The office downstairs doesn't have a space for a cubicle."

"It'll be fine."

"Fine isn't good enough. If you can't do what you need to do here, then that means you'll have to go there." Cody didn't know why he was getting so worked up about office space.

Summer put her hand over his. "We'll figure it out."

David pushed his empty plate away. "I heard you're hiring a personal assistant, too, to help with the day-to-day stuff. I could use someone to stock my fridge, clean the apartment, run errands."

"Your work schedule is insane," Brooke agreed. "And your fridge is a sad wasteland where condiments rule and food turns into gross science experiments."

David shrugged it off. "Alex thought the green mush that used to be mashed potatoes was cool."

"Yeah, well, next time we come over, you need to have snacks. And wine."

"Alex really shouldn't be drinking that stuff," David teased.

Brooke bumped her shoulder into his and shook her head. "I drink the wine and you get lucky."

"I know for a fact, you don't need the wine for me to get lucky."

"Gross," Cody said, putting his hands over his ears. "Please make them stop," he implored Summer.

"Should I tell your sister that you're going to get lucky later?"

"Ew." Brooke scrunched up her lips.

Then they all laughed.

Cody caught David's eye. "You two seem really good together."

David and Brooke shared a loving look and smiles.

Summer addressed Brooke. "Alex told me this morning that you're all going to his friend's birthday party together."

Brooke blushed. "We're making it a point to spend more time together."

It seemed that their relationship was quickly moving ahead.

And it felt like Cody's relationship with Summer wasn't getting to where he wanted it fast enough. And other times, he wondered if they'd ever get there, but didn't know why he felt that way when everything seemed great between them.

Brooke leaned toward him. "Are you worried about Summer going back to Texas and how that will work for the two of you?" Leave it to his sister to read his mind and ask the hard question.

"I am," he admitted.

Summer put her hand over his on the table and squeezed it.

"Our circumstances are complicated. The reality is, I live and work in a different state. You've known for weeks that I have to return, yet we've just started making plans to join our lives in a way that works for both of us."

He wanted to explain why he'd held off, but she put her hand up to stop him from interrupting.

"The circumstances of me getting to know my family, while also starting a relationship with you, made us both wait on the long-term stuff because we needed to know if this was something we both wanted to hold on to. For me, it feels like we're moving in the right direction toward what we both want."

"I think so, too. But I also can't deny that I'm concerned things will fall apart if we're not communicating what we need."

"Aw, look, David. He learned from his past mistakes." Brooke gave Cody a sincerely absurd grin of approval.

Cody rolled his eyes, then turned back to Summer. "Just because this relationship is going to take a lot of effort doesn't mean we can't make it work."

"We're both worried about the same thing. But we're also both holding on to the other. That's what matters. It's not about the office space or how many days we spend here or there. It's about us making each other a priority," Summer said.

"I can do that."

Summer put her hand on his cheek. "I can, too. No matter how much my grandfather grumbles."

"I'm more worried about your mom."

"She's newly married. She'll be happy for at least another six months."

"So are you going to Texas with Summer when she's due back?" Brooke asked.

Cody nodded. "That's the plan. I spend Monday to Wednesday

with her in Texas. She spends Thursday to Sunday here with me. We'll alternate weekends depending on what's going on with family here or there."

"I hope you both have frequent flyer miles." David held up his beer to them.

Summer put her hand over Cody's on the table. "It's about finding balance between our two lives."

"And not sleeping alone," Cody added. "You got up earlier than usual this morning and I couldn't sleep without you."

"I noticed when you found me in the office."

He'd wanted to drag her back to bed with him. "Your grandfather ruined the plans I had to show you what a good morning it could be."

Summer chuckled. "With him, there's always something that can't wait and needs my attention."

Cody shook his head. "He's afraid you're going to leave him." The second he said it, he realized Brooke had been right. He was so desperate to find a way to make this work because he feared Summer would leave him for her job.

"I care about the company and the people who work there. I can't just leave it behind, Cody."

"I know. And I understand what that means for us. Though things might get a bit more complicated when we have kids."

Summer's eyes just about popped out of her head. "What?"

"You heard me. I'm not saying now. But someday. Soonish. You want a family. I want one. I'm just putting it out there."

"Don't you think you should *put a ring on it* first?" Brooke said.

"Soonish," David added.

Cody picked up his beer and held it out to Summer. She clinked it with her wine glass, both of them grinning and sharing a look that said it all. Yes. Soonish.

Because they still had a way to go before the I do's and a baby shower.

But things were definitely headed in the right direction. Cody felt he had learned from his past mistakes in relationships, and this one would go the distance. Because that's what he wanted: a life with Summer.

$\mathcal{C}$ody pushed open the heavy wood door and walked into the foyer, stopping short so he didn't collide with Natalie. "Are you on your way out?"

"No. I was waiting for you."

He closed the door and stared down at Nat, who looked up at him expectantly. "What's up?"

"Summer's not here."

"I know. She left first thing this morning." She'd been up before dawn to catch her flight to Texas. He hadn't heard from her all day.

He'd hoped they'd have this last week to finalize their plans for her return to work. Instead, she'd been suddenly called back home to handle an emergency: an acquisitions deal she'd been working on nearly two weeks. It was only supposed to be an overnight trip, but he worried once she was there, she'd give up the last of her vacation here without them having a solid plan in place for how they'd continue their long-distance relationship.

They came together every night desperate for each other, but something felt off. Maybe it was him. He admired how hard she worked, that getting the deal done and doing it right mattered to her. He appreciated that when they were together, she was there. Present.

And maybe that was it.

When they weren't together, it felt like he was out of sight, out of mind.

He didn't like feeling that way.

Natalie followed him over to his side of the house. "I thought maybe you and I could catch up on our series. It's been a while. A whole new season came out."

"Sorry. Can't. I've got Alex tonight." He dropped his briefcase in the office, noting that Summer had taken all her files and stuff with her. The room still smelled like her, but there was nothing else there.

"Is Brooke going out with David again?"

"Yes." They made a point to get together at least three times a week. Somehow they managed to do that with their busy schedules and having to think about Alex's needs, too.

Cody headed for the stairs.

"What's wrong?" Natalie blocked his path in the hallway.

"Long day." He hoped that got her out of his way. He needed to change into clothes that could withstand a boat battle with Alex at bath time.

"She hasn't even been gone a whole day and you're upset."

"I just miss her."

"You better get used to it, because this is how it's going to be. Probably worse, because it won't be just a day here or there, but all the time."

"We have a plan to be together."

"Uh-huh. Until you're needed here while she's needed there."

"Nat." He sighed out his frustration.

"Why her when you could be with someone who's here, who wants to be with you all the time, who doesn't put something else first?"

"That's not what she's doing."

"Isn't it? Her grandfather beckons, and off she goes."

His frustration skyrocketed. "It's not like that."

"How long before it's easier for her to just give in to him and do what he wants because you're so understanding and patient?"

He tried to rein in his temper. "I get that you're looking out for me. I appreciate it. But this is between Summer and me."

"She's going to break your heart. I can already see it happening. You deserve so much more. You deserve someone who is here for you always."

"Is everything all right?" Brooke asked, coming down the stairs with Alex.

"Fine," he automatically answered, though the word came out clipped and sharp.

Natalie shook her head at him. "Making excuses for her doesn't change the reality of what's happening." Natalie pressed her lips tight. "I want you to be happy."

He'd never been as happy as he'd been these past few weeks with Summer.

But he couldn't deny that what they'd had here was about to drastically change.

Did that mean it would change the way either of them felt? He didn't think so.

But the reality was that their relationship wouldn't go the way he thought and they would spend time apart. Maybe it would be a good thing.

Not if he felt the way he did right now, missing her, wondering what she was doing and why he hadn't heard from her at all.

"Cody," Brooke prompted him to tell her what was going on.

Natalie squeezed his forearm. "I'll see you at dinner."

Brooke stepped up to him as Natalie walked away. "What's going on with you two?"

"Nothing." Cody reached for Alex, picked him up, and held him close. "How was your day, little man?"

"Good. I fed crickets to the class lizard. Mom said I could sign up to bring him home for a weekend."

"I can't wait to meet him."

Brooke leaned up and kissed Alex's cheek. "Be good. Go to bed on time."

Alex bobbed his head. "I will."

Cody set Alex back on his feet. "Head on over for dinner. I'll be there in a minute. I just want to change clothes."

Alex ran off.

His sister stayed put. "Do you miss her?"

"Yes."

"That's a good sign."

"Why?"

"Since Amy, you haven't cared if someone had other plans and couldn't see you. You weren't waiting for a call or text, hoping to hear from them. I know what it's like to miss the person you love. Maybe this is the first time since Mom left and Dad died that you're really feeling it. But she'll be back tomorrow. She can't stay away from you because she loves you."

Hearing that made his heart jump in his chest. "How do you know that?"

"Because everything she's done since she got here is to show you that she does. She's arranging her life to be with you. Yes, sometimes things will pull you in opposite directions, but what you share will always bring you back together."

He liked the sound of that. It felt very much that way. But . . . "I haven't heard from her all day."

"Did you call her?"

"No. I figured she was busy."

Brooke gave him a look.

He was being ridiculous. "I'll call her."

She poked him in the chest. "Don't let the little things trip you up and tie you in knots."

"I don't want her to feel like I can't go a day without her."

"I think she'd be really happy to know you can't."

He wrapped her in a hug. "Have fun tonight."

"Oh, I will. You'll have to save the sexting for after Alex goes to bed."

He released her with a soft push to get her to go. "Leave before I pretend to be sick and you have to stay home."

"Not a chance," she said over her shoulder.

"You look happy."

"I was going for sexy, but happy is always good." She kept going, waving to him over her shoulder.

He had to admit, she did look great in dark jeans, black boots, and the white blouse that hugged her curves, even if she was his sister.

He blew up that train of thought and any hint of him thinking about her out with his best friend. He pulled out his phone instead and called Summer.

"Hi, sorry I missed your call. Leave me a message and I'll get back to you as soon as possible."

He wanted her to do just that physically, as well as over the phone. "Hi, sweetheart, I just wanted you to know I miss you. I'm thinking about you. Call me back. Doesn't matter how late." Yeah, he didn't sound desperate at all.

But who cared?

Just hearing her voice made him think of all the good times they'd shared and how much he liked her. Loved her? Yeah. That, too. Otherwise he wouldn't be this desperate to hear her voice, smell her sweet scent, see her beautiful face, or touch her soft skin.

Yeah, he had it bad.

And he liked it that way.

Instead of going up to his lonely room to change, he headed over to the other side of the house for dinner.

Alex was playing some intricate patty-cake game with Haley. Nate and Miranda had just finished putting the food on the table and sat.

"Thanks for making dinner," Cody said to Miranda.

She smiled across at him. "I missed having Summer's help. I guess I've gotten used to our time together in the kitchen, catching up on the day, talking about whatever."

"I'm sure she's missing your cooking tonight."

"Have you heard from her?" Nate asked.

"No. She's probably busy with her grandfather. I just left her a message. I'm sure she'll call later tonight."

Natalie put her hand on his arm. "Of course she will."

Nothing in her voice sounded patronizing, but it sure did come off that way to him, because he knew Natalie thought Summer wasn't going to call.

And he couldn't seem to let that thought go all through dinner; all through Alex's bath and the epic boat battle he lost because he was in his head, wishing and hoping Summer proved Natalie wrong; all through the five books he let Alex swindle him into reading instead of the usual three because Cody didn't want to go up to his room and sit in the quiet wondering what kept Summer so busy she couldn't return his call.

He leaned over Alex and kissed him on the head. "Good night, buddy. See you in the morning."

"Will Aunt Summer be back then, too?"

"Not until after you're home from school."

Alex nodded, then turned on his side and snuggled into the covers.

Cody left Alex's room, closing the door all the way because Alex preferred it that way, then headed down the hall to his own room, taking off his soaking wet shirt as he went.

The second he walked into his room, his night got a hell of a lot better. He approached the bed and the woman in it. "I'm so glad you're here. I dreaded having to sleep alone."

"Who are you talking to?" Summer asked from behind him, not in front of him.

Suddenly the light went on and he went perfectly still, his joy that Summer had come home early overshadowed by the gut punch of seeing someone else in his bed, thinking he'd been talking to her.

Natalie rose up on her knees wearing a skimpy pair of black undies and a pushup bra that barely contained her . . .

He laser focused on her face, not wanting to see anything else. The look of pure joy in her eyes turned to embarrassment, then rage when her gaze shot past him to Summer.

Cody turned his back on Natalie, not wanting to see anything more than he already had by accident.

"What are you doing here?" Natalie asked Summer.

"I'd like to know what you're both doing."

Cody was about to answer when he caught his sister and David's surprised expressions as they took in this absurd scene from the doorway next to Summer.

"Oh, shit," David and Brooke said in unison, showing how much in tune they were with each other.

Cody focused on Summer. She had a death grip on the strap of her purse hanging from her shoulder. She'd dropped her overnight bag at her side. Man, she was a sight for sore eyes even with the anger and suspicion flashing in hers. Behind that, he saw the fatigue.

Summer hadn't taken her eyes off her sister in their bed.

All Cody wanted was for Summer to look at him and see the truth. "This is not what it looks like."

"You look nearly as half naked as she does," Brooke pointed out.

He held up the wet shirt in his hand.

It was Summer who spoke sense. "Bath battle."

Brooke and David backed out of the room, leaving him with one woman in his bed and the other looking like she might follow them out the door any second.

Panic shot through him, but he tried to remain calm and not light a match to this volatile situation.

"You heard him. He wants me here." Natalie's words shocked him.

When he'd entered the room, he'd thought he'd been speaking to Summer, not Natalie.

Summer's gaze swept up his bare chest to meet his eyes. "Explain."

He really didn't like that quiet, hurt tone.

"Natalie!" Nate stood in the bedroom doorway, Miranda next to him, though her scrutinizing gaze was on Cody, not her nearly naked daughter.

He guessed he could thank Brooke for the newcomers to his room. Natalie shifted behind him.

He hoped she'd pulled the sheet up and covered herself. He couldn't take his eyes off Summer. "This is not what it looks like."

Summer remained very still. "You said that already." Tears gathered in her eyes.

"Please don't cry." His chest ached with dread and his anger built. He tried to keep it in check, because he really needed to keep it together and tell Summer the truth. "It was dark. I thought she was you."

Doubt clouded her eyes. "You weren't expecting me."

"I thought you came home early to surprise me."

"I did."

"I see that. And I'm so damn happy you're back. I missed you." It took everything he had not to go to her and wrap her in his arms. He didn't think she'd welcome it at the moment.

"I got your message when I landed, but I . . ." Tears ran down her cheeks.

Every single one of them tore his heart to shreds. "You wanted to surprise me. Yeah. You don't know how much I appreciate that." It meant so much to him. He took a step toward her. "I didn't do anything. In another second or two, I would have realized she wasn't you. Please. You have to believe me. I would never cheat on you. Ever." And it made him sick and angry that Natalie would think he would and put him in this position.

"I believe you," Summer said, looking him right in the eye. Her gaze went past him to the bed. "I'm just incredibly hurt *you* would do this to me," she addressed Natalie. "And to the person you so obviously love."

Cody, as always, didn't acknowledge that land mine, just steered clear of it.

"You're going to break his heart," Natalie said matter-of-factly, like it was inevitable.

Cody didn't believe that for a second. Not when they had the possibility of forever, and they both wanted it this much.

Summer frowned. "He'll forgive you for this, because he loves you, too. Just not the way you want him to. I'm sorry you think I took him from you. But he was never yours in that way."

"He could be. I'm the one who's always been here. I'll always be here. You'll be running a corporate empire."

"That's enough, Natalie," Nate said. "You should not be in here. Like that."

"I'm an adult. I can do whatever I want." The childish tone didn't exactly reinforce Natalie's statement.

"Then think like one," Summer admonished. "Our dad runs a business and has a very successful marriage with your mother. Am I not capable of the same thing? Just because I have responsibilities doesn't mean my relationship with Cody isn't important. I spent the whole day working my ass off to get done what needed to be done so I could get back here to him. I don't know why you keep insisting that I'm leaving and I'll hurt him when I've done everything I can to show him how much I care. I know you see it; that's why you're so afraid of losing him. But you won't. You just don't get to have him the way you want. That doesn't mean he doesn't care about you, it just means that you have different feelings for each other. And you need to respect that. And my place in his life."

Astounded by her words and how she tried not to hurt Natalie's feelings, Cody took Summer's hand, feeling the slight hesitation before she squeezed his hand back. "I couldn't have said it better." He'd have said it with a lot more expletives and anger. Starting with *What the fuck were you thinking?* Because he never saw this coming.

"Apologize," Nate instructed Natalie.

Cody couldn't see Natalie's face; he didn't dare turn around when she wasn't dressed properly, and he feared his anger would take over and he'd say something he'd regret.

How Summer managed to keep her head, he didn't know. But he did know her hurt and anger ran deep and they weren't done hashing this out.

"I won't apologize for the way I feel or for trying to show Cody that there's someone here who will always put him first, and it's not her."

Miranda went to the bed. "That's enough. Put your nightshirt on. Out. Now."

Cody turned, keeping his back to Natalie as she climbed out of the bed and walked behind him and out the door with her mom.

Nate hung back. "Cody."

Cody met the man who'd helped raise him eye to eye.

"We'll talk to her." Nate glanced at Summer, then back to him. "I'm sorry she put you in this position. I really don't know what else to say."

"Summer already said it. I'll forgive her. But I need some time. Right now . . . I'm just angry and hurt she'd think I'd ever cross this line or cheat on my girlfriend. Her sister," he snapped, and raked his fingers through his hair. "Just go. I need a minute." His emotions were too raw and wild inside him.

Even worse, Summer stood there like a statue, her cheeks tear-streaked and pale.

Nate turned to her. "Honey . . ."

"I'm fine." The words came out too fast to be believed. The choked tone didn't help, either.

"I've got her," Cody assured Nate, though he wasn't sure how true that statement was at the moment.

Just as Nate left, Brooke and David showed up at the door, carrying a tray with a bottle of wine, two glasses, and some food.

"We thought you might be hungry after your long day, Summer." She nodded, but didn't say anything.

Cody had never seen her so closed up.

He went to his sister and took the tray. "Thank you for thinking of it. You should check on Alex, make sure all the noise didn't wake him up."

Brooke took the hint and turned to leave with David.

He set the tray on the table by the fireplace, then turned back to Summer, who hadn't moved an inch. She was between him and the door, looking like she didn't know which way to go.

He took one option away and closed the door before he turned to her again. "Say something. Please. Anything."

"I . . ." She stared at the bed.

He stepped into her line of sight. "How was your day? Mine sucked. I missed you so damn bad, I couldn't get anything done. All I did was think about you, wondering what you were doing."

She met his gaze, hers accusing. "And if I'd ever come back?"

"No. But did I want you here with me? Yes. Desperately."

She sighed. "Because all the times Natalie reminded you I was leaving haunted you."

Damnit, he hated that she read him so well. But he also loved that she knew him so well, too. "Yes. But then I talked to my sister and she said something that made a hell of a lot of sense. She said sometimes things will pull us in opposite directions, but what we share will always bring us back together. So instead of continuing to think you were too busy to talk to me, I left you that message letting you know I wanted to talk to you. Even though you didn't pick up, I knew you'd contact me as soon as you could. You did me one better and you came home early because you wanted to be back with me."

"I shudder to think what might have happened if I hadn't."

His anger returned. "I can tell you exactly what would have happened. I'd have dragged her out of our bed and tossed her out on her ass, and she and I would not have been friends anymore. I'm not sure we are right now, but you managed to stay calm and keep me from tearing my relationship with her to pieces."

"You'd have been well within your rights."

"And I'd have regretted it. You knew that, so you took control of the situation when I felt anything but in control."

She raised a brow. "Are you okay now?"

"No. Not even close. I won't be okay until you are, because I know that shook you."

Tears welled in her eyes again. "I don't want to be here right now."

"Then let's go." Cody went to his dresser, pulled out a T-shirt, and put it on. "Where do you want to go? A hotel? Texas? Paris? Your place in Wyoming? Belize? You tell me where and I'll make it happen."

Summer's shoulders went lax. "How about we just go to the guest room?"

"You are not a guest here. This is your home. And I'm sorry you don't feel like it is right now."

"She came into our room." Her voice cracked. The words shook with her disbelief, anger, and sadness.

He picked up the tray his sister made for Summer and headed for the door. He looked over his shoulder and found Summer still standing in the same spot. "We have another bedroom just a short walk away. No one will bother us there." Not that he thought anyone would dare come up here again tonight.

Summer shook her head. "I'm not letting her run me out of here."

Cody wanted to fix this. "We've made a lot of good memories here in this room. Let's make some more." He took the tray back to the table by the fireplace, set it down, and grabbed the matches. He lit the paper and kindling between the logs he'd already laid and blew to get the flames burning hotter.

Summer's purse thunked on the floor behind him, the lights went out, then she joined him by the fireplace, taking a seat in one of the chairs. He sighed out his relief, turned from the flames, and knelt in front of her.

They needed this, the two of them tucked away in a room, in the quiet, together.

He met her sorrowful blue eyes. "Are you mad at me?" He hoped not. He hadn't done anything wrong.

She shook her head. "No. Of course not. I'm just . . ."

He put his hands on her knees, hoping the contact eased her the way it did him.

She put her hands over his. "I just wanted to come home and surprise you and have it be this nice thing, and you and I would be so happy to see each other and fall into bed and . . ."

"It was nice. And I am incredibly happy you're back. And I am going to take you to bed because I always want you desperately."

She leaned in, holding his gaze, showing him everything in her eyes that she was feeling inside. Her pain wrecked him. "I've tried really hard to make a place for myself here."

He cupped her cheek. "You have a place here no matter what."

She leaned into his touch. "I wish it felt as permanent as you make it sound."

"It is."

The disbelief in her eyes contradicted him.

He shifted and grabbed the open bottle of wine. He pulled out the cork, poured them each a glass, and handed her one. "Let's have a picnic and talk."

"I don't want to talk about it anymore."

"Good. Because I don't, either." He slipped his hand beneath her leg and gave it a gentle pull. "Sit down here with me."

She slid off the chair and joined him on the soft rug, the warmth of the fire spreading to them and through the room. He set the tray between them.

She pulled off her shoes and set them aside.

He picked up a cracker, stacked a piece of cheese and summer sausage on top, and handed it to her. "How was your day, dear?"

That got him a soft grin. "Terrible. My flight this morning was delayed by half an hour. It was raining when I landed. My grandfather was not pleased I arrived late for the meeting, though he was impressed with my questions about the acquisition and insights on why we weren't going to pay more than the company was worth. Since I was in town, my mother insisted we get together for dinner and has left me several unhappy messages about my ditching her to come back here early. My grandfather also expressed his displeasure about being left with my grumpy mother because of me. But you know the thing that really sucked today?"

"Coming home and finding your sister in our bed."

Her gaze softened. "I love that you keep saying *our* bed."

"It is because you and me, we're together. No one will come between us. Not even her."

She nodded and took a big sip of wine. "And though my business went well today despite the annoyances that popped up, the thing that sucked was missing you and wishing you'd come with me."

He leaned in and kissed her softly. "I missed you, too. I wasn't looking forward to sleeping alone. More than that, we hadn't spoken. I just wanted to hear from you, to know how your day went, to talk about the business and family stuff, and to know you were okay."

"I'm sorry. I should have called or texted, even if it was just to tell you I only had a minute and everything was fine. Next time— because we both know there's going to be lots of next times—I will communicate better with you."

"I'll do the same. I could have called, texted, or emailed you. Instead I obsessed over the fact that you hadn't and that it meant something when it didn't. I missed you sitting beside me at dinner. I wanted you to play water war with me and Alex. And the thing I wanted most, I still get to have."

"What's that?"

"This. The time we spend together alone, talking and making love before we sleep side by side. I get to wake up next to you and be the first person you see and you're the first person I see. I love that we start and end our day together."

This time, she leaned in and kissed him. "I do, too. Why do you think I rushed back here to you?" She grinned, then stuffed another cracker with cheese and sausage into her mouth.

He held his glass out to her. "Thank you for coming home early."

She clinked her glass to his. "There's no place I'd rather be than with you."

They sipped their wine and finished off the food, letting the quiet surround them and the events of the evening fade into the background of their minds.

Summer set her empty wine glass on the food tray, then looked directly at him. "Cody." She didn't need to say anything more.

He took her hand and settled onto his back on the soft carpet, the fire blazing beside him. Drawing her up and over him, he slid his free hand up the back of her neck and in her silky hair and kissed her. "Is this what you wanted?"

She straddled him, rocking her hips, moving against his hard cock. "Yes. But more."

"Absolutely. Lots more." He leaned up and kissed her, sliding his tongue along hers, tasting the wine on her lips. He pulled the blouse from her pants and up and over her head, diving back into the kiss he'd hated to interrupt. She pressed her breasts to his chest, giving him all the access he needed to undo the bra clasp at the back and pull it off her, too.

He kept kissing her and rolled her to her back beside him so he could undo the button and zipper on her slacks and push them and her panties down her thighs. She kicked them off the rest of the way.

She broke the kiss, rose, and went for his shirt as he undid his pants. It was all hands and pushing and pulling until he was naked on his back and she straddled him again.

The firelight cast soft shadows and bright light against her skin, highlighting her beautiful face, the cascade of her dark hair, the swell of her breasts, the dips and hollows he wanted to explore.

He stared up at her looking down at him, his erection pressed against her wet folds, her hips rocking ever so slightly against him. "Keep doing that."

She did and planted her hands next to his head and leaned down and kissed him.

He gripped her hips, holding on as she moved over him, making him want to be deep inside her, but holding out while she pleasured herself against him. He felt it in how she positioned herself to maximize the gratification and heard it in the soft sighs and moans he captured with his lips.

And when she was close, she rose up and took him in deep again and again, the rhythm building as her body caressed his. And then that wonderful tightening happened and his body begged for release, but he held back, wanting her to join him. He reached between them, found the swollen nub with his thumb, rubbed against it as she moved over him, her dark hair brushing her breasts, blue eyes filled with passion locked on him as the climax hit and her eyes closed on a moan of pure pleasure. He followed her into the surge, holding her hips to his. His body spasmed as he filled her. They were locked together in this perfect moment.

She collapsed on top of him, their breaths sawing in and out, his arms banded around her, their hearts beating against each other's.

They didn't say anything.

They didn't need to. Their bodies had said it all.

In the quiet, their hearts connected, the fire crackling and popping and keeping them warm, he held her, knowing nothing got better than this.

Eventually, they both needed the comfort and warmth of the bed. He left her only long enough to remove the tainted bedding and replace the sheets and blankets before he helped her up and followed her under the covers, pulling her close, wrapping her in his arms. He held her until they both fell asleep.

She was still lying in his arms when he woke up to her soft blue eyes on him. "I love waking up to you."

"Every day I wake up to you is a good day." He held her, hoping today was a better day for both of them.

He didn't know what was going to happen when they confronted the events of last night, but he knew no matter what, they'd deal with it together.

He hated the discord. He didn't like that his relationship with Summer sparked it.

He didn't want to tear apart the family because he'd finally found someone he wanted to make a life with.

He wanted all of them to be happy for him and Summer. For the most part, they were, but one person could ruin all that for the others. He'd like to convince Natalie that Summer was the only woman for him, but that seemed to be the thing that hurt her the most. And while it was flattering that she had such big feelings for him, it meant that he'd disappoint and hurt her.

He hated that.

He wished he could avoid it all together.

That was why he'd always kept things friendly and uncomplicated and never acknowledged Natalie's flirting in any way.

"It's not your fault."

He should have known Summer would read his mood. "I know. It's just a complicated mess right now." He didn't like complicated or messes because they were hard to fix.

He wasn't sure this one could be resolved, because Natalie had crossed a line and jeopardized his relationship with Summer. She'd put him in a really bad position. Luckily, he and Summer were strong enough to work it out.

Natalie let her feelings overshadow her good judgment.

He could forgive her impulsive mistake.

In time.

When? He didn't know.

Chapter Forty-Three

*N*atalie had avoided the mind-melting lecture last night by locking herself in her room and shouting at her parents to leave her alone, humiliation burning inside her.

Since she'd caused the embarrassing scene, she'd remained in her room, trying to come up with a way to make things right.

Natalie could only imagine what Cody was thinking about her. It made her heart race and her throat clog every time she thought about how he wouldn't even look at her last night.

In the morning light, sitting in the kitchen, nothing had changed. And, she feared, everything had changed.

"Are you ready to talk?" her mom asked, walking in, dressed and ready for a day Natalie didn't really want to face.

She met her mom's disappointed gaze. "I did what I did because I love Cody. I am not ashamed to say that or of what I did." Humiliated she'd been caught by her parents, yes.

Her mom's eyebrow shot up. "Really? You aren't remorseful that you wanted Cody to cheat on his girlfriend *with you*, Summer's sister, after he was completely devastated by Amy's betrayal and would never do that to someone else?"

Natalie went still, everything inside her going cold. Her heart clenched. That's not what she'd meant for him to do at all. She just wanted him to pick her. "I wanted him to see that he had a better choice than someone who has a life in a different state."

"Cody is a grown man, who knows his own mind and heart and what he wants. He chose her. But you couldn't accept that." Her mom's eyes softened. "He's much older than you. He's in a different place in his life than you are in yours." Her mom had pointed that out before and Natalie still didn't care.

"That doesn't mean it can't work. People who are different ages do it all the time."

"You're right. But those people are attracted to each other. They build a relationship."

"I have a relationship with Cody. We're best friends. We used to spend so much time together. Until *she* showed up."

"If you were really Cody's friend, you'd be happy for him."

"She's going to hurt him."

"You don't know that." Her mom patted her hand. "It seems to me they've been dedicated to finding a way to be together."

"So he's just going to move to be with her."

Her mom gave her a sympathetic look. "Yes. That's what couples who are in love do."

"He doesn't love her."

"You don't want him to love her, but he does. You've seen them together."

And she hated every second of it. "It won't last."

Her mom sighed. "Some things do. Others don't. But do you really think throwing yourself at Cody is going to change his mind about the way he feels about her?"

"I thought, if he just gave us a try, he'd see I'm the better choice."

"Sneaking into his bedroom, putting him on the spot without there being any signs from him that he'd welcome you there . . . You thought that was better than going to him and talking to him about how you feel and what you hoped could be between you.

That would have been the adult move. A hard one, yes, but the one that would have ended with you two still being able to move on without the hurt you caused him and Summer, and yourself."

Natalie deflated. "You really don't think he could have feelings for me?"

Pity filled her mom's eyes. "I know that's what you hoped, but that's not how Cody feels about you. You just didn't want to see it. He was too kind to squash your hopes and break your heart, because he does love you, sweetheart. Just not like that." Her mom pressed her lips tight. "And I hate to tell you this, but he won't be the only one you want who doesn't want you back." She put her hand over Natalie's. "But one day, there will be someone who loves you the way you love them. And it will feel a million times stronger and magical and special, and you'll want to hold on to it and that person forever. I know that someone is out there for you."

"Do you think that's how Cody feels about Summer?"

"What do you think?"

Natalie rolled her eyes. "He's been obsessed with her since she got here."

"Sometimes it's like that. You find someone that just draws you to them."

"I thought he just felt sorry for her and it would wear off."

"Instead, they're making plans for their future together."

Yes. Plans that would take Cody away from Natalie. From all of them. Maybe she'd already pushed him away. "Do you think he's really mad at me?"

"How would you feel if Haley tried to steal your boyfriend? A man you loved, who loved you back equally. How would you feel if Haley was trying to mess that up for you when it's all you'd ever wanted for a long time?"

"That's not what I was trying to do."

"But that's what you did," her mom snapped.

"I just wanted him to pick me."

"He'd already picked her." The gentle tone didn't soften the blow one bit.

Natalie wondered something. "Why isn't Dad in on this?"

"I asked him to let me handle it. He's upset because his two daughters aren't getting along and one hurt the other."

Natalie's heart sank and the anger returned. "He took *her* side."

"Does it feel like I took yours?"

She folded her arms across her chest. "Not really."

"Because this isn't about sides. It's about taking responsibility for the hurt you've caused. Your father is upset that you and Summer are hurt and angry and upset. He doesn't want either one of you to feel that way."

Natalie slid off the stool.

"Where are you going?"

"To apologize." Natalie knew this was only part one of the ongoing lecture/lesson her mom had in store for her, but the rest could wait. She needed to see Cody. She needed to make him understand she'd never meant to hurt him.

But when she reached the foyer, she stopped in her tracks and stared across the glass-enclosed entryway at the closed double doors on the other side.

Chapter Forty-Four

*D*o you have any idea what time it is in New York City?"

Summer didn't feel like playing this game today. "It was just after eleven PM your time last night when I found Natalie in Cody's bed ready to seduce him."

"No fucking way."

Summer could still see it so clearly. "Cody walked into his dark room and thought it was me. I arrived home from my rushed trip to Texas to surprise him and caught them both off guard." Summer raked her fingers through her hair. "She thought he'd take her up on it. She really and truly believed he'd cheat on me to be with her."

"Of course he didn't."

Summer appreciated that Lucy knew Cody was kind and honest. "She hurt him. Deeply. Badly. I know they'll work it out eventually, but . . . It's a mess here."

"What about you two?"

"At first, I was just stunned. But we talked about it. It actually brought us closer together. But I'm afraid this is going to tear a rift in the family."

"She needs to make this right. Not you. You didn't do anything."

"I know, but it feels like my being here set this in motion."

"Even if it did, she's responsible for her actions. Is your dad pissed?"

"I don't think he or Miranda knew what to say or do last night . . ."

"That must have been humiliating for your sister, though she deserved that and more."

"I don't want her to hate me because I'm with Cody."

"He made it clear from nearly the second you two met that he wanted you. You fell in love. That's not something you do to hurt someone else, it just happens. She needs to respect the boundary of your relationship. While he has history and a connection to her, he wants to build a life with you. Don't let her pathetic stunt chip away at what you and Cody want for your future."

"You're right."

"I always am." Lucy's confidence knew no bounds. "I know this sucks. You're worried about everyone else, including Natalie, I'm sure. But you need to remember she hurt you. Don't just let her off the hook. If you don't nip this in the bud now, who knows what she'll do next."

"I'm hoping this is the wake-up call she needed to see reality."

"I hope so, too. Otherwise the holidays together are going to suck."

Summer knew Lucy was teasing with an ounce of truth thrown in. Because if they didn't fix this situation, things could get a lot worse. "Tell me what's going on with you."

"I fired the interior decorator and hired a new one. She's amazing. And the contractor who works with her . . . Oh. My. God."

"Did you get a date?"

"Tonight. A concert at the Garden." Lucy loved music and dancing.

"Have fun. Text me that you're safe and home later. Then call me tomorrow with all the details."

"You know I will."

Summer heard a knock on the doors leading to the foyer. "Hey, I've got to go."

"Love you, babe."

"Love you back, Luc."

Chapter Forty-Five

*I*n Natalie's whole life, she'd never seen the doors to Cody's side of the house closed. Ever.

Her gut tightened with dread as she approached them and tried the knob. Locked.

Her heart sank. Panic shot through her.

She knocked. And waited.

Finally, the snick of the lock sounded and the doors opened slowly. Only it wasn't Cody who appeared, but Brooke, looking just as disappointed in her as her mother had been. "In all the years we've lived here, there's been an unspoken rule of privacy. We don't go upstairs to your rooms without being invited or asked to do so. The same applied to all of you coming over here. You broke that trust and hurt Cody and Summer." Brooke's frown deepened. "I have never seen him as happy as he is with her, and you tried to take that from him."

"I wanted to be the one to make him happy."

"I know. He knows that, too. He tried to spare your feelings. He knew there was a line and he never crossed it, because he didn't want to give you hope where there was none, because he was your friend and that's all."

The sinking feeling and sadness grew as reality thumped Natalie right in the heart. "I realize that now."

"I hope you also understand what your thoughtlessness cost you."

She couldn't lose Cody. "I can fix it. I just need to talk to him."

Brooke's eyes filled with pity. "He's already left for work."

"Did Summer go with him?"

"She's on a call in the office here. Would you like me to see if she'll see you?"

That stung. "I'd like to talk to Cody first."

"Then you're going to have to wait."

Natalie didn't like the dismissive tone or that she'd inadvertently made Brooke mad at her, too. "I'm sorry."

"I know you are. But some lessons are hard and come with consequences we don't expect or anticipate. You hurt my brother and my friend. I don't take that lightly. No one should ever meddle in someone else's relationship. You wouldn't like it if someone did it to you."

"She did. Cody and I had a great relationship until she showed up."

Brooke stood taller and narrowed her gaze. "Summer never took Cody away from you. She never interfered when you two were spending time together. I appreciated the way she tried to get to know each and every one of us here individually. She's tried the hardest with you, because she saw how much you cared about Cody. She wanted to prove to you that she'd treat him right. And she has. Maybe their relationship isn't the way you think it should be, but it seems to be working for them. That's not for you to judge or put your expectations on. They get to decide what's right for them and what makes them happy. Cody didn't ask your opinion because he knows what he wants. We are family. Here to help and support when asked; otherwise, it's none of our business."

"I don't want to see him get hurt again."

"I don't, either. But did you ask him if he was unhappy or feeling hurt by Summer? Did you see that in any way when you saw them together? Or were you just jealous and acting out?"

The demanding tone set Natalie off. "Why are you being so harsh?"

"Because I want you to understand that for all your worries that *she'd* hurt him, *you* were the one who actually did."

Natalie felt that like a knife to the heart. "I didn't mean to."

"But you did." Brooke echoed her mom's words, as if Natalie needed to hear it again. "I know you want to make this right. I hope you can in some way. Just know you changed things with Cody. It won't ever be what it used to be. Maybe it will be better. It could be worse. Either way, you need to accept how he feels and what he wants going forward."

"If I can just talk to him, I know we can work this out."

"It should be in person, when *he's* ready. Don't bother him at work."

"I won't. I just . . . It sucks to wait."

"I know what you mean. I've wanted to see him really happy for a long time. These last few weeks, he's been happier than I can ever remember. I saw him let go of the past and look forward to the future. Like you, I saw that it meant he wouldn't be here with us all the time. I knew I was going to miss him. But I was also so happy for him. I hope you get to that place for him, otherwise there's no future friendship for the two of you, even though he will always want your happiness."

Natalie turned to go with a heavy heart, but turned back as Brooke started to close the doors again. "You don't have to do that."

"I think a reminder of people's personal space is still in order. At least until Cody feels comfortable being here again." Brooke closed the doors on her.

Natalie walked away, needing time alone to think. And plan.

Not that her other plan had worked so well. But when it came to apologies, "I'm sorry" wasn't going to cut it this time. Not if Cody didn't even want to speak to her.

And then there was Summer. Her sister.

Until now, she hadn't really thought of her in that way. Summer had been a nuisance. An unwelcome disruption. And yes, in Natalie's eyes, a rival.

But to Cody, she'd been the woman he couldn't resist. The one who made him happy.

And though Natalie didn't want to admit it, a good sister. She'd helped Natalie pick out that killer dress. She'd helped Natalie study for finals. She didn't freak out when Natalie took her car. She didn't even make a huge deal out of Natalie not taking her to the hospital after it turned into a big thing. She praised Natalie for calling for help instead of lecturing her about being drunk.

She'd even encouraged Natalie to take her photography seriously as a career path. Natalie probably wouldn't have even thought about it. Now, it's all she thought about.

Well, besides Cody.

The embarrassment came back in a wash of heat to her face and anxious butterflies in her belly. She felt so foolish for sneaking into his room. He'd barely spared her a split-second look before he turned away and never looked at her again.

She'd tried to be bold.

She wanted to believe that if Summer hadn't come home and walked in on them, something totally different would have happened last night.

But the reality of it was that her mom and Brooke were right. Cody would never cheat on anyone, even for her. And she'd hurt him so deeply he didn't want to speak to her right now.

Maybe ever.

Her heart broke all over again.

I need to fix this.

She just wished she knew how.

Chapter Forty-Six

Summer overheard Brooke talking to Natalie. She'd also been surprised to see the doors closed, but understood Brooke's desire to protect Cody from another ambush.

He'd been up early and out the door this morning before anyone else in the house stirred.

She didn't blame him. Truth be told, she was still too angry to talk to Natalie reasonably and rationally.

But that didn't stop her from getting up and walking over to Miranda's kitchen. Miranda stood by the windows facing the ocean, a quiet, thoughtful look on her face.

"Is everything okay?"

Miranda's lips scrunched. "It's hard to answer that. What happened last night . . ." Miranda turned and faced her with a frown. "It shouldn't have happened. She crossed a line. But I also understand why she did it."

"I do, too. Love can make people impulsive."

Miranda gave a sharp, single nod. "She didn't think it through."

"I imagine she's embarrassed and maybe a little scared that Cody won't forgive her and things will be different now."

"They are different now." Miranda caught herself after that sharp retort and took a calming breath. "They're different because you're here."

Summer wasn't sure she liked this change in direction, or that Miranda seemed to be blaming her for sparking Natalie's escapade last night. "What exactly are you saying?"

"I'm happy that Nate has this chance to get to know you. I hoped the girls would see you not as a rival, but as someone they could look up to and be friends with because you were already grown and not going to change their lives here. I guess I was naïve in thinking that."

"You don't see me as someone they can look up to and be friends with?"

Miranda caught herself again. "Yes. Of course, I do. It's just, your being here upsets Natalie. Look at what she's done. If not for you being here, being with Cody right here in this house with two impressionable teenage girls . . ."

"Cody and I have never flaunted our relationship, nor have we been inappropriate around any of you. In fact, we've gone out of our way to be discreet because of how Natalie feels. So much so that Cody was the one who came to me upset that I was holding back being affectionate with him in even the simplest way because I was trying to spare Natalie's feelings."

Miranda sighed. "I appreciate that. I do. But Natalie is sensitive. Especially when it comes to Cody."

"You've seen how Natalie feels about him, yet you've let it go on."

Miranda narrowed her gaze. "Maybe it's time for you to return home and give Natalie some space to work this out with Cody."

Of course, the mama bear in her wanted to protect her child, Summer thought.

Miranda continued, "They've been friends practically their whole lives. I don't want to see them torn apart over this. And I fear that with you here, Natalie will do something more drastic to get his attention."

The hurtful words made Summer's heart ache. "So instead of making Natalie see that what she's doing is wrong, you want me to leave, so she can have Cody all to herself."

"Yes," Miranda said. "It will give them a chance to mend this. Natalie is in a vulnerable state right now. She's hurting."

What about me?

Miranda wasn't concerned about her. She wasn't concerned about how Cody would feel if Summer left. Miranda just wanted her daughter to be happy again.

Summer had done the whole make-everyone-else-happy thing her whole life and it had gotten her nowhere.

"Did it ever occur to you that Cody would leave with me?"

Miranda folded her arms over her chest. "He'd stay if I ask him to."

That's how insignificant I am. She asks, and Cody stays. That's what Miranda thinks.

"You and your daughter have a lot in common. You both think putting Cody on the spot will get you what you want because he's such a good guy and he loves you and wants to make you happy. You're asking him to choose between me and you, just like she did last night."

That caught Miranda off guard. She seemed to realize she'd spoken without thinking things through.

"Well, I'm sorry," Summer went on, "but I'm not willing to do that to him. No. I won't leave. Cody and I have been making plans for when I have to go back to Texas, and I'm not changing them because you want to blame me for what Natalie did and make things easier on her by not having me standing by Cody's side when she apologizes to him."

"I'm trying to find a simple way to fix this, so that no one else gets hurt."

"But it's okay if I'm hurt by you asking me to leave."

"I'm asking you to be the bigger person and give Natalie some space and time with Cody to fix things."

"If I do that, then I'm hurting not just Cody, but Dad, too. I promised him I'd stay the six weeks. We've gotten so close."

"Of course, he'll miss you. So will Cody. But you'll be back. I'm not saying forever. I'm just saying for right now."

Summer shook her head. "No. I'm not ready to leave. Especially when things are the way they are between me and Natalie. I want to fix that just as much as I want her to fix things with Cody."

The look on Miranda's face spoke volumes. She didn't believe that would happen.

Summer turned and walked away, feeling like all the ground she'd gained cultivating a relationship with Miranda meant nothing when her heart and dedication was with her girls and didn't include Summer. Miranda would choose her family, even Cody and Brooke, over Summer.

She went back to the office with a heavy heart to work on the acquisition she hoped would be an answer to some of the issues she and Cody faced.

He called her two hours later, and she picked up on the first ring.

"I've been thinking about you all day," she confessed. In between reading financial reports and market analyses, her mind kept going back to him.

"Same," he said. "I'm outside. Want to go for a drive, get an early dinner, maybe make out on the beach?"

Yes, her heart shouted. "Only if you turn that maybe into a definitely."

"I like the way you think."

"Will there also be wine?" She could use a drink.

"Absolutely. Come and get me."

She was already around the desk and headed for the front door. "Did you have a good day?"

"No. I wasn't with you. Hurry up."

She giggled because he had to see her rushing down the path to his car. "Impatient much?"

"You look amazing and I want to kiss you."

She pulled open the car door as he leaned over to her side. She met him for that kiss. The second his lips pressed to hers, they both moaned in sheer pleasure and relief to be so close again.

He slipped his hand up to her cheek and into her hair. "I missed you."

She slid into her seat. "Missed you more."

Cody grinned, kissed her again, then put the car in gear, hit the gas, and they sped off down the driveway ready for a good time together.

Away from everyone else.

She knew that's why he hadn't come into the house.

"Cody."

He put his hand on her thigh. "Yeah, sweetheart."

She wanted to tell him about what Miranda had said and asked of her, but kept it to herself because she didn't want to upset him more. "I'm glad you came home early."

"I wanted to surprise you."

She grinned at him. "It was a nice surprise."

"There's another for you in the back seat."

She turned and spotted the huge bouquet of red roses. "They're lovely. Thank you."

"I just wanted to see you smile."

"I do every time I look at or think about you."

He squeezed her thigh. "There's this taqueria down the road. It's got the best food. Plus we can walk down to the beach and eat tacos on the sand and watch the ocean for a while if you want."

"That sounds perfect."

An hour later they were sipping sangria from takeout soda cups through straws, with their toes in the sand, taco wrappers stuffed in a bag as the seagulls called out overhead and the ocean crashed against the beach in front of them.

They didn't talk much, sitting next to each other, her arm wrapped through his, her head on his shoulder.

Her phone broke the peaceful atmosphere.

Cody glanced at the incoming text. "Your mom again?"

"Haley." Summer sat up straight, her eyes locked on the message.

HALEY: Come home. Your mom is here! Dad is not happy.

"Oh, shit. We have to go home. Now!" Summer scrambled up and grabbed the garbage bag, her purse, and cup on the go.

"What's the rush?"

"My mother is at the house."

"Okay."

"With Nate."

"Oh, shit." Cody swiveled and stood at the same time to run after her.

If her mother was in town, guarantee, this was going to go bad. Very bad.

Chapter Forty-Seven

Summer and Cody heard raised voices the second they opened the front door and headed toward the Weston family living room.

"I'm taking her home," her mother said.

"Summer's a grown woman. She can make her own decisions," Nate shot back. "And anyway, she's better off here than with you."

"That's not true. You've met her, you spent time with her. Now it's time for her to return to her real life."

"She has a life here with us, too," Nate snapped.

"I gave her everything you couldn't. She's going to run Sutherland Industries soon. That's her legacy."

"A company isn't what she needed. She needed her father," Miranda pointed out, surprisingly standing up for Summer.

Though maybe it was more that she was taking Nate's side, Summer thought cynically.

"She's done quite well without him." Jessica always lashed out when confronted with uncomfortable truths, like the fact that Summer had wanted and needed her father her whole life.

"How could you do this?" It sounded like her dad had asked that more than once and not gotten an answer that made sense. Because what her mother had done was wrong and inexcusable.

"I was eighteen. A kid. I made stupid mistakes. And I've paid for them."

Summer glimpsed Natalie just inside the room, looking like she could relate to Jessica in this moment.

"She won't speak to me." Sadness filled her mother's voice. "She came home to help her grandfather, but left before we could speak."

Summer walked into the room with Cody by her side. "I left without seeing you because my anger is unrelenting and my feelings are too raw. And I wanted to be here." At the sound of her voice, everyone in her family turned to her.

"Your life is not here." Jessica gave her a pointed look.

Summer wasn't a child anymore, and she'd grown past the point of capitulating to her mother. "My life is where I say it is." She shook her head, disheartened that her mother came all this way, knowing there was a fight waiting for her. "Why would you come here like this, just to upset everyone?"

"Because *I'm* upset. My daughter won't answer my calls. You don't respond to any of my texts. Your grandfather calls and asks you to come home and you're on a plane, there and gone, without ever giving me a chance to explain."

Her dad sank his teeth into that. "Please explain to me why you didn't tell me we had a daughter, without giving me that bullshit line that I didn't have the means to care for her. I may not have had the financial resources you do, but I would have done what I could and certainly loved her better than you ever did. I would have given her stability and a family like she wanted."

Her mother's arms went rigid at her sides. "She had everything she needed."

"Except me!" Raw pain filled those words.

Summer appreciated that he stood up for her and his rights, but it was all for naught. "I'm a grown woman now. I make the decisions in my life. I get to decide where I am and where I want to be and with whom."

Her dad took a breath and nodded, knowing she meant those sentiments for him, too.

She looked her mom in the eye. "I told you I was taking six weeks to be here with my family. I needed time away from you and the company and to just get to know them. I needed to figure out who I am now with all of them as a part of my life."

Jessica held her arm out toward the foyer. "You've done that, but now it's time to return to reality."

That set Summer's back teeth to grinding.

"Reality," Nate scoffed. "The reality is you kept us apart for no good reason. Even worse, you did it because you were selfish. You're a coward. You knew she'd hate you for what you did."

"She doesn't hate me."

"You're delusional, too." Miranda rolled her eyes. "You thought you could get away with this, that Nate would never find out about her."

"He wouldn't have if my father hadn't meddled." The haughty look on her mother's face grated.

Even worse was the pain of knowing her mother really didn't want Summer to know the truth and be with Nate.

"Thank god he did," Nate snapped. "At least Charles had a conscience. You don't care who you hurt, including your own daughter."

"That's not true. I gave her the best of everything."

"And yet she's lived her whole life feeling less than and unhappy."

Wow. Was that how her father saw her? Was that how they all saw her?

Her mother wiped that away with a wave of her hand. "You barely know her."

"And whose fault is that?" Miranda cut in, her dad nodding.

"What's done is done. I didn't come here to defend my choices. I came to collect my daughter."

"You could at least apologize," Nate interjected.

Her mother held her hands up, a diamond tennis bracelet sparkling along with the gigantic wedding ring, and something came over her that changed her expression to one Summer had never seen. Contrition. "There isn't a word for how sorry I am."

Summer felt her mother's deep remorse and saw it written all over her face.

The atmosphere in the room changed.

"I never intended to hurt Summer, or you. I simply wanted to leave the past in the past and move on with Summer. Do you have any idea what it's like to carry the mistake you made at eighteen year after year? How hard it is to look into your daughter's eyes and not be able to give her the one thing she wants because it means disappointing her again?" She met Nate's intense gaze. "You want to make me pay for what I did? Believe me, there isn't a day that goes by that I don't think about it and what I've done. I've had to bear Summer's discontent for a long time, knowing I'm the one who caused it."

"Yet you didn't do anything to assuage your guilt or make our daughter feel better by telling me about her, because you don't think about anyone but yourself."

"If that's how you feel, then I guess you understand this wasn't personal."

Nate took a step toward her mother. "Oh, this is very personal, Jessica. You thought I was beneath you. You thought I didn't matter. You thought I wouldn't want my own daughter. You thought because I didn't have money I didn't have anything to offer her. But the deeper truth is that you feared she'd rather be with me than you because I know how to love someone and you don't. So go back to Texas. Enjoy your money and your new husband while he lasts and before you go looking for another dead-end relationship, because who could love someone who doesn't love you back." Nate's words hit home.

Jessica put her hand to her chest, frowned, and quickly hid the hurt in her eyes, then went on the defensive again. "Oh, I'm leaving and I'm taking Summer with me."

"No, you're not," Nate snapped.

"You can't just take her away from Nate again," Miranda said over Nate.

Natalie spoke her mind into the din, telling Summer, "Maybe you should go."

Miranda heard and added, "This mess is getting even worse. Our daughter was half naked in Cody's bed, throwing herself at him because of you."

"You did what?" Haley's eyes rounded with shock.

"Stay out of it." Natalie glared at her sister, then turned to Miranda. "How could you just blurt that out?"

Nate cut off whatever Miranda was about to say. "We'll talk about this later."

Haley stared wide-eyed at the scene, sadness and worry in her eyes.

Summer felt for her youngest sister. This had turned to chaos with everyone's emotions so high.

"You can't have her," Jessica shouted at Nate.

He shouted right back. "You can't make her go."

Cody stepped forward. "Enough!"

Nate turned to him, then looked at Summer, regret and remorse in his eyes. "I think we all need to take a moment."

Cody agreed. "This whole thing has gotten out of hand." Cody raked his fingers through his hair and met Summer's gaze. "What's happening here? This isn't right. People yelling at each other. Your mom wants you home, Natalie wants you gone, your grandfather wants you in the office."

"Miranda asked me to leave this morning," she blurted out, her heart still aching because of it.

Nate glared at Miranda. "You did what?" He held his arms out, gave her a what-the-hell look, then dropped them. "How could you?"

Miranda tried to explain. "Nate, I'm sorry, but ever since she got here, Natalie has been acting out."

The pain and worry in Cody's eyes held her attention. "How did it come to this? Everyone upset . . ."

Because of her, Summer filled in, her heart sinking.

Because Summer and Cody were together, Summer wasn't in Texas where her mom and grandfather wanted her, Natalie was heartbroken, and Miranda wanted her gone.

Miranda put her hand on Nate's arm, imploring him to understand. "I just wanted a little time without Summer here, so we could sort this out."

"She's right," Cody said, shocking not just Summer, but Nate, too, judging by the look on his face. "This has to stop before it gets any worse."

Those words hit Summer like a sledgehammer to the chest. She stiffened her knees to catch herself before she crumbled and gave in to the pain. Every heartbeat punched against her ribs. She tried to breathe, but it felt too hard to fill her lungs past the lump in her throat.

And with the pain came anger that he'd say something like that to her after all they'd shared and promised each other.

It hurt so much she didn't know what to do with all the turmoil inside her.

"This is too much," Cody said. "We don't yell in this house. We don't fight like this. We don't hurt each other." He'd had enough.

That hurt even more.

Miranda looked at Summer with her thoughts so clear in her

eyes and face. Like Cody, she blamed Summer for this strife, just like she blamed Summer for what Natalie had done.

All this friction because Summer had come and changed things.

Cody's gaze held a plea. He hated that his family was in upheaval. He needed the return of the safety and sanctuary of this home and the family he'd known all these years.

Summer loved him, so she took control, despite how her heart was breaking, and gave him what he wanted. "Mom, you had no right to come here uninvited, especially when you knew your presence would only result in this."

"I just wanted to see you."

Summer shook her head. "You want me to forgive you the way I always do, without any real consequences for what you've done. You want me to love you more than I love Dad and appreciate the life you gave me because you want to think you gave me the perfect life. But you didn't. Though it is nice to hear that you actually do feel guilty about it. I appreciate that you apologized to Dad. But it's not enough, and you know it. You're going to have to earn it."

"I am sorry, sweetheart." Her mother really meant it this time.

Summer needed time to let it sink in and settle, because there was a lot more going on here than just her mother's betrayal.

She looked at the rest of them. "I get that you all think my coming here is what caused all this trouble."

"That's not true," Nate said, a plea in his eyes to believe that.

"Miranda thinks so." She turned to her stepmother. "You actually asked me to leave, thinking that would make everything go back to normal." She turned to Natalie. "You think I'm trying to take everything from you. The spotlight. Dad. Haley. Most of all, Cody. You've faked an ankle injury, reminded Cody every chance you get that I'm leaving, playing into his fear that someone he cares about will leave him again like his mother did, like Amy did. And when that wasn't working fast enough to get him to back off, you snuck into his bed to show him who really cares about him. The one who's here, because you thought my leaving to attend a meeting in Texas proved your point so well. You're probably plotting right now how you can turn this to your advantage, too."

Natalie shook her head, her eyes filled with remorse. "I'm not. I swear."

Summer didn't believe her.

She turned to Cody. "She doesn't have to do anything this time, though, because all those things you said to me: We're in this together. We'll find a way to make it work. That the thing you never thought you'd find was right in front of you.

"You meant them as long as this was easy and I was here. The second I left town, you had doubts. I wasn't even gone a day."

Cody winced.

She let the rest fall from her lips. "Today, the family is upset once again, and your first instinct is to say we should take a step back. Like that will make this all go away. I have felt alone and out of place my whole life, but never so much as you made me feel right now." She looked at all of them. "You want a moment, you can have it without me taking up space, your time, being in the way, or asking you to believe that I just wanted to be a part of your lives, to be included like I belonged.

"But now I see it, the truth is so obvious. I don't." She turned to Haley. "Except with Dad and you." She went to Haley. "Thank you for taking me into your heart with acceptance and love. You are so special. I love you so much." She turned to the rest of them. "I love all of you. But as usual, that's not enough."

She turned and headed back to the foyer.

"Summer, wait," Cody called out. "Don't leave like this."

"Go ahead and blame me for leaving, but you're the one who pressed stop on all those plans we talked about."

Cody held his hands out wide. "Look at what's happening here."

She turned to him and spilled the truth he didn't want to admit. "Yes. Look what happened. My mother had a long-overdue argument with my father. Natalie hurt you, but I'm the one Miranda blamed and asked to leave. In this chaos that could all be worked out with cooler heads, you found a path to leave me before I can leave you because, let's face it, that's what you're always expecting will happen. None of what happened tonight would have changed us or the way I feel about you, but you somehow think it does. You love your family. I've seen it every day that I've been here. I get that you don't want to lose that and you want them all to be happy always. I just wish that included me."

"It does."

"If it did, you wouldn't need to step back and take that moment. You said you'd always say what you mean. I heard you. I'll give you what you want."

"What about the deal?" her dad asked. The one Cody knew nothing about. And now never would.

"What's the point?" she asked her father, knowing he'd understand. "Thank you for these last few weeks. I've really loved getting to know you. This isn't the end. It just can't be like this, here. I'll call you."

"This is your home," he reminded her.

"I know you want it to be. That will have to be enough for me." She walked out, knowing no one was coming after her, but hoping someone would.

And that someone was the bravest of them all.

Haley rushed out to the driveway just as Summer opened her car door. She threw her arms around Summer and held on for dear life. "Please don't go."

Summer held her sister and kissed her on the head. "I just can't be here right now. But I'll come back to see you. You'll come see me."

"We'll go to your house in Wyoming, like you said." Tears filled Haley's eyes and clogged her throat.

"Someday. I promise." In fact, that sounded like the perfect place to spend the next couple of days collecting herself before she returned to work and went on with the life she'd been given, even if it wasn't exactly the life she wanted. Because Cody wasn't in it anymore. And the love and family and life she thought she'd build with him remained a dream while reality broke her heart yet again.

Chapter Forty-Eight

Cody stared toward the entrance to the foyer, shell-shocked and confused. *What the hell just happened?*

He must have said it out loud, because Jessica answered. "They say we pick partners who are like our parents. In this case, Summer chose someone who is so very much like me."

He did not want to be compared to her in any way, shape, or form. He was nothing like her.

And then she proved him wrong. "You don't want to get hurt, so you don't trust, but you so desperately want to be loved. And you love her. But you've loved all of them longer. You don't want to lose them, so you cut Summer loose, because you know they'll always be here for you. They've proven that, and you're still wondering if Summer will choose her life in Texas over you. Which proves you haven't been paying attention, otherwise you'd see it's the people in Summer's life who mean everything to her. The rest . . . the job, the money, the properties, here or there or anywhere . . . it's just stuff. But the people she cares about . . . they're everything to her. She would do anything for them. Even forgive me for being a bad mother. She loved you even though you were waiting for her to choose a job when she always chose you.

"She read you like a book. And you did what she expected you to do but hoped with her whole heart that you wouldn't. You chose everyone else, instead of her. Not even, *and her*. You disappointed her. Worse, you hurt her. Believe me, I know how deep that cuts because you really do care about her, it's just you're more concerned about yourself."

"Stop talking." He meant it to sound like an order, but it came out more like a plea.

"The truth hurts. I know. She throws it in my face all the time. I can't seem to help myself and the things I do, though I really do try. She knows that. But it doesn't erase what I've done."

"No, it doesn't," Nate interjected. "Just tell me why?"

Jessica shrugged a shoulder. "The same reason he let her walk out of here. I loved you. I didn't want you to see that I didn't deserve the way you loved me, so I left before you left me."

Cody swore under his breath. He hated that she was right.

He'd spent his whole young life thinking his mother left him because he hadn't been good enough, worthy enough for her to stay. Then he'd worked his ass off to prove her wrong, doing well in school, being the best at sports, taking over where his father left off at the company, working hard to not just earn his spot but prove to everyone that he had what it took to take the company to greater heights.

And when he'd failed at his relationship with Amy, he'd kept things casual with other women so he didn't have to feel that failure again, that he wasn't good enough to hold on to. So long as he kept things simple, women adored him. They thought he was smart and funny and charming, and he always aimed to please in bed. He never left a woman thinking he wasn't a good guy.

He was upfront with them about this just being fun while it lasted. He had other priorities. Work. Family. The long term was for later.

But Summer had been different. From the beginning, he'd been clear with her that he wanted more. He told her she was the one he wanted. He wanted to be her everything, but wondered if her job and life in Texas appealed to her more.

And tonight, instead of stopping the arguing and telling everyone to remember that Summer hadn't asked for any of this and just wanted her time with her dad and space from her mom until she was ready to forgive and move on, he'd done what they all did and blamed her for the discord.

If she wasn't here, none of this would have happened.

And because she was here, he'd learned that he could care about someone so much that even the thought of losing her made him crazy and say and do stupid things. And lose her.

He was so afraid of getting his heart broken again, he broke hers instead.

He ran from the room, into the foyer, and out the open front door to the driveway where Haley stood, tears streaming down her cheeks. "Where is she?"

"She left."

"Where did she go?"

"I don't know."

"Did she say she's coming back?"

Haley turned on him, her arms rigid, hands fisted. "Why would she?" Haley glared at him. "I thought you loved her."

"I do," he said, without even thinking about it.

He'd never said it to Summer, though.

He'd held that back. Another useless way to protect himself.

Because if he had told her, maybe she'd believe it. Maybe she'd have stayed after she called him out on his bullshit, the way she had with Natalie, understanding where the bad behavior came from and giving him a chance to do and be better.

What the hell did he just do?

He pulled out his phone and called her. Voice mail. He hung up, then turned and found Haley walking into the foyer, her shoulders slumped.

He ran back inside and found Jessica on her way out. "Where would she go?"

She shrugged nonchalantly. "Where can't she go?"

That stunned him.

She had properties all over the world. She had the money to live anywhere she wanted for the rest of her life without having to work.

She could literally give up her job and life here and build a new one somewhere else. Or everywhere else.

She could get on a plane, find that island with a warm beach, cold drinks, and no phones . . . and someone else.

He turned and walked away.

Jessica would be no help to him.

Summer didn't want anything to do with either of them.

He passed the room where she still kept her clothes, even though she'd been sleeping with him. He'd never offered her space in his closet, not even a drawer in his dresser. She didn't even shower in his bathroom. All her stuff was in that room. Separate from his.

How could he let her light up every inch inside him yet never give her any space around him?

They talked about how they'd spend time here and in Texas. She'd talked about him moving his stuff into the master suite at her condo in Texas. Yet if she left a sweater in his room, he returned it to her room downstairs.

Now he didn't have to wonder why she stopped leaving things in his room.

He walked down the hall and looked in at the office and all her files stacked on the credenza he never used, not left on his desk, even though he hardly worked from home since she got here.

Without even saying anything, he'd somehow conveyed very

clearly that he didn't want her stuff in his space, even as he tried to convince her he wanted her. She'd become so adept at reading people and how they felt about her, she'd seen the conflicting messages he sent her without being conscious of it.

She never said anything, but he knew she hoped in time he'd change.

He hadn't. Not in time to stop this from happening.

He went up to his room, slammed and locked the door. He didn't bother to turn on the lights. He let the deafening quiet surround him.

He could smell her in here. The soft floral scent of her perfume. Sweet and light, it hung in the air. He bet he'd smell it on the sheets. But he couldn't look at the bed where they'd made love and slept together.

He didn't want to be reminded of Natalie's stunt, either.

He wanted Summer back so bad he felt the need of it in every cell of his body and aching beat of his heart.

He had no idea how to accomplish that when he'd fucked up so spectacularly by not putting her first, by not choosing her above everything else.

It had to be devastating to see her parents fighting like that. He couldn't imagine how she felt about Miranda asking her to leave. She hadn't even told him about that. Probably because she'd been consoling him over what Natalie did.

She put him first. She picked him over everything.

He hadn't meant to hurt Summer. He'd just wanted everyone to have some time to settle down and get back to normal. But how could they when Summer had changed things?

For him, for the better. He liked his new normal with her.

And still he'd sacrificed it for a peace that wouldn't come without her, because if she wasn't here, how could anything be resolved between any of them?

How could he breathe easy again without her?

She left him because he'd proven he wasn't good enough for her. He pushed her right out the door. Because why would she stay with someone who didn't try each and every day to show her she was wanted and needed and everything to him?

She put her heart on the line, wanting so desperately for him to be the one who never disappointed her the way her mother and grandfather did.

He was just like them.

But he wanted to be better. He wanted to make it up to her. But how? He had no idea where she'd go, or whom she'd turn to.

Well, that wasn't exactly true. She had Nate, Haley, and her grandfather. She had friends. But somehow, he'd gotten lucky enough to be the one she counted on most.

They'd built their relationship on the understanding that they'd both been hurt by their parents and had trouble trusting others. He swore to always tell her the truth, but he never told her the one thing she deserved to hear.

Now it might be too late.

Would she ever believe him again?

He grabbed the bottle of whiskey and took a swig. The burn down his throat was nothing compared to the ache in his chest.

He stared at the ocean view he loved so much and wished he was staring at Summer's beautiful face instead, seeing the joy in her eyes when she smiled at him, because she was always happy to see him.

The ache got worse and so he drank more, hoping to dull the pain that would never leave as long as Summer wasn't with him.

A knock sounded on the door.

"Go away," he barked.

"It's me," Brooke said. "I heard what happened. Let's talk."

"Not now. Just leave me alone."

"Cody," she begged.

He turned and shouted over his shoulder, "Just go!"

He'd screwed up and hated himself for it. He felt as if he had no reason to do anything anymore, not if it meant not having Summer by his side.

But maybe if he drank a little more, maybe he wouldn't feel anything at all for a while. Because this heartache, pain, and misery sucked. And he had nobody to blame for it and the impending hangover but himself.

$\mathcal{S}$ummer called Lucy as soon as she left the house.

"Do you know what time it is in Monte Carlo?"

"It was about six forty-five when Cody imploded our relationship." Summer hit the highway going north to the San Jose airport.

Lucy paused for a second. "I'm sorry, what?"

Summer's tears made it impossible to talk.

"Okay. You need to take a breath and tell me what happened."

Summer could barely see or catch her breath. She turned off the main highway onto a side road that ran along huge produce fields. She stopped the car next to a sign that had the name of an artichoke producer. Sure enough, the dark green, sharp-leafed plants in the nearby field had fat artichokes topping them.

"You need to talk to me, Summer." Lucy's concern had turned to a desperate plea.

"My mother showed up."

"Oh, well, that's all you needed to say. What chaos and pain has she wrought this time?"

"The usual. She demanded I go home to Texas with her. She fought with my dad about what happened."

"You mean what she did."

"Yes. But then she stopped all the excuses, let her defenses down, and she apologized."

"Like, a real one?" Lucy sounded as surprised as Summer had been.

"Yeah. I really felt it."

"Well, that's something. But it doesn't tell me why Cody broke up with you. Not after you two seemed so solid after what happened with Natalie."

"Well, that all got more complicated when Miranda asked me to leave."

"What? Why? That wasn't your fault."

Summer filled Lucy in about her conversation with Miranda, the fight between her mom and dad, how Miranda had actually stood up for her during it, how things got out of control and everyone was yelling. And how Cody thought they all needed some space and time to work things out.

"What the fuck?" Lucy huffed. "Nothing can be solved if you're not there."

"Exactly." Summer raked her fingers through her hair. "But Miranda, Natalie, and Cody were all ready to blame me for the strife when all I did was try to be included in their lives. I didn't mean for any of this to happen."

"Of course you didn't. Do you really think Cody wants to end things? I really thought, based on everything you told me about him and your relationship, that he really loved you."

He'd never said it. Then again, neither had she. But she'd felt it.

He'd made it so clear to her in the way he opened up to her, the things he said, the plans they'd made.

While she had been talking to Lucy, Cody had called her . . . and then the text messages started coming in.

CODY: Come home. Please. Please. Please.

CODY: I'm sorry.

CODY: I messed up.

CODY: I need to see you. There's something I need to tell you.

CODY: Please come home.

Summer wiped away a fresh wave of tears. There were a lot of "pleases" in those texts, but what she loved most was that he asked her to come home, meaning to him.

So she did.

She turned the car around and got back on the highway headed back into Carmel. She berated herself for doing exactly what her mother always did, running away instead of facing a problem head-on. That wasn't Summer's way, yet she'd walked out instead of claiming her place in the family and in Cody's life. She let him drive her away when she knew deep down that was not what he wanted.

He was scared.

And now that she'd called him out on it, he regretted it.

"What were those noises? Is he calling you?" Lucy asked.

"He texted me and asked me to come home."

"You bet your ass you're going back, so he can apologize and you two can work this out, because I've never heard you this happy about anyone. You knew this wasn't going to be easy—nothing is—but what you two have is worth fighting for."

"I know that. And I'm pretty sure that's how he feels, too."

"Good. But you should still make him grovel."

Summer found a smile and a laugh. "I just want him."

"You deserve to be happy. I think if you two work this out, with him, you will be."

"You are the best friend I could ever have."

"I know. Right back at you."

"Love you, Luc."

"Love you back, babe." They ended the call, Summer knowing that no matter what, Lucy always had her back.

Summer couldn't wait to see Cody, but she also wanted to reconcile with Miranda and Natalie and see if there was a way for them to finally come together as a family.

Chapter Fifty

*N*ate stared at his wife and two daughters, completely taken aback by what had just happened. He read the worry in Miranda's eyes. He hated to see Haley so distraught, tears rolling down her cheeks. Natalie folded her arms across her chest, looking defiant but also remorseful.

And then there was Jessica. She stared back at him, regal as always, but the pain and sadness got to him, despite his best efforts to remain angry.

Summer didn't need that added turmoil in her life.

Maybe Jessica understood that her string of bad decisions had culminated with Summer not feeling like she belonged with either of them, and that's not what Jessica ever wanted.

Jessica breathed in, then simply said what he needed to hear. "'I'm sorry' will never be enough, Nate. I know what I did. I know what it cost you. There were a thousand different moments where I could have told her the truth, and all those moments were when I thought to myself, *If only Nate were here to see this*." Tears rolled down her cheeks unchecked. "I don't expect you to forgive me. I don't deserve it. I know you love her. I know I kept that from her, just as I kept her from you. I wish I could go back and change it. I didn't do it out of malice. It's just . . . I made a stupid decision, and then things went too far and it felt like I couldn't turn back. By the time I was older, wiser, but still so scared of losing her, I felt like I couldn't fix it. I felt like you'd take her and she wouldn't want to be with me anymore. That was the lie I told myself. Because that's not true. We can love more than one person."

"I know what you mean," Natalie interjected.

Nate stared at his daughter, who held Jessica's gaze.

Natalie turned to him and Miranda. "I thought she'd take Cody and he wouldn't love us anymore. I didn't want to lose him, so I did something stupid and thoughtless and I pushed him away all on my own. I didn't mean it." Tears streaked down her face.

Haley, always the loving one, went to her sister and wrapped her in her arms.

Jessica met his gaze again. "There's a lot of love here, Nate. She needs this. She needs you. I'm so sorry. I'll leave you with your beautiful family." She headed for the door.

Nate called out, "Jessica, wait."

She turned to him.

"I accept your apology. I hope that in the future when we're together to support our daughter, we'll be able to do so as her mom and dad without animosity and with all the love and pride we have for her."

Jessica smiled. "I'd like that." She gave a regal nod, turned, and left them.

Nate wondered what happened to Cody, though he could probably guess Cody was locked away on the other side of the house, also trying to figure out how this night ended with Summer walking out the door.

And Nate had a good idea how it started and turned to Miranda. "What were you thinking asking Summer to leave? You blamed her for Natalie's behavior. You made her feel unwelcome here."

"I made a mistake," Miranda confessed. "I'm sorry. Like Cody, I just wanted all the trouble to cease and for things to go back to normal."

"So she leaves, then what? Natalie doesn't have an opportunity to own up to what she did and apologize to Summer, so they can work it out. How does that help things?"

Natalie stepped away from Haley. "I will apologize to her and Cody. I see now that what I did was all about me and what I wanted. I never took into account how it would make Cody feel. Or Summer. I never really gave her a chance, but she was always nice to me anyway."

"Because you're my sister," Summer said, walking into the room. "And I love you. But you can be a spoiled brat." Summer's eyes softened and a slight grin tugged at her lips, showing that while those words were true, she didn't mean them to hurt Natalie.

Haley ran to Summer and threw her arms around her. "You came back."

"I don't like the way I left things. I needed a minute to calm down." Nate stared at her. "We all did."

Miranda stepped forward. "Summer, I owe you a huge apology. I'm so sorry. I never should have asked you to leave. You were right. Nate and I should have addressed Natalie's feelings for Cody in a more direct manner before things went too far."

Summer pressed her lips tight. "Cody should have done the same." She turned to Natalie. "Everyone in this family loves you so much, none of them want to upset or hurt you. I don't want to do that, either, and I know that my presence here threw you. But what you did to Cody and me, it hurt, most especially because you're my sister and I want us to be not just close, but best friends."

Natalie's eyes teared up again. "If you'll give me another chance, I'd like that very much. And I want you to know, I am truly sorry for what I did."

"I know you are."

"And I want you to know that, yes, my feelings for Cody run deep, but I understand now that they aren't the same kind of feelings you two share. I'm sorry if I messed that up for you."

"Cody and I will work out our issues together. That's what couples do," Summer added, making it clear that she and Cody were together and Natalie needed to stay out of it.

Nate opened his arms to Summer.

She closed the distance and walked right into them.

"I love you." He kissed her on the side of the head. "Please say you'll stay a little longer. If it helps, your mother and I came to an amicable understanding."

Summer leaned back. "I'm happy to hear that. But first, I need to talk to Cody."

Chapter Fifty-One

Cody hadn't moved from his spot on the floor, back against the bed, his view of the ocean doing nothing to ease him as he held his phone to his chest, hoping and praying Summer either walked in the door or at the very least texted him back. He'd given up drinking three swigs in. The booze helped numb some of the anxiety, but not the heartache.

God, how could he be so stupid and thoughtless and reckless with his relationship?

Time apart only made him want her more.

He should have said what he really meant, and that was that everyone who thought Summer was to blame for anything needed a reality check.

Well, Summer had given them all one.

Natalie needed to grow up. Miranda and Nate needed to stop coddling Natalie. Jessica needed to take responsibility and show a little more remorse for her actions. She also needed to give Summer the time and space she needed to find her way to forgiveness. Because it would come in time. Summer had a good heart. She loved her mother despite all of Jessica's many flaws.

He hoped Summer forgave him, too.

In his heart, he knew she would, but the waiting was killing him.

Someone pounded on his door again.

Hoping it was Summer, he jumped up, caught his balance—maybe he did have a bit too much to drink—and rushed to the door, unlocking it and throwing it wide. The smile about to cross his face dipped into a frown. "Go away," he grumbled, trying to close the door on Natalie.

She shoved it open and grinned from ear to ear. "She's here. She's downstairs. Come on." She waved him forward. When he didn't move, she grabbed his hand and pulled. "What are you waiting for? Go get her back!"

He stumbled forward and caught his footing, walking with Natalie. "Why are you doing this? You hate that we're together."

Natalie stopped in her tracks in the middle of the hallway and gave him a sad look. "I'm sorry about what I did. I didn't think it through. I didn't think about how you'd feel. Or how she'd feel. I just . . . care about you so much. I want you to be happy. And maybe I got a little mixed up about things. Because I saw how happy you were with her and it kind of felt like you picked her over me. And I know that's stupid and childish—and then I acted that way." Her gaze went to the floor. "I can't stop thinking about it. Who does something like that? Throwing themselves at another person?" Tears gathered in her eyes. "I can't believe I did that."

"Now you know you'll never do it again. Because if someone really likes you in that way, you don't need to go to that extreme."

Her mouth twisted. "I know that now."

"Then be grateful you learned that lesson with me and not some jerk who'd throw it in your face or tell his buddies or something."

She nodded, remorse in her eyes. "I lost my head and got jealous. I hope you can forgive me one day, because I know you love Summer."

"I do. More than anything, I need her to know that she can

count on me and trust me to always be there for her. And I didn't do that for her tonight."

"Everyone makes mistakes. She'll forgive you. She loves you. She knows you love her. She wants to please everyone, but most of all, she wants to make you happy, because you make her feel that way." Natalie frowned, then grinned at him. "You two really are meant for each other."

"And how does that make you feel?"

"Like I want someone to look at me the way you look at her."

Cody hooked his arm around her shoulders and pulled her in for a hug. "I want that for you, too, Nat. You deserve that and more. Never settle for anything less."

Natalie pushed him away. "Go. Hurry up. Don't keep her waiting."

"I don't even know what to say."

"Yes, you do. It's just three words. But they mean everything."

Cody rushed past Natalie and took the stairs on the run. He sprinted across the foyer and into Nate's living room, where he found Summer talking quietly with Nate and Miranda.

Nate saw him coming first and grinned.

He stopped dead in his tracks when she turned to him, hesitation and uncertainty in her eyes. He couldn't take his eyes off her. "Can we talk?"

"Sure." She didn't move.

"Here?" Well, why the hell not. Everyone was always in their business, they should hear what he had to say so that they'd all know what Summer meant to him.

He took a steadying breath. "I don't know how we're going to do this."

She raised a brow, and her eyes filled with disappointment and sadness.

He'd clear things up for her. "You're brilliant at what you do."

This time shock widened her expressive blue eyes.

"You're amazing at everything, because you try so hard to always get it right."

Out of the corner of his eye, he saw the look of approval on Nate's face.

"I wish I was more like you in that way. Maybe then I wouldn't have messed this up so badly by saying something so colossally stupid. It was the biggest lie I've ever told. Seeing my family like that, it messed with my head. I don't like seeing them upset and at odds. It makes me feel like . . ."

"You'll lose them," she finished for him. "You wanted it to stop."

"Yes. I just wanted everyone to accept you and let go of the anger and pain your mother caused and for all of them to be happy for *us*."

"So we could all be a family."

"Yes."

"And what about the fact that my life in Texas and the company matter to me. I will need to be there just as much as you'll need to be here."

"When I said come home, I meant to me. I don't care where we are, for however many days it's here or there or anywhere, so long as we're together."

"Then there's something you should know," she began.

"What?"

"Charles wasn't the one who called Summer back to Texas," Nate said. "She called him, asking if she could make an acquisition and Sutherland Industries would partner with you and me."

That got him to tear his gaze from Summer and look at Nate. "What?"

Summer filled him in. "My father wants more than anything for me to be happy. He wants the same for you. So during our long lunch talks he filled me in about your company. What you do.

What you make. What you hope to achieve in the future. He told me about a company you've been keeping your eye on and want to eventually buy."

"It's in Austin," Cody blurted out, not believing where this was going. He glanced at Nate. "We don't have the equity to buy them."

Summer continued. "You do if Sutherland Industries backs you." Summer looked very proud of herself. "I propose a partnership, since Sutherland Industries already owns a large share in W. L. Robotics. The thing is, someone high up in your company would need to oversee the acquisition and transition of leadership to bring the new company under W. L. Robotics."

Cody caught on real quick. "I'd need to be in Texas to do that."

"You'd carry out your father's hopes and dreams of expanding the company while my dad continues to do what he loves most, tinkering with his toys."

Cody grinned because Nate was like that with his projects and prototypes. Cody took care of the business side of things so Nate didn't have to.

"Austin is a long way from the Sutherland offices in Dallas."

"They have offices in Austin," Nate pointed out.

"This was the deal you mentioned earlier?" he asked Nate.

"Yes."

Summer added, "He trusted me to make the deal, because he knew how important it was for me to find a way to make this work for both of us."

"I don't know what to say." He held up a hand. "Yes, I do. Forget everything else. The deal. Our families. All of it. The only thing that matters is that I love you. I want to make a life with you, whatever that looks like, wherever that is. And I know you love me, too."

"How do you know?" Summer asked.

"Because you came back, even though I said something dumb

and hurt your feelings. I'm sorry, Summer. I was careless with my words and it nearly cost me everything, because without you, nothing else matters."

.   .   .

Summer couldn't stand the distance between them one second longer and launched herself straight into his arms. The kiss they shared was filled with passion and relief to be together again, tinged with a hint of whiskey.

Suddenly, applause filled the room.

Cody broke the kiss and turned them sideways without letting go of her.

Nate and Miranda grinned at them. Natalie and Haley had bright smiles to go with the happy clapping.

At first, Summer wondered if Natalie was just doing this to score points with Cody, but then she saw the relief and joy in her gaze directed at Summer. She looked truly happy for them.

Summer left the comfort of Cody's arms and rushed her sisters, taking them into her arms and hugging them fiercely. "Thank you for being happy for us." She released them and gave them a wide smile.

Cody came to her and wrapped his arms around her from behind, his hands on her belly.

Natalie looked from him to Summer. "I'm sorry I got in the way. I'm sorry about all of it."

Summer gave her a nod. "Sisters?"

Natalie nodded. "Sisters."

Miranda smiled at all of them. "Well, it's late." She made a big show of yawning. "We should all get to bed."

Natalie got the hint. "Come on, Haley." She tugged her sister toward the stairs, but then stopped short and turned to Summer and Cody. "You two look perfect together." She and Haley disappeared, leaving her and Cody alone with her dad and stepmom.

"She's right, you know. You two have what it takes to make your relationship last." Her dad held her gaze. "Your mom is looking for perfect. But sticking together, talking, working things out when it's hard, that's what marriages are built on." He squeezed Miranda to his side.

"Who said anything about marriage?" Summer asked, not making assumptions, but also hoping she and Cody took that leap when they were ready.

Cody turned her into his arms and held her close. "Summer, I'm never going to let you go."

Chapter Fifty-Two

Summer reached for her ringing phone on the nightstand next to Cody's bed. She barely grabbed it before Cody rolled her onto her back, buried his face in her neck, and settled back into sleep.

She saw Lucy's name on the caller ID and swiped to accept the call, even though it wasn't even dawn yet. "Do you have any idea what time it is in Carmel?"

"Hey. I've waited hours to hear what happened with Cody and your family."

"All is well in the family. My mother and father have called a truce. Natalie apologized to me and Cody."

"And Cody?" Lucy asked, breathlessly awaiting her answer.

Cody grabbed her phone and put it to his ear without moving an inch away from her. "Cody wants to make love to his girlfriend, since someone woke him up, and he loves her so much he can't help himself." He ended the call with Lucy squealing and giggling, then rose up and looked down at Summer. "Would you have rather talked to her than—"

She kissed him to shut him up. "You. I pick you."

He grinned and her heart melted. "I love you."

She pulled him down until his lips were a fraction of an inch from hers. "Show me."

And he did that early morning—and every day after that.

One year later . . . A Summer wedding

Never let it be said that Charles Sutherland didn't do right by his Ladybug. Especially when it came to throwing her the wedding of her dreams.

He'd been right about Cody. The man never left her side. They spent their time between their beautiful Carmel seaside home and the house they bought together in Austin. Summer worked at the Sutherland offices there while Cody oversaw the expansion of W. L. Robotics. They found a balance that worked for them.

And Summer finally had her whole family around her.

Which meant her sisters Lucy, Natalie, and Haley were all waiting for her at the altar, along with Brooke standing up for Cody as "best man," with her new husband, David, and little Alex at their side.

Nate stood on Summer's left. Charles stood on her right.

She'd never looked more beautiful than she did in her wedding gown with the full white skirt, cinched waist, and cap sleeves. His princess.

She wore the beautiful diamond solitaire necklace Cody had given her this morning as a wedding gift. The stone was the same round shape and size as the engagement ring he gave her the day he proposed on the beach on their six-month anniversary.

"Ready?" Nate asked as the wedding march began to play.

She smiled up at him, her eyes bright with joy. "More than ready to spend the rest of my life with him."

Charles grinned and spotted Jessica sitting up front with Roger and remembered how Jessica had sworn no matter what, she was going to make this her last and best marriage.

Charles didn't outright believe her, but he had hope in his heart that she'd finally be happy.

He knew Summer would be for the rest of her life. Because when she loved, she loved big and with her whole heart. And she had found someone who did the same for her.

When he set her up to meet her father, he had no idea he'd also brought the love of her life into her lonely world.

Yes, he took credit for that, too.

Why wouldn't he? What wouldn't he give to make his Ladybug happy?

So when the officiant asked who gave this woman, he had no trouble answering, "He stole her from me." A collective gasp went up from the guests. But Summer only smiled. "But if he makes her happy, I'll let him keep her."

Cody took Summer's hand and leaned into him. "I'll never let her go. And I will always do my best to make her happy."

About the Author

New York Times and USA Today bestselling author Jennifer Ryan writes suspenseful contemporary romances about everyday people who do extraordinary things. Her deeply emotional love stories are filled with high stakes and higher drama, love, family, friendship, and the happily-ever-after we all hope to find.

Jennifer lives in the San Francisco Bay Area with her husband and three children. When she finally leaves those fictional worlds, you'll find her in the garden, playing in the dirt and daydreaming about people who live only in her head, until she puts them on paper.